I0646770

2023 | Volume 7

U.P. READER

Bringing Upper Michigan Literature to the World

A publication of the
Upper Peninsula Publishers and Authors Association (UPPAA)
Marquette, Michigan

UPPAA

U.P. Reader
Volume 1 is still available!

Michigan's Upper Peninsula is blessed with a treasure chest of writers and poets, all seeking to capture the diverse experiences of Yooper Life. Now U.P. Reader offers a rich collection of their voices that embraces the U.P.'s natural beauty and way of life, along with a few surprises.

The twenty-eight works in this first annual volume take readers on a U.P. Road Trip from the Mackinac Bridge to Menominee. Every page is rich with descriptions of the characters and culture that make the Upper Peninsula worth living in and writing about.

Available in paperback, hardcover, and eBook editions!

ISBN 978-1-61599-336-9

www.UPReader.org

U.P. Reader: Bringing Upper Michigan Literature to the World — Volume #7
Copyright © 2023 by Upper Peninsula Publishers and Authors Association (UPPAA). All Rights Reserved.

This is a work of fiction. Names, characters, places, and incidents are the products of the authors' imagination or are used fictitiously. Any resemblance to actual events, locales, or persons, living or dead, is entirely coincidental.

Cover Photo: by Mikel B. Classen.

Learn more about the UPPAA at www.UPPAA.org

Latest news on *UP Reader* can be found at www.UPReader.org

ISSN: 2572-0961

ISBN 978-1-61599-733-6 paperback
ISBN 978-1-61599-734-3 hardcover
ISBN 978-1-61599-735-0 eBook (PDF, Kindle, ePub)

Edited by- Deborah K. Frontiera and Mikel B. Classen
Production - Victor Volkman
Cover Photo - Mikel B. Classen
Interior Layout - Michal Šplho (Amorandi Design)

Distributed by Ingram International (USA / CAN / AU / UK / EU)

Published by
Modern History Press
5145 Pontiac Trail
Ann Arbor, MI 48105

www.ModernHistoryPress.com
info@ModernHistoryPress.com

CONTENTS

About the Cover: "Painesdale Rock Shaft House #4"

by Mikel B. Classen

This is a mining shaft at Painesdale. Constructed in 1902, it is the #4 shaft of the Copper Range Company and is the oldest still-standing rock-shaft house on the Keweenaw. Located nine miles south of Houghton on the corner of M-26 and the Painesdale-Chassell Road, this mine once extended nearly 5,000 feet underground and had forty-eight levels. The Copper Range Mining Company had several mines in the area, also called the Champion location, but this is one of the only ones where most of the mine buildings still remain standing. The Quincy mine in Hancock is another.

An old blacksmith shop and machine shop still stand nearby. There are also the old offices of the Champion Mining Company, now abandoned, sitting on a hill west of the mine called in its heyday, "Snob Hill." A bit of investigating will turn up the remains of another shaft and a hoist house along with relics of railway equipment, mining artifacts and other buildings scattered about.

The shaft and mine operated into the 1960's, one of the reasons it is mostly still intact. Like most mines and mining companies, the profits were up and down. World War I and World War II gave the mine a boost in profits and business, but eventually, like all of the copper mines, it went bust and now sits marking the bygone era of the copper boom.

The town of Painesdale was named after Albert Paine, president of the Copper Range Mining Company. It was built between 1899 and 1917 by the Champion Mining Company. Today the town is not the boom town it once was, but it is still a small community. In 1916, the town reached its peak with about 200 homes. Today many of them still stand and are occupied. When visiting Painesdale, keep in mind some of the relics are on private property and should be respected as such.

A few years back, the historical shaft was being threatened to be turned into scrap. Members of the local community decided that this would not be the case and organized a local group to save the history and restore the town's heritage. The Painesdale Mine and Shaft Inc. was organized and are actively trying to restore the buildings and relics that surround them. Free tours are available by appointment and the organization is looking for donations to help with the restoration. They can be contacted through email painesdalemineshaft@yahoo.com or snail mail: P.O. Box 332, Painesdale, MI 49955. They also have a website at https://www.pasty.com/copperrange/sos.htm

Learn more about **Mikel B. Classen** in our Author Bios section at the back of this book

Janet

by Sharon Kennedy

◆❖◆

I met Janet quite by chance when I was at the Riverside Cemetery in Sault Ste. Marie. It was one of those overcast days when rain could come at any minute and force me to take cover underneath the branches of some old oak or maple and hope lightning skipped around me. Janet had her camera, too, and I watched as she tiptoed around the graves and carefully avoided stepping on old sunken markers. Once she did and I zoomed my lens in on her face, on the guilt clearly spreading itself over her features. She crossed herself, and I saw her lips move in supplication of the dead. Perhaps she said something like, "I didn't mean to step on you" or "Please forgive me" or any one of a dozen apologies people might utter at such moments.

Eventually the rain did come. Janet ran for shelter, seeking a marble bench by a mausoleum in the gloom of a willow tree. I thought she felt safe there, concealed from the downpour and I hesitated before joining her. Would I frighten her? Repulse her? Would she run into the rain to escape me or would pity show in her eyes as she looked at me? Would she pat my back and smile the way people do when they think a pat or a smile can hide their disgust? But no matter. I was driven to her and made my way to the bench.

She looked at me when I took my place next to her, but other than a quick "Hello" she was silent. We waited, watching the rain, and I fancied I could smell her fear. I drew one leg up sharply underneath my chin and rested it on the bench while I struggled with my cart and photo equipment, cursing my mother's womb where I had grown twisted. Janet, not much younger than I, sat huddled into herself, wisps of her curly brown hair sticking to her small face. The face, I had noted, was unremarkable—hazel eyes set deeply within their sockets, a rather long and sharp nose, a small mouth, and hardly any chin. Her neck, though, was long and graceful as it rose from her coat. An agreeable face, I thought, befitting someone generally satisfied with life.

"We really shouldn't be here," I ventured. "You often hear of people getting struck by lightning when they shelter under a tree." She remained silent and I smelled her perfume. To this day, I remember the smell of rain and that perfume and wonder what became of her. "It's only a shower," I tried again. "It will soon pass." Still, she stayed behind her thoughts, but when I spoke, I turned to her and lost myself in the porcelain face that had suddenly become beautiful. We sat thus for perhaps a quarter of an hour. The rain fell softly, and no thunder or lightning ensued, and it was not unpleasant. Her breaths came in long sighs, and I felt her relax. Without warning, she wept, carelessly dabbing a tissue at her eyes and cheeks. I wasn't sure what to do. Although nature had damned my body, she had seen fit to give me a kind disposition. My natural instinct was to reach my hand over hers and say comforting words until the weeping subsided. But I am a freak. An accident of genes. Who was there to comfort her from me?

Allow me to speak of myself for a moment so you will better grasp the setting. I am twenty-nine years old but look much older. My red hair is thinning as are my eyebrows and lashes. I wear very thick glasses over colorless, myopic eyes that droop at the corners much as a basset hound's. My head is large, my forehead protrudes over my nose, and my nose itself is large and bulbous. My mouth is twisted in a perpetual grin and my teeth are crooked. My complexion is muddy and pocked. I have no cheekbones, no chin, no neck to speak of, and the weight of my head leans over my small frame. I only hope to reach five feet tall, but it's obvious I will never get there.

Mind you, though, I could live with the way my face looks. I've gotten used to it, as have one or two others who call themselves my friends. It's my body that frightens me as I know it does others. Sometime during my stay in the womb, the signals got mixed up and my right leg misread the blueprint. For instead of growing straight as the left one did, it grew very little and what did grow got the wrong message. My shin hangs from my thigh much as your hand would if you held out your elbow and swung it. My little shin jerks my little foot, and I am forced to hop when I walk. My little foot is six inches off the ground and suspends itself, defying gravity. Often, I use crutches, but more often than not, I prefer to utilize my good limb. I hop down the street with my right leg leaning on my cart where my camera and books are. Except for the curious who stop, stare, laugh, or grimace, people leave me alone.

Mind you, I am not telling you this for sympathy or whatever. I only feel you must be told to understand why I hesitated to comfort the poor creature next to me who still wept as if her heart would break. I was afraid to breathe lest I scare her, but I was getting a cramp in my leg and wanted to move. It was impossible, though, to vacate the bench without much havoc and the last thing I wanted to do was create a scene. Actually, the fair maiden seemed to take little notice of me, so wrapped in her own woes was she. As rain continued to fall, I leaned on my cart and jerked my little leg over the good one. Then I whistled. It seemed the right thing to do.

I have always preferred taking pictures in a cemetery. It is not the calm, peaceful setting I treasure as much as the interesting events that take place. I am often on hand during a burial and get spectacular shots of mourners.

You may or may not be surprised at the number of smiles that show up where one would expect tears. Mourners go from one extreme to another, and I have not yet decided which I prefer probably because I have had no one to mourn. The young woman next to me was not at a burial; that much I knew. She did not stop at any specific grave, at least not while I watched her. Since her camera was with her, I surmised she was simply on a photography assignment for class, and the gloom of the place overtook her. She touched her eyes with the wet Kleenex and emitted a very deep sigh. Good, I thought. She's coming round.

"Oh," she said as if she had just noticed me. "I hope I didn't frighten you."

She was looking me straight in the face, and I did not see as much as a flicker of disgust or amusement. What a remarkable person, I thought. As she gazed at me, the right side of my mouth started twitching. Still, she paid no attention.

"Have you lost a loved one?" My words sounded hollow as they left my throat. The twitching was making me nervous.

"Yes. No. Well, I'm not sure. I mean, I call her my twin sister but I'm not sure if she's my twin or me. To tell you the truth, I don't think I even have a twin."

Her eyes looked away and I felt her mentally leave the bench. She continued to knot the Kleenex, then shred it, then roll the shreds into tiny balls that she put on her lap. It was a pink tissue which seemed appropriate for such a delicate creature. Her coat was rose colored, as was her handbag. Even her shoes showed a trace of pink. Rose colored blush was brushed on her cheeks. The farther away she looked, the more peaceful her face became until the few lines surrounding her mouth disappeared. *She is beautiful* was all I could think. I yearned to hold her. Water filled my eyes for how could I, a freak, expect to embrace this beauty?

"Did you hear me?" She sounded annoyed that I had remained silent. "I said I don't know whether it's my twin sister or I that is dead."

"Yes, yes," I stammered. "I heard you, but I thought you were just, well, just musing."

"I tell you something as crazy as that and you think I'm musing?"

"Well, no, I guess not, but well, I don't know."

"I tell you I don't even know for sure if I have a twin sister let alone whether or not she's dead or I'm dead and you think that's not crazy?"

"Who am I to judge?" She was furious now and thought I was making fun of her, which, of course, was the last thing on earth I would do to such a beautiful girl. She stood up and the pile of pink balls rolled to the ground. She placed her hands on her slim hips and glared at me, bending until her nose was level with mine. My mouth twitched madly, and I was powerless to stop it. *She's going to laugh when she sees it*, I thought. I shrunk from her until my back caught the tree trunk and I almost fell. She grabbed me.

"Oh, no you don't," she screamed. "You're not leaving here until you've answered my question." She was out of control now. Gone beyond all reason. "Am I or am I not crazy?" Her pink hands were around my throat, and I could hardly breathe. She was the most enchanting mortal nature had ever made, and she was touching me—a freak—and it didn't matter that I was choking. Her perfume covered me. I lost myself in it as I let my neck go limp in her hands and slumped forward unto her breast. I had never known such bliss in touching another human being. I wished the moment would last forever, but, of course, I knew it couldn't and as quickly as she had encircled my neck, she let go.

"I hate you," she screamed. "I hate you. I hate all of you here, so dead, so silent, so condemning, so mocking. Why won't you tell me who died? Me or Janet?" She crumpled to the ground. It was all I could do to keep from kicking her with my little foot that was jerking uncontrollably. She lifted her head and leaned against my left knee. I noticed a tiny braid held in place by a pink ribbon mixed in with her curls. Her coat opened, exposing a pink locket hanging from her neck. She wore no blouse or sweater. I saw her small bosom. Her nipples stood erect like tiny strawberries. She was a naked vision of beauty. I held my breath.

"You're right," she said. "There is no Janet. I am Janet and I am both dead and alive and I come here to take pictures of the grave where I'm buried, except I can't find it. I visit all the cemeteries in the area looking for my grave, but it's not anywhere. It's lost like me. Please take me home."

She whimpered like a child and clung to my knee. At last, I drew breath. The rain fell, then let up, then fell again and still she did not move. *She doesn't notice me*, was all I could think. *She doesn't see me at all. It's not me she's clutching but an apparition from her past.* I wondered if the tombstones surrounding us would claim the name of Janet. I wondered if Janet was lying cold beneath the earth around us. The long branches of the willow danced in the calm afternoon breeze. The rain stopped and I felt chilled. I wanted to retreat to my rooms on Portage, start a fire in the grate, brew a pot of tea on my hotplate, develop my negatives, and sleep. I had my own troubles, but Janet clung to me.

"Please take me home," she said again. She shifted herself, releasing her hold on my knee. I seized the opportunity, hopped from the bench, leaned on my cart, and moved away. Before I left the graveyard, I turned and looked at the beautiful girl who had suddenly become plain, resting in a pink haze, her drab, wet hair hanging flat against her head. A thought flashed through my mind that I could make love to her, that she wouldn't even notice when I opened her coat and thrust myself into her body, but then I thought *what a foolish idea*. Why would I want to make love to one so obviously unstable? To one so freakish?

"Please take me home," she pleaded. Without hesitation, I hopped away, eager to be rid of her.

"Please take me home," she called again. For the first time in my life, I thanked the man and woman who made me. As I continued to hear the plaintive cries, I knew—even in my misshapen, ugly body—I knew I was happier, more content and more beautiful than Janet or whatever she called herself had ever been or was ever likely to be.

Learn more about **Sharon Kennedy** in our Author Bios section at the back of this book

Quale and Agnes

by Sharon Kennedy

The fading sun shines through lacy beige curtains and brings a quiet glow to Quale's living room, turning her surroundings into a welcoming cocoon. She wraps herself deeper into her yellow cardigan, stirs a little Irish cream into her coffee, and turns to Spike who is reading yesterday's newspaper, quite oblivious to Quale's obvious suffering. She hates him and his cool indifference.

"I didn't think it would end like this," she says. "I thought I'd awaken one morning, and Mom would be gone — that I'd find her asleep in her chair with a peaceful look on her face and her plastic crucifix clutched in her hand. Sweetie would be purring and licking her arm, trying to awaken her, but knowing as an animal instinctively knows, that her mistress has gone someplace the cat cannot follow. It wasn't supposed to end like this. Dear God, not like this."

"How long are you going to cry?" Spike asks as he glances her way. "Your ma's okay. She's happy living at the home. It's you I'm worried about. Snap out of the dumps, will you?" Spike has heard Quale's complaints for weeks. Her constant rehashing of her mother's move to the nursing home isn't good for their shaky relationship.

"I can't help it," Quale answers. "This is the first spring in seventy-nine years she hasn't been home to see the daffodils bloom. It doesn't make sense that she lives in a healthy body while her mind disintegrates. If she had died, it would be so much easier."

"But she didn't die, and life goes on. Besides, the home has flowerbeds. She'll be watching daffodils bloom from a different window, that's all, and she won't even know the difference. That should give you some comfort."

"Why? Why does life go on and why should knowing Mom doesn't know where she is bring me comfort? She worked hard all her life and look how it ended. Life makes no sense. It's crazy—everything ends. Everything. All her hard work amounted to nothing. Her life amounted to less than a stick of kindling."

"Stop it, Quale. Stop it or you'll be sitting in a wheelchair next to her, dribbling your chicken noodle soup on your bib, and filling your Depends with urine."

"You don't understand. You didn't live with her. We shared this house for nine years. It wasn't until she moved in with me that I remembered everything about her that I thought I had forgotten. I loved her, then I hated her, then I forgave her then I loved her again. She's been gone for two months. Give me time to mourn. Please. I need more time. That's all I'm asking."

"But you're not getting better. Every time you visit her, you come home an emotional wreck. You can't live her life. You have to go on and think about us. How about we go to the casino? I still have a little time before I catch the boat. What'd you say?"

"I say close the window. I'm cold and I can't stand the noise from those four-wheelers. This sideroad used to be so quiet—no more than three cars drove by in a day. Sometimes it was three days before one car would go by. Now the quiet is gone. I hate it here now. Strangers live on the road that used to be ours. Kids break the windows in the old house and sleep like thieves in the barn's haymow. Everything's changed. I hate it. I hate the way things turned out. It isn't fair. Please close the window. I said I'm cold."

"You're not well, Quale. You're living in the past. You need to see a doctor."

"What do I need a doctor for? To tell me cancer is eating my body? Or the polyps in my nose are malignant? So, what if a doctor says I need an operation? And if I survive, what then? What then? If they heal my body, and I lose my mind, what difference will it make? Why bother with a doctor? What's the point?" Spike closes the window.

"Here, put on this sweatshirt and drink your coffee. Dammit, Quale, you've got to pull yourself together. You're all I've got. I need you. Don't quit on me. Did you take your Xanax?"

"Xanax, Prozac, Tetracycline, four aspirins, three Butterfingers, a bag of gas station popcorn, and a pot of coffee. That's what I've taken today. Tomorrow will be the same except for the candy. Maybe I'll eat a bag of Switzer's black licorice."

"Do you think this is what she would want? That she'd be happy knowing you're ruining your health? Did she give up when your dad died?"

"No, but he died quick. He escaped a nursing home."

"Then be like she is. Be strong. She's adjusting to her new life. She seems happy. It seems to me you might be a little jealous that your ma has adjusted to the situation better than you have. She wouldn't want to see you in such misery."

"I've been strong all my life and for most of it, I've taken care of someone other than myself. I'm fifty-three years old and I'm tired. If I eat junk food and pop pills, then so be it."

"What do you want me to do?"

"Nothing. You're never around long enough to do anything anyway. Always complaining how much you hate the life of a Great Lakes sailor, but you love to boast about being one."

As usual, Spike feels useless because he is. He looks at his watch. Nine-thirty. The ship will lock through in an hour and if he's not on it, it will sail without him. The freighter *Joe Block* waits for no man. Spike knows when he's licked. "Okay," he says. "You don't want to go to the casino but come here and let me love you before I leave." Spike heads for the bedroom but Quale won't follow him. How can a woman make love to a man she despises? The years of manipulation and verbal abuse and passive-aggressive behavior have taken their toll. Quale no longer feels any emotions for Spike other than contempt and fear. She feigns concern as he puts on his jacket and gets ready to leave.

"Be careful," she says. "Dusk is when deer feed alongside the road. Promise me you'll be careful." Twice this spring Spike has hit a deer. Quale is much less concerned about his welfare. It's the poor animals that have her sympathy.

"Don't worry. Don't worry about anything. I'll call as often as I can, but you know when we're on Lake Superior heading for Duluth, I can't get a signal on the cell."

"I know," Quale says. She turns away after he kisses her cheek. She listens until his truck is gone and then closes her eyes. Soon she is sleeping, and her dreams reveal what she tries to keep hidden. Her dreams take her to the old barn, but it's much larger than it was. Mom and Dad and Spike are with her. They're walking along the south wall of the haymow because the floor isn't safe. Years of neglect rotted the wood. Quale watches as the mow falls to the ground. Her parents disappear amid old milk bottles, curry combs, pictures of herself when she was young, and boxes of broken glasses. She grabs everything and runs to the house, but it isn't the house, it's the old red building Dad used as a work shed. When she puts the items on a table, they roll away like human heads roll from the slice of a guillotine.

Quale sees herself in the mirror she holds in her dream. Her face is lined, wrinkled, looking much older than she is. She tosses the mirror aside and returns to the haymow. Female bodies lie on the hay. When she looks closer, they open their eyes, and their arms reach for her. Their faces are white, and their eyes are colorless. A shudder runs through Quale as she thinks of the movie *Je'Accuse* and wonders what she has done to earn the wrath of these dead women. They go for her throat. Mom and Dad and Spike have disappeared so there is no one to help her. She does not struggle as the dead women strangle her. Resistance is pointless.

Quale cries in her sleep and awakens. In her mind's eye, she sees Spike as he is—a handsome, tall man whose eyes are empty. Five years ago, when they first met, she asked him why he had empty eyes, but he didn't understand so he didn't answer. Quale's eyes take her to the picture of Jesus hanging on the wall. In every Catholic home, the same picture is tacked or taped to a wall. The eyes of Jesus follow her as she moves from the bedroom to the kitchen. His eyes are full of love and hope and compassion and understanding. They are not the eyes of a stranger.

"It's just You and me now," Quale says as she pours water into the tea kettle. "I guess You'll have to do." She pushes back the linen tablecloth, takes a China cup and saucer from the cupboard, and puts a teabag in the cup when the water is hot. She opens the cookie jar and places three oatmeal cookies on a fancy plate and sits at her place, staring at the same picture of Jesus that hangs from a nail pounded into the west wall.

"I suppose You'll do," she repeats as she stirs sugar into her cup. "What choice do I have?" Quale looks past the picture and thinks of Spike as he drives north on Mac Trail towards the Soo Locks where he'll board the freighter. Then she thinks of her mother. She sits for a long time and wonders what they are thinking. Eventually, she finishes her snack, puts the dishes in the sink, and draws the drapes. Evening has descended. The house is cold and dark. Quale no longer sees the eyes of Jesus watching her, but she feels His presence within her. At least she thinks it's His presence, but maybe it's only the Xanax.

Spike calls at midnight. She doesn't pick up the receiver, and the call goes to the answering machine. "The night is clear. Superior is smooth as glass," he says. "All is fine. I love you." Quale erases the message and closes her eyes. She sleeps soundly until 6:00 a.m. When she awakens, she hopes the day will be different, but that's a hope void of hope. How can something be different when nothing changes? She dresses, makes coffee, eats some cookies, sits at the kitchen table, and waits for the day to end. This is the life of Quale as she searches for meaning in the emptiness surrounding her. Emptiness occasionally broken by the appearance of a man she loathes. She longs for the safety and security of her youth when she was unconcerned about the future and the sorrow it would bring. Her eyes fill with tears.

Meanwhile, at the nursing home in Sault Ste. Marie, Agnes pushes her wheelchair down the hallway until she finds her room—B4. It's an easy number to remember because it reminds her of bingo and the number that always comes up. She just finished a good breakfast and is looking forward to watching her favorite show on the small television in her room. She likes the banter between Kathie Lee and Regis. It's not quite nine o'clock so she does what she does every morning. She opens the drawer of her nightstand. A feeling of pride rushes through her as she looks at the contents. There are so many things in it. She counts each treasure as she removes it.

Number one is a bottle of gold-colored cologne. Number two is the holy card of Mary. Number three is her rosary. Number four is a Mother's Day corsage. Number five is a new pair of socks. The counting continues until Agnes reaches thirty-one. The number is high because she counts all the tiny bits of discarded candy wrappers and all the ribbons from various presents. Everything she owns is spread on the twin bed that is not hers in the room that is not hers. She smiles and tells her roommate that all her possessions are from someone whose name she doesn't recall but who must love her very much to be so generous. The roommate agrees. Agnes puts everything back in the nightstand that is not hers. Then she leans back on the pillow that is not hers and smiles as her show comes on.

She spends her days watching shows and talking to her new friends. When the afternoon soaps come on, she wheels herself to the glass patio door that looks out on the garden. She watches the flowers grow and smiles when she sees the daffodils have finally bloomed. For the first time in her life, Agnes is happy. She no longer has to care for or worry about anyone. Her health is good as is her appetite. She doesn't remember the home she shared with her daughter because she doesn't remember either one. She gives a contented sigh as she wheels herself to one of the tables. It's time for bingo. B-4 is the first number called. Agnes finds it on her card and quickly covers it. She hopes she picked a lucky card. If so, she'll win the blackout and the main prize, a bag of Hershey's Kisses. The caller yells "B-8." Agnes covers it. The man next to her pats her hand. "You're on a roll," he says. Agnes smiles. "I-21" is the next number. She covers it. The smile spreading across her lips would melt snow. She's never been so happy.

Learn more about **Sharon Kennedy** in our Author Bios section at the back of this book

Historical · ishpeming girl on motorcycle

Memory Trails

by Ellen Lord

Rural roads were a childhood theme, backstory for so many memories.

We rode in a red Jeep Wrangler to the old camp west of Kenton in the Upper Peninsula of Michigan. Doors were off and I rode shotgun. It was back-country rocky, tufts of wild grass along the centerline; jackrabbits darted across the road, partridge flushed in the forest. The last three miles of two-track were rutted, muddy after a deluge of rain. An eagle soared high above the tree line. Dad said this was a good omen. It was the summer of '57. Sweet July. Just me and dad on a grand adventure—suspended now in time.

Long ago, that camp was used for logging during the Great Depression. Grandpa Cameron had draft horses, hired crews to harvest pine and hardwood. I've seen pictures of those wiry souls with their rough hands and hardscrabble faces. Sepia photos show sinewy men, smiles on most, as getting a picture taken was a special event. They were a tough bunch, mostly local guys from Irish or Finnish families; a few were vagabonds of dubious origin. They were known as 'Jack-Pine Savages'. The big draft horses all had names: Stony, Big Red, Buck.

•••

Years later, Garner Road meandered west of Stephenson, Michigan. I'd take solitary walks to a gravel pit, then hike into the forest. My favorite old maple stood on a high ridge and was a 'climber'. I would get my first foothold and then, up I would go. I was a scrappy kid, tomboy—calluses on my hands and pine pitch under my fingernails. A thick branch would hold me as I gazed over forest and field. I'll always remember swaying in a soft breeze and feeling free. It became a meditation for me—the beginning of a life-long practice to retreat to wild places whenever I could. It was the summer of '65.

•••

As the years unfold, I continue to yearn for unpeopled spaces—to commune with the lakes, rivers, and forests. Of course, I cherish idyllic days, but I love big storms—how they surge with bluster—a sky dance of thunder, lightning, and rain. I walk most days; early morning is best. There is nothing more spectacular than a Michigan sunrise. I have seen bobcat drink by a river, muskrat slide along the shore, and deer gaze from the shadows. I walk and walk as sun sequins the trees. I pass a long stretch of marsh, deep tangles of forest, and listen to delicious vignettes of birdsong. No matter where I go, I don't need much—just a backwoods trail and a span of northern sky in Michigan.

Primitive trails are a lifetime theme, backstory to my changes.

Learn more about **Ellen Lord** in our Author Bios section at the back of this book

Two Riders

by Ellen Lord

"There must be some kind of way outta here
Said the joker to the thief" — Bob Dylan

We left Ann Arbor at dawn
on a long rising road in Michigan—
hitchhiked US-23, going north
to hunt at his camp in Curran.
Shotgun cased and slung,
he yearned for something wild—
I just wanted to get away.

It was October, fall colors vibrant
in the hills. So eager for adventure,
we believed this could be *our life*—
free to journey where we pleased.
His eyes flashed mischief
as wistful drivers waved goodbye.
Luck and rides came easy—
for I was young, and he was beautiful.

What I remember most, is how sunlight
shimmered above the highway,
like we were traveling to a distant sea—
an unexplored horizon, so far away
from where we were destined to be.
It was a mid-semester college interlude—
two small town desperados,
trying to traverse a big town world
on a quest to be the right size.

Learn more about **Ellen Lord** in our Author Bios section
at the back of this book

The Giant Flower

by Deborah K. Frontiera

Scout Bee #2100 buzzed into the hive bursting with excitement. She danced in circles indicating the direction of the sun's rays and distance to her incredible find. Translated from the language of bees, it went something like this.

"You'll never believe the Giant Flower I found—absolutely filled with never-ending sweetness! I've never tasted nectar so sweet. Or so much of it. Not far from here hanging from the house of the two-legged giants."

"Calm down #2100," said Lead Worker.

#2100 stopped her dance and rested—something difficult for a hive scout, or any worker bee, to do.

Lead Worker then questioned her further. "Now, please describe this supposed 'Giant Flower'."

"It's large, very large, and reflects the sunlight in places, but is opaque in others. It's red with yellow blossom openings. I headed for a blossom first, and found them not living, but the scent of nectar was SO strong. I tried to sip from the hole, but my proboscis could not reach the sweetness. It's hanging in front of the shiny smooth place we can't get through."

"So how do you really know what is there?"

"It was sticky beneath my feet! Then I discovered a narrow crack between the top and bottom half of the huge red part and the bottom of it, just enough to slip my sucking tongue in. Oh, I can't tell you how sweet it is!"

Lead Worker buzzed, still skeptical, but also thinking. Finally, she said, "Come over here, #3421! Go with #2100 and check this out. Report back immediately."

The two bees left their hive in a hollow of a dead tree in the forest. A few weeks before, a bear had raided the hive and stolen over half their supply of food and eaten many larval and pupating bees along with the honey. Those remaining had worked so hard to repair the damage and build more honeycomb deeper in the hollow, where hopefully, the bear could not reach it again. The Queen had immediately laid eggs to replace the lost young. Now the new larva would soon pupate and then emerge as young workers. The Queen's immediate assistants were concerned that if they didn't have more scouts and gatherers to work extra hard to replace their food supply, the hive might not be able to survive the next winter.

Scout #2100 slowed down a bit flying around a balsam tree to check her position in the angle of a patch of sunlight coming through the branches. She turned to make sure #3421 was still following as she changed direction slightly. Ah, there it was, perhaps twenty feet from the tree line. #3421 could smell the sweetness and grew as excited as #2100 had been when she entered the hive.

"Here," #2100 buzzed to her companion. "If you turn upside down by this crack, you can get your proboscis in better." She demonstrated the technique she had done herself not long before.

#3421 copied the position and took a long suck. "WOW! You weren't telling a tale! We must lead the others here."

A few minutes later, a large group of bees followed #2100 and #3421 to the remarkable find. Back and forth the gatherer bees zoomed. To the Giant Flower, suck up a load, buzz back to the hive, deposit the sweetness into an empty cell (which the Queen would soon fill with a new egg, and nurse bees would cover with a layer of wax) and back to the Giant Flower. They worked at a feverish pace until the sunlight left the Giant Flower in shadow and almost until it was too dark to find, vowing to return the next morning for more.

For the next few days, many gatherers spent the entire day sucking nectar from the Giant Flower. On the fourth day, #3421 noticed something troubling, which she reported to her Queen. "When we first went to the Giant Flower, I could see red liquid on the inside, which we were sucking out at the bottom of the of the flower, about 2/3 up the scc-through part of the thing. Now I see it is about half as much. I think we will eventually empty it. Great as the amount is, it will run out."

The Queen was silent for a moment and then called for the Lead Worker. "#3421, please tell Lead Worker what you just told me."

So, #3421 repeated her observation. "How many days more do think there will be of gathering there?" Lead Worker asked.

#3421 was silent for a moment, then replied, "Well, based on the rate of collecting we've been doing, I'd say not more than four or five days."

Lead Worker and Queen stopped buzzing to think.

Finally, Queen stated, "Starting tomorrow, send only a third as many workers to the Giant Flower to continue collecting there. Send all the scouts out to search for more sources of nectar. While the Giant Flower has definitely saved us from our losses to the bear, we can't depend on only one source of nectar."

#3421 and Lead Worker nodded and flew off to carry out Queen's instructions.

The following week, the bear attacked the hive again, but because the bees had built the new comb farther inside the tree, the bear could not reach it. The bear tried to rip the edges of the hive entrance to reach farther in. Though the tree was dead, the wood was not so rotten that the bear could rip the wood away easily to reach farther into the hole. The bees gave the bear's nose such a stinging that the bear retreated growling in complaint. To be certain it would not return, #2100 and two other scouts followed the bear. It licked its nose, still growling and then settled for easier food in a patch of wild blueberries.

"You should say thank you," buzzed one of the scouts. "We pollinated those white blossoms in the spring to make those berries for you."

The bear paid no attention to her.

"You have to remember," said one of the other scouts, "bears do not understand our language. It's useless to try to reason with them."

"I know, but one can always try." #2100 was an eternal optimist.

The bees at the Giant Flower could no longer reach the nectar with their proboscises and had about decided to leave when a friendly harvester ant climbed down the string from which the Giant Flower hung. She had labored long to climb up the wall to where the string was tied, up the string, across from where the string was hooked to the eve of the Giant Two-Legged Creatures' dwelling, and down to the Giant Flower. The bees, being insect cousins to ants, understood the ant's telepathic message asking if she could share their bounty.

One bee told her their dilemma. The ant looked at the hole in the middle of one of the fake blossoms. Yes, she thought she could crawl in and check out the situation. She pushed her body through the hole and landed with a sploop in the pool of nectar remaining at the bottom. *"Oh, oh, oh, there's so much here,"* the ant's telepathy told them. *"I can see the crack you used and, no, you won't be able to reach it. BUT I can't swim! I can't get out! I shall drown in this nectar."*

The bees buzzed around in frustration as the ant struggled to reach the edge, which was too slippery to climb up. There was nothing they could do to help. The ant's telepathy grew weaker and then stopped.

"What a shame," one of the bees said. "But what a way to go!"

"Perhaps we should stop buzzing for a while in respect for her heroic actions," said another.

"Here comes another ant," buzzed a third. "We should warn her not to crawl in there."

The bees buzzed around the second ant, gently so she wouldn't think they wished her harm. The ant stopped, listened, thanked the bees, and turned to go back up the string, across the top, down again, then down the wall to the ground. Then it headed for an ant hill not far away. The bees assumed they would report it all to their Queen.

Not long after, scout #2100 happened to fly to the opposite side of the Giant Two-Legged Creatures' dwelling and spotted another Giant Flower! She flew over to investigate. While not as large as the one they had already harvested, it was shaped in a way that

did not allow any way for a bee to get at the nectar. Hummingbirds, rivals with the bees, landed, sucked away at it, and gave #2100 a mean look. She retreated. But she returned to check out the situation briefly every day. A Two-Legged female took down the Giant Flower one day and brought it back filled to the top with nectar. #2100 sighed and wondered why she didn't fill up the other one again.

Life went on in the beehive. Late summer and then fall flowers bloomed, and the bees gathered more nectar. They still checked the Giant Flower from time to time, but the Two-Legged did not refill their flower. Did she mean for that nectar to be only for Hummingbirds? That seemed so wrong. The bees needed nectar, too. The days grew shorter, the mornings colder. The maples turned bright red and the birches yellow. Queen declared it was time for her to stop laying more eggs for that season. She directed her workers to continue gathering their winter

food supply until there were no more flowers.

The day came when #2100 saw a Two-Legged take down both Giant Flowers but she didn't bring them back out. She took in their outside chairs and her mate pulled their boat out of the lake. When #2100 reported seeing that, she heard a long sigh from the whole hive. Queen said their work for that year was done, decreed the usual rationing of stored honey, and told her workers to rest for the cold season to come. But #2100 made up her mind she would watch and hope that the Giant Flower would be refilled in the spring.

Learn more about **Deborah K. Frontiera** in our Author Bios section at the back of this book

Spring Haiku Trio

by Deborah K. Frontiera

Free water exists
"Snow and bitter cold will end,"
Promise ice pancakes.

Fiddleheads sprout up
Playing spring's first symphony
Glorified in green.

Arbutus confirms
Fills air with sweetest fragrance
The promise fulfilled.

Learn more about **Deborah K. Frontiera** in our Author Bios section
at the back of this book

Charles Uksila:
From Calumet to a Career
in Hockey and Figure Skating

by Bill Sproule

Charles "Charlie" Uksila was one of the first American-born players to play in the Stanley Cup playoffs as a member of the 1915/16 Portland Rosebuds, and after he retired from hockey, he went on to a fascinating career in figure skating. Uksila was born in 1887 in Calumet, Michigan. His parents, Charles "Carl" and Anna (Niemela), immigrated from Finland to the Copper Country in the early 1880s when his father got a job as a laborer for the Calumet and Hecla Mining Company. There were fourteen children in the family.

While attending Calumet High School, Uksila participated in hockey, fancy skating, and speed skating, and after high school he played left wing on the Mohawk (Michigan) team in 1910 and 1911 when they won the Copper Country Senior Championships. He would also put on skating performances and barrel-jumping demonstrations at the new Glaciadom in Mohawk on Sundays during the hockey season. The family lived in the Osceola area of Calumet and there was an Osceola station on the Houghton County streetcar line, so it easy for Uksila to travel to Mohawk (six miles north of Calumet) and other ice arenas in the area. Like his father, he was also a laborer for the Calumet and Hecla Mining Company but moved to Portland, Oregon during the Copper Country strike of 1913–14. A childhood friend and former teammate, Jack Herman, had moved to Portland a couple of years earlier and encouraged Uksila to join

him. Herman was also manager/coach of the Portland Multnonah Amateur Athletic hockey team in a Portland-based amateur league, and he recruited him to play on the team for the 1914–15 season. After the season, Uksila signed a professional contract with Portland of the Pacific Coast Hockey Association (PCHA), and he played two seasons with the Rosebuds (1915–16 and 1917–18).

The PCHA was founded in 1911 by Frank and Lester Patrick with three teams – New Westminister, Vancouver, and Victoria. The Patricks built new arenas with artificial ice surfaces in Vancouver and Victoria, introduced several rule changes, and were willing to pay the best players to head west. The New Westminister team relocated to Portland in 1914. In the same year, an agreement was also made where the champions of the PCHA would play the champions of the National Hockey Association (NHA) for the Stanley Cup, and the location of the championship series would alternate between the two leagues. The Seattle Metropolitans joined the league in 1915. In March 1916, the Portland Rosebuds won the PCHA championship and traveled to Montreal to play the Canadiens, the NHA champion, in a five-game series in Montreal's Westmount Arena. This series marked the first time that a U.S.-based team played for the Stanley Cup. The Canadiens were an impressive team that included four players who were later inducted into the Hockey Hall of Fame

– George Vezina, and three former International Hockey League players, Newsy Lalonde, Jack Laviolette, and Didier Pitre. The International Hockey League (IHL) was hockey's first professional league. It was founded in 1904 and operated for three seasons with five teams – Calumet, Portage Lake (Houghton), Pittsburgh, Sault Ste. Marie Michigan, and Sault Ste. Marie Ontario. Lalonde played one season with the Canadian Soo team, while Laviolettte and Pitre each played three seasons with the Michigan Soo team. The Portland team included future Hockey Hall of Famers, Ernie "Moose" Johnson and Tommy Dunderdale, and two American-born players – Charlie Uksila and Tom Murray.

Portland won the first game in the series 2–0, before dropping the next two games but then the Rosebuds tied the series with a 6–5 victory in the fourth game. Uksila scored a goal on the legendary George Vezina in both Portland victories. The Canadiens defeated the Rosebuds 2–1 in the deciding fifth game to win their first of what would be many Stanley Cup championships. The Montreal Canadiens are the all-time leaders having won the Stanley Cup 24 times.

An interesting story related to the Rosebuds trip as they traveled from Portland to Montreal is a stop in Houghton, Michigan. The Portland team, with Uksila, played an exhibition game against a Michigan Upper Peninsula All-Star team of players from Calumet, Sault Ste. Marie, and Houghton (Portage Lake). The local newspaper billed Portland as World Champions by virtue of their league win over the Vancouver Millionaires, the 1915 Stanley Cup champion. The All-Stars included Jack Adams, Hugh "Muzz" Murray, Billy Coutu, Len Bailey, and Elmer Sicotte. Jack Adams was born in Fort William, Ontario (now Thunder Bay) and played one season in Calumet. He went on to play in the National Hockey League and had a long career as coach and general manager of the Detroit Red Wings. He was inducted into the Hockey Hall of Fame in 1959. "Muzz" Murray was born in Sault Ste. Marie, Michigan where he played several years before joining the Seattle Metropolitans in the PCHA. He was a member of the Seattle team in the 1919 Stanley Cup series that was cancelled because of the influenza epidemic. He played three seasons with the Seattle Metropolitans and was inducted into the U.S. Hockey Hall of Fame in 1987. Billy Coutu was born in North Bay, Ontario, played two seasons in Sault Michigan, and later played several years for the Montreal Canadiens. He was the only player banned from the NHL for life as a result of his attack on a referee during the 1927 Stanley Cup series. Canadian-born Len Bailey from the Portage Lake team played rover for the All Stars, and another Portage Lake player, Elmer Sicotte, was the team's left wing. Sicotte would later serve as head coach for the Michigan College of Mines (now Michigan Tech) in their first two years of intercollegiate varsity hockey. The game was played at the Amphidrome on Friday, March 17, 1916.

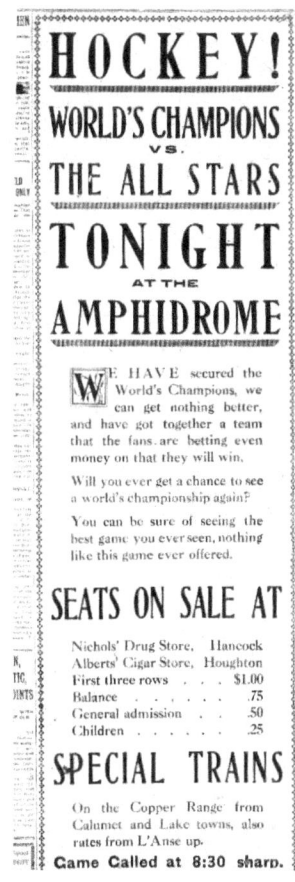

Advertisement in Houghton Daily Mining Gazette, Friday, March 17, 1916

The Amphidrome in Houghton (MTU Archives and Copper Country Historical Collection)

Charles "Charlie" Uksila in a Vancouver Millionaires uniform, 1918-19 season (Houghton County Historical Society)

The Amphidrome on the Houghton waterfront opened in December 1902. At the time, it was the finest arena in the Midwest with seating for 2,500 hockey fans and room for 600 standees.

The All Stars lead 4–0 before Portland scored their first goal in the second period. Portland went on to win 7–6 with four goals by Charlie Tobin and three by Tommy Dunderdale. Len Bailey scored four goals for the All Stars and Jack Adams added two goals. The local newspaper reported, "The biggest hockey crowd of the season", and "The exhibition showed the crowd the finer points of hockey and it was distinctly pleasing, no matter what the result."

Following his first year with the Rosebuds, Uksila stepped away from professional hockey and played one season with an amateur team in Portland. It was during this time that he served in the U.S. Naval Reserve and began skating with his younger sister Lena. She had learned to skate in the Copper Country, and they were contracted to skate in ice shows at the New York Hippodrome with several of the top international skaters. Among the skaters were the famous Australian ice dancing team of Bobby and Louise Jackson. Bobby Jackson had played hockey in Australia, so it was easy to establish a close friendship with Uksila as they were mutual friends with Australian Tommy

Dunderdale, one of Uksila's Rosebuds teammates.

Uksila rejoined the Rosebuds for the 1917–18 season, but Portland suspended operations at the end of the season. He was then recruited by the Vancouver Millionaires for the 1918–19 season and among his Millionaires teammates were former International Hockey League players and future Hall of Famers, Fred "Cyclone" Taylor and Hugh Lehmann. Taylor played two seasons with the IHL's Portage Lake team and Lehmann was goalie for one season with the Canadian Soo team. As a young boy growing up in the Copper Country, Uksila had no doubt attended IHL games in Houghton or Calumet and saw these players in action.

Uksila retired from hockey after the season and started a new career barrel jumping, speed skating, teaching skating, and giving figure skating exhibitions throughout the United States and Canada with his sister Lena. In the 1920s, newspapers started to refer to ice skating as "figure skating", instead of fancy skating, and skating shows became a popular form of entertainment. Local skating clubs presented carnivals in which members would participate in various skating performances, and the carnivals in larger cities would often feature guest skaters who were national, world, or Olympic champions. There were also sev-

Hotel supper club skating show would have a male and female soloist, an ice dancing team, a chorus line of skaters, and a live orchestra. (Houghton County Historical Society)

Charles and Vida Uksila (Houghton County Historical Society)

eral professional skaters who would barnstorm and skate between periods of hockey games or during club carnivals. It was about this time that professional skaters performed in miniature ice revues at hotel supper clubs on portable ice stages called "tanks". A typical show would have a male

and female soloist, an ice dancing team, and a chorus line of skaters performing on a small ice surface. A live orchestra would provide music for the show. The Uksilas and Jacksons were among the popular skaters for these shows.

Through their friendships with the Jacksons and Tommy Dunderdale, the Uksilas were invited to Australia a couple of times in the early 1920s. Lena was a member of the instructional staff of the Melbourne Academy of Skating and would perform ice dancing and skating exhibitions with Charles. She was billed as the "woman champion ice skater of the world". Charles was also asked to provide training and coach a hockey team. During a second trip in 1923, Lena married Herbert Furst and remained in Sydney. Charles returned home and married Dorothy "Vida" Blunt and they teamed and continued to do figure skating performances in arenas, at fairs, and in hotel supper clubs throughout the United States and Canada.

One of the famous skaters of the 1920s was Norwegian Sonja Henie. She won her first major competition, the senior Norwegian championship, at the age of ten. She then placed eighth in a field of eight at the 1924 Winter Olympics at the age of eleven. At fourteen, Henie won the first of an unprecedented ten World Figure Skating Championships and then went on to win the first of her three gold medals at the 1928 St. Moritz Olympic Games. She defended her Olympic titles in 1932 and in 1936, and her world titles annually until 1936. During this time, she was in demand as a performer at skating exhibitions and carnivals throughout Europe and North America, but she had to be careful to retain her amateur status for Olympic competitions and could only accept travel and other expenses related to her appearances.

After the 1936 World Championships, Henie gave up her amateur status and began a career in acting and professional skating. She dreamed of becoming a movie star. Following an ice show that her father organized in Los Angeles, Darryl Zanuck signed her to a long-term contract with Twentieth Century Fox, which made her one of the highest-paid actresses of the time as she starred in a series of box-office hits. She also signed a contract with Arthur Wirtz to lead a professional skating touring company, the "Hollywood Ice Revue". During the Depression, the Chicago-born Wirtz partnered with James E. Norris to purchase several arenas. In 1932, they purchased the Olympia Stadium in Detroit and its hockey franchise, the Detroit Falcons, and renamed the team the Red Wings. A few years later, they purchased the Chicago Stadium, New York's Madison Square Garden, and the St. Louis Arena. Wirtz and Norris saw Sonja Henie as a way to fill their arenas. At the height of her fame, Henie brought in as much as $2 million per year for her skating shows and she had numerous lucrative endorsement contracts to market skates, clothing, jewelry, and other merchandise branded with her name. These activities made her one of the wealthiest women in the world in her time.

The first large scale, professional skating touring company was also founded in 1936 when Eddie and Roy Shipstad, and Oscar Johnson formed the "Ice Follies". Their show included elaborate production numbers and novelty acts, and one of the show's features was a chorus line that included intricate maneuvers by a group of skaters. This was the start of synchronized figure skating.

In 1940, members of the Arena Managers Association were so delighted with ticket sales at their arenas for the "Ice Follies" and Sonja Henie's "Hollywood Ice Revue" that they met in Hershey to form their own ice show to play in their buildings. They adopted the name "Ice Capades". Charles Uksila was hired as skating director and choreographer, his wife Vida was hired as wardrobe mistress, and through their business contacts, a group of skaters were assembled, and a traveling show was put together. The world premier was a ten-night stand in New Orleans in June 1940 followed by a six-week engagement in Atlantic City. In the fall, new stars were added, and a new production was developed for a tour that opened in Pittsburgh on November 5, 1940. The twenty-five-city cross country tour with a cast of over seventy-five skaters starred British Olympic figure skater, dancer, and actress, Maria "Belita" Jepson-Turner. Ice Capades grew rapidly and prospered for almost fifty years as the public flocked to see the unique thrills and beauty of skating, from solos and romantic pairs to large precision groups, all interspersed with comedy and variety acts in a family-friendly spectacle. However, interest declined in the 1980s and Ice Capades went out of the business in the early 1990s. The Uksilas traveled with Ice Capades for ten years before retiring to the San Francisco Bay area. Charles died at the age of 76 in 1964, and he was inducted into the Upper Peninsula Sports Hall of Fame in 1974 - an amazing career of hockey and figure skating.

Learn more about **Bill Sproule** in our Author Bios section at the back of this book

Michigan's Dogman

by Maria Vezzetti Matson

"Don't forget my pasty before crossing the Mackinaw Bridge," I tell her," stop at the Mighty Mac Pasty Shop."

Just thinking about the Cornish meat pie makes my mouth water—flakey golden crust enclosing juicy rutabaga, carrots, beef, and onions. You didn't have to be a Cornish copper miner to enjoy them. I hear my mother's tired laugh over the cellphone.

"I bet sis is glad to be back at the university. It's lots of driving for you in one day. It'll be dark and icy on the roads, Ma. Be safe. Don't worry about us. Grams' snug in her chair and watching the news. Surprise her with some fudge."

I tell Ma I love her, say goodbye, and place my cellphone into my flannel shirt pocket. I'm the man of the house, so I need the phone. At twelve, not many of my friends own one.

Looking through the picture window, I see daylight dimming into dusk. The dark snow clouds tell me winter in Northern Michigan is here to stay.

Bang-bang-bang, it's the sound of a shotgun.

"Illegal hunters still out hunting, Grams. Strange, it's almost dark."

The adjacent wildlife preserve looks mysterious with leafless dark branches and dense dead undergrowth. The evergreens provide a windbreak but create a wall of black contrasting with the falling snowflakes. It looks haunted. The wind blows. I worry about branches falling and cutting off our power.

"Grams," I call out, walking into the lighted room, "what's happening on the news? What's the weather report?"

My Grams is cranky, hard of hearing, and kind of lives in the past. But she's lovable, too. She grunts at me and points to the tele-vision. We got her to read captions instead of blasting up the volume.

I read the bright red headlines, Michigan Dogman Sighting Alert.

The interior lights flicker, the TV dissolves into a black screen, and the electricity goes out.

"I'll get the flashlight, Grams, don't worry."

Her eyes are wide open in disbelief, and she remains focused on the lifeless TV. Her lips are moving, trying to communicate some message.

"Save it until I come back." I find a flashlight and get a blanket for Grams. The heat's off, too. Who knows how long the power will be out?

I find my warm snuggles, the onesie dog bodysuit. It's easy enough to slip on over my clothes. Taking off my shoes, I place my feet into the dog-like paw slippers, use my hands to pull the sleeves along, zip it up to my neck. I decide to leave the attached hood, with the floppy dog ears, hanging down my back. I place my cellphone in the front pocket. I can't resist growling.

Returning to the darkening living room, Grams squirms in her chair and points her knobby finger to the window. Why? She's irritated, anxious, and stares out the window.

The snow carpets the lawn. Surrounding the yard is the snowcapped rustic twig fence. It does little to protect us from visits by rabbits, deer, or an occasional coyote.

"Did you see someone outside?"

I feel the tension in the small room, then decide to put her at ease by getting on all fours, flipping my dog hood over my head, and crawling. She'll like my joke.

Grams notices a dog-like movement creeping towards her. She springs to a standing position and begins to scream. I jump up and run to help her. Grams' eyes close, shoulders sag, and in slow motion, her body begins to collapse. I catch her. Put her in her chair. She isn't moving.

Is she dead? Did she die of fright?

I'm distracted by an unearthly howl outside, and a scratching sound like animal claws on our front door. The blackening darkness of evening surrounds the house inside and out. I grab my cell phone. Using its flashlight, I aim at our front door.

The small fan-shaped glass window on top of the wood panel reflects the light. I see two yellow circles. They remind me of car lights shining on deer eyes. Crazy, what deer are seven feet tall? Can it be a coyote on its rear legs? The yellow globes disappear as I hear Grams' moan.

In a telltale whisper, she asks, "Did you see it? The Dogman!"

I point the flashlight at my face thinking she won't be afraid.

She shrieks, "Don't hurt me! What do you want this time?"

"Grams, Grams, it's me."

The electricity returns, lights flicker back on, and the TV colored image reappears on the screen. Placing her hand over her heart, she begins to whimper. Her head trembles. She murmurs the words, "not again, not again."

Something spooked her in the news. Was it the Dogman Alert? What's going on?

A glass of water might help calm her. I go to get one. Wisely, I take off my comfy onesie. If Dogman's on her brain, I don't want to look like a dog boy.

I return with the glass of water and hand it to her. Unmuting the TV, we listen to the news broadcast on Channel Nine. A cartoonish sketch of a werewolf looking beast with bared teeth fills the screen.

The newscaster says, "Sightings of the legendary Dogman are surfacing again. The man's body with the dog's head appears in a ten-year cycle with years ending in the number seven. Lumbermen in 1887 were the first to report seeing it."

Gram's ghostly white face freezes in horror. "See?" she asks while pointing to the picture window, not the TV.

I glimpse a bison sized shadowy figure. It's on four legs and dashing behind the trees. An eerie human-like scream or howl makes us shudder. Shining my flashlight in the direction of the sound, I spot two large yellow eyes peering back at us. In a blink, they're gone.

"The Dogman," she says, "He knows where I am now."

"Huh?"

"Years ago, your Gramps and I saw him. No one believed us, just a myth they told us. Gramps went hunting for him. Saw two, wounded one."

"Is this true?"

"Got the newspaper guy to come and take photos of the huge muddy footprints. Found a trail of blood, but no Dogman body. They laughed at us and said we made it all up. Fake news."

I stifled a laugh. Older people always tell stories and exaggerate. Her Dogman story must be another tale. My skeptical face makes her angry.

"You don't believe me. You're like all the others." She mutes the TV and turns her face away from me.

I feel guilty making her so upset and wonder if there's any truth to her story. I start to walk back toward the kitchen with her empty glass and pass the front door. I flip the outdoor lights on for my Ma. I wonder if I should shovel off the sidewalk.

Opening the front door, a pungent odor of rotten eggs, feces, and something like wet dog fur enters my nostrils. Then I gulp, not believing what I see.

The damage to the exterior of the door is significant. Deeply gouged slashes crisscross the once perfectly polished oak door. My eyes drop down to the snow-covered sidewalk leading to the front porch. The giant canine-looking hind leg footprints stop at the front door. The deep wolf-like tracks are filling up with snow and won't be visible much longer. A distant creepy snarling noise comes from the wooded preserve.

I'm frightened. The thought of the Dogman makes me shiver. Reentering the house, I double-lock the door.

Grams gives me a knowing look and says, "See, I told you so!"

Learn more about **Maria Vezzetti Matson** in our Author Bios section at the back of this book

Captive Spirit

by Tamara Lauder

She wondered if anyone else ever noticed or if he did it just for her. Twice a year, Sorel went to the zoo, once with her class, and once with her family. She loved seeing all the animals—but the tigers—well, they were her favorite. There was a white tiger. It was spectacular. His short white fur seemed so soft and slinky, quite different than her grandmother's coarse white hair.

Sorel saw her grandmother's hair once, first thing in the morning. Gram, as they called her, didn't know Sorel sneaked a peek as Gram was going to the bathroom. Her hair was standing straight up and out, like the bristles on Sorel's hairbrush. Sorel didn't know that hair could do that, at least not without lots of hairspray.

"Sorel!" her teacher said loudly. "C'mon, we have to move along."

Sorel could have stood there for hours watching the white tiger with the black stripes. Sorel looked back as her teacher pulled her by the hand. She could see the tiger's eyes meet hers. The reflection of his eyes, from the morning sunlight shining into the dark cave, penetrated her soul. He was trying to tell her something. Sorel just knew it.

There he went again. His head! It wriggled through the cage, his eyes fixated on Sorel as though sending her a message. Sorel broke free from her teacher's strong grip and ran toward the cage.

"Sorel! Come back here! You have to stay with the other children. Come back here!"

Sorel paid no attention to her teacher's cries as she ran back toward the cage. Mrs. Miller would understand once she saw what was going on. She was a nice person. Sorel ran as fast as she could to stay out of reach of Mrs. Miller's outstretched arm. When Sorel reached the cage, the tiger was gone. In Sorel's effort to preserve her freedom from Mrs. Miller, she must have missed the tiger's head squirming back into the cage. *How did I miss it?* Sorel wondered if Mrs. Miller saw it.

"Sorel! You absolutely cannot do this again! We talked about this before we came. Now let's go. We have to catch up with the rest of the class."

"But, Mrs. Miller. Did you see it? Did you see it?"

"See what Sorel? There is nothing here. The tigers must have gone back inside of the cave. C'mon now. We have to go."

"But—"

"Sorel. We talked about this. Let's go."

Mrs. Miller's tone had quieted down from her first outburst when Sorel had first run off. She now addressed her in her usual gentle tone. Sorel wondered if Mrs. Miller did see the tiger with his head outside of the cage, his large sleek body still inside, and just wouldn't admit it. Mrs. Miller never told Sorel that it was "just her imagination" like her family did; therefore, Sorel remained suspicious that Mrs. Miller did actually witness the sighting but felt too embarrassed to side with an eight-year-old. At the very least she never made Sorel feel badly about her experience. That is one of the reasons she liked Mrs. Miller so much. She was stern, but kind. She never put any of the students down or made them feel ashamed for something that they did.

Every experience is meant to be learned from; Mrs. Miller would say when one of the students made a mistake. Sorel wished everyone was like that, especially her family. Sorel's head was always full of ideas, pictures to draw, stories to tell about the things that she witnessed. There just wasn't enough time in the day to get everything down on paper, so Sorel would hide under the covers at night with a tiny flashlight that Joey, a friend of hers at school, took from his dad's garage. *He won't miss it,* he told her. *He probably doesn't even know that he has it. His garage is such a mess. Plus, my mom is always telling him to get rid of that junk.*

Joey was a good friend. He seemed to understand Sorel. He wasn't the best student, but Mrs. Miller never made him feel bad. She would just always smile as she handed him his paper and say, *I know that you can do better next time Joey, because you got one more right than last time.*

Sorel would help Joey with his homework sometimes, but he usually had to rush home and help his dad at the family hardware store. Joey didn't like working there any better than Sorel liked having to study all the time. In the springtime, when they got a chance, they would escape to the creek and play in the gushing water. Each year they tried to make a raft out of the old logs that drifted and settled along the side of the creek. They would tie them together with old string Joey found in his dad's cluttered garage. They never floated very well. They knew if they ever got caught, they would be in big trouble. Sorel's mother, well, was worried about everything all the time, but in this case, she would worry that Sorel would drown in the creek. Joey's dad, well, he would have been mad that Joey was wasting time and didn't rush right home to help him in the hardware store.

Sorel was a good student—good, being the key word. She was a good student because she did her studies like she was told and had to study a lot to get the grades she achieved. They did not come easily. She would try to resist the rules of studying every night, but never got her way. All she really wanted to do was draw, write stories, or just stare into the sky. If she could have, she would have arranged a stakeout near the tigers' cage so she could witness the white tiger's head wiggle in and out of the cage bars and then draw a picture of him. Sorel wondered if he would ever escape; if she would go there one day and the cage would be empty. She hoped so. Sorel's nightly prayer was that he would one day be free from human captivity and expectation. Sorel felt a special connection with him. Every time she visited, she could feel his glassy eyes penetrating deep inside of her, asking for her help. She didn't know how to help him now, but maybe one day she would, when she was older. In the meantime, Sorel decided to keep on praying.

Year after year her class and her family would visit the zoo, but then high school began. The yearly visits to the zoo stopped. The family visits to the zoo stopped. Sorel and Joey didn't see each other very much either because Sorel was busy with homework, sports, and music. Joey was occupied working at his dad's hardware store after school. Sorel didn't have time to help him anymore with his homework, as she struggled to keep up with her own. They were also both taking different classes.

Sorel thought about the white tiger often. She could visualize him inside the cage behind the bars, eyes sad, watching the passersby. Then she would remember his head, outside of the cage. At this point in her life, she wondered if it was real. She began doubting herself, but then noticed how her spirit lifted as she thought about the tiger with his head outside of the cage. She remembered his eyes, not just how they looked at her, but how they made her feel. They were calling to her. She felt her spirit begin to lift as she thought about those moments. She wondered if the tiger was still there, or if he had escaped, as she had prayed for every night as a young child. Life had gotten so full of stuff, that she was forgetting about everything she loved doing, the people she enjoyed doing them with, and the things that made her feel alive—like the tiger with the beautiful white soft fur coat with black stripes that wiggled his head out of the cage, maybe, just for her. She never really knew if Mrs. Miller ever actually saw it. She never said. At this point, she didn't even know if Mrs. Miller was still teaching. Sorel knew she would never have the courage to ask Mrs. Miller if she ever saw the tiger's head outside of the cage bars.

Sorel decided that she would make a trip to the zoo sometime soon. She would ask Joey, to see if he could get away from his dad's hardware store long enough to go with her. Joey was never with Sorel when the tiger actually had his head out of the cage. He was usually up ahead, with the rest of the class, where Sorel was supposed to be as well. Sorel was not sure what Joey would think about her sightings in the past, so she decided to keep her motivations a secret and just preface her idea as a fun visit to the zoo for old times' sake. Joey had always been "cool" with whatever Sorel was into when they were kids, but their time together had been limited since high school started, so she wasn't sure about his outlook on things at this point.

Joey seemed excited about the invitation. With a lot of persuasion from Joey's mom, Joey's father reluctantly agreed to let him take a Saturday afternoon away from the store. Sorel was excited, but a bit nervous at the same time, wondering if the tiger was still there. Sorel and Joey took off walking to the zoo as soon as Joey got done working for the morning. It was about a mile walk. Sorel was hoping that things would not feel weird between Joey and her, since they had not spent much time together recently.

Sorel decided to just start any conversation she could think of. "When do you do your homework Joey, if your dad has you working in the store all of the time?"

"Oh, I don't do much. I'm too tired when I get home. I usually just eat, go to my

Encaged

room, and fall asleep as soon as I start studying."

"Does it bother you?"

"Does what bother me?" Joey looked puzzled.

"Not getting your homework done?"

"Weeell, I don't get the best grades, if that's what you're askin'. You know that Sorel. Plus, I don't have you to help me anymore." Joey kicked a pebble on the sidewalk and then looked at Sorel and smiled. "My pop isn't real happy about my grades, but Mom gets on him real good if he says anything to me. She tells him he can't say anything if he expects me to keep working in the store all the time."

"Well, do you like it?"

"Like what? Bad grades, or workin' in the store?"

"Working in the store, silly?" Sorel chuckled. She had forgotten how much Joey used to make her laugh.

"Not really, but it keeps my dad off my back, and off my mom's too, so I just do it. Plus, *you* know... I don't really like studyin' anyhow."

"Me either!"

"What? You've always studied Sorel. What are you talking about? You're a good studier. I wouldna made it through eighth grade without ya."

"Well, Joey, it's kinda like you. It just keeps everybody off my back if I just do what they want and be what they want."

"Well, I don't intend on being a hardware store worker my whole life, if that's what you're thinkin'. I'm just workin' there til I can get outta the house and don't have to listen to my dad complain that I'm not workin' hard enough. Then I can do what I want."

"Well, whadaya wanna do Joey?"

"Oh, I don't know yet, but I'll know it when it comes along. I haven't had a chance to do anything else but go to school and work in the hardware store. Why the third degree about school and homework anyhow? Aren't we supposed to be here having fun?"

"Oh ya. Sorry."

They had finally reached the gate into the zoo. Sorel handed the young gatekeeper enough money for both her and Joey. The gatekeeper was a young woman. The older woman that kept the gate for all of Sorel and Joey's previous visits to the zoo was not there. She had always been really friendly, was always smiling and asking the kids about school, and seemed to remember everyone's name. The unfamiliar young gatekeeper put her cell phone down with one hand, swooped her long brunette hair back with her other hand, and then took Sorel's money. She made no eye contact with Sorel. Sorel started to walk away, but then turned back.

"Where's Betty?" she asked the young woman.

"Huh?" The woman seemed annoyed by the interruption, as she was already reengaged with her cell phone. "Who's Betty?" she asked sarcastically, finally making eye contact with Sorel.

"She was the gatekeeper. Here at the zoo. For years. Betty was her name."

"Oh. I have no idea."

"Well, thanks." Sorel felt a bit disheartened, as she was envisioning Betty being a part of the day's experience, for old times' sake.

The young woman made no parting response and continued her cell phone activity.

"Let's go," Sorel said to Joey.

"But I gotta pay."

"Don't worry about it. I got it."

"Gee! Thanks Sorel. You didn't have to do that."

"Sure I did Joey. You're losing out on work wages today to come with me. So, thanks."

"Are you kiddin'? You're the one doin' me the favor. Where we goin' first?"

"To see the tigers." Sorel tried to contain the excitement in her voice as she led the way.

"Oh ya, I remember you used to love looking at the tigers, especially that albino one."

"It's not an albino," Sorel said in an annoyed tone.

"Well, what is it then?"

"It's an infrequent genetic—"

"I remember Mrs. Miller getting mad at you for always taggin' behind," Joey said in a very animated tone. "That tiger ever get his head back in the cage that one day?"

Sorel stopped dead in her tracks, her annoyance about her precise researched answer being rudely interrupted, now replaced by panic. "What did you say?"

"The white tiger? Did he ever get his head back in the cage that day that Mrs. Miller got mad at you for laggin' behind?"

"Did you see it?"

"See what?"

"The tiger's head?"

Joey laughed. "Of course, I saw the tiger's head. I don't remember any headless tigers when I looked in the cage."

"Nooo!" Sorel grabbed Joey's arm and twisted him around, so he was looking at her. "Did you see the tiger's head out of the cage?"

"Oh thaaat. No. I didn't personally see the tiger's head out of the cage, but I know that's what you saw."

"Why? Did Mrs. Miller tell you that's what I saw?"

"Don't get so worked up. No, Mrs. Miller didn't tell me that."

"Did Mrs. Miller see the tiger's head out of the cage?"

"No. Well, I guess I don't know for sure if Mrs. Miller saw anything, but I overheard you talking to yourself one day at the zoo, after Mrs. Miller pulled you back to the class."

"Do you think anybody else heard me?"

"No, I don't think so. I wouldn't worry about it. The rest of them are all fuddy-duddies anyhow. They wouldn't get it."

Sorel didn't quite know what to say at this point. She was uncertain from their conversation if Joey believed that the tiger's head really was out of the cage when she was there, or if he thought it was all in her imagination. What did he mean by *they wouldn't get it*? Sorel wasn't sure but was too embarrassed to ask at this point. She decided to leave it alone because they were almost at the tigers' den. It felt like old times, talking with Joey again. It was easy and comfortable. Joey skipped up ahead and arrived at the tigers' cage first.

"Is he there?" Sorel yelled.

"I don't see anything yet. They must all be in the den."

Sorel got to the cage and grabbed the bars looking inside.

"Don't get your head stuck inside," Joey said with a smirk on his face.

"I think I see him. Inside the cave," Sorel said, ignoring Joey's comment.

"Oh yeah." Joey pressed his face against the cage trying to get a better look inside. "I think he's coming out."

Sorel's heart skipped a beat. Out of the dark cave sauntered the tiger with the soft-looking smooth white coat with black stripes. He seemed to be walking slower than she had remembered, but after all, it had been several years since she had been to the zoo.

"He's as beautiful as I remember him, just a little slower," Sorel said, almost in a trance.

"Yup, he's pretty cool. He is older though you know. My granddad walks slower each year I see him. You know that tiger years are like a bunch of people years—"

"Yeah, yeah, I know Joey. Save me the lecture about how old he is. Isn't he just magnificent?"

Joey was about to comment when the tiger came right up to the cage where they were standing. Joey backed up.

"Sorel, be careful, he's right there! He could swipe you with his paw."

"He won't hurt me," Sorel commented.

"How do *you* know?"

"I just know."

Just as Sorel said that, the tiger fixated his glassy golden green eyes on Sorel as he turned his head from one side to the other, as though studying her carefully.

"He seems to like ya," Joey interjected.

Sorel spoke softly to the large white cat. "How have you been? I'm so sorry that I have not been here to visit lately. You know, school, life, well… it's just been busy. No excuse I know. I've thought about you a lot though. Well, all the time, in fact."

Joey didn't say a word. He just listened intently to Sorel's conversation with the tiger. Joey stared at Sorel, then at the tiger, then at Sorel again. The tiger made a guttural sound as he rotated his head around, like a house cat when they want to be petted. Sorel smiled. Her heart felt warm. She could feel the tears well up in her eyes. She bent her head down to the tiger's head level and leaned forward toward the cage. She whispered, hoping that Joey wouldn't hear, "I've

Captive Spirit

been praying for you, that you escape some-day." The tiger made another head rotation with a gentle guttural sound, as if to thank her.

Out of the corner of her eye, Sorel could see Joey straining to hear her, trying not to make it obvious.

"I don't know what you said to him, but I think he's tryin' to talk back to you." Joey's comment sounded sincere, not sarcastic, like Sorel was dreading that it might.

Sorel and Joey stayed at the cage, just watching the tiger for at least thirty minutes. Finally, Sorel decided they had better move on to some of the other animals before Joey started thinking she was weird.

"Well, I suppose we better go, huh Joey?"

"Weeeell, I suppose. If you want to? I don't mind staying here a bit longer if you want Sorel."

"Oh, that's okay. We better go see some of the other animals as well."

Sorel and Joey stayed at the zoo for an-other two hours, but nothing was as satis-fying to Sorel as the white tiger. Sorel knew that they better be going home, but she re-ally wanted to go to the tigers' den by her-self, to see if the white tiger would wiggle his head out of the cage. She didn't know if he would do it if somebody else was with her.

"Oh Joey, I think I dropped my barrette at the tigers' cage. I'm gonna run back and see if I can find it."

"Oh, I'll come wi—Uumm, I'm gonna go to the bathroom. How bout I meet ya at the gate?"

"Great! I mean… great. That'll work. I'll meet you there." Sorel was trying to disguise her relief, but she really wanted to make one last visit to the tigers alone and didn't want to hurt Joey's feelings.

Sorel took off running back to the tigers. The white tiger was laying in the yard. His eyes were closed as he basked in the sun. His white coat shimmered in the sunlight. Sorel felt at peace—relaxed—something she had not felt in a while. The tiger made her feel calm, hopeful for things her heart yearned for, but she felt she could not speak of—things she was starting to lose sight of.

She felt connected to the tiger somehow. He had to yearn for his freedom someday. Sorel closed her eyes too, as the sun hit her face. It felt warm against the cool fall air. She could feel goose bumps perfuse her arms and legs, tingling as they arose. Sorel opened her eyes. To her surprise, the tiger's face was right up to the cage. Sorel was a bit stunned, as she had not heard him walk toward the cage.

Sorel's mind went from one thing to the next. First, she imagined herself in a snowy landscape watching his white coat slither along the ground waiting to pounce on an unsuspecting deer. Next, she was in Afri-ca as the tiger crouched in the tall grass to blend in, waiting for a zebra. She real-ized in that moment, that silence was the key to his survival in the wild. *How else would he be able to catch prey?* While a ti-ger's mighty roar and ferocious bite brought them respect and power, their real success and survival depended on their silence. Humans had taken so many opportunities away from him.

With his head tilted sideways, he stared at Sorel with sorrowful eyes. A guttural sound, just like before, came from deep inside his throat, commanding but gentle. Just like when she was a kid, it felt as though he was trying to tell her something.

For the first time in years, Sorel didn't feel alone anymore. She felt a bond with the mus-cular white cat that she could not explain to anybody, not even Joey.

"Sorel!" Joey interrupted her daydream as he was yelling her name and running toward her. "Sorel!" He stopped to catch his breath before continuing, "I thought I better check up on you. You were takin' a while. I wanted to be sure that you were okay."

"Oh. Sorry Joey. I didn't realize that so much time had passed."

"Oh, that's okay. I thought I better make sure no weirdoes snatched ya. You'd be a good catch."

Sorel smirked. "Thanks for checking on me. I just got caught up in the warmth of the sun and, well, just stuff. I'm ready to go."

Joey and Sorel started walking toward the gate where their visit had begun. Sorel drug her feet a bit and kicked pebbles along the way. She could hear Joey chattering in the background, but her mind was still in the snowy deer hunt and the African zebra herd.

"Sorel. Look! The moon is green."

"Huh? Oh ya, a huh."

"Sorel, you're not payin any attention to me. You didn't hear a word I said. I just said that the moon was green, and you agreed. Plus, it's daylight out."

"Oh, I'm sorry Joey. I didn't mean to ignore you. I guess I'm just a little distracted."

"I know you were hopin' to see the tiger poke his head outta that cage, but he's not gonna, ya know."

"Why do you say that, Joey? You think I'm crazy. Don't ya? You think it was all my imagination."

"No, I don't. I never said that. Plus, it doesn't really matter what I think, Sorel. All that matters is what you think. That tiger's head can't get outta the cage no more cause you trapped it inside."

"Whatdaya mean Joey? What are you talking about?"

"You know, with all the stuff they got ya doing in school and at home. Ya know, it's just like the hardware store is for me. It's just stuff. It traps ya. Ya can't get out."

Sorel and Joey kept walking in silence until they reached the gate. They said goodbye to the new gatekeeper, even though she didn't seem even remotely interested in goodbyes. She did look up from her cell phone though, for a brief moment, and waved. No smile though.

Once they were out of the gate and far enough away so the gatekeeper wouldn't hear them, Sorel asked Joey, "Remember how Betty used to wave like crazy when we all left the zoo?"

"Oh ya! You'da thought she was gonna wave her hand off. It was funny. She used to say goodbye to each one of us too. How'd she ever remember all our names?"

"I don't know. It's not really the same without her, I don't think," Sorel said.

"No. You're right. It doesn't feel the same as it did when we were kids."

They kept walking down the sidewalk toward home. The sun was beginning to lower on the horizon portraying a pinkish purplish backdrop. Sorel sighed as the colors flashed through her head on a watercolor canvas. Joey just looked straight ahead, seemingly as impressed with the intensity of the colors.

"Pretty, huh?" Joey said.

"It's beautiful! Joey…"

"Yeah?"

"Never mind."

There was silence between them again as they continued walking. They were almost at Sorel's house when Joey spoke. "Sorel, you gotta let the tiger outta the cage."

Sorel chuckled. "What are you talking about Joey? You want me to break into the zoo and cut the bars of his cage open?"

"No. I mean *your* tiger. *You*, Sorel. *You* gotta break outta *your* cage. Once you do that, the tiger at the zoo will stick his head outta the cage again. You'll see. Just remember though, you're runnin' outta time."

"Whatdaya mean, running out of time?"

"It's like I told ya. Tiger years go quicker than human years. Remember? And he's getting' older. So, hurry up."

"Joey, how'd you get so smart?"

"Well, I'm not smart like you. I guess I just know different kinda stuff. You know … the kinda stuff they don't tell ya in school, just to screw with your head."

Sorel laughed. "Joey, you are somethin'. How'd we ever lose touch?"

"Well, I guess you're always busy and I haven't wanted to bother ya."

Sorel didn't respond, so Joey interjected, "But I'm busy too. My dad sees to that."

"Yeah, I suppose so. Well, what are we going to do about it?"

"Maybe we'll just have to make more trips to the zoo before that tiger kicks the bucket. You wanna see him escape, right? Well, let's help him do it."

"You would do that Joey? You would do that with me. You would do that for him?"

"No Sorel. I would do that for *you*."

Learn more about **Tamara Lauder** in our Author Bios section at the back of this book

The Wonder of Snow

by Tamara Lauder

I look outside at the snowy landscape and marvel at its beauty. The white tufts of snow glisten as the bright sunshine hits their surface between the shades of the tall pines. Giant white mounds sit above the birdfeeder, birdhouses, and the large oak tree stump in the middle of my yard. Snow is nestled tightly on the trees where the branches meet, most snow blown off the needles from the brisk wind the day before.

After several hours of shoveling, yooper-scooping, and snowblowing, the thick blanket of white is removed from its place of origin to its designated spot for the season. The chickadees and goldfinches, waiting patiently for the feeder to be replenished, no longer flutter in front of the window where I sit each morning to observe and peacefully drink my coffee. They now gorge themselves on the feast at the newly filled feeder.

A backcountry ski is the gift that my husband and I treasure with each new snowfall bestowed upon us. While only the second substantial snowfall of the season, the snow is deep enough to leave our skis buried beneath, as we trudge through the precious white gift. Our legs burn as we propel through the fourteen inches of heavy fresh snow that lay atop the twelve inches of once fluffy old snow. The sensation in our muscles intensifies the excitement, as one explores the environment amidst the infrequent blue sky and bright sunshine touching the crystalline deciduous tree branches. Magic, it seems, as it appears as though myriads of white lights are strung meticulously on even the smallest of branches. The days now short, the sun barely reaches above the treetops for a brief period of time each day, requiring one to ski in a variety of directions and terrains to experience the warmth of the sun hitting your face and reaching the ground at any given moment.

The silence is powerful. The wind, after delivering the storm, has died down and leaves the winter paradise for all to treasure. Many snowbirds have migrated, leaving serenity for the local birds that stay for a period of time. As the climate changes, so might migration patterns, but for now, the silence that the snow brings is the remedy for the soul that searches for healing and rest from the busy seasons.

How is it that such a single tiny flake of snow can have such a positive impact on the world? A single flake can make any person, but especially those who have never seen snow, smile, cry, and direct their hands and face toward the sky, longing for more of the tiny miracle. When many single tiny flakes happen at once, an accumulation of snow covers the bareness and dirt, leaving everything feeling fresh and new. Once the ground is covered, each additional snowfall leaves a clean white blanket offering new and exciting opportunities for some, and much needed rest for all.

I wonder if one tiny flake of kindness could do the same? Could one single act of love make someone smile, laugh, and hold their hands up toward the sky, longing for more? I wonder if many tiny random acts of kindness and love could cover up the bareness and the dirt that the human race experiences, leaving everything feeling fresh and new? Once the groundwork is covered, would each additional act of love and kindness leave us feeling clean, give us hope for new opportunities, joy for those we have, and rest from that which makes us weary? I wonder if one's feet being buried beneath such precious gifts would make one's heart burn with excitement and see the lights strung meticulously all around them in what once felt cold and exposed? I wonder, in the wonder of snow.

Learn more about **Tamara Lauder** in our Author Bios section at the back of this book

Two Goldfinches

Expanding Horizons – Seeking Harmony

by Tamara Lauder

By "The Great Water"
as one looks out onto the horizon
from the hill on the old family farm
there are lush green trees that surround,
as the sun meets nature's promotions
daylight nestles, miners settle,

pinks and purples blanket their rest
the cool fresh breeze from the Superior lake
quenches the heat of the day,
bringing solace to the present generation
and those of the past

and those,
still to come to terms with
what lies before them
and comes without asking

yet,
questioned if enough.

Pasties and strawberries nourish the body
the sauna, cleanses the soul
wondering,
which of the offspring will stay
to preserve what is and what has been.

•••

On "The Great Plains"
as one looks out onto the horizon
from the prairie on the old family farm,
the landscape—the book
drought—the reader telling a story
of scorched crops covering the fields

as the sun falls off the edge of the earth
for nothing,
stands in its way.

Blood-orange paints the sky—a sign of old
the hot wind blows night and day
no relief as one retires
but hope, brings solace to those of the
    present
and those of the past

and those,
still to come to terms with
what lies before them
and comes without asking
yet,
questioned if enough.

Cold beer and Braunschweiger nourish the
    body,
sauerkraut and potato dumplings, a favorite,
will wait until the seasons change and the
    sun relents,
shelter from the brutal sun cleanses the
    soul
wondering,
which of the offspring will stay
to preserve what is and what has been.

•••

With "Marriage"
one looks out onto the horizon
as two old family farms meet
embracing each heritage for what it brings
distant from their original dwelling,
hearts unite attempting to maintain
some semblance of what was and what is

adjusting to changes brought by
those who thought it was enough
yet,
change what was to what
brings harmony between two worlds of
    difference.

A multitude of colors blends the two souls
as they explore their way about
other horizons, other heritages,
finding solace somewhere in between.

Food and beverage nourish the body
as the soul searches
for harmony connecting two worlds
and,
similarities in mankind,
independent of diversity
wondering,
which of the offspring will stay
to preserve what is and what has been.

❀ ❀ ❀

Learn more about **Tamara Lauder** in our Author Bios section
at the back of this book

Historical Autrain Lake Camp

Victorian Nightmare

by Tyler R. Tichelaar

Like his brother John, Chad Vande-laare loved Marquette history, but what he was really passionate about was everything Victorian. He loved Victorian carpets and wallpaper, Victorian furniture and Victorian dishes, and most of all, he loved Victorian houses. His greatest yearning was to live in a Victorian home—something along the lines of the house in *Meet Me in St. Louis* or the Winchester Mansion in California, or at least one of the big Victorians on Ridge Street in Marquette like his brother lived in.

Chad was very jealous that his older brother John lived in a Victorian house, and not just any Victorian house—the Robert O'Neill Historical Home. Robert O'Neill had been a famous novelist in the mid-twentieth century. He had not been Victorian, but his house was. He had befriended John when he was an old man and John was first starting out as an author. He had been so impressed with John that he had left him his Victorian mansion.

"It was left to me in trust," John had explained to Chad many times. "It's not really mine. I just have the right to live in it and be the caretaker. The house itself belongs to the Robert O'Neill Historical Trust. It's kind of a pain in some ways, actually. I mean, I love the house, but it's a lot of upkeep, plus we have to have several of the rooms open to the public for tours."

"Still, you get to live in it," said Chad.

Chad was also jealous because the house had once belonged to Marquette's pioneer Henning family. It had been built in 1868 by Gerald and Sophia Henning. John and Chad were Gerald Henning's great-great-great-grandchildren by his first wife, Clara. The Hennings had sold the house to Robert O'Neill's great-aunt and great-uncle when they left Marquette back in the 1870s, but as far as Chad was concerned, it should have stayed in the family. He was glad someone in the family had it again, even if it was John and not him, but he still wished it was him. And it could have been him, too, if John hadn't gone and married Wendy. Then Chad could have convinced John to let him live with him, and he would have been in charge of decorating decisions and restoration and simply would have enjoyed living in the house every day. But, unfortunately, John had married, and had a couple of kids too—Neill and Madeleine. The kids were teenagers now, and Chad loved them, but deep down, he felt resentment toward Wendy, and it didn't help that she ignored his decorating advice even though he knew more about Victorian furnishings than she and John put together.

To compensate for his lack of a Victorian mansion, Chad did the next best thing. He rented an apartment in an old house on Ridge Street. The house wasn't really a Victorian mansion, but it was a big house built on the property where the Longyear Mansion had once stood.

Unlike the Hennings, when the Longyears had decided to leave Marquette in 1903, they hadn't sold their house—they had taken it with them—to Brookline, Massachusetts. Their son Howard had drowned in Lake Superior, and Mrs. Longyear couldn't bear after that to look at the lake, which the house overlooked—especially not after the city decided to run a railroad track along the lakeshore where she wanted to build a memorial park dedicated to her son. And so, Mr. Longyear had suggested they move away and relocate the house too, and Mrs. Longyear had agreed. The mansion had been disassembled brick by brick—Chad's great-great-grandfather, Charles Dalrymple, had been one of the workers hired to help in the tremendous effort. One-hundred-and-ninety railroad cars had been required to transport the home to its new location.

Chad wished the house had never been moved. Marquette had never seen such a grand home before and likely never would again—at least not a vintage Victorian mansion. The Longyears' Lake Superior sandstone palace had contained sixty-five rooms, leaded glass windows, parquet floors, and an octagonal entry with a Tiffany stained glass dome. A library, music room, extensive porches, and a bowling alley in the basement had made it a true millionaire's mansion of the period. The property had been landscaped by no one less than Frederick Law Olmstead, and when the Longyears had moved in at Christmas 1892, the house had the distinction of being the first in Marquette to have electric lights. What a Christmas to remember that would have been! The only thing Chad loved as much as Victorian houses was Christmas. For Chad, to have been present on that spectacular day would have been the epitome of intoxicating happiness.

But the mansion had been moved, and it was replaced with several homes built in the first decades of the twentieth century, which were not Victorian but Edwardian and Georgian. Renting an apartment in one of them—decades after it had ceased to be a private residence—was the closest Chad could come to his Victorian dream. Nor was his apartment all that grand. Sure, there was the original woodwork and a few nooks and crannies. There was even a window with leaded glass at the top, but it was no Longyear Mansion. A remodeled living room and an open kitchen/dining area, a bathroom, a bedroom, and another small room somewhere between the size of a bedroom and a walk-in closet was all the space Chad had. But he did have a Ridge Street address, like his brother, and that meant something in Marquette.

Chad did everything he could to make his apartment as Victorian as possible. He wasn't able to change the bathroom fixtures, the ugly carpeting, or the horrid wood paneling some philistine had stuck up in the 1970s, but he could make everything else as Victorian as he wanted. He bought replica Victorian wallpaper for the rooms after getting his landlord's permission. He bought Victorian-looking throw rugs for the floors. He bought Victorian furniture at antique shops. He filled the walls with Victorian sconces and nineteenth-century photographs of Marquette. He even went to the Marquette County History Museum and bought reprinted photographs of rooms in the Longyear Mansion to hang on the walls. He bought candelabras, Victorian silverware, Victorian glassware, Victorian lamps, a replica victrola, and even a Victorian pickle dish because while he hated pickles, the Victorians had loved them.

Before long, John pointed out to Chad that if he would quit spending so much money on old Victorian stuff, he might be able to save enough to buy a little house for himself, but Chad did not want a little modern-looking or even twentieth-century house. He wanted a Victorian mansion, and he wasn't going to settle for anything less, so he kept buying Victorian knickknacks and bric-a-brac for the day when he would get one, whenever that day would be.

Some of Chad's possessions were quite impressive. Since he lived in Marquette, he managed to buy a dresser that had once belonged to George Shiras III and an end table that had belonged to one of the Kennedy sisters. He had touristy plates from the Hotel Superior and a large map of Marquette from 1886. He had antique books that had belonged to Marquette pioneers like Matthew Maynard, Amos Harlow, and even Carroll

Watson Rankin—he knew this as a fact for they had written their names in them. He had many beautiful books with gilded bindings by nineteenth-century authors no one remembered. John, who had a PhD in literature, was unimpressed by his brother's elegant collection, other than the first edition of Captain Marryat's *The Pirate* that Chad had picked up at a garage sale. But it didn't matter—Chad didn't read much beyond Victorian decorating magazines.

As the years passed, Chad's antique collection grew. End tables in the living room had Victorian candy dishes and lady's fans upon them. The bathroom had a Victorian man's mustache kit. The bedroom had a settee Queen Victoria herself would have envied. And for Christmas, Prince Albert could not have planned a more splendid tree. Charles Dickens might have popularized Christmas, but Chad had perfected it. He would have even had real candles on his tree if they would not have triggered his smoke detector.

For years, Chad had not invited his family over since his apartment wasn't that big and he had not wanted his nephew and niece to break anything—but now Neill and Madeleine were teenagers, so he invited everyone over the evening after Christmas. His parents, brother, and brother's family were served Christmas cookies on silver Victorian dishes, and they drank hot chocolate out of the rose teacups Grandma Whitman had gotten when she married—they were only Depression era, but they were family heirlooms, so Chad made an exception for them.

"Your apartment is so full of stuff it's starting to look like Lucy and Maud's house," said his mother. Lucy and Maud were her cousins, and Lucy was a pack rat.

"Please," said Chad. "They only have modern junk."

"You have nicer stuff," said Wendy, "but you do have a lot." She was perched on a Victorian settee next to John, afraid to sit back because it was an antique and Chad had warned her the back wasn't very sturdy.

Chad's father was less subtle than his mother. "Why don't you get rid of that old piece of junk?" he asked, gesturing toward the hutch cabinet.

Chad's eyes grew large with horror. "That was made by great-grandpa!" he exclaimed, as if his father should remember that.

"Whose great-grandpa?" asked Chad's mother.

"Your grandpa, Will Whitman," said Chad.

"Oh, really?" his mother replied, looking puzzled.

"Mom, it was in your grandparents' house all your life," Chad replied. "Alan gave it to me when he sold the house." Alan's father, Great-Uncle Bill, had lived in the Whitman family home until he died and then the house was sold out of the family. Chad had not wanted the house because it wasn't Victorian, and he couldn't afford it anyway, and it was over in North Marquette, the wrong part of town for him, even if his family had lived there for decades.

"I don't remember it," said his mom about the cabinet.

"You do have too much stuff," said John.

"The Victorians loved clutter," Chad told him. "Really, you need more in your house."

"Did they also love ugly wallpaper?" asked Madeleine. She was fourteen now and developing an attitude. Chad remembered the nasty girls he had gone to middle school with, and she sounded just like them.

"That is a William Morris pattern," he informed his niece.

"Who cares?" she said.

"Madeleine, don't be rude," her mother told her.

"We have William Morris wallpaper in the O'Neill House," her father reminded Madeleine, "in the library."

"Yeah," Madeleine said, "but ours isn't ugly."

"I like it," said Neill. Chad liked Neill. He was the peacemaker in the family and the one who usually took his side. Neill actually seemed interested when Chad would talk to him. He was almost like the brother Chad wished John would be sometimes, but John was an older brother, so usually disapproving because Chad had not been an overachiever like him. Neill was an older brother too—he was eighteen now and in his freshman year of college—but he was protective of his sister rather than controlling, and very mature for his age, Chad thought. His remark gave Chad the confidence to say to his brother, "I never thought your house was really persuasive as a Victorian home. You definitely need more Victorian items in it."

"But the O'Neills weren't Victorian," said Wendy. "More people come to visit the house because it belonged to Robert O'Neill, the famous author, than because it's historical. Of course, the O'Neills had some Victorian family heirlooms, but the library is the only room where they preserved the Victorian charm."

"Besides," added John, "too much stuff scattered about would be a liability—someone might trip over it. Even though we rope off parts of the rooms for tours, there's always someone who doesn't obey the rules. You should be careful yourself with all the stuff you have in here."

"Yeah," said Chad's father. "You could easily trip over something and kill yourself."

"I'm not going to trip over anything," said Chad. "I know where everything is. When I turn off the TV at night, I don't even turn on a light to go to bed. I can see just fine and know my way around here."

"That's good," said Neill. "I never turn on a light either at night. I can see fine in the dark."

Chad smiled at his nephew.

"Well, we should get home," said Chad's mother. "Now that Christmas is over, I need to catch up on my sleep."

After they left, Chad turned off all the lights and only left the Christmas tree on. He sat on the couch listening to his *Victorian Christmas Carols* record while trying to imagine what Christmas for the Longyears would have been like. Eventually, sugarplums began dancing in his head and he knew it was time to go to bed.

•••

A couple of weeks later, Chad was taking down his Christmas tree and decorations. As he was carrying a giant box of ornaments from the living room to the closet in the spare room, he couldn't quite see where he was and tripped over the edge of the living room rug. The box of ornaments box went flying, with the lid coming off and the ornaments strewing themselves down the hall. Chad did not fare better. He tried to right himself, grabbing at a little round end table to break his fall, but his efforts only sent the lamp teetering off the table while the table itself fell forward in front of him. Chad went sprawling over it, his hands reaching out to try to stop his fall, but they came in contact with the frame of his giant portrait of Queen Victoria, causing the picture to hang sideways. Queen Victoria was not amused.

Neither was Chad.

"Ow!" he shrieked as he lay on the floor, his feet elevated behind him on top of the table. For a moment he lay there, recovering from the shock of the fall. Then he started to pull his legs off the table and onto the floor. He managed to get into a sitting position, and then sliding one leg under himself, he tried to stand on it and pick himself up, but he instantly fell to the floor with a scream as excruciating pain shot through his toe.

Instantly, Chad was sure he had broken a bone. He managed to twist around to look at it and found it poking out at an odd angle through his sock. His foot was throbbing like hell. He managed to try to stand on his other leg and succeeded at pulling himself up by leaning against the arm of the couch. But when he tried to walk on the hurt foot, the pain was so unbearable he had to plop himself down on the couch. Fortunately, his cellphone was on the coffee table where he could reach it.

Chad knew he had to see a doctor. Since he had hurt his right foot, he wouldn't be able to drive. He thought about calling his mother, but she was a worrier, and he was trying to convince her to stop driving anyway, so he called his brother. When John didn't pick up, Chad thought about calling Wendy, but she was probably out with John somewhere, so he called his nephew. Once Neill answered, Chad explained the situation and Neill said he'd be right over to take him to the emergency room.

"Your dad is going to love this," Chad said on the way to the ER.

"Why?" asked Neill.

"He told me I'd trip over something in my apartment."

"Actually, I think Grandpa said that," Neill replied.

"It doesn't matter," said Chad. "Your dad is the one who first brought it up."

Neill decided to keep his mouth shut rather than get caught up in his father and uncle's petty squabbles.

A few hours later, an x-ray confirmed Chad had broken a bone in his foot. The ER doctor told him to stay off it and scheduled an appointment with an orthopedics doctor for him tomorrow. Neill promised to take him to the appointment since the university was still on Christmas break and he worked evenings at his job.

Neill helped Chad into his apartment and got him settled before he had to go to work. He suggested calling his father to come spend the night with Chad, but spending an evening with John was the last thing Chad wanted. He figured he could just sleep on the couch, if need be, and the pain killers were helping now, so he was sure he could make it to the bathroom and back. Neill cleaned up the spilled Christmas ornaments and righted what had fallen over, even straightening Queen Victoria before leaving for work.

A few minutes later, John called. Neill had earlier texted his father about what had happened while Chad's foot was being x-rayed.

"How are you feeling?" asked John.

"I'm okay," Chad replied, waiting to hear, "I told you that you'd trip over all that Victorian junk," but instead, John just asked if he needed anything.

"No," said Chad.

"Did you tell Mom and Dad?" John asked.

"No. They'll just worry."

"Well, you'll have to tell them."

"I'll call them later."

"Okay," said John. Chad could hear him hesitating, as if trying to decide whether or not to lecture his little brother.

"I'm really tired," said Chad. "I'm going to take a nap and then I'll call them this evening."

"Okay," said John. "If you need anything, let me know. I'll be home the rest of the day."

"Thanks," said Chad and disconnected.

•••

The next day, Neill took Chad to the orthopedics doctor, and they got him a pair of crutches. The doctor said the bone should heal by itself if Chad stayed off it, but he warned Chad to stay mobile and keep his foot elevated so he didn't get a blood clot. Afterward, they came home, and Neill stayed to finish taking down the Christmas decorations while Chad lay on the couch and told him where to put everything. His mother had offered to come help, but Chad didn't want her hovering over him. Sometimes he felt like Neill was the only one in the family he could cope with. Neill was always respectful to him. He didn't fuss like Chad's mother, or tell him what to do like John, or roll his eyes at him like Madeleine.

As Neill worked, he asked Chad about some of the historical photographs on the wall. Chad told him they were images of rooms inside the Longyear Mansion. Neill knew about the mansion, but he enjoyed hearing the extra details Chad shared.

"I wish I could have seen it," said Neill.

"So do I," said Chad, "but I have the next-best thing. I get to live on the property."

Additional talk about the Longyears led to Chad mentioning how after the family had left Marquette, they had built the Stone House at Ives Lake adjacent to the Huron Mountain Club north of Marquette. The family had spent many a summer there. When Chad was just a small boy in the 1970s, his grandfather, Henry Whitman, had been the caretaker at Ives Lake.

"I wish I could go up to Ives Lake," said Neill. "I've never been to the Huron Mountain Club at all. You and Dad are lucky to have memories of being up there as kids."

"I'm surprised your dad has never taken you up there," said Chad. "Being well known as a local historian, I would think he would know someone there."

"Probably," said Neill. "I should ask him. One of my classmates had a brother who worked up there one year. Wouldn't it be cool if I could get a job up there this summer? I'm sick of making pizzas."

"Actually," said Chad, "I know someone up there. Let me make a call and see if he knows how you can get a job there."

"Really? That would be awesome," said Neill. "You're the best, Uncle Chad."

Chad appreciated how Neill always seemed so grateful whenever he did something for him. He was so different from his father. Whenever Chad tried to discuss Marquette history with John, John was always correcting him about a date or a family connection or some other minor detail. Neill was different. He valued what Chad had to offer.

"I have something for you," said Chad. He directed Neill over to a bookshelf where a rock a couple of inches in diameter sat on a shelf.

"I got that up at Ives Lake," said Chad. "Geologists go up there to study the rocks, and one time when I was a kid, my grandpa took John and me inside the Stone House and there were a bunch of rocks on a table. He told us we could each have one. I don't know what John did with his, but that one was mine. I want you to have it."

"Really?" said Neill.

"Yes," said Chad. "No one else would appreciate it."

"Thanks," said Neill. He didn't know what kind of rock it was and neither did Chad. They had never seen anything like it, all brown but with two different shades and quite smooth rather than rough. It was definitely a rare stone, whatever it was. Neill tried to refuse it, but Chad insisted, so finally Neill pocketed it, thinking it cool to have something connected to Ives Lake, the Longyears, and his great-grandfather, as well as his uncle. "I'll have to ask my dad if he still has his."

Neill didn't have to work that evening, so he stayed for a while. He went to Togo's to get them subs for dinner, and then they spent time looking at historic photos of Marquette.

"I know my dad knows all this history stuff," said Neill, "but somehow it's more interesting talking to you about it."

"Well, I appreciate your enthusiasm," said Chad.

"You don't just lecture me about Marquette history like my dad," added Neill. "That gets old fast."

Chad knew exactly what Neill meant.

"Well, I better get home," said Neill. "Do you need anything before I go?"

"No," Chad replied. "I'll be fine."

"Okay. Good night then," said Neill, leaving Chad propped up on the couch where he planned to sleep that evening since it was easier to get up from the couch than his bed. He picked up his laptop from the coffee table and emailed his friend at the Huron Mountain Club about Neill, giving him Neill's phone number. Then he watched a little TV before drifting to sleep.

•••

In the morning, Chad woke and lay there on the couch for a while. He had to use the restroom but being on his foot hurt so much he decided to wait until he really needed to go. He lay there in the dim early morning light and admired his Victorian sconces, the imitation Victorian curtains, his replica victrola, the blue glass candy dish from the 1860s, and his gilded books on the shelf. Queen Victoria seemed like she was still asleep since he couldn't see her in the early morning light, but sometimes he thought the spirits of the Longyears must still be here, except Mrs. Longyear, who had chosen to leave and never return. How he wished he had been able to see the Longyear Mansion in reality. The black and white photographs hardly expressed how richly the house had been furnished, how very grand it had been, and how exquisite it would have been to live in that late Victorian world.

Finally, Chad could resist nature no longer. He carefully swung his legs off the couch and onto the floor. He put his weight on his good foot, holding onto the couch arm as he stood up. Then he took his first step on the foot with the broken bone. Suddenly, a searing pain hit his chest. That couldn't be from his foot. Would it go right up his body like that?

"Oh!" he screamed as another excruciating pain hit his chest. He was shocked by its vehemence. What was happening? Was he having a heart attack? His leg was also throbbing now, but not his foot.

The doctor's words came back to him. "Stay mobile so you don't get a blood clot." But he hadn't been very mobile.

"Oh, no," he cried out as his whole chest felt like it was about to explode. He bent over the coffee table and his fingers fumbled, trying to grab his cellphone as the pain became relentless, causing him to lose his breath.

Chad managed to swipe open the phone, and then he tried to go to his phone directory. Who should he call? Should he call 911? Probably. He couldn't believe the pain. It was so bad he couldn't focus to bring up the keypad to dial. Somehow, he had gotten on the call log screen. He could see the last call he had made was to Neill. He hit the phone icon next to Neill's name and heard the phone ring.

A new lightning bolt of pain shot through him as he heard his nephew say, "Hello."

"Neill, I'm in trouble.... I—I—I've got pain—I...."

And then he fell forward onto the coffee table, and the phone went flying out of his hand.

"Uncle Chad! Uncle Chad!" shouted Neill when he heard the sound, but Chad did not hear him.

•••

Everything seemed foggier, but the light was brighter. The sun was up, but who had opened the curtains? Queen Victoria was fully visible now. She still did not look amused, and Chad did not remember her picture being below him. How did he get so close to the ceiling? And who was that? Who was lying on top of his coffee table?

And then he heard a pounding at the door and someone jiggling the doorknob, and in a few more seconds, he saw the top of Neill's head as his nephew entered the room and went to the man on top of his coffee table. Was the person drunk? What was he doing there?

"Uncle Chad!" cried Neill, and then Chad saw more people enter the room. People in uniforms. Police. EMTs.

Oh, no! thought Chad.

The room grew even brighter as the people around the coffee table seemed to fade into the distance, and...was that Grandma?

John was right, thought Chad. *I hate that John is always right.*

Learn more about **Tyler Tichelaar** in our Author Bios section at the back of this book.

Historical · Yachting the Tahquamenon

Worth Fighting For

by Emilie Lancour

I've been doing a lot of work to heal myself; figuring out who I am and the fact that I am lovable, and I have a high self-worth. I'm figuring out that I was put here for a purpose and trying to learn what that purpose is. In all of this, a lot of questions about my childhood have come up. A lot about the memories I have and how they fit into a timeline. And about the memories I don't have. I don't remember being at the courthouse or meeting with anyone about the adoption. I don't remember you and him fighting. I don't remember changing my name at school. I don't remember a time without Dad and my sisters. I don't ever remember not feeling loved.

I have grown up believing that you asked him to revoke his parental rights so that Dad could adopt me, and I never really thought about his side of that and if he fought for me or how that all worked. I'm wondering when you first started thinking that adoption might be the road to take. I'm wondering when you talked to him for the first time about the adoption and what his reaction was or was it all done through the courts. Obviously, I can't ask him anymore.

I wonder how long after he signed the revocation did it take for my actual adoption to take place? A friend of mine got the papers in April and still does not have an adoption date. I always thought it was a few months but now thinking it may have been years.

There's always been something with my name in the back of my head. I remember standing under the clothesline with you and you telling me that I got to choose what name I wanted. I don't know when that conversation took place, and I don't know what my thinking was. Something related to my name is really strong in my body and I am not sure why my name seems to define me when it is really just a word.

I feel like there are a lot of gaps in what I remember about being little. I don't feel like I know if I was planned or wanted from day one. Did you and him talk about having a baby? I remember you saying that I was one of the only good things that came out of your marriage. I don't know if I was part of the reason for the divorce.

I don't know how much custody he had and how much he honored that. I know a lot of that was done through lawyers. I do remember being at his house and of course lots of time with grandma and grandpa and cousins. I don't remember ever missing birthdays or holidays with you. I love that I have so many memories of birthdays and holidays with you and grandma and grandpa. I love our traditions.

I don't know how much Dad was involved with making a decision about the adoption. I mean obviously he wanted to adopt me, or he wouldn't have gone through with it, but I wonder if he was part of the initial process of asking for that revocation. I assume the two of you were paying all of my bills because it looks like child support was an issue. I remember you talking about being in a car accident and wondering what would happen if you were gone...would he get custody, and would I have a relationship with my sisters?

I 100% know that everything that happened was out of love and that he did give me up to have a better life. I know you did it to protect me and make sure I was always going to be with family. I love the life I had.

He told me that when I talked to him a couple months before he died that he signed the papers out of love and to give me a better life, so I assume he felt that he wasn't able to do that. I think that alcohol was a lot of the reason he couldn't be consistent in my life. I have always thought that he couldn't figure out love with being married so many times and not being able to be a dad and grandpa over time. I now think he was a very loveable person and I guess I need confirmation that he did want me; that he fought to be my dad; that he tried. At the celebration of life for him, so many people shared what a good person he was and how he would do anything to help someone out. I was angry that I didn't see that side of him. I remembered the inconsistency. The lack of communication for years at a time especially when I was older. I think I can see that part of him now. I remember him making me burgers and fries and having a gum drawer, listening to Billy Joel and making salt dough ornaments, reading *Harold and the Purple Crayon* and him singing "Dear Little Dolly" and "Hush Little Baby". He gave me a job in college, and he came around a lot when my kids were little. He let people stay in his house instead of their car. He must have some redeeming qualities for you to have married him and for others to have done the same. He must have been okay for me to spend time with him because I know you would not have let me go with him if not.

I need to know that you fought too. And that Dad fought to change things legally. I need to know why the adoption mattered when Dad was always my dad ... I have no memories without him in my life. Was it all about the legality or were there more concerns about him? Was there abuse? Were you worried about him hurting me physically? Was it the alcohol? Was that always a concern? Was it just to keep us together?

I loved spending so much time with Grandma and Grandpa and know that a lot of that had to have started because you were a single mom. Thanks for keeping me when I know you had other choices. I love the relationship that I have with Dad and the fact that we celebrate the adoption every year. I love you and how you have always been a huge part of my life. I love memories of the trips we took and how honest and open you have always been. I guess what I'm just looking to know is that everyone was fighting for me and what was best and how my memories fit with reality. I need to know I was worth fighting for.

Learn more about **Emilie Lancour** in our Author Bios section at the back of this book

Historical · ironwood football brother Ben

Dying Autumn White
by M. Kelly Peach

Dying autumn white
Silence waits in mourning

Winter comes purely
Like magic—a mist riding

Upon a unicorn
Wind of lightest treading

Crystal scintillant fields and
Clouds of smokey wreathing

Snow flies before it falls
Is noon pale but night glinting

In Echoless Regions
by M. Kelly Peach

In Echoless Regions
   of falling starsilk
      and frozen
          moon particles drifting
            in whispered whiteness,

I am awestruck by
   pallid mantle's purity
      and soundless
         tranquility.

Quiescence,
   like a soothing balm
      heals my ragged soul,

As hyperborean murmurs
   encloak crystalline
      calm nights
        in the aftermagic
          of a midwinter's snowfall.

Learn more about **M. Kelly Peach** in our Author Bios section at the back of this book

Bestseller

by Richard Hill

Though I'm a live-and-let-live sort of guy, some people just get under my skin. They reel you in with their charm and BS, then play you for a sucker. Take this mystery writer from Upper Michigan I met last summer at an art fair. He goes by the name Tony James and lives somewhere up by Munising. This guy did some horrendous things to the trust of his readers that I just couldn't let pass. I made it my personal mission to expose this imposter and put an end to his deception.

Ever since I was a teenager, I've been a big-time mystery fan, reading everything from John LeCarre and Dashiell Hammett to Lee Child and Stephen King. I've always liked solving riddles, following clues, and tripping up criminals. I guess it goes with the territory—I'm a retired investigative reporter from the *Detroit Free Press* and can't seem to get it out of my head once I smell a rat. I spend my summers just west of the Soo in a little rundown cabin on Sullivan Creek, out near Raco—mostly fishing, reading, and recovering from my divorce a year ago. I bought this little shack right before the Covid-19 pandemic swooped down on us. To avoid isolation and pure squirreliness up here in the U.P., I try to broaden my horizons, for what it's worth, by getting out to a few art fairs and festivals during the summer. That's where I first ran across Tony James, the curious mystery writer.

It was the latter part of August last year, a rare hot and muggy day in the U.P., and the Blueberry Art Festival was underway in Par-adise. The three-day show included an eclectic mix of entertainment from magicians and chainsaw jugglers to folk music and blueberry pie-eating contests. I was strolling through the art fair, eating a fresh brat smothered in sauerkraut and mustard, checking out the stained-glass work, photography, and comical lawn ornaments made from discarded machine parts, when I bumped into a bold and colorful display of books for sale. A large yellow sign with prominent black lettering read: "Book Signing Today by Best-Selling Author Tony James." On several nearby easels were an oversized portrait of the author and a blowup poster of a book cover, *Death Warmed Over*. A long display table featured about a dozen mystery novels with names like *Icebound* and *Frozen Remains*. I was immediately drawn in.

Mr. James noticed me taking an interest in his books and approached me.

"Are you a mystery reader?" he asked.

He was an average-sized guy somewhere in his late forties and wore a wide-brimmed Panama hat and wire-rimmed sunglasses.

"Sure," I said, "I like a good murder mystery now and then."

"Well, you're in luck then. My books are all murder mysteries that take place mostly in the U.P. and Northern Michigan. This one's my latest, *Death Warmed Over*, and I'm offering a special discount on it today."

As I glanced at the titles on the table, I noticed that the name Tony James was splashed on every front cover in large letters whose size rivaled the title itself. It reminded me of the way some well-known writers on *The New York Times* bestseller list designed their book covers for maximum attention. I wondered why I'd never heard of this guy—not that I'm familiar with every prominent mystery author—and asked him how long he'd been writing.

"Only six or seven years now, but I've been lucky; my books have been selling really well. It's hard keeping most of my titles in stock."

"Really? I don't know why I've never run across any of your books."

"Oh, they're out there all right. My books are very popular. In fact, a couple months back, I was signing my books at the Barnes & Noble stores in New York and Chicago. Had people lined up around the block. This is my first time at the Blueberry Festival—thought I'd try something different."

"So," I said, "you must be pretty successful."

"Well, I keep quite busy. My wife, Sarah, helps me out in the summer when we do art fairs and festivals. She drives a school bus during the year and helps edit my writing whenever she can find time. Saves us a bundle in the long run."

I chose a couple mysteries to purchase, paid Mr. James, and wished him well. As I walked away, something about this guy didn't smell right to me. I'm familiar with plenty of mystery writers, yet I'd never heard of him. And if this writer was so successful, lining readers up at bookstores in New York and Chicago, why was he spending so much time selling books at summer art fairs? I decided to check up on a few things. Once you've been an investigative reporter, it's hard to shake loose your gumshoe habits, even though you're retired. Just have to do a little more digging around and see what turns up. Something unexpected usually does.

For several days, I holed up in my little cabin back in the woods, hoping for a few days of quiet and relaxation. By this time of year, the mosquitoes and black flies had mostly died off. Between drinking coffee and splitting wood for the cook stove, I read both mysteries I'd picked up from Tony James. The writing in both books was fast-paced and suspenseful—not exactly page-turners, but they definitely held my interest. After

years of writing for a metro newspaper, I had trained my eye to pick up errors; they seem to jump out at me. As I read further, a few punctuation goofs began to pop up regularly. I'm not trying to be picky, but in my experience, even some of the bestsellers from major publishers in New York have a few errors. I would guess any published manuscript that they spend big bucks on has been spell-checked and scanned for mistakes by at least three or four editors. Their reputation and professionalism are at stake. And still, a few errors show up when the book hits the street. Unless you're an English major, two or three minor mistakes are probably acceptable to most people.

By the time I finished the second book, I had come across quite a few more factual errors, repetitions, and misspellings. It absolutely floored me. This James guy was a very good writer, but his book was obviously never edited. Now, this might not bother some people; they just want a good story that keeps them turning the pages. But it stops me in my tracks. People are paying good money for these books; readers deserve better.

Out in the woods, I wasn't getting reliable reception on my smart phone, so I drove to the library in the Soo. Hunkering down at one of their computers, I searched around for Tony's books and found them on Amazon. For so-called bestsellers, his books had very few customer reviews. However, when I came across Tony James's website, it was a different story. Many of the individual mysteries highlighted on his site were bursting with effusive, glowing reviews: "Spine-tingling page-turner; I couldn't put it down," "Gripping and powerful tale of murder and revenge," "Mr. James is one of the finest mystery writers of our time." And these brief comments were attributed to *The New York Review of Books*, *Kirkus Reviews*, and the *San Francisco Chronicle*—heady words from some first-rate publications. Something was not passing the old reliable sniff test.

As I paged through his website, it was obvious Mr. James knew how to market his books. He was running contests and giveaways on his site and on Twitter and Facebook as well. Oddly enough, I couldn't locate any upcoming dates for signings at bookstores, but he had lined up numerous fairs and festivals for months in advance. In the first few pages of the books I had purchased were words of praise from the likes of Steve Hamilton and Lee Child: "Stunning piece of writing," "A thriller that will sweep you off your feet." With comments like these, shouldn't this guy be showing up on *The Late Show with Stephen Colbert* or *Oprah Winfrey*? I was growing more than a little suspicious.

When I returned to my cabin, I called my old friend Meghan at the *Free Press* in Detroit. She owed me a small favor, so I asked her to do a little background search on Tony James. I explained the situation and relayed my suspicions. She was intrigued.

"You know, Mac," she said on the phone, "for a guy trying to uncover the mystery behind a mystery writer, you must have a lot of time on your hands."

I laughed. "Listen, Meg, I'm just following my nose. As a reader, I just want to make him accountable and find out what makes him tick. Is there anything crazy about that?"

She said she'd check around and see what she could find. Meanwhile, I emailed *The New York Review of Books* and *Kirkus Reviews* and asked if they'd ever reviewed any books by Tony James. I mentioned that I was a former investigative reporter following up a lead. A few days later, I received answers from both publications; they had never heard of Tony James.

Why, I wondered, would an up-and-coming writer risk his reputation and good name by quoting bogus reviews and blurbs on his website? Was this the price of fame, at any cost? Wouldn't any aspiring author have qualms citing high praise from bestselling writers? Praise that was totally dreamed-up? This was really some gutsy marketing campaign, little white lies that weren't intended to hurt anyone but had snowballed into eye-popping fabrication.

By the end of the week, Meghan from the *Free Press* called me back with some unflattering news. It seems that Tony James had a colorful past and a good reason to get away. He'd been a newspaper journalist in Cincinnati and had written a series on a homeless

man who had struggled on the streets and finally turned his life around. Supposedly, this homeless fellow had grown up in an abusive family with alcoholic parents and moved out at an early age. He'd supported himself washing dishes and sweeping floors, but he had persuaded a friend to start a Go-Fund-Me page on the internet to raise money so he could launch a homeless shelter for others. Money poured in from sympathetic readers, and the shelter was an enormous success. The readers all loved the stories and asked how they could help out. At one point, however, as the story goes, this high-minded homeless fellow decided to abscond with all the funds, simply vanished without a trace. Quite a story, no doubt. Just one little problem: It was complete fiction—total fabrication.

Tony James was a big hit at the newspaper, that is, until a suspicious editor thought it all sounded too good to be true. Upon fact-checking the story more closely, he learned that Mr. James had masterfully blended fact and fiction, often sensationalizing many of the important details. More scandalously, he had plagiarized the writing of other reporters and blown this story totally out of proportion. After a fiasco at the paper, they had no choice but to fire him.

Meghan was out of breath relating this tale and said she would drop a copy of the newspaper clipping in the mail. Now it all started to make sense. Maybe James had fled southern Ohio and moved to the Upper Peninsula to bury his past and start over. That would explain why he'd written for the newspaper under the byline of Harry Logan but had changed his name to Tony James when he began writing mysteries. The blur between fact and fiction was making me dizzy.

When the mail from Meghan arrived, I pulled out the newspaper clipping: "Reporter Fired for Submitting Fake Stories." It was a tremendous scandal ten years earlier that had nearly ruined the credibility of a major newspaper. The readers were understandably quite angry and upset at having been deceived so easily. Apparently, the fallen reporter had no choice but to clear out of town.

When I visited the Soo library a week earlier, I'd noticed a flyer posted for an upcoming talk by Tony James on his latest book, *Death Warmed Over*. I decided to show up that evening and expose this charlatan in front of his loyal fans. As a reader, I was appalled at being duped by promotional lies and hyperbole. His fans needed to know the truth.

About two dozen people attended the late summer event. As the evening proceeded, Mr. James gave a reading from several chapters in his new book, talked about character development, discussed plotting choices, and elaborated on his Upper Peninsula settings. He described his habit of writing 1,000 words per day in order to produce two 75,000-word novels a year. Near the end of his talk, he pointed to a display table of his books which he offered to sign for anyone. Then he opened it up to Q and A from the audience.

I was about to raise my hand and ask Tony James if the name Harry Logan meant anything to him, but several people spoke up quickly and said that his stories had really inspired them to continue writing their own stories. Another woman asked if there would be a sequel to his latest book. Someone complimented the writer on his choice of so many familiar U.P. settings. It soon became obvious that a lot of fans truly enjoyed this man's writing. They were inspired and greatly entertained by his work. And, I had to admit, I thought he was a very good writer as well but felt he had crossed a line and gone too far with his self-promotion and sloppy editing.

I raised my hand.

"Mr. James, you self-publish all of your books, is that right?"

"Yes, I do."

"With your wide popularity, is there any reason why you don't simply find an agent to give you more national exposure with a larger publishing company?"

Tony James looked at me like I'd thrown him a trick question. "Well, I prefer to self-publish so I can control the whole process. There's more in it for me, from the cover design to marketing. It's been working just fine so far."

He seemed to sense some kind of trap and quickly called on someone else. Soon people who wanted to buy a copy of his new thriller milled around the display table, waiting for the author to sign their books. I wedged my way in and handed Mr. James a sealed envelope with a copy of the newspaper clipping I had received. Mr. James looked at me nervously, and I said, "I'm a former investigative reporter, and I think you might find this interesting." Then I turned and left.

I'd had a slight change of heart. Why humiliate this man, I reasoned, if I could at the very least get my point across? Most readers, apparently, found more good in his writing than bad.

A few days after his talk, when I pulled up Tony James's website, all the false attributions and reviews had been stripped out. The internet pages for his Amazon books had also been scrubbed clean of any bogus blurbs and glowing commentary. He must have known he was about to be exposed, again. Fame and a consuming drive to write a national bestseller must have obsessed him so badly that he was willing to do almost anything for the spotlight of attention. A few white lies, a little embellishment here and there, he probably thought, were a small price to pay for a writer climbing the ladder of literary celebrity.

Surely, I'll run across Tony again at some art festival or book signing. I hope he understands that I was just trying to even things out for future readers. They deserve that much. If Tony could somehow spring for a good editor to clean up his punctuation and misspellings, perhaps find a good publisher to promote him, I'm sure his books would eventually start climbing the charts. After all, everyone deserves a second chance.

For now, I'll keep my eyes open and follow my nose wherever a mysterious clue leads. These summer art fairs have been a good distraction for me though. I seem to be attracted to bright and shiny, dangerous things. And lately, for some reason, I've been mesmerized by the chainsaw juggler, but I keep a safe distance. I know when to back off.

Learn more about **Rich Hill** in our Author Bios section at the back of this book

The Robin's Nest

by Richard Hill

Spring arrived late that year. By early May, the snow had melted and the bare ground reappeared. The buds on the birches and maples swelled in anticipation of their imminent explosion of green. After six months of frozen isolation, life was returning to the U.P.

Day by day, the birds revisited their upper Michigan haunts to do what nature had asked of them. Many had traveled thousands of miles on the journey north. On the crossbeam jutting out from a remote log cabin that faced Lake Superior, a pair of robins chose a spot for their summer retreat; it was on a high perch over the back porch, just under the roof's eave. This seemed like a splendid place to build a nest, a safe and quiet location with a grand view of the lake.

The two robins gathered moss, mud, and twigs for several days, foraging for building materials in the nearby woods. A special excitement spurred their tireless efforts, like the nervous energy before company arrives. Before long, they had fashioned a fine, comfortable nest for their summer home. Now they needed to fortify themselves for their coming labors.

Every morning, the two robins combed the dewy grass for their breakfast of worms and grubs. They needed to build up their strength and reserves for starting a new family. Before they tugged each worm from its den, the robins stared cautiously left for a few seconds, then right, trying to detect any predator's movement that might threaten them. It was a survival mechanism that had saved them countless times. With each worm in their beaks, they flew to a nearby branch to finish off the meal. For several hours each morning, the robins continued this ritual before returning to the nest to rest.

At last, the mother robin laid her eggs. The father skittered anxiously from tree to tree, then back to the nest, attending to her every need. When the eggs finally hatched, three fuzzy little heads popped up with open beaks stretching skyward. Back and forth, the pair of robins played a tag-team match, bringing as many worms and night crawlers to their hungry brood as they could find. The youngsters displayed a voracious appetite and kept their parents busy hunting and retrieving enough to supply their demands.

When she had finally satisfied their hunger, the mother settled into her nest, content, and gazed out at the calm lake waters. The swaying birch trees and the tall aspens provided a shady and secure cover from the heat of the sun as well as camouflage from predators. Out in the bay, the long ships passed by silently, downbound for the Soo Locks. Each evening at sunset, the loons and the Canada geese gathered on the waterfront to perform their nightly rituals, calling to one another and splashing playfully in the reed beds.

Then one morning, without warning, a large black raven appeared; it had discovered the nest. The raven had watched from a distance, biding its time, as the two robins retrieved food for their young. Another raven, part of a pair, distracted the mother robin in her nest and prompted her to take flight away from her young. When the moment was right, the predator struck swiftly. In a flash, the first raven darted for the nest under the eave, snatched one helpless baby robin in its beak and flew away with its prey. The two robins squawked after him in a rage but were powerless to stop the thieving raven, which was three to four times the size of the robins. A few minutes later, the thief returned for the rest of his plunder, leaving behind an empty nest. The angry robins dove at the raven, pecking at him, attacking from every possible angle, but they were overmatched; the damage was done. Up and down the waterfront, you could hear their plaintive cry. Their nest was now empty; in an instant, the robins' family had vanished.

So quickly, so unexpectedly, from tranquility to despair. The robins had fulfilled their promise to nature, but nature had dealt them a cruel blow. The randomness of nature seemed heartless and unfair at best. The mother robin returned to her empty nest and quietly settled in. She waited there day after day as if hoping something would change. Her mate flew excitedly throughout the nearby woods and back to the nest in an effort to protect his partner from further harm. Hours slowly passed, days drifted by, and still she sat on her barren nest staring numbly at the other birds on the waterfront, as if refusing to give up hope. But nothing changed.

Dark clouds gathered in the bay and a summer storm moved in from across the lake, soaking the pine boughs and birches. A brief shower cleansed the evening air, and soon the sun broke out. Next spring would offer a fresh start for the robins. Perhaps, next spring, their luck would change.

Learn more about **Rich Hill** in our Author Bios section at the back of this book

Robin's Nest

White Knuckles/ Black Wheels

by Richard Hill

◆❖◆

Driving the roads of the Upper Peninsula for five or six long winter months has never been my favorite pastime. I've spun out on icy roads, slid into ditches, and dodged absent-minded deer for years. So, I was not looking forward to venturing out to hunt for another used car in the middle of January.

My son, who lived in Traverse City, had recently been involved in a car accident and totaled his vehicle. Fortunately, he came out of it without a scratch but needed another car soon for work. My wife Judy and I had planned to sell our Corolla when summer returned in about six months; so, we worked out a deal with my son, and the Corolla soon migrated to Traverse City.

We usually purchase another used car every three or four years, and always, if we have anything to say about it, in the warm summer months. Why make car buying an unpleasant experience. In more agreeable weather, you might look forward to washing and waxing your new wheels, blasting the AC, and cranking up a few tunes on the radio. Waving to your admiring neighbors, you cruise down the street with a carefree attitude. You can't do this when it's ten below zero.

I drove a white Kia Soul and liked the way it handled, and its price range as well; so, I considered buying a second one, something with about 50,000 to 60,000 miles on it. For several years, *Consumer Reports* had posted good reviews about this particular car, and so the hunt was on.

Before long, we came across a 2014 Kia Soul on the internet at a car dealership in Traverse City. We made the three-hour drive from the Soo, test-drove the car, and sat down with a young salesman to hammer out a deal. Just one little problem. The salesman told us their prices were firm; they supposedly had set them at rock bottom so buyers would not have to dicker. How they arrived at these consumer-friendly prices, no one knew. But they were definitely not negotiable. However, I had diligently done my homework earlier by studying current dealer prices on *Kelly Blue Book* for this particular car, and these folks were nearly a thousand dollars too high.

They were asking $10,995. Judy and I offered an out-the-door price of $9,500, all sales taxes and fees to be included. They flat out refused, claiming their price was as low as they could go on this particular vehicle. Finally, I said, "All right, throw in a set of snow tires, at your wholesale price, and we'll pay what you're asking." The young salesman, perhaps thirty, looked like he needed a drink and a day off.

"Mr. Hill," he said, in a voice that had just cleared puberty, "maybe that's how they did things back in *your* day, but we run this business different today." That's odd, I thought. Since time immemorial, the market price for anything had always been whatever a willing buyer negotiated with a willing seller. I was stunned, but before I could respond, the salesman's boss suddenly appeared—a middle-aged man with fiery red hair, a slight girth, and a tie much too tight. He must be *the closer*, I thought, who would show the rattled youngster how to smooth things out and wrap up the deal. The boss smiled and reiterated the cast-iron price and asked what he could do so we could drive that Kia Soul home today. I wanted to ask whether his rock-bottom car prices were delivered from the heavens on stone tablets by an old grey-bearded man, but I hesitated. Maybe that's the way they did it *back in my day.*

Stubbornly, I insisted on a slightly lower price, and the boss stomped out of the room, probably to pop a few antacid tablets. Five minutes later, the boss returned with a clipboard in his hand and tossed it across the desk to me. Glaring at us, he blurted out, "That's our best price!" He had budged, but barely. He stared across the room at me, arms folded, fists clenched at his side, red-faced, and sweating profusely. This felt like the showdown at the OK corral, and he was not backing down. I thought I saw a puff of steam hissing from his ears.

I had always heard, with regard to material possessions, that one should never fall in love with anything that can't love you back. When I looked over at Judy, she shook her head in disappointment, apparently upset by the boss's aggressive demeanor. Standing up, we said we had another vehicle to check out across town and thanked them for their time. Petrified, the two salesmen stood there in silence as we drifted out the door.

Five days later, back in the Soo, the young salesman called me back, offering the Kia for $200 less. On the internet, we had noticed that the *Car Gurus* website tended to show a price about $200 lower every couple weeks if the car remained unsold. So, on the phone, I offered a price that was another $250 lower than what he was asking. After all, I had already driven to Traverse City and back to the Soo once. There was a long silence; he was speechless, probably reluctant to confer with his boss. Ten days later, the salesman called again, offering to reduce the price another $200. Now, the car was closer to the price we had offered two weeks earlier. By this time, we had already moved on to other prospects.

Persistently, I had my mind set on purchasing another Kia Soul and finally located one online at a Grand Rapids dealership, 295 miles away. Since it was mid-January and barely above zero, I was reluctant to drive that far just to look at a car. On a lark, I called the dealership and asked if they might possibly consider meeting us halfway for a test-drive. I assured them that I wasn't wasting their time, that I was serious about buying this type of vehicle. To my surprise, the salesman agreed to drive the Kia to Gaylord, only about 100 miles south of the Soo. It was January after all, and maybe winter car sales were a bit sluggish. Personally, I would much rather hunker down near a crackling fire with a good book and a cold beer. But the hunt was underway.

We scheduled a rendezvous in Gaylord for 3:00 p.m. the next day, but a major snowstorm was moving in fast, and we had to cancel. Because of Judy's work schedule teaching school, we reset our test-drive for three days later. But once again another blustery January day emerged, and we grudgingly had to cancel. This unpredictable winter weather was typical for Michigan, and it seemed Mother Nature was never going to cut us a break. Maybe we'd have to wait until spring to find a car, or else locate someone with a dogsled and a team of huskies.

Then two days later, on a beautiful cold but sunny morning in the Soo, I called the salesman in Grand Rapids and asked how his weather was. Nice and sunny, he said, hoping I would agree to meet. Upon checking the afternoon forecast for the Gaylord area, however, we learned more snow was expected. I shouldn't have been so surprised, considering that Gaylord is located in the heart of northern Michigan's snow belt, averaging nearly 150 inches of snowfall every winter season.

Having slid off the road on black ice and having driven through too many blinding snow squalls with nothing but hope and a prayer, I was not eager to enter the fray. But my wife insisted that we go; it was her only day off and the weather outside looked just fine to her. We needed another car soon. Besides, I thought, don't those weather forecasters get things wrong half the time? "I say we go for it," she said bravely and with a little too much conviction. It's hard to refuse a strong-willed woman.

With blue skies and cool, sunny weather, we headed down I-75, excited to finally go for a test drive. As we drove south of the Mackinac Bridge, the sky darkened, and the wind picked up speed. It began snowing slowly at first, sweeping across the roadway in a ghostly manner, an ominous shift in the weather pattern. We slowed to 40 mph, then 30 mph, as the gathering storm built up steam. As I focused intently on the disappearing roadway, I said to Judy, "Keep your eyes on the centerline; let me know if I'm wandering off."

Finally, approaching Gaylord, we limped towards an exit and tried to locate the Family Fare supermarket where we had agreed to meet. In the blinding snowstorm, it was near impossible to find the store parking lot, let alone see any of the traffic signals or stop signs. It became a surreal free-for-all in which all normal driving rules were suspended. Why would any sane person be out in this weather anyway? Inching our way along, we found the store at last.

Two salesmen had driven from Grand Rapids to meet us, one in the Kia, the other one following in another car. The driver in the black Kia showed up first, but his fellow driver had been seemingly lost in the storm. We waited a few minutes to see if he would show up, but the salesman was anxious for us to test-drive the car before the blizzard got any worse. With a maelstrom swirling around us, a leisurely spin around the block seemed like the logical thing to do. We had driven 100 miles to get here; they had driven nearly 200. We had to make the most of it.

Tossing me the keys, the salesman climbed into the back seat as we hopped in the front. I broomed off the accumulated snow on the car windows and taillights and crept cautiously out to the main street for a trial run.

I crawled down the street at fifteen or twenty mph, barely able to distinguish a red light from a green one at intersections. My heart pounded and my muscles tensed like I was going into battle. I wanted to click my heels three times and magically transport us to the Land of Oz, or wherever there was green grass and no more snow. We soon pulled over, switched places, and Judy took the wheel. She promptly stepped on the gas like it was a bright, sunny day. "Oh, my," said the salesman in the back seat, "you're a very aggressive driver." She took that as a compliment and gunned the engine for a few more blocks down the main drag. The salesman, cringing behind us, must have assumed Judy had some kind of radar capability or x-ray vision; it was a near total whiteout.

In the middle of this storm, Jimmy Buffett's "Margaritaville" drifted from the radio speakers. I could see myself lying on a white sand beach in Key West, sipping a gin-and-tonic, watching the sailboats out in the bay. It was all very soothing until, suddenly, the car fishtailed and nearly smashed into the car in front of us. From the back seat the salesman sighed, "So, have you had enough?"

I was quite relieved when we returned to the supermarket for some hot coffee and serious negotiation. Judy and I had already agreed beforehand that if you really liked the car, do not go gaga in front of the salesman—just nod; it may save us a few dollars. The *lost* salesman had called his partner, having passed us in the snowstorm driving the opposite way. When he finally joined us for coffee, he raved about how fine the weather had been all the way from Grand Rapids until just outside of Gaylord, when all hell broke loose.

After discussing the pros and cons of this particular used car, the *lost* salesman said, "I sure hope you are planning to buy this car because I sure as hell don't want to drive it all the way back to Grand Rapids." Was this a new sales tactic—an appeal to sympathy? Judy laughed; I tried to maintain my composure. I glanced over at her: remember, no gaga. So far, so good.

The salesman originally wanted $10,000 for the car, a price that was close to the Kelly Blue Book. I offered them $9,500 out-the-door. We finally agreed to $9,700, and I wrote them a check.

Still the storm surged outside; snow swirled under the streetlights and piled up in the parking lot as evening approached. I insisted that we lay low at a nearby motel for the night and drive back to the Soo in the morning. But, since our friends lived only about ten miles up the interstate, in Vanderbilt, Judy thought we should stay the night with them. "Just follow my taillights down the road," she said. "We'll be fine." I could've used a shot of Jack right about then. Not wanting to push our luck any farther, I said, "I can't see even ten feet in front of me, and you want me to drive ten miles?" I could see that resisting her was hopeless and climbed into our new marshmallow of a car.

It took us forty-five minutes to reach Vanderbilt, without going off the road. Our friends welcomed us in from the storm with hugs, dinner, and a glass of wine. We were the last ones they expected to show up in the middle of a blizzard.

What I remember most about our fearless but foolhardy car-buying trip were the white knuckles and my death grip on the wheel; it was like driving blindfolded in the dark. I wouldn't recommend car shopping in the winter. Buying a used car is tough enough already without having to compete against Mother Nature. But don't take my word for it; check with your wife first.

Learn more about **Rich Hill** in our Author Bios section at the back of this book

Eagle Harbor Foley store ride

Mail Order Ministry

by Roslyn McGrath

Your mail order ministry melts many hearts
with its handouts of corrugated cardboard,
Styrofoam sheeting, and plastic
packages. It delivers truth
to the masses in the form of wishes
taking shape through elegant
equipment, painstaking
assemblage, engineering miracles
and wheeling through many miles to land
at their doors.
You are a tale as yet untold.
You are an Amazon.
And I am your warrior sheep.

Recipe

by Roslyn McGrath

Dribbles of honey swirl
through golden yolk,
porcelain grains,
liquid vanilla,
thick violet ooze,
shining oils.

Plump berries
and fine-ground cinnamon
add to the mix poured
into fluted parchment cups.
Heat is the final
ingredient, baking batter
into gold-violet yum.

Learn more about **Roslyn McGrath** in our Author Bios section
at the back of this book

Shelf Life

by Becky Ross Michael

A child's sweet voice from the next room sang along with the *Sesame Street* theme song about a sunny day sweeping the clouds away. Beth gazed out a small kitchen window, taking in the gray winter sky. *Looks like more snowy than sunny days.*

On the countertop lay a cookbook and four venison steaks seasoned according to directions. No matter how she cooked it, Beth disliked the flavor of that meat and cringed thinking about those poor deer. *That's what I get for marrying a hunter.* Near the cutting board, a selection of colorful root vegetables waited. *Maybe some homemade biscuits?*

Floor mopped, furniture polished, and carpet vacuumed. Guests would join them for dinner.

As her daughter navigated a yellow tricycle on the cement floor of the cold basement, Beth readied a load of laundry. She faithfully checked the pockets of her husband's clothing, pulling a folded slip of paper from a pair of pants. Holding her breath in expectation, Beth opened the note and scanned the feminine handwriting.

After digesting the words, she hid the proof behind ancient jars of strawberry jam, forgotten by previous tenants. *I wasn't crazy, after all.* Pulling away cobwebs, Beth also discovered a dusty tin of pork shoulder "meat" on the rough wooden shelf.

Change of dinner plans.

Peddling in faster circles, the little girl was lost in a happy world of make-believe. A good mother might protect her daughter from reality longer.

Grandma and Grandpa collected the child somewhere between laundry and dinner, happy to have an overnight visitor. Their station wagon crawled away into the early twilight as snowflakes fell.

In the background, a news report on the TV took on a strange tone while Beth removed a block of processed cheese from the refrigerator. Instead of reporting on the day's events, the newscaster seemed to whisper an assurance to Beth that she was doing the right thing.

By the time two vehicles squeaked onto the snow-packed driveway, aromas of dinner filled the kitchen.

Beth's heart accelerated. Her head pounded.

As he sniffed the air with feigned approval, her husband's eyes fired unspoken questions. He removed his boots and bumped a 12-pack of his favorite brew onto the table. "This should be good with the venison you promised us," he claimed.

"Sorry," Beth told him and their company, removing a pan from the oven with shaky hands. "The steaks didn't thaw in time, so I came up with something else."

Her husband's face colored when he glanced at the rectangular baking sheet. *Anger or embarrassment?*

Removing their outdoor apparel, the visiting couple took in the scene without a word. Beth moved the steaming, open-faced sandwiches onto plates with a spatula, adding stale potato chips from a wrinkled bag.

She served and joined the others at the narrow table, clutching a glass of water. *Alcohol feels too risky.*

The small group chewed in silence. After swallowing a large gulp of beer, her husband's mistress finally forced a smile in Beth's direction. "This is good! You'll have to give me the recipe."

"It's easy," Beth answered, though nothing would ever be easy again. "You just open the tin and cube the meat..."

"I notice yours has only the melted cheese and no meat cubes," interrupted the lover's clueless husband.

"I wanted to make sure there was plenty for all of you, first. And there's vanilla ice cream with strawberry topping for dessert," Beth added.

What a shame if one of those deserving souls ended up sick. No matter. She wouldn't think about that. Beth smiled, musing that tomorrow was the day to start making plans for spring and for her sunny days.

Learn more about **Becky Ross Michael** in our Author Bios section at the back of this book

Mackinac Island 1880

A Call in The Night

by Julie Dickerson

Christmas Eve! Magical words full of anticipation and excitement! And everyone wishes for snow that night. It is only right that Santa flies through the sky with the snow falling around his sleigh and reindeer. The wish for a carpet of white and a snow-frosted landscape is only fitting for this enchanted night. But it was not so for our family!

How my sister, brother and I wished it would not snow. Our father was the one who drove the snowplow. He cleared and salted the roads in winter. He was often called away to do his job any time the unpredictable Michigan weather required the job be done.

But Christmas could not be celebrated with Dad not there. It just wasn't right. So, we would wait for him when he was absent on Christmas morning. How hard it was after waiting all through the long, dark December days. How frustrating knowing that all around town our friends and their families were opening gifts and celebrating! Begrudgingly we waited until he returned from plowing the roads for Christmas Day.

So, this evening we were hoping the snow would not come. We busied ourselves with getting ready for our traditional Christmas Eve. We went to our Grandpa VanRaemdonck's for dinner and gifts. Our Uncle Max and Aunt Pat came with our cousins. The sparkling, silver Christmas tree from the department store glimmered in Grandpa's parlor with the light that went round and round and turned the tree different colors: red, yellow, green, and blue. It was marvelous to

watch. We would never have a tree like that. Ours was always a scotch pine cut from the woods.

We talked and laughed, and Grandpa would play the organ. We stared out the windows as he played, looking across the street where all the houses were glowing with Christmas lights and the warmth of their Christmas festivities. It was a different world from our home in the country. We enjoyed our visits into town to see Grandpa's world.

At last, it was time to open our gifts from Grandpa. As we opened them, we talked with our cousins about Christmas morning. This was just the prelude to the glories of gift opening tomorrow! Our excitement put a bounce in our steps as we walked around Grandpa's big front porch and down the steps.

"See you tomorrow," said Eric, my cousin, as we got into our cars. His family would be over on Christmas Day to exchange gifts among our families and share tales of our Christmas morning. As we drove home, we noticed snow was starting to fall. It came toward our windshield like daggers piercing the night. It was hard to see, so Dad dimmed the lights. "I hope this doesn't keep up," said Mom.

We all echoed her hopes in our minds without saying a word. Reluctantly we went to bed and conjured up memories of Christmases past.

We were all sound asleep when the phone rang. Dejected, we knew what it meant. Only Mr. LaClare, Dad's boss, called in the middle of the night. Dad answered the call as he stumbled out to our phone on the wall. We heard him say, "OK", in a sleepy voice.

Off he went into the snowstorm where the wind made drifts of snow across the road. He headed toward the County Road Commission garage where he would climb up into the big snowplow truck with his route in hand. He would drive into the darkness with the snow steadily falling and swirling around. It was a lonely job. If the snow stopped, he could be done in a few hours. If the storm raged on, he could be gone a long time. A blizzard once kept him at work for days.

Luckily, the storm wasn't a blizzard this night so Dad was home by 8:30 a.m. Christmas morning. This was much later than the 5:00 a.m. starting time we had chosen for Christmas but that was OK. Dad was tired but always a good sport. He drank some coffee as we started opening our gifts. And Mom reminded us that our cousins' gift opening was over and ours was just beginning! It didn't matter now. Dad was home and we could start Christmas.

We always had stockings that were full to the brim and most toys we wished for turned up under the tree. Joy filled our living room as we enjoyed gift giving. Breakfast was always homemade tea rings, a once-a-year tradition.

After we ate, we asked Dad if he would have to go out next Christmas Eve. We voiced our dislike of his job and its interference with our plans.

"You never know about Michigan weather," Dad told us. "In the winter snow and ice come and it is my job to make the roads safe for travel. If guys like me don't do their jobs, others can't get to their jobs, or to hospitals, schools, or all the places people must go. Without people to clear the roads, no one could get to Christmas gatherings safely. Someone has to do that job, don't they?"

Though it was a hardship at times, we had learned how important Dad's job was. We were proud of him. Whenever Dad had to leave on Christmas, we knew others could get to their celebrations safely because of workers like our dad. Our fun would only be a bit delayed. Knowing our dad helped others was a good feeling for this Christmas day. And it made it a little easier when the phone rang in the middle of the night!

Learn more about **Julie Dickerson** in our Author Bios section at the back of this book

12 On Lake Superior at mouth of Hurricane Creek showing logs to be rafted, near Grand Marais, Mich.

Historical · Hurricane River Logging

Lost and Here/ House of Autism

by Julie Dickerson

❖❖❖

We all read *The Prophet* in college; Gibran spoke of the House of Tomorrow, the place your children would live, where you could not visit, not even in your dreams. And I dreamed of children. And my precious babies came and grew up and I came to see it true; they live in the House of Tomorrow. I could not imagine their world. But my daughter also lives in the House of Autism. She is locked in its walls, and I cannot get her out. I stand outside with offerings of therapy, communication devices and medications that the sorceresses tell me will cure her.

I hold my love in a jeweled box, hoping it will entice her out. There are so few windows in her house. She doesn't see my offerings. She does not value them. It seems she most values her solitude and her music and her music machines. They are so predictable and have no expressions to decipher. To her, I may be incomprehensible. I may want what she does not understand or need.

And I live in the House of Normal. A place that barely exists anymore. What is normal? But all mothers still wish this house for their babies. And I have a need to be there at times, though I have guilt to say it. I have a need to be a wife, sister, or friend at times. Or a carefree Mom to my "normal" son.

To run from the House of Autism tears my heart. But I cannot bring you here, to the House of Normal. You cannot get in. No matter what I do. And do you even want to know its walls and rooms?

Do I long for something meaningless to you? Your confounding condition shuts you out. Shuts you out of conversations, planning your dreams and all the things I want to do for you, all the things that happen in the House of Normal. Or, perhaps, you want to tell me how much you long to talk to me.

We are both locked out. And both chronically sad. I wish you could be in my house. The House of Tomorrow, for you, scares me. No one will be trying to reach you when I am gone.

Learn more about **Julie Dickerson** in our Author Bios section at the back of this book

Soo WWI marchiing band

Michigamme Grades

by John Adamcik

The Stretch seems long enough,
but consider that
either side
is only half an hour ride
to the greatest of the lakes:
one that knows no equal,
the other a namesake.

And that you're halfway from the bridge
to the foci
of this wild estate.

Halfway to Michigamme.

Where I first learned
Quiet
and a cartographer's perspective.

One can get lost in one's
thoughts
in the middle of somewhere
in the middle of a summer's night.

My compass points to this sylvan shrouded
lake haven.

A place where time and essence meet
in a dance
with the Milky Way
and the flapping of a preening loon.

A place where, nearest on this earth,
one can find the rest that stills the soul.
Where you can shuttle off to the Keweenaw
    Rift
for a pastie and soak in Brockway vistas
    that belie
glacier-scraped flatlands downstate.

Or sojourn to a pristine stand of pines and
    cast
a caddis into a ripple or pool,
like Papa or Traver.

It is here,
at these Michigamme Grades.

Here you can retrace the voyageurs'
Grand paths and
follow First Nation early winter trails for
    venison.

In my heart I have broken rock,
laid the stones flat,
heaved timbers and placed rails thereon.
I see it inside me.

My spirit often carries me
this way,
and I am eager to return.

Onward, Inward, Upward, Home

by John Adamcik

Father was at work
the day I stepped upon the
   boards
and felt my heart freed
and watched the waves
and counted stars
and wondered.

Mother had the younger
   ones
that called her name
and meals to make
and clothes to mend
and wounds to bind
and hope.

The welcome was not fam-
   ily
or friends
or kindness
of the sort I might have
   thought.
But it was a welcome
of necessity,
and that was something.

The work was damp
and dark
and hard;
tight spaces full of
danger and
opportunity.
A nation built upon
this ore, rising
in pieces,
then pellets,

loaded on the ships
like those of us who struck
the rods and breathed
the heavy air.

My headlamp was
an oily comfort,
but yielded
no room for me to show
my heart,
for I had signed my very
   self
for passage and for
a future.

My love was there, at Fa-
   ther's house
one respite day;
a meal and laughter
under orange-green maple
   leaves.
Like those around us, she
   and I
did share a common
   tongue,
(though she was born
   here).

My prospects did not
overshadow love,
and she promised we
   would
walk as one;
faith and family,
bound by paper
and blood

with smiles
and laughter.

We counted seasons
and hardships
and loss
and joys
and grew silver on the
   wings.
I've never known beauty
like her eyes
upon my own,
her hand on
my cheek.

They were home that day,
when news arrived.
A furious *dunamis* -
collapse of earth
and spirit
and dreams
and stillness.

The lapsenlapset
know my name
and see photos.
When I was young
and strong
and unafraid.
I am unafraid now,
and full of love.
And very much alive.

Softer Echoes of a Frozen Roar

by John Adamcik

While not a voice of thunder
from a distance, still
a gentle growl and rumble
greets the mind.
Blurred in scope,
one imagines cataracts and pools
aswirl
with tea-stained runs.

Winter underfoot;
safe at times
yet shrinking in the light—
the chill fades.
Shall we trust ourselves to trod
the inviting phase beneath
while life flows an
ever-widening path?

Breathing in and holding,
the spark of a tenuous time
captures our momentary
pause.
Hope is full and bright
and the smallest green
upon the fringes
speaks truth.

Another moon,
and we shall be closer.
There will be the fragrance
of motion,
bringing the cycle forward.
Gravity and time
and the necessity of
that humbler attendance.

Learn more about **John Adamcik** in our Author Bios section
at the back of this book

The Bottom of the Cider Barrel

by August Whitney

"What happened?" Roger asks, crouched over the hospital bed, wearing a control freak's look of frustration.

"Well, I don't know," you say. "I was tired. My back hurt. I dropped my pill case behind the toilet and gassed myself trying to pick them all up, I guess."

He rubs the baseball sized tumor peeking out from under his shirt cuff. He starts to say something else but stops. It has all been said before. You're both frustrated with saying the things there are to say. He reaches out his good arm and rests it on your hip brace. He has tears in his eyes.

"Ellie, my love, I think we have to move out."

You nod. You reach out your good arm to rub his good arm. "Hey, hey. We made it. Honey. We're here. You're still here. Honey. What a life we've had! I remember it all! Don't you? Don't you remember?"

He smiles and coughs and wipes his nose. "Oh, I remember. But I don't... it's not– something spilled out along the way. You just aren't the same in my head." He starts to cry again. "It's been seventy years, Ellie. I'm hooked. You got me. I don't know what I'm going to do."

"Oh, Roger," you say, "We're not going to die tomorrow. Or, well, you won't." And just like that, as the wrong words like slippery fish pass from your lips and land in his eyes, you know he *must* be the one to die first.

•••

They take you home on a Sunday. The maple tree in the front yard is a blazing orange and yellow; leaves crunch underfoot on the sidewalk. The swing bench on the front porch creaks when the wind kicks up. You can hear it from the couch where Roger deposited you. He's down in the basement, so out of sorts that he mercifully forgot to put on the Packer game.

On the way home from the hospital, you'd agreed to call your eldest daughter and give her launch authorization on the retirement facility in Marquette she'd been pushing for at least a year. Sons and in-laws would fill the place in a few days and empty it by the following weekend. And that would be that.

•••

You met him in a rather unromantic way; you each were looking for a quick fix at the time. He made a joke about a doobie and you laughed, and that was pretty much it. When he brought in Tarot cards, he purportedly stole from the trinket shop on the corner, and asked you to read his palm, you nearly asked for his hand right then and there. Things were different back then; you were streaky and emotionally all over the place. For weeks you slept together and did a bad job acting too cool to really like each other. At the end of the summer, he was making pancakes when you had to run to the bathroom and weep. You told him you loved him. He said he loved you too, but not with the same gusto. It wouldn't be until later that he was really sure.

• • •

He'd decided to love you by the time you finished school. He came to your graduation and suffered through car rides with your family and friends. You went up to his dad's place on Keweenaw Bay for a weekend. The following week you left for a summer job in upstate New York. After a month you were ready to quit. You called him in tears after getting screamed at in a meeting.

"My love, my love," he said. "Hey, hey, hey. You're so okay. Screw that guy, I mean, really, forget about him, but baby, baby, hear me on this one, I happen to know from experience. Getting yelled at is part of the job. I'm so sorry baby."

"I know, I know. Ughhh. I hate that it affects me so much."

"Doesn't make it okay, but I just want you to know that this guy probably thinks that that interaction was ordinary. You're all good. All good, baby."

Later during the phone call a roommate came in who was at the meeting. Roger asked the kid why he hadn't stuck up for you. The kid got righteous, at which point Roger got litigious, and after five minutes of going at it you were hysterical again, so the kid left. Roger realized he screwed up.

"Hey, baby, baby, I'm so sorry, I'm just trying to stick up for you! Hey, hey, it's okay. Ellie, Ellie, breathe for me," and so on and so forth for several hours. He was patient; he knew about your past, about what certain guys and family members had said and done.

You cried and cried. Not just that time–there were many instances, those days, of uncontrollable tears. Roger was solid as a rock through it all. Occasionally he got frustrated, but most of the time he was brilliant. "I'm like your sponge, baby. I'm here to soak up all the bad stuff. Let me soak it all up, baby. I'm here. I'm right here. I'm not going anywhere. I love you so much." And he meant it.

• • •

He wakes you up in the late afternoon, gently. He didn't actually wake you up; you heard him approach, hobbling up the basement steps and across the floorboards. You always let him wake you up, even if you're already awake. You're the snoozy one of the two of you. There has always been an element of flirtatious song and dance in his efforts to wake you from your naps. It was a sad day when, because of your busted hip, he could no longer wake you up by tickling you. And you had been sad about it, too! The devious gaslighting bastard. That's what you tell him, and he grins his gap-toothed grin and gently pokes your ribs through the blanket.

"I made you a grilled cheese," he says.

"Well, okay then," you sigh, and then you both laugh, and begin the odyssey of rising and limping to the kitchen; you lean on him, he leans on the furniture whose layout he knows so well. It was a minutes long journey, plenty long to look at pictures resting on side tables and hung in frames on the walls, at trinkets from here and there, the detritus of half a century and more.

You know you hope the move will kill him, you just can't decide on whether or not you want to die too.

• • •

About fifteen years ago you thought you had him beat. Unable to resist such offers, he took up a buddy on an invite to ride around the Great Lakes on the back of his massive Harley. It was early June. Roger wanted to camp, and you had to get a doctor to tell him, with you in the room as a witness, that he wasn't allowed to sleep on the ground anymore. He had some rather poetic things to say about it afterward, but you could tell he was devastated. Sleeping rough in the woods was one of his all-time favorite things. You heard him and his buddy (whose control of their own volume was inversely related to how cranked up they were) talking about doing it anyway. Apparently, there was some new fancy schmancy blow up pad that was meant for people with problems.

On the way out the door he gave you an extra-long kiss. Later, in the emergency room in Thunder Bay, you wondered whether he'd anticipated the crash. An arm was mangled, and they had to do a bunch of skin grafts. Wounds got infected. He forgot to take certain crucial meds at seemingly crucial junctures. You knew you weren't ready then. And he pulled through, thank God.

•••

On the flip side, you knew about his past, too. He was very open about it, and you loved him for that. About the hospitalizations, about the attempts, about the shrinks that drove him crazy with their patronization and their buttoned up, sterile attempts to wade into his messy psyche. In the early days, he always said that you would get your turn. Part of his skill with hysteria came from his own father's skill with him: he was always quick to credit his father when you thanked him for caring for you so well during your episodes. He was brilliant when his own life was moving forward. But in the winters, he shut down and was useless in a crisis. He was always good at telling you he loved you. But in the winter, that was all he could do, and that wasn't enough, but it had to be.

•••

"What did you put in this one?"

"Muenster, ched, red pepper flakes, minced garlic. The classic."

"It's incredible. I should eat up all the butter so you can't."

He smiled. "Perfect." He tried not to watch you screw up your features in pain as you swallowed. He tried to watch the shaking leaves in the rattling branches out the window. The weight of the half empty glass shook your hand and you had to bring your head down close to the table to drink. His fist clenched over a red cloth napkin. "I'm glad you're hungry today. I'll leave the other half just in case."

"You should eat it. Go ahead and eat it."

"Are you sure? I had plenty of turkey and rice for lunch. I should really not."

There was no reply.

"I'll leave it just in case."

"Thank you darling." You put your shaking hand on his.

It would be crass, you've decided, to take the Lord's work into your hands and hasten his end. And you really should eat while you've got the appetite, painful though it is. You are only half joking when you say you married him for his grilled cheeses.

•••

The most romantic thing he ever said to you came in an insulting package. It was fifty years ago, your first or second winter, and you each were reading quite a bit. He was deep into a novel about a Confederate soldier hiking home across rural North Carolina. Some old man compliments a young man's choice of wife by saying, "It makes as much sense to marry a girl for her looks as it does to hunt a bird because you like the way it sings." Roger tried to dress it up by talking about your hourglass body, and he was right about that– still it stung, at the time. Now that your hip is broken along with your appetite, it's easier to understand what he meant. You are the type of lady who learns. You are the type of lady who understands who needs to die first.

•••

The following morning, your daughter and her husband arrive to start packing up. They're all gung-ho in a way that seems premeditated and vaguely sinister– Laura and her husband are acting like they have something to hide, or that they're getting away with something. Roger doesn't like it at all, and prickles. They won't let either of you touch a thing. You knew this and avoided the confrontation by sitting on the swing on the front porch. Roger joins you in a huff.

"It's like watching them divvy up your organs while they all still work. I almost flipped a table in there just now."

You rest a trembling hand on his knee. "We went through it all, remember? Everything we want is staying."

"Collecting dust in Laura's garage."

"Well, yes, darling."

"A man shouldn't have to watch his own bookshelf get torn down."

"Hey, hey, hey. Shhh. Shh." You stroke his hair. "We can set up all the books just like they were in your new room. We'll do that first." This was apparently the wrong thing to say. He composes himself after a minute or two.

"Will they let us crash together?"

"I don't know."

"That alone might do me in."

"You're telling me, darling."

Roger sits bolt upright as if struck by lightning. He jostles the creaky swing as he hauls himself to his feet.

"What's up baby?" you ask.

"My clubs. My ... uhhuh" His breathing is labored. "My clubs. I need to check on my clubs."

"Aren't they going to Laura's, darling?"

"Like hell they are!" He turns and shuffles toward the front door. You swallow everything about not having a car, or someone to drive him, or a course close by to play, or a heart strong enough to do more than hit five or ten balls at the range anyway.

Roger always hated guys who took carts. "Just walk," he said venomously. "Are your legs broken?" There were scenes made with groups of younger guys who wished he would play faster. There were awkward insinuations from the guys who could still bear it to go out there with him. It was a control thing, and that only goes one direction with age.

You could hear him now, taking all this out on Laura's husband, who was a douche, and always took a cart, sure, but none of that was his fault any more than the color of his hair.

•••

He talks Laura into leaving a sack of potatoes and a pan and some butter for one last dinner. She reminds him to be ready by eight for the drive on over to the facility tomorrow.

He puts on a B.B. King record when she leaves and turns it way down low, so as to not wake you from your afternoon nap. You wake up anyway and listen to him chopping potatoes, greasing the pan, frying them, spicing them, frying them some more. You hear him sneak a few for himself even though the salt and the carbs and the butter will wreck his insides. He goes in the fridge and gets a glass, and you hear the hiss-crack of a can of beer. He goes to the bathroom for several minutes while the potatoes burn.

You battle your way through a few bites for his sake; he blames himself for burning them, but the truth is that you wouldn't have eaten them if they were perfect. After dinner you both decide to get drunk. You sit together on the couch and listen to John Prine, and talk, and talk, and talk. You cry when he tells you about his beloved uncle; just before this man's death, Roger was talking to him on a late fall day out behind the farmhouse in his orchard. He quoted a Keats poem about a farmer at the end of October squeezing the last bits out of the bottom of his cider press, tasting the sweet sorrow in the last bits of light and warmth before winter comes and all is dark. The man was dead two weeks later, before the season's first snow flew.

When silence falls on the room it's almost unbearable. You finish a bottle swig for swig, and he passes out on the couch. You fairly crawl into bed.

It turns into one of those nights where the minutes are hours long. Every time you think light is breaking in the east, the blackness just remains until you turn over. You hear Roger get up to piss. He joins you in bed, and for the rest of the eternal night, gets up to piss every twenty minutes. You each nuzzle each other as you can but are rendered silent by the night. You aren't quite sure if you're having a lifelike dream or if you're just awake. Eventually your thoughts meander inward and then he's shaking your shoulder, the sun beaming savagely through the window and landing on the rumpled bed sheets.

He's waiting with his coffee and your glass of water. You suggest that you sit on the swing, on the porch, and he agrees.

"Oh, baby," you sigh, slouching over to lean on him. "What are you thinking?"

He squinted into the sunlight. The wind raised a wisp of white hair on his head; it settled in a goofy way. "I feel like a scared little boy on the first day of kindergarten. I want my books and my golf clubs." He says this last in a whiny voice and laughs at you, but you can see the twist of agony as his head turns every time a car growls around the corner.

"They might have a foosball table," you suggest.

"That's true. They might."

"I'll have to find a place to read in the sun. A nice chair."

"I'm worried about the food for you. I tried to tell them– the kid with the paperwork didn't seem like he was listening. I might have to get someone to do special grocery runs."

You give him your warmest, most radiant smile. "Thank you darling. I'm sure it'll be fine. I'm sure they've had people like us before."

He coughs and starts to rise. "I'm just going to check the, uh, the basement. I'll be right back. Just make sure there isn't any, I mean, that we're all set. I mean, it's just.... I don't want to have to come back here once we're gone."

"Okay, darling."

You watch him hobble up the steps and into the house. As soon as he's gone, Laura's car pulls around the corner.

•••

You married him for his brains, not his brawn, but in hindsight it was his instincts that were the most valuable. They were also cruelly on the money when it came to nutrition at the facility.

The food was crap. Barely even worth the Sisyphean effort of getting it down. They tried fluids, which your body promptly rejected. It wasn't just the foods; it was stage fright as well. It was like trying to eat in the cafeteria on your first day at a new school. By the end

of the week multiple major organs failed. The second day in the hospital, they moved you to full time oxygen. On the morning of your third day, they asked if you wanted to speak with a priest.

"No, thank you."

Roger was there day and night. You slept most of the time. You told him about the whole priest thing. That afternoon he left and snuck home, returning in an hour with a grilled cheese. You smelled it before he even had it out of his pocket. He gently nudged your shoulder to wake you, but of course you were already awake. You sniffed. He smirked and you smirked back. He handed you the sandwich and you took a bite. You hated the look of concern that sprouted on his face. He could tell you lacked the energy to properly chew it.

"I hope I didn't interrupt a good nap."

"No, my love, you're fine."

"How are you feeling?"

Your face screws itself up. "Oh, I.... Oh, oh, oh. I failed you baby. I'm so sorry."

"What? What's up, baby? Hey, hey, hey, what's going on?"

You try to muster the energy to choke out what you mean. "I mean... What are you going to do, baby?"

He smiled. "How do you mean?"

"Like, literally?"

A look of horror flashed across his eyes but disappeared as quickly as it came. "Well, Ellie, I'll cross that bridge when I get to it."

"No, baby, no, I need more than that. I need... I need to know you'll be okay."

He looked at you with adoration across the blur of tears. "Of course, I won't be okay, baby. I mean... I'm sorry, but things are going to be horrible. Don't make me think about that right now."

"No, please, Roger, listen. I fully intended to outlive you. Our whole lives, ever since we were twenty, up until last month. I mean, think, think with me, all the drugs and the motorcycle crash and the heart attack and... Oh, oh, it wasn't supposed to be like this! You were supposed to... I'm sorry, my love. I'm so sorry. I'm sorry I can't be there for you all the way home."

He strokes your hair and wipes your eyes and says nothing for a good long while. He squeezes your hand tightly and kisses it at thirty second intervals. Your hand which had been kissed in an identical fashion for seventy years. "It's okay, my love," he says at long last. "It's all okay." And he sounds like he means it.

You calm down after a while and it occurs to you to ask again. "Seriously, Roger. You must have thought about it. What are you going to do?"

You are immediately warmed by the glint in his eye. "What," you demand, as his grin widens. He reaches out and squeezes your hand.

"Well, baby," he says, "I'm going to go on an adventure. Sam says he wants to drive to Duluth while the leaves are still pretty. From there I'll fly to New York where Leo Tyler's waiting with his boat. He's sailing to Sweden in November–"

"*Sweden?* In *November?*"

"Oh, sure, it'll be a blast. We'll stop off in Portugal and watch those knuckleheads who surf those hundred-foot waves. From there we'll head up to Scandinavia, where his wife is. That's the brilliant bit, right? I needed to get to Sweden, and he was going anyway. There's a place in Stockholm, a river I think, where my father told me you could drop an unbaited hook and pull fish all day long, as many as you can eat. If I survive that long, I think I'll go see about that. If he wasn't exaggerating, I'll stay a while and eat fish all day. If he was, I'll head on over to Amsterdam. I'll get some kids in an alley to shoot me full of Jesus. And then I'll meet you wherever you're at."

You nod weakly. A transatlantic journey with the son of an old buddy in a small boat sounded like just the thing. If it didn't kill him, it would be the reason he survived. Your eyes close.

He strokes your hair and kisses your forehead and tells you he loves you over and over. Eventually all the sounds blend together– the buzz of the electric lights, the hums and the beeps of the infernal machines, the screech of gurney wheels on a freshly polished tile floor. It wasn't so hard to breathe after a while. You slept, and when you awoke, you were ravenously hungry and a young Roger was there snoring next to you, and you realized, thank goodness, that you were dead.

Learn more about **August Whitney** in our Author Bios section at the back of this book

Historical · Keweenaw Cliff Mine deserted

Free in the Harbor

by August Whitney

He was our friend, they said. And then they began to play.

•••

Just before summer I remember sitting in church on Easter Sunday in Houghton with Ronald and my dad. It was beautiful outside. I wept during the last hymn especially given all the talk about bringing the dead back to life. Because for all the fancy spiritual philosophical mental gymnastics you can do to keep dead people alive in your head, it's just not the same when they're dead and you aren't. I hear them all in the music, the voices, and the organ, which is why it makes me sad sometimes. I'm not ready to die yet. But I miss my buddy, Joe.

•••

Today was the last day of the kayak season. As we haul boats in from the dock to the cellar, I look around—Greg, Terrence, Matt—and all I can think about is how little I remember. We've been sweating on this dock shoulder to shoulder since May, and all I can remember are the highlights, the greatest hits. If that's all they remembered about *me*, well—but before that thought sent me swirling, I caught a whiff of cigarette smoke and went to join Terrence, who was surely "checking the water levels", as we did, out back, "making sure they were safe".

•••

There's some refuge taken in a common state of mind—at least *now,* when we're smoking, we know for sure we are not alone. But somehow the process of calcifying this feeling into memory forces all its comfort to burn away, leaving only the foggy head and the dormant synapses which refuse to yield the mercy of a word, detail, anything to remind you that they are real, or at least were at one point, and not just a story you heard somewhere.

•••

Death surrounds anyone who is paying attention—then, of course, so do other things but death should really be on the front burner.

Months ago, I was getting on the Amtrak from Boston to Chicago. I walked through the dry sun out to the train and got on and sat down. A family with two little boys came in behind me. The boys each hugged an older couple who'd walked onto the train with them. The older couple then hugged the parents and left the train. The train rolled away from the station. The mother told the kids to sit down, stop horsing around. The kids sat and spoke in hushed tones. The younger of the two boys started to cry.

"What's wrong buddy?" asked the father.

"I miss Grandpa and Grandma," sobbed the little boy. He cried harder as the father picked him up and wrapped him in a hug. "I miss them too, bud. I promise. They're coming out to Stillwater in two weeks, though, remember! They're staying with us until Christmas."

The boy considered this between sniffles. "Ok. But, but, what if something happens?"

The father had no answer. "We'll see them soon, bud. I'm sure of it."

The boy sobbed. I turned in my seat to face him. "Hey, bud. I miss my grandma too. I came out here to visit her, too."

"Oh really?" said the mom as the boy looked at me. I nodded and reached out to give the boy knuckles. His mom smiled and asked where I lived.

"Houghton, Michigan. I live with my father. My grandma's ninety-four and they hadn't seen each other in a year or two. It might be her last time out to the Midwest, and… " I coughed and the mother tactfully handed me a tissue.

"I hear you," she said. "They always miss their grandma and grandpa real bad when we have to leave."

The little boy and I cried together. I thought of the coming weekend working kayaks in the harbor. I wondered if I could spare a night in Chicago on the way home. My buddy Trevor lives there with his parents in an apartment by the lake, and he's leaving for the army at the end of the month. There's already a huge party planned, but I figured it'd be easier to say goodbye for five years if I saw him in Chicago a bunch first, when he's not in the middle of his last night of freedom, because lasts never count if you're aware of them as lasts. Or do they count doubly? Sometimes it's hard to tell, but increasingly I believe it's the former.

•••

I remember when I found out about Joe, the first thing I remembered was our conversation on the porch the weekend I visited two years ago. It was the end of a long night. He was wearing that bright purple tracksuit of his. We decided to head out to the porch and smoke a cigarette.

"There's this girl in my chem lab," he'd said. "I'm so close, man. So damn close."

"Alright," I replied. "No more art majors?"

"Huh? No." I could tell he was confused.

"You know, like freshman year? The girl with the teal hair?"

"Oh, yeah. No, none of that."

"I hear ya."

Confusion played across his face. "Can I tell you something kinda personal?"

"Sure."

"I'm a, uh. I'm a virgin."

Long pause. "Wow," I said, wishing I had more time to calibrate an answer. "But what about the teal haired girl? Or the one, what was that one? That was my favorite, man. The girl who banged her head on the wall and started crying! None of that happened?"

His face twisted up and I wished I'd held my tongue. I was just surprised, since those stories he'd told us had such vivid detail.

"No, man. None of that happened."

"Well, shit! It's all good. Girl in your chem lab, right?"

"I suppose." But I'd embarrassed him, I could tell.

We smoked and things lightened up. He told me more about the girl in his chem lab, who he actually really liked apart from the likelihood of sleeping with her. Maybe that's what he'd meant by "so close"—not that he was so close to sleeping with her, but so close to feeling like he could, feeling like he cared about her, and in the right way. That was the last substantial conversation we ever had. When I got the news, my first thought was, "Damn, I wonder if he died a virgin."

•••

During Grandmother's week in Houghton, things were lovely and tense, as always. Ronald, our Nigerian asylum-seeking houseguest, was delighted to meet her after five years staying with my father, but he was also preoccupied with violence in his home country and threats to his family, from whom he was likely separated for life. He conducted this utterly serious business over facetime with various relatives in his blue penguin pajamas at all hours of the day.

One afternoon I was out at the farm gathering properly sized sticks for the woodchipper, expecting Dad to roll up about half an hour before he did. I remember now—it wasn't a problem that he was late (because normally it would be, for me, emotionally) because I had fallen asleep with my back against a pine listening to the wind scrape over the tops of the trees. I walked up through the woods and then through the long grass to the driveway by the shed when I heard him pull up.

He got out and immediately wrapped me in a hug. I was grateful for this but also guessed that something was up. He said he was sorry for being so hard on me. I told him it was fine, he wasn't hard on me, which was true. We took our places on either side of the truck bed to talk—in my memory he is wreathed in chokecherry leaves.

"I'm sorry bud, I'm just a little... I'm staring it in the face right now," my father said. "I was driving down the hill, you know, over by that McDonalds across from the Walmart at the top of the hill?"

"Yeah?"

"Well, there's this guy, he hitchhikes all the way over from Painesdale to that McDonalds every day apparently. I picked him up today. He was looking real uh … haggard. He didn't talk much, wouldn't give me anything but his name, Roy, and a few short answers. He told me he hitchhikes every day from his place in Painesdale to the McDonalds in Houghton for a cup of coffee. He was in Vietnam, judging by how old he was. There was fire in his eyes the whole time. I've seen him out there before and seen him inside the McDonalds too."

"So, every day he just hikes over, nurses a coffee all day then hikes back?"

Dad swallowed hard. "I think that's all he can handle."

"Shit," I said. "I'm surprised he finds a ride every day."

"I thought the same thing. I asked him about that, actually. It's funny. He goes 'Yep, every day, 'cept Sunday when I go to church. Somebody always gets me. You just gotta be patient. Sometimes it's the first car, sometimes it's the hundredth. They always get me.'"

"Jeez."

"Anyway, let's get on these lingonberries. I've neglected their weeding for far too long."

And so, as the long summer sun sank slowly through the pine boughs that smothered our land, we crawled around on our knees, each with a trowel, attacking the weeds which had sprouted up over the last few months. I kept my eyes peeled for "runners"—little sprouts of lingonberry that spread between the larger bushes. They mature into full bushes themselves and spread their own runners, and eventually the patch will all be one big bush.

As my hands dirtied and my nose grew accustomed to the rich odors of the forest and the orchard nearby, I thought of Dad's hitchhiker and what circumstances might have brought about his wayward mission to McDonalds and back six days a week. It reminded me of the previous winter when Dad had to tell me to stop offering Ronald rides to work at the grocery store, despite the icy roads and freezing temperatures.

"Think about it, Jack," he'd said. "Ronald is a patriarch. That's why his family is always on facetime with him all hours of the day. He's been gone from Nigeria a decade and they're still on him every day for things. He told me once, I asked him, 'Ronald, wouldn't it be easier to just let them decide things for themselves back in Nigeria?' and he said, 'John, they would call me anywhere. They would call me no matter if I were on the *moon*.' So, he's the man, and being over here utterly reliant on us for shelter is probably pretty emasculating. His half-hour walk to work through the blizzard is the one alpha-male bit of toughness he gets in his life. Let him have it. It's alright. He understands the world differently. He's the one indefinitely separated from his family. He knows how to survive."

At the time I felt bad for offending Ronald by offering, as though in the offering I had implied a lack of manhood, but I realize now that not offering would have been strange too. I remembered riding the bus in Milwaukee in June. In my imagination, my father's hitchhiker resembled in some respect a man I'd met on the bus, and walked a little way with afterwards, him talking, me listening. Or rather, I don't know whether they looked the same, but surely the shape of their warped hearts did.

•••

About a month into the kayak season, I started listening to Stan Rogers again. The "first time" was all those years in the car with Dad crisscrossing the Midwest on the way to hockey tournaments. He and Mom were together then, and sometimes even kissed in church to trick me into thinking them happy. At first it was merely nostalgic to play the old music I recognized, but then I branched out. Every morning, with songs of the old harbors stuck in my head, I unlocked the kayaks and ate my breakfast under the cottonwood tree behind the shipping container next to the boat yard. One song was about an old fishing village that had crumbled thanks to the massive trawlers who overfished and crowded out the traditional fishermen. The town was empty, the boats rotting on the shore, and every day the whales swam free in the harbor, unbothered by the happenings of days gone by.

It was easy to project these songs onto my life. I'd sit on the dock and smell the stinky river in the morning, watch the seagulls over the harbor and hear their cries. My life as a child had long since ended. No mom, no hockey, new city, possessed of only a far-flung group of buddies who were dying off one by one before their time. And here I am, just like Stan says, free in the harbor. Free, and crumbling under a desolation of the heart.

●●●

After church on that Easter Sunday, I was a wreck. Eventually I ended up with Dad in his room. I was tearfully trying to say something about how once you know someone is gone and the memories attached to them are a different kind of valuable because they're all that's left, those very same memories become like sand in your hands on a windy day, slipping gracefully away in the tiniest pieces bit by bit, impossible to hold on to and even harder for the trying.

"I know, buddy," he said. "I know. It's so hard, but we really all will end up in the same place. I was thinking about Heaney the other day …" He got up and pulled a pair of socks on. "Real quick—this is important, and I'd like to continue, but just for a second—you think a drive out to the farm might do you some good?"

"Sure. Yes."

"We don't have to do any chores. The woods might be soothing."

"You're right. Let's go."

On the way down the stairs, I remembered Brendon Heaney. I'd played hockey with him when we were both fifteen. He went to work at the local rink where my dad, when he wasn't teaching, was managing and driving the Zamboni. He worked with my dad for a year and a half, then turned up dead of an overdose at a friend's house. Apparently, there was some history of opiate abuse. He'd recently been kicked out of the house. All I could remember was the kid who got bullied in the locker room, who couldn't make a breakout pass, who was nice to me but always managed to say the wrong thing.

Dad told me about Heaney's last days. How he'd fought with his dad about going to rehab. How he'd gone to live with a friend, only to come home when his parents called the friend's parents and withdrew their permission. How during their last shift together, my dad noticed that his boots were untied the whole time and his eyes remained out of focus and his hair was greasy from the lack of a shower. Sometimes Brendan just had greasy hair, but he'd always combed it anyway. The day of their last shift together, he barely even pushed it out of his eyes.

Apparently, it wasn't even suicide. Things got better before they got worse, and Brendan agreed to go to rehab the day after his last shift with my dad. He went two days without using. Then, the night before he started rehab, the urges took over. He tried to make a home-brewed concoction that allegedly worked like a "tide-me-over"—a little dose to imitate the good stuff he didn't have on hand. The evidence was inconclusive as to whether he screwed up the recipe or administered it wrong. He was dead within the hour, having destroyed his insides.

"That must have been unbelievably painful," I said, shocked, as we turned onto Coles Creek Road.

"Unimaginably painful. I remember his funeral. Everyone was in hockey jerseys. I spoke to his dad for a long time. I felt bad because he wanted to talk, you know, knew I'd been close with Brendan at the rink. He screwed things up a lot there towards the end of Brandan's life. I think he knew it, too, but he was just so … bewildered."

We sat with this for a minute. He pulled into the driveway at the farm, and we got out and stood facing each other over the truck bed, listening. Dad talked about how you never know, you just gotta keep answering the bell and trusting that things will not always be how they are right now. Easter Sunday is always a trigger, he said. Bringing the dead to life, even in the spiritual way of Jesus, was awfully tempting; the warmth of spiritual healing and love are so deceptively close to how it feels when they're actually alive, right in front of you, ugly and sad and wrong but at least *tangible,* something entirely outside of you, something capable of saving you, too, from the depths. Once they're gone, Jesus be damned, they're gone, and everlasting life exists on an entirely different plane than this one.

I had assumed Brendan died of an overdose. The actual details brought things strikingly into reality. He boiled his guts to death. Maybe not intentionally, like when Joe dropped a plugged-in toaster into a bathtub full of water. Not like that. But still fundamentally the same—grasping for something, anything, an escape from the way things are, the way life is. No, the way life *feels.*

•••

Last Christmas, when the farm up the hill was under deep snow, my buddies came to stay in Houghton. In the winter, there's not much to do beyond skiing and snowshoeing, so we spent all afternoon having a massive snowball fight in Freda out on Lake Superior, using the bulging mounds and ridges of ice as cover. Red faced and jubilant we drove into town and settled in at the KBC. The talk shifted from the Bears woes at QB to a gruesome story from Grant about a cyst on his ass that burst during a piano recital. Trevor lamented his future sobriety and lack of greasy food in the military—he'd decided on the Army but was waiting for medical waivers to process. When the lights flashed for "last call" we left.

We were all pretty greased up walking home up the steep hill of Bridge Street. We rounded the corner at the Seventh Day Adventist church, seeing the warmth of the attic lights beyond the steeple. We crunched up to the porch and bundled inside. We took off our coats and stamped our boots in a cluster by the door. I turned around at a creak on the stairs, and there was Ronald wearing a very serious expression.

"Ronald, hey!" said Trevor.

"Hello, you guys," said Ronald, his eyes cast down and aside.

"Hey, Ronald," I said.

"Hey, Jack. How are you?"

"Oh, I'm great. We just got back from the KBC, which was excellent. We show-shoed around all day and explored that old crushing plant out in Freda, then had a snowball fight on the frozen lake. It was wonderful."

"Oh, yes. That is good."

"How are you, Ronald? How was work?"

Trevor and Grant had shed their heavy clothes and stood by politely at the foot of the stairs.

"Oh, well, it was good. I am upset because of the violence in my country. It's ,.." He trailed off.

"What happened?"

"Oh, I heard about this," said Grant. "Didn't Boko Haram just kidnap a bunch of Nigerian girls or something?"

Ronald's jaw set. "Yes, they kidnapped and murdered a lot of schoolgirls. Nigeria ... I am at my wits end for my country. The leadership, always there are kidnappings, the violence ... I do not know what to do for my family ... you here should know. You are lucky. You have so much."

"I hear you, Ronald."

"No, no. It is more than that." There was fire in his eyes now, and his voice rose with passion. "It is more than that. They take everything from you. When they kidnap you, kill you, they take everything. It's so bad, so, so bad in my country."

"I'm so sorry, Ronald."

"Ah, yes, well, for me I am ok, but in Nigeria." He shook his head and launched into a monologue.

"You must understand, you three, over here. You have your life. You have everything. Life in Nigeria is not given, and people are not free. I spend all I can keeping my family free and for what? My countrymen go and kidnap and murder and ... you, here, have your life. There are others who think over here you have much more than just your life, but they are wrong. They are *wrong*! That is all you ever have. In Nigeria, many have nothing, and those still in possession of their lives spend all their energy trying to retain it." He paused, looking at us with a boring, burning gaze. "*All you have is your life. And you have it.*" He looked down. "I am very upset about the situation in my country. I am, very ... frustrated."

"Oh, Ronald. I hear you."

"Thank you, Ronald," said Trevor. We all felt a great gulf between us and him.

"No, it is good, thank you," said Ronald. "I am just ... I wish one day to take you to my country when life is sacred again. I remember so many beautiful things ... Ok, I am going to go upstairs." And he turned around, in his blue penguin pajamas, and walked back up to his room, leaving us to ponder the possession of, if he was right, the only true thing that mattered.

•••

When my train, which left the crying little boy and his family in Toledo, dropped me off in Chicago, Trevor was there to pick me up. Sitting outside Union Station, I tried to make time telescope so I could remember with specificity every single moment of our last visit before he left for the Army. His ship date was set for August eleventh. I was lost in thought when he pulled up to the curb, and I kicked myself for not savoring the anticipation of seeing him before he arrived, then immediately spaced out for the first few moments he was talking, forgot what he'd said, and panicking, suddenly felt like everything was slipping away all too quickly.

We zoomed north of the city to his beautiful apartment in Edgewater, just past downtown. I hugged his mom and did my usual lap around their apartment to see the paintings—mostly French and Italian farmhouse/countryside/river-under-a-bridge type stuff they'd gotten from one or two artists they liked while abroad. There were some figures and abstract paintings, too, mostly cool tones, done by an uncle who lived in Virginia. After a few minutes, Trevor and I took the elevator to the roof and smoked. The view from his twenty-story roof was spectacular all around—the city to the south, layers of buildings fading into white in the distance on a sunny day, Lake Michigan a rich teal blue with little white triangles sailing to and from across it, to the west the El click clacking its way north, like a model train from this height, planes soaring in out over the lake, headed over our heads to O'Hare. We went downstairs after a long while to watch TV and wait for our friend Charlie to come by.

"God damn do I love this couch," Trevor said, sinking back in front of the TV and wrapping himself in a blanket. I felt a pang of sympathy for him, who would be sweating his guts out in Oklahoma for basic training in two weeks, but he looked utterly unconcerned about that.

Charlie showed up after a few minutes and we went to dinner. It was a jovial meal, telling stories about our mutual boys and asking after those we kept in poor touch with. Charlie asked Trevor a zillion questions about the army, and Trevor gave him a zillion and one answers. Beer glasses started to crowd out the table. There was a brief silence when the food came, and expressions of approval at it. We paid and left for Mickey's, Trevor's go-to dive bar around the corner. We started drinking heavily. I had the round of my life in darts, winning all three games of cricket. I barely remember the last one. We spent twenty minutes in front of Trevor's building saying goodbye. Back upstairs we fell asleep on the couch in front of the TV.

I rose with the sun flashing bright on Lake Michigan, residual pink burning away, the water sparkling more and more until, way off in the distance, it was a pure reflection of the sun and sky. I pulled on my shoes and gathered my things. Usually, I felt awful at this point, like everything was slipping away and that I should've videotaped it or written it all down immediately. But as I walked over to Trevor's sleeping form on the couch by the window facing north, I didn't feel any of that. A bit sad, perhaps, but full, too. I nudged his shoulder.

"Mpfff."

"I love you man. I'm taking off."

His eyes still shut, he offered a hand. I squeezed it twice and let it fall. He snorted and rolled over.

As my Greyhound bus rolled out of Chicago I wondered—why is it that before I always grew inconsolable when I left Chicago and my buddies, but now things were bearable? I thought about my last year and a half with Trevor. We'd left school, been unemployed, worked shitty jobs, and gotten each other through it. The army was his ticket out of the cycle. Mine had been more subtle, with the advent of the kayak job. But here we both were, out from under the thing that we'd needed each other for. How many dinners had we shared, how many hugs from his parents, how many times had I walked into their apartment and known, *known,* that everything was going to be alright? And my stomach still turned from the whiskey he'd bought us, and my feet wore the socks I'd borrowed from his third dresser drawer, and though it ached with melancholy my heart was still stretched to the max with all the kinds of things a heart is meant to hold.

•••

One day in the middle of the summer at the height of my Stan Rogers phase, I decided to read his Wikipedia page. I was stunned to learn that he'd died young. I'd assumed he was either still alive or had lived his share; his music was rich with age. But his little plane had caught fire on the runway headed to a folk festival, and the entire flight suffocated from smoke inhalation. He was thirty-three, and I thought of my old friend Derek who'd been killed in a skiing accident.

•••

On the day of the first river roundup, I'd been thinking about Joe and Brendan and Derek on the bus to work. It felt wrong to inhabit a world where all three hadn't made it past twenty when some of the people on the bus were either so fat or so destitute it was hard to imagine how they'd survived.

It was hot, and the event launched from the docks at five in the afternoon. A pontoon boat with a string band would play a few songs, then head north past the harbor to a riverside restaurant, then further north to another place, then down the river to a bar. My company rented kayaks to those who wanted to follow the band the whole way up the river and do a bar crawl. I got to paddle along as a chaperone to the boats people left on the docks as they went inside the bars to get drinks. It was a chaotic event, but the music was excellent, and the river cooled off in the evenings as the sun sank below the tops of the buildings. Once we were on the water, I was glad to be.

It happened suddenly. We were paddling between the first and second stop, the band trolling along slowly so that we could keep up. They were a bluegrass band. They took a drink after the third song was over, as we passed into the beginning of the heart of downtown. Speedboats wove in and out of the thick kayak traffic on the river. Along the bridges people stopped to watch and listen. The front man paused to say a few words.

"Well, y'all, we appreciate you being here with us tonight. Music is one of those things that bends the rules of time and space. We need a little bit of that right now. This next one goes out to our dear buddy Ethan, who passed away recently. He played the fiddle for us. He did most of the work on this next song. He was our dear friend. This one's for Ethan."

And the fiddler's bow danced into the number, his fiddle moaning, and the rest of the boys hustled to keep up. It was a slower, sadder song. It was about being a little boy, catching minnows in the shallows of a lake with your friends, and then one day coming back and realizing you couldn't catch them anymore, that your hands had become too slow. And you keep going back and trying to catch minnows, if only to ratify the memory of catching hundreds as a boy. But you can't, and one day you realize that catching minnows alone is impossible, and that all the little boys you used to catch them with are now men who don't care about catching minnows anymore.

Learn more about **August Whitney** in our Author Bios section at the back of this book

Final Irony

by Tricia Carr

Michigan's Upper Peninsula – 1957

Father James staggered around the side of his camp with an armful of firewood. He dumped it next to the wide flat stump that served as his chopping block and paused to wipe his hot forehead; then his eye was caught by a small shape squatting on the other side of the narrow channel and his brows knit themselves into a frown. So that child was still here, was he?

This lake was strictly off limits to the neighboring children at the new air base and Father James and the other weekend residents had had enough difficulty with them in the past few months to make him regard this child with little patience. Besides, surely he'd been there for a good twenty minutes now, not even playing or fishing, just looking at the lake.

The priest hesitated a moment, then called out, "Hey! Little boy! Hello!"

The child looked up and Father James saw that he was very young; seven maybe; certainly not more. The white-blond hair so common to the Upper Peninsula Finnish population fell into the boy's eyes and his face was still round and babyish. The man's impatience increased. *Where* were the parents of these children who wandered around? Didn't they even notice when their little kids were gone for stretches of time?

"Are you lost?" Father James shouted across the water. The child shook his head.

"Are you looking for someone?"

The child seemed uncertain, and the man's suspicion increased.

"I'm waiting for my friend!" the child called after a moment. "He wanted me to wait for him."

The priest glanced up the beach. There were no permanent houses here; only summer cottages or camps, and all of them except his were empty this weekend.

"Where is your friend?" Father James called.

"He went in the lake," the child shouted back.

The priest's mind froze.

He threw one glance across the shining flat silver of the water and stumbled for the beach, kicking off his shoes and shouting to his housekeeper as he ran.

"Here?' he yelled to the child, "He went in here?" He splashed in as the boy nodded, then hit the lake's abrupt drop off and dove. "In the lake—" Oh God! And that kid had been hanging around for so long—

He forced himself down and forward, his hands groping. This narrow section was deep in mud and a fine black silt that churned up immediately and made seeing impossible. He surfaced gasping a few feet from the other shore.

"Can he swim?" he shouted. The child's eyes widened as he stared at him, then he picked up the man's fear and his face went pinched and scared.

The priest dove again, the water now so heavy with silt it was a black curtain he pushed through. He focused his mind on the

Scandinavian look of his parish kids and his eyes strained to catch a glimpse of anything light—clothing, skin, hair—anything. He dove again and again, back and forth across the narrow channel, during the long forty-five minutes it took the rescue team to find this hidden lake and take over.

Then he waded out of the water and dropped heavily onto the grassy edge. He was middle-aged and getting portly, and his chest hurt, and his breath came in great sobbing gasps.

A policeman left the group surrounding the blond child and came over to him.

"I—don't suppose there's any doubt?" Father James asked when he could speak. "There really is a child in the water?"

"Looks that way, Father," the policeman said. He hesitated a moment, then added gently, "I'm afraid there's really not much chance; all this time, and this other kid says his friend is only five years old."

Five! Oh, my dear God!

"From the new air base, I suppose?"

The policeman nodded briefly.

"WHY didn't he say something? I was right here working around the house! If he had only yelled—"

The policeman shook his head unhappily. "He never realized, Father. His friend said, "Watch me!" and he—watched. He's just a little kid too. He doesn't really understand what's happened even now."

The two men fell silent, watching the others search the channel, and then a murmur went through the group as the team found the boy and brought him out. The constricting band in the priest's throat tightened. He stood up numbly and went to look down at the tiny shape and the final irony of his frantic search through the night of the mud and silt stabbed him.

This child was black.

It had never occurred to him.

He had rarely seen a person of color in this remote area peopled so largely by the descendants of Scandinavian and European immigrants. But now it was the fifties, and the new air base was being built here, bringing new jobs and new people—

It had never occurred to him.

The rescue team took the quiet body and the dazed little boy and left.

The priest sat on his beach and cried.

Learn more about **Tricia Carr** in our Author Bios section at the back of this book

Press photo of icebound freighters in Mackinaw Straits

soft forest symphony
by t. kilgore splake

◆❖◆

everything makes noise
only poet hears
autumn leaves turning color
fresh snow falling
spring buds growing
small birds in flight
standing in their shadows
becoming part of nature
enjoying wilderness music

we love it
by t. kilgore splake

◆❖◆

storm blowing out of canada
fierce alberta clippers
below zero saskatchewan screamers
snow knee high and rising
foot or more accumulation
many losing tempers
making unkind remarks
graybeard poet declaring
"we love it"
making storm less severe
enjoying blizzard beauty
life feeling better

those who stayed
by t. kilgore splake

◆❖◆

copper mines shut down
water pumps turned off
sudden economic depression
widespread unemployment
many leaving area
escaping down highway
railroad train seat
greyhound ticket south
moving to big city
detroit and milwaukee
factory jobs and paychecks
some working boats
great lakes shipping
hauling iron ore and grain
others joining service
army navy air force
twenty-year plan
early retirement pension
those who stayed home
working in forests
topping trees
pulping timber
few on family farms
gambling on seasons
to make ends meet
many miner shadows
riding tall stools

drinking self to death
desperately praying
price of copper rising
mines reopen
shafts pumped out
after many aa failures
twelve-steps tries
offering soul to jesus

Learn more about **t. kilgore splake** in our Author Bios section at the back of this book

Astronautical: A Yooper Translates the Song of the Space Whales

by Elizabeth Fust

I know someone else has heard it too. Jane Rowe Schoolcraft's Ojibwe name, Bamewawagezhikaquay, means 'The Sound the Stars Make Rushing Through the Sky.' She's my favorite poet, and from right here in Michigan's Upper Peninsula. Whoever named her must have known, must have heard the song. Anyway, this was how I heard it, so now you can listen and see if you hear it, the song between the waves and the wind.

It all started because it didn't glow right, out there half covered in the sand and lapping tide under the starlight.

Not orange like the Yooperlites I was looking for. Not blueish purple like the litter and fuzz you find from adventurers after a day at the beach. Not silver like a wet rock in the moonlight. Green, and then gold, under the violet light of my torch and a moonbeam.

The water seemed to bend around it, slow with a gravitational longing to touch this foreign object. I was drawn in too. It was a deep wade out there, then I had to put the UV flashlight away to grab the object with both my hands. It was warm. Warm in the frigid post-first-snow water of late autumn on Lake Superior. It was smooth. Smooth but not from the water. Something else had shaped the object. Then as my hand followed the slope of the warm metallic object, it was sharp, broken apart from something.

Up on the beach again, I set it on a driftwood log and studied it as the tide came in. Green, with gold swirls, etched in repetition. It had a meaning to be sure, but none this Yooper knew. I was not so content as to let this remain a mystery of the universe. This northern wild held many wonders with answers contentedly to never be known, but this didn't belong here, and an answer called it home.

There happened to be a coven of maddened scientists who called themselves engineers and astrophysicists. They spent their time sending things to and bringing them back from space, all from our rugged shore. Outlandish though they were, they could help this quest. And besides, they were a rather fun group in their own Mad Hatter's Tea Party sort of way. The way you expect Yoopers with a passion for something to be.

They passed my beach-found token hand to hand, examining it under lights and through spectacles.

They all concurred. It hailed from space.

But from where therein had it originated?

They scratched their heads and beards and fiddled with glasses. Then all shrugged. "Just go up and find out."

This seemed a good enough idea to me.

There are enough boatmen and spacemen and lakemen out there that I need not go into the particular details of preparing for my journey, how I readied my rowboat with the outboard motor and converted my great-grandfather's diving helmet to be a space helmet. There were setbacks, as in any do-it-yourself project, but before long, my bird dog and I were ready.

It was on another full moon night that we returned to the beach, and just after a storm to boot, which is the best condition for starting a journey. Gallie, the bird dog, led the way as I tugged our little craft to the water. Pensive Rowe, our little craft, went smoothly down the slipway and into the cool lake, settling into a contented float on the still lake. The moon favored us, and we set in at the trace of its moonbeam. The bauble, protected in a sack knit from propylene rope, glowed through the fibers when touched by the beams of this heavenly friend. We followed the trace of the moon deeper out into the lake until the beach was barely visible and then disappeared entirely.

There was no breeze, so as I let rest the oars, our only movement was backward to the shore.

"Well, Gallie, about time we go on up, eh?"

Gallie let out a lone pure howl that stretched with the waves.

I switched on the starboard engine, and we pushed forward in the moonbeam. As the boat skimmed out deeper and the waves got bigger, the little craft began to skip and jump on the waves. With each airborne shutter we glided a little longer in the air, and then like a skipping stone that comes to rest in the sky and not the water, we were coasting up the moonbeam into the night sky. As we did, the auroras came out to wave us goodbye, not even the moon could dim their well wishes.

At first, Gallie was cautious to peer over the edge, but the more we ascended, the more her tail wagged. Before long she threw her paws to the side to peer back down to the shrinking earth and then up to the growing moon. Don't worry, she was wearing a harness, safety first, of course. We were both strapped in to ward off the effects of zero gravity.

It got a little toasty on the way up, but a nice chill wrapped around us as we crested Earth's atmosphere. It was like the first cold day at the end of summer when you know you have three weeks or so of fall weather before the snow comes in October and it's time to harvest the garden.

Together, Gallie and I stared back at the pale blue orb we'd just come from. I could see my home from up here, but then, I considered the whole of it my home.

Something nearly clipped the side of our craft while we were absorbed in admiring our Earth.

"Oh, dear."

Another something was approaching.

"Hold on, Gallie." I revved the motor, but I didn't know if we would be fast enough.

We pulled up and ahead just as the orbital debris zipped through the spot of space we had just been.

"Evasive action, Gallie, we're in a debris field."

Now, in preparing for this trip, I had done my research, as any traveler should. In research, and from the notes of eccentrics back on terra firma with their glasses and mustaches, I'd learned that this particular band outside of Earth's atmosphere is called low Earth orbit. The challenge in this region is all the bits and pieces and hunks of whatever humankind has managed to throw into space and that is no longer serving the purpose of whatever it is that we put it up there for in the first place.

"Gosh darn it all." I said to Gallie, "The first thing you're taught as a kid is to pick up after yourself. When do folks forget that sort of thing?"

In my research, some said nets, or harpoons, or magnets were the way to go. Malarkey. Sounds like it would make more of a mess. A machine isn't the same as a fish. You need to approach that sort of situation gently, really wrap your head around it first. So, I decided Gallie and I would subvert the whole issue entirely, there was only one foreign object we were concerned about today. I considered it approaching the problem one step and one alien object at a time. Take care of one debris object, but how to manage the debris field to do it? We'd been white water rafting before and this didn't seem much different, just needed to apply some quick thinking, maneuvering, and speed was all.

Now, in the space of time it took me to write the last bit about orbital debris and for you to read it, we would have been dead in the water. Well, dead in space. So, there's no need to think we paused and hesitated at that moment. No, Gallie, good girl like she is, put both paws to the throttle and revved. After regaining my balance, after Gallie's quick thinking, we switched places.

Gallie would bark a warning, one for starboard, two for port, and a howl for above or below, and I'd maneuver while I kept my eyes peeled as well. It was a surefire debris field, probably all from one satellite that had met an untimely end. We didn't escape unscathed; you can still see the holes shot clean through my stalwart vessel.

And then, as quick as it had begun, there was peace.

Once again Gallie and I turned to face our home, looking a little smaller now, and we could see the bits of glinting, gleaming metal shards reflecting the sun and disappearing in the next round of their destructive orbit.

"Good girl," I said and gave Gallie honorary ear scritches for her hard work. I didn't want to remind her then that we would have to face the debris once again on the way back home.

Now, we had a new problem. We were almost out of fuel.

We had prepared for debris, but not a squall of that magnitude, and all that maneuvering had cost us precious resources. It put us in a self-made doldrum.

"Hold to a moment, Gal." And she nosed the motor to its off position.

"Let's just sit an' enjoy the view for a bit."

She sidled up close and licked at the chin of my diver's helmet, and I knew she knew I was putting on a brave face. Dogs are smart like that.

Since we were there, we did enjoy the view. I leaned back and looked out to the stars. Still really so far away, just so many more of them. Not so much twinkling as burning.

I lost track of time, and track of my thoughts. No words could begin to say what those bright burning stars made me think so deeply, and feel about my home behind us, about humankind, about God, the universe, and love. And about joy. Burning as bright as those stars, but unlike them, unable to die.

Gallie's ears perked, then her head snapped up from its resting place on her paws. She sat at attention.

Our ship rocked.

It was a gentle, long sway. I sat up, slowly, trying to move as little as possible as I pulled myself upright.

Gallie stuck her nose over the starboard side.

I gasped in a breath, and it rushed out again an exclamation, "Mother Mary Star of the Sea, there be a space whale."

It spanned far and wide enough to block the view of Cassiopeia and the Big Dipper. As more stars blinked in and out of view, I realized there was a whole pod of them surrounding us.

Gallie growled.

"Don't worry, girl, they're peaceful creatures to all—save the Captain Ahab types."

Reassured, she leaned out a little further. Then, each inching forward at an adagio pace, she and the mother space whale booped noses.

"Well, I suppose this is how they expect to greet earthlings now." So, I leaned out and booped noses with the space whale too.

The space whale sang a bit, and though I don't speak any dialect of whale, across all things that speak it's not too difficult to know when the message is, "Hello, what are you doing here?"

"We're on a mission to return something somebody out here seems to have lost. It made its way down to my shore, and finder's keeper's aside, we thought it seemed important enough to try and return." After my speech, I said, "Just a jiff."

I carefully took the object from its safe-keeping bag and held it out to the mother space whale and her pod.

They hummed together, a tale of loss and longing.

"You know what it is?"

The mother space whale hummed louder.

"Do you know who it belongs to?"

She hummed louder still, swished her head, and began to move under us and past us.

"Turn the ship, Gallie, they're going to be our guide."

Gallie kept up with the route of the whales, which wasn't quite straight but wandered left and right and up and down as they sang, like a dance across the map of space. I kept us propelled forward. My mind didn't drift away so much as just stop, looking out at those magnificent space whales against an unending backdrop of stars, listening to their concert, aware of nothing else.

The mother space whale swished her tail, and all the other whales stopped behind her. Gallie and I did as well.

Now only she sang, low and strong. Though I don't speak any whale, as I said before, I still had the impression of collective consciousness in that what she was saying was, "Hello, we're here."

There was a moment and space felt tight in that beat of time. The stars rippled then shed their light, slipping away to show a golden hull with a statuesque sweeping prow of a space whale—except its snout.

"Ah, yes, I see. This belongs to you." I retrieved the debris once more and held it out.

All were silent, even Gallie.

So silent. Without the song of the space whales to buoy me, I searched for a song in my memory to sustain me and my mind snapped to the lapping of the waves, caught by the silence, and pulled to home.

"Home," collective consciousness translated. This ship just wanted to go home, but they couldn't, not without their missing piece.

"I've kept it as safe as I can for you, I hope it's alright." I held it aloft on open palms.

What appeared to be a golden mist, like from a lighthouse in a fog, beamed out just to the debris in my hand, then it lifted up the prow piece and pulled it back to the ship. The golden mist beamed out from the eye of the space whale figurehead, which swept around and lifted the debris to the hole where it was missing. Then suddenly it wasn't debris anymore. It clicked into place. Then the ship was no longer gold but alive with iridescence. The choir of whales raised their voices to the heavens, for above this still were heavens more.

Joy too does not need a translation.

Space whales sound close to what I imagined angels do, and in space, you could hear the echo of Earth and space whales mingle together. One creation, all together.

The mother space whale turned back to us with a bow of her head.

Gallie bowed to her, then I as well.

"Well, I'm glad that all worked out for you. Now," and I thought about those lapping waves, and the feel of that fog out by that lighthouse, "I'd like to be getting back home too, nice as it is out here. I feel a bit of a, well, fish out of water."

Space whales can laugh, I learned then.

She sang to a contingent of her pod, who surrounded us, then with her own snout nudged us around and gave us a push toward home.

With one of the space whales pushing us, our fuel scarcity didn't matter, and Gallie had no need to run the rudder. She gazed back at the mother space whale till she was out of sight. Gallie allowed herself one

mournful, longing cry of farewell for a friend, and then turned back to face home.

I liked this part of the trip. Sitting tight against Gallie, watching our pale blue dot grow bigger and bolder.

"Dagnabit," I said as something shot over our heads. "I forgot about this debris."

One of the whales sang to us. I looked out and saw the space whales anew in the glow of our planet reflecting the sun. Their hides were pockmarked, and in some places, you could see the debris that had pierced them over decades. A fury warm enough to heat all of space sparked inside me. Our presence in space, its debris, had touched the pod and had not been gentle in its reach.

With a swoop, one of the whales dipped down alongside us, then another. They were our shield. As fast and as dangerous as this debris was, and even as it marred the incomparable splendor of the space whales, they, unlike any other creature or craft in space, were stronger than the debris.

With their propulsion and protection, we were soon through the debris field and just outside Earth's atmosphere. Our atmosphere.

"Thank you," I called to them as they fell into formation behind us. "We'll never forget you. I mean it." I let myself have one of those mournful sobs as well, and a tear formed at the corner of my eye, welling up on my face because tears can't fall in outer space. It floated away and danced inside the diver's helmet before settling against the interior.

They sang to us, and I knew they returned the sentiment.

Our journey had not been long, but I felt the wear of all I'd learned, the fatigue of experience. And also, the energy to go home again and make the world—no, I knew now the world was too small—to make the universe a better place. That is the song of the stars that go rushing through the sky.

I turned on the motor and turned Pensive Rowe towards Earth.

"Come on Gallie girl. Let's go dip our toes in the lake."

Learn more about **Elizabeth Fust** in our Author Bios section at the back of this book

NONFICTION

A Yooper Wonder in My Backyard

by Ninie Gaspariani Syarikin

It happened towards the end of August 2016, almost a year after I moved up to Houghton in Michigan's Upper Peninsula from the nation's capital. I just returned from there, as a matter of fact, attending an eight-day teachers' workshop at Georgetown University. As a habit, a day or two after recuperating from my journey, I would walk around inspecting my yard, the small woods behind my house, the stacks of cut rocks nicely arranged to fortify the soil at the higher ground from erosion, and my basement for any sign of a leak or possible flood. Basically, only to ensure I would find my property just as I had left it.

Sometimes I would find two deep holes on the ground in the size of about three inches in diameter. I would try very hard to peek inside what could be there, but the holes were so jet-black and bottomless that they evoked eerie feelings if the occupants might be long snakes, although I had never seen one slither in my property. Indeed, I would rather see the face of a tiger than a serpent, which to me, the comparison of the two was between 'majestic' and 'terror.' As if it could suppress my fear, I would immediately cover those holes with soil densely, then place big stones on top of them, or stab them each with a piece of long wood with a similar diameter. And to convince myself that I had conquered my imagination, I would exclaim: "There, whoever and whatever you are, stay right there; never come out!"

However, some weeks later, I would see the holes again; and much later I discovered that the animals housed there were squirrels or rabbits or their other kind. Since then, I never bothered. I welcomed such lovely companions. Yes, live and let live! Although had they been that Ophidia, I might have sought to kill them first before they attacked me or implore the local authority to seal the holes with concrete.

That August afternoon, though, I did not find any creatures that disturbed me; but, yes, I did find something that baffled me.

In my backyard, a completely round, white, pure white as snow, a size of a soccer ball, sat silently a thing or a creature that I had never seen before in my long life of almost fifty-eight years and more than a quarter of a century living in the United States. I was awed, captivated by its strangeness and peculiarity. I thought it was a plastic ball that some children left after play, but the structure and design of my property were not for any casual footballers or curious trespassers. No shortcut paths to go anywhere: on the left, some distance to my neighbor—a house full of students of Michigan Tech—with some big old and small young trees on our border, including an apple tree; on the right, a longer distance with another neighbor—a couple who were an emergency doctor and a pediatrician—with a row of trees on our border, in addition to their very large yard and a garage in between; and behind my house, a much longer distance to the neighbor's house on West Douglass Avenue with my and their backyards hugely combined, bordered by a long row of big trees secured by a wire fence to prevent erosion from their higher ground position. So, the only open area for pedestrians was solely my front yard and sidewalk of West South Avenue.

I became suspicious of that full round pure white soccer-ball-like creature that perched quietly on the soil on the verge of autumn. Could it be a bomb? Was a bomb white, by the way? I had no clue since I had never seen one. But again, it had no protruding wires or ticking sound. It stood alone plainly with a few yellowish and brownish leaves around because of the fast-approaching fall season in this region.

I was still wary, even after being sure that it was not a plastic soccer ball. I slowly approached it. In my mind, there were only three categories of visible living beings in the world, namely humans, vegetation, and animals. I contemplated whether this creature was a plant or an animal. If it was a plant, it had no leaves or stems whatsoever; if it was an animal, it was clearly bald without legs, hands, or tentacles.

I remained standing, afraid to touch it with my fingertips while avoiding coming in close contact. I used the tip of my boots to poke it around. It flipped and I saw it slightly uprooted. It had a short stem on its base, covered with a little black earth, so I figured that it grew out of the soil. My forehead wrinkled in confusion. I wanted to step on it to crush it with my boots but feared it would explode or burst into some danger, perhaps poisonous liquid, gas, or fire, so I stopped. Besides, I came from a culture that believed that even still vegetation had souls that could balance and imbalance environment. That you could make them your friends or enemies. So, I merely kicked it mildly and it glided towards the base of a tree.

From that spot, I continued to every corner of my yard. To my surprise, that creature was not alone; I found eight others with various measurements, but most were soccer ball size. One was partly hidden by fallen leaves, another rested under a tree looking like a moon on earth, the other grew among green bushes, and one other emerged amidst a pile of dead bark. Altogether, nine white balls. For a moment, I felt scared, almost a

sensation like my piece of land was suddenly plagued by chicken pox. Or a suspicion like my outer space was invaded by aliens. Uninvited but not intrusive. What calmed me most was the fact that they were motionless, not aggressive animals. So, I did not really sense imminent danger. To cater to other demands of life, I left, leaving them to nature. Live and let live, was my motto.

Several days later, I returned to my backyard and discovered that the first creature had perished. The ball plummeted, ruptured, and turned brownish and powdery. Its pearly beauty had vanished and seemed to be integrating with the soil. So did the other eight. Still, I could not decide whether it was a plant or an animal. As I had seen in its prime time, if it was a plant, it had no leaves or stems; if it was an animal, it was totally bald without legs, hands, or tentacles. And to cater to other demands of life, I had forgotten all of them and soon got busy surviving the winter snow of the Upper Peninsula.

One day, the following year approaching summer, it occurred to me to research whatever those nine giant earth pearls were. But where would I start? I did not even know their name. What was the keyword I should type in the Google search bar?

Determined to find out since they might visit again, I typed "what are those big white balls on soil," and another version: "giant white balls on soil," which gave me a clue word "mushroom." I refined the search to: "giant white ball mushrooms" which then gave me a better and closer answer and photos: "giant puffball mushrooms" or "Calvatia gigantea" with its link on Wikipedia.

I was astonished. One link brought me to another to another and to another. "Giant Puffball Mushroom Information and Cultivation" with its link: www.mushroom-appreciation.com/puffball-mushroom-identification.html, and then how to cook them: "2 Delicious Ways to Prepare and Cook Giant Puffball Mushrooms" with its link www.wikihow.com/Cook-Giant-Puffball-Mushrooms.

When I went to YouTube, it became wild; it turned out that lots of people had already been enjoying them in their kitchen and in their yard barbeque! I typed "how to cook giant puffball mushrooms" in the YouTube search bar and out came numerous video links. Giant puffball mushrooms were edible! I was astounded.

I became excited! Wow! It was a mushroom, and I had always loved eating mushrooms since I grew up in Indonesia—any kind of edible mushrooms. When I was little, my young mother and her friends would go hunting mushrooms in the forest after the rain and they would bring home plenty. And these giant mushrooms on American soil, what better source of food? Free food in my own backyard! I did not know.

Regret seeped in me. I wasted those nine giant earth buttons. I, who usually, was very prudent with food. But how would I know? I then promised myself to be more careful in the future. And I was also looking forward to "harvesting" in autumn.

However, to my disappointment, in early autumn 2017, Giant Puffball Mushrooms did not emerge in my backyard. I combed the area, yet none I saw. I wondered why not after the unexpected visit in droves the previous year.

"Let's go hiking and foraging," I urged my son Ibrahim who happened to be home from his globetrotting.

Forever an adventurer, he went out without waiting for me. I was busy at home, anyway. After some time, he called me with excitement:

"Ummi, I found some."

"You found Giant Puffball Mushrooms?" I exclaimed.

"No, not really," Ibrahim corrected me. And my heart sank!

"Please don't kid me," I snapped.

"It's not that mushroom but Bear's Head mushrooms," said he.

"What's that?" I got irritated. "Bring me Giant Puffball Mushrooms, I am telling you!"

"We found none of that, but this Bear's Head mushrooms," he sounded delighted.

"We?" I wondered aloud.

"Yes, some people were foraging here, and they found the spot with lots of Bear's Head mushrooms. They were kind to invite me to pick with them. There's too much."

The thought of a field of growing mushrooms thrilled me. "What's your location? I can come and join you."

"No need, Mi, we are almost done. I got plenty."

Oh, not plenty enough, I thought with shameful greed.

That evening, Ibrahim told me that they had found the Bear's Head mushrooms in the grasslands not very far from the Michigan Tech campus. The mushrooms looked more like clusters of meaty beards. After cleaning it, I mixed it with eggs, all-purpose flour, chopped onion and garlic, turmeric powder, coriander leaves, and some spices and fried it into patties. That was for our dinner that we ate with rice.

I was glad to know that there were other edible mushrooms in the wild in the Houghton area but was still very eager to taste the Giant Puffball Mushrooms which I had no luck with this year. I did some self-introspection of why they did not grow; was it because I offended them last year when I kicked one with my boots? Kicked a source of food, and I was sorry to find out much later. Which in the human world was a rude act. But I did not know what it was then, not to mention a little fear of the unknown.

Nevertheless, my curiosity was satisfied when Mark, Ibrahim's friend, who lived in Hancock dropped by one day.

"Hi, Ib, Ninie, guess what I brought you."

In his hands was something wrapped in aluminum foil.

"What?" I responded with inquisitiveness.

From the way he carried and presented it to me, I could see something he valued. When I opened it, there were five large slices of white 'meat' about one inch thick. My eyes were wide open, afraid to guess wrong.

"Giant Puffball Mushroom!" Mark affirmed almost with pride. "I found two while hiking."

"Oh, how lucky you are to have found it and generous of you to still share it with us," I praised him sincerely. I was touched since it meant my desire was answered.

"Alhamdulillah," I whispered automatically as a Muslim. Thanks to Allah! Then I proceeded to tell him what I had experienced.

"It's not plenty to find," Mark remarked, "At least now; but when you are lucky, you get it."

"But then how come last year there were nine balls in my yard, Mark? Nine balls! It was just that I did not know any better," I protested his sentence of "not plenty," refusing to accept his assessment and willing it that the Giant Puffball Mushrooms were mushrooming in at least the Keweenaw Peninsula.

The few slices that Mark gave me, I flour-coated and fried steak as large as it was originally cut and ate with mayonnaise. To be honest, its taste was not that spectacular; it went according to the spices that you put, like soybean cake or tofu. It was meaty, though. A soccer ball size mushroom, what meatier could you expect? Plus, the fact that it was provided by nature.

I subsequently did lots of reading on how it could be possible to grow them, since it was not sold in American supermarkets. I also reasoned that since there were nine balls in my yard and they perished in each of their spots, surely the spores would have stayed for future seasons. But, no, from what I gathered, Giant Puffball Mushrooms were directly a work of nature, not something to be able to cultivate.

So, I watched the video shows on YouTube with envy of how many YouTubers were able to find some in the meadows or even harvest in the woods behind their house.

In early autumn 2018, about four buttons emerged in my yard. Oh, how fantastic they looked, like the moon settled on earth. Four beautiful moons. When I spotted them for the first time, they were not big, so I thought they were still very young. I was willing to wait patiently until they became a soccer ball. Almost every day I walked by and looked at them with expectation. However, it turned out later that I miscalculated. When I approached, ready to pick and savor the prized mushrooms, they were no longer solid and dense; they already decayed. My gloved fingers easily ruptured them. Too mature. Too late. I learned my lesson.

In the autumn of 2019, I got two medium balls. Not satisfying but I was grateful. At least knowing that my yard was still attracting those "aliens." Hopefully, in the future, they will land in droves. Learning my lesson, this time I did not wait for them to grow bigger. I picked them right when I spotted them.

I savored them. I cut them into cubes and sauteed them with shrimp and broccoli. In order to eat them sparingly, I added tofu cubes. Not only was I able to eat them while being fresh, but the meat was also plenty enough that I could freeze for future use.

The years 2020, 2021, and 2022 passed by without Giant Puffball Mushrooms visiting me. I felt gloomy seeing the bushes and small woods behind my house experiencing the uneventful situation. I certainly hoped that by now their "anger" towards me had subsided since I had educated myself about them. Besides, Nature runs its own course.

The squirrel holes were still showing from time to time, albeit moving inches from one place to another, but I no longer stabbed the holes with a piece of wood or weighed them with rocks. I just covered them with light plastic covers, the base of my plant pot containers, just because I disliked seeing dark holes, though now I knew the occupants. When I ventured again to the backyard a few days later, I would see the holes again and the plastic covers had been moved a few inches away. Then I would cover them again; not to be mean, but I purely used the movements as a method of communication with my squirrel and rabbit friends. And I was sure they understood.

I still pondered and longed for the 2016 explosion. Ever an optimist, I believed that in future years, during autumn, Calvatia gigantea would sprout again with charm as I had not changed the landscape or the essence of my land. In other words, I did not alter their habitat. Perhaps they were on hiatus now to teach me a valuable lesson, maybe also for a soon prettier parade. You never know. As a Muslim, I could only utter: Insha Allah, God willing. He is ultimately The Ar-Razzaq, The Provider.

Learn more about **Ninie Gaspariani Syarikin** in our Author Bios section at the back of this book

On the Death of Two Finn Patriarchs

by Mack Hassler

Denver Leinonen, 1932–2021
We seem to hear from death too much these
   days.
Her ugly little knock will not let us rest,
And always those we lose seem the best.
We stop and search our wits to load with
   praise.
But seldom such a hero falls and mutely
   lays
Himself to rest as this colossus. We must
Admit death wins when such a hero whom
   we trust
Goes silent, whose voice we cannot raise.

I know for Denver work has taken many
   years
And will go on. He will not let us stop.
His stories would repeat. His faith and hope
Were filled with energy. His time for tears
Somehow was hidden. And though he'd
   mumble
At the end, I never knew his step to stumble.

Russell Tarvainen, 1937–2021
Our friend Russell got the call from God
Yesterday while tilling up his yard
Far north where he was born. Let us regard
The utter loneliness of waking sod
Embracing him. This quiet giant stood
For crowds of Christians, ancient true and
   hard
Realities of patriarch and bard
Seldom voiced but always large and good.

In fact, he typeset Finnish text for books
But never setup as an intellect.
Still, we watched his leadership in church
Where language never was a check
Against belief, where solid stoic looks
Always seemed to validate the search.

Innovations on History

by Mack Hassler

[This poem derives from my discovery of the work of Graham Robb, b. 1958, who already has done substantial biographies of Victor Hugo and Balzac as well as several books of "adventure history" that blends what can be read with what can be experienced through archeology. Hence the poem below.]

History

"…another great forest, the *Arduenna,*
   'the largest
in all of Gaul,' was said to be 'more than five
hundred miles wide.' This was the eroded
mountain range now called the Ardennes,
which straddles the Franco-Belgian border."
Graham Robb, *France, An Adventure
   History* (2022), p.11

In the gloriously civilized seventeenth
Century, *les voyageurs* headed West
From Montreal into bug-infested
Domains. Canoes like dinosaur teeth
Carried them alike in rapids and in calm
   beneath
The Great Lakes dome. These French
   truly blessed
And with their black-robed priests professed
Belief to conquer hatred, grief and death.

Can manly saints like these navigate
Adamantine planet cores from one
Curved surface roughly through to the
   opposite?
Mormons meet ancient brothers and run
Beside them on modern deserts of Utah.
Transported bodies representing history's awe.
Such queries, furthermore, are the coin
For transported heroes to enable Tolkien
With his magic of linguistics to join
The Great War of Middle Earth with the
   Ardenne
Battles we still must fight to beat back
   the predators.
History is a tale of wolves and never-
   ending wars.

Learn more about **Mack Hassler** in our Author Bios section at the back of this book

Ghosts in the Calumet Theatre

by Donna Searight Simons

Red Jacket, Michigan -- October 1919

Richard Weyburn took a bow at Calumet Theatre's stage center. All of the main floor seats were filled and most of the seats in the two balconies were occupied as well. He smiled as the audience gave him a standing ovation. He bowed once again, then stepped back, allowing his co-stars to revel in the same enthusiastic response to their performances. The curtain closed for a final time, while Richard affectionately slapped the backs of the actors, telling them how they did a great job.

Richard and his cast had just performed the Shakespeare's *As You Like It*, and it always amused him to observe the actors speaking with a British accent, and wearing capes and tights, just like people did from the 17th century. He walked across the stage, admiring the sylvan set that brought the play to life with painted backgrounds of trees clumped together in nature's delight.

At the tender age of twenty-two, Richard had already made a name for himself as a playwright, as well as acting and directing plays across the country. He was visiting his home near Calumet Theatre in Michigan's Upper Peninsula and loving every minute of it.

As he headed toward his dressing room, he bumped into the theater manager. "Oh, hello Mr. Cadbury," said Richard, shaking the manager's hand.

"I remember when you were in high school working for me as a janitor."

"I told you I'd perform on your stage someday," said Richard, sweeping a hand toward the stage, "And here I am."

"It was a satisfactory performance," said Mr. Cadbury, always one to understate a situation. He smoothed back his wavy red hair and carried an aloof expression, making it difficult to know whether he was happy or irritated. Richard assumed his former boss was currently pleased.

Suddenly, they heard a prop crash to the floor, causing both men to jump. "One of the stagehands must have dropped something," said Richard looking up, then down, then shrugging his shoulders.

"Or it's one of our resident ghosts causing mischief again," smirked Mr. Cadbury.

"Huh?"

Mr. Cadbury tried to hide a secret smile. "Go get dressed, Richard."

Richard agreed. "These tights are chafing my legs."

Mr. Cadbury shook his hand again. "I look forward to your next play."

"Yes, Sir," Richard said, saluting him like he was an Army sergeant. Mr. Cadbury walked away, chuckling under his breath.

Richard found his small dressing room, closed the door, and changed his clothes. It felt good to get out of tights and into trousers once again. He sat down and faced a mirror, then took a cloth to wipe the makeup off his face. He noticed a photograph with a picture of a woman hanging on the wall behind him and turned from his chair to stare at the image. The woman was middle-aged and attractive.

Richard walked to the portrait and noticed that the woman's eyes seemed to follow him no matter where he stood. Richard shuddered.

As he removed his cape for a more modern shirt, he heard something fall. He turned around. The photograph had fallen to the floor, causing the glass to crack. He picked up the photograph, wondering how it fell. He tried to put it down but found himself drawn to the woman in the frame through the crack. Black and gray curls framed her face, and she seemed to stare at him.

Suddenly, he heard a knock at the door. "Be right there," Richard said, placing the damaged photograph on a table. He opened the door, finding a girl he used to court in high school. "Sally Jane, what are you doing here?"

The beautiful woman smiled, her blonde hair perfectly coifed in a bun. "Richard, I heard you were in town, so I watched your performance." She drew him in for a tight hug. "Of course, I sat in a box seat."

Richard squirmed. He had cut off their courtship during high school because Sally Jane was so hoity-toity, and here she was once again, trying to win him back. "I'm engaged to Victoria," he warned.

Sally Jane couldn't help the gasp that had escaped from her. Obviously, she had been hoping to form a relationship with him again. She regained her composure before speaking. "Where is Victoria? I'd love to see her again. We were such friends in school."

"I never knew that," said Richard, knowing that Sally Jane was lying. "In any case, Victoria is in New York, performing on Broadway at the Lyceum Theatre."

Sally Jane clapped her gloved hands. "How marvelous. I'll convince Mother and Father to take me there for a visit some time." She looked at the table and picked up the broken photograph. "What happened here?"

Richard shrugged. "I was changing clothes when it fell off the wall."

Her eyes darted back and forth like a detective. "I wonder if this theater is haunted?"

"Of course not," said Richard, retrieving the photograph from Sally Jane. "I'll let Mr. Cadbury know what happened." Richard waved a hand in front of him, escorting her out. "After you."

Sally Jane was enjoying the limited attention from her former beau. She followed him to the front box office. Richard opened the door to find Mr. Cadbury working his usual late hours. "I don't know what happened," Richard admitted as he placed the damaged photograph on his former boss' desk. "It just fell."

Mr. Cadbury frowned as he rubbed his freckled nose.

Sally Jane tried cozying up to Richard as she said, "It could be ghosts."

Richard introduced Sally Jane to Mr. Cadbury. The two shook hands as Mr. Cadbury said, "Sally Jane has a point, you know."

Richard laughed out loud. "Mr. Cadbury, since when do you believe in ghosts?"

Mr. Cadbury shrugged. "Are you aware of Helena Modjeska?"

"Who?" Richard and Sally Jane asked simultaneously.

A smirk washed over Mr. Cadbury as he looked at his former employee. "She was an actress who performed here years ago."

"I worked here as a janitor during high school," Richard reminded his former boss. "Wouldn't I have remembered working in a haunted theatre?"

Mr. Cadbury shrugged. "Maybe, but don't you recall mysterious items falling to the floor?"

Richard closed his eyes momentarily to search his memory bank. "Not particularly."

Sally Jane grabbed his arm. "It does sound spooky, Richard. Perhaps we could solve the mystery together?"

Mr. Cadbury frowned. "I thought you told me that you were engaged to be married, young man?"

Richard gently pushed the young woman away. "I am, and I wish Victoria were here right now."

"But she's in New York," Sally Jane reminded him. "And I'm here in Red Jacket. Would there be any harm in the two of us investigating this?"

Richard sighed loudly. He could indeed see a lot of harm, but he always tried to be a gentleman. He looked at Mr. Cadbury for advice. "Where do I start?"

Mr. Cadbury smiled, which was a rarity. He was clearly amused at Richard's predicament. "Ask your mother about Miss Modjeska."

•••

The next morning, Richard found the only empty seat at the long dining room table. He sat down, dining with his family and boarders. His parents owned a boarding home filled with copper miners. His mother, Marie, was busily placing food on the table for all to enjoy. Following grace, Richard scooped scrambled eggs onto his plate. The boarders took turns asking Richard questions, getting re-acquainted with him.

Finally, his father, Paul, warmly touched his shoulder. "It's good to have you home again, son."

Richard beamed. "The Copper Country is my favorite place to be."

Marie drank some of her coffee. "Have you and Victoria set a date yet?"

"Ma, we're too busy with our careers. Victoria and I both travel around the country."

One of the boarders, Cecil, nicknamed Cece (he told everyone it rhymed with peace), was always forthright with his opinions. "Time to say your wedding vows."

Richard cleared his throat, wanting to change the subject. "Pa, how do you like being a senator?" His father had been elected as a Michigan senator two years prior.

"Sometimes I feel like I can make a difference," Paul admitted. "Other times, it's a lot of grunt work trying to handle unhappy people."

"You mean unhappy women," Cece gruffly said. "You need to help 'em get the right to vote."

Paul shrank into his seat. "Some of my constituents don't seem to want that." His wife put her hands over his.

"Paul, it's 1919," Marie reminded her husband. "It's time to give us the vote."

"By the way, who is Helena Modjeska?" asked Richard.

"Who?" asked Marie.

"Mr. Cadbury said you would know who she is."

Paul began, "Her name does sound familiar—"

"She was an actress," Cece barked, specks of eggs flying out of his mouth. "She per-

formed at Calumet Theatre a few times before she died."

Marie looked deep in thought, then her face brightened. "I have met her before! She attended some of my women's group meetings. She spoke at the Chicago's World Fair '93 about the plight of women in her native Poland. She seemed to care very much about women's issues."

Paul looked at his son. "Why the interest in her?"

"After my play ended last night, her photograph fell to the floor in my dressing room."

Marie rolled her eyes. "Isn't that a bit melodramatic?"

"Ma, I swear it's true."

Marie stood to clear away the dishes, with her husband dutifully helping. Cece rose from his seat to go to work at the copper mines, and the other miners followed him out of the boarding home.

Suddenly, they heard a knock on the front door. Richard opened the door to find Sally Jane once again. "Hi, Richard, can I come in?"

Richard hesitated, as he really didn't want to be more than an acquaintance to her ever again. But he allowed her in the foyer, as his mother approached. Her eyebrow was slanted quizzically.

"Hello, Sally Jane," said Marie. "We're just finishing breakfast. Would you like a cup of coffee?"

"Yes, Ma'am."

Marie led them to the dining room table where Paul was pouring coffee. He handed a cup to Sally Jane.

"Thank you, Mr. Weyburn."

Paul, ever the gentleman, held out a chair and motioned for the young woman to sit. "We haven't seen you in a long time, Sally Jane."

Marie plopped herself into a chair. "Yes, ever since you and Richard ended your courtship years ago." It was evident that Marie still didn't like Sally Jane.

Sally Jane pursed her lips, but then tried to relax as she took sips of coffee. "Yes, well, I realized you were right about something, Mrs. Weyburn."

"And what might that be?" asked Marie.

"I regret that I haven't supported your women's cause yet."

"Marie still holds NAWSA meetings," said Paul.

Sally Jane uncharacteristically took Paul's hands into her own. "I know you are going to Lansing soon to cast your vote on the 19th amendment. I beg of you, sir, to vote in favor of it."

Paul quickly retorted, "I must vote the wishes of my constituents."

Sally Jane's eyes filled with tears. "With all due respect Mr. Weyburn, all of your constituents must have the right to vote. I'm still an unmarried woman. Sir, I want the freedom to either work at my family's store, perhaps attend college, or to marry at some point. When women don't have the vote, you force many of them into marriages that make them unhappy. I want the same rights you have."

Marie grabbed Paul's arm. "Paul, I've been trying to tell you the same thing."

"My fiancée is in New York," offered Richard. "But I know she wholeheartedly believes in women's suffrage."

T-Bone, the black Labrador, jumped up and down at Paul, wanting to play. Paul chuckled. "Even T-Bone seems to agree."

"How about Helena Modjeska?" Marie reminded everyone. She quickly told Sally Jane about the dead actress' past interest in women's causes.

Sally Jane nodded. "She most definitely would have wanted Mr. Weyburn to vote for universal suffrage."

"The actress is dead," snapped Richard. He rarely was annoyed with people, but his patience was just about up with his former girlfriend.

Sally Jane stood with her hands firmly on her hips. "It's no coincidence that her photograph fell in your dressing room last night, Richard."

The grandfather clock chimed nine o'clock when Marie spoke up. "Paul, your train leaves in two hours. If you want help packing and driving you to the station, I insist that you at least think about what the women folk are trying to tell you."

As his parents walked upstairs, an uncomfortable silence developed between the former romantic pair.

"Richard," she finally spoke, "Let me come with you to the theater to give this mystery a crack."

The young man shot an uncomfortable gaze at the floor. "Sally Jane, I need to rehearse with the actors."

"Please, Richard," a sense of desperation forming in her eyes. "Ever since we graduated from high school, my days consist of helping my parents run the general store. I'm bored and I'm tired. I want something different in my life."

"I'm engaged to Victoria."

"I promise not to do anything to interfere with your relationship with Victoria. Give me a chance."

•••

As Sally Jane and Richard entered the theater, they rushed to Mr. Cadbury's office. "I thought rehearsals didn't begin until the afternoon," said the surly theater manager. He was much too serious for someone only in his mid-thirties.

With confidence that she only recently discovered, Sally Jane stuck out her hand to shake Mr. Cadbury's. "We met yesterday, sir. I'm interested in that broken photograph and the dead actress."

"Ah, yes," said Mr. Cadbury, gently touching the cracked photograph on his desk. "I had almost forgotten."

"Did you ever meet her?" asked Richard.

Mr. Cadbury put a finger to his mouth to encourage his memories. "I had just started my job in 1905 when Miss Modjeska performed here in *Mary Stuart*."

A chilling rush of air shot through the room. Sally Jane shivered. "Did you feel that?"

"I sure did," Richard admitted. "This place is giving me the creeps."

Suddenly, the threesome heard someone whistling the tune, *Oh Susannah*, but without any music. Mr. Cadbury darted from his office, with Richard and Sally Jane following close behind. He threw open the auditorium doors so that they could investigate.

"There's nobody in the orchestra pit!" exclaimed Richard. The whistling finally ceased.

Mr. Cadbury's forehead furrowed, and his face turned red. "Enough with the pranks, Richard."

"It's not a joke, Mr. Cadbury!" Sally Jane said, standing up for her former beau. "Richard wouldn't do that."

"We need to un-haunt this theater before the next performance," warned Mr. Cadbury. He turned the door handle to leave the auditorium, but it wouldn't budge. "What is going on?" asked Mr. Cadbury, in disbelief. He tugged at the handle several times. "How can this be locked? There's nobody else here!"

Suddenly, the lights went out, causing Sally Jane to scream.

Richard felt around a wall and flicked the switch on and off, with no results. "Did you forget to pay the electric bill?" he asked, trying to inject humor into the situation.

"I don't believe this," said Mr. Cadbury.

"I'll get us out," Richard offered. "Sally Jane, you stay here with Mr. Cadbury."

"How can you see anything?" wailed Sally Jane.

"Don't worry," said Richard, feeling the wall and inching his way toward an exit. "I worked here long enough during high school to know where I am."

Mr. Cadbury felt the wall to locate Sally Jane and clumsily found her shoulder to pat. "It'll take Richard a few minutes to exit out back and come in through the front entrance."

"Okay," Sally Jane said, but her hands shook.

Mr. Cadbury found one of her gloved hands and gently held it. "I'll protect you."

"Why is this happening, Mr. Cadbury?"

"Perhaps someone or something wants to stop the next performance?"

•••

In total darkness, Richard slowly walked, patting the walls. He finally felt fabric. He knew it must have been the stage curtain. He turned, continuing to pat the walls until he felt a doorknob. He opened the door and saw a glimmer of light in his dressing room, leading his gaze to the wall where he found Miss Modjeska's cracked photograph. Goosebumps rose over Richard's shaky

arms, but he found and lit the candelabra. The candles burned quickly, in fact so fast that the wax was already dripping! The candelabra shone on the photograph. Was Miss Modjeska crying in the picture, or was it the dripping wax? Richard's hands shook. Behind the photograph, he found an old letter, and grabbed it along with the candelabra to escape the theater.

Richard cut through the blackened stage and out a side door, then ran back inside to let out Mr. Cadbury and Sally Jane. Mysteriously the lights turned back on when he opened the auditorium door! "The door was already unlocked," Richard announced. "Maybe it was stuck when you tried turning it?"

"It wasn't stuck," said Mr. Cadbury, growing more determined to solve the mystery.

"At least the creepy whistling stopped," Sally Jane offered.

"Indeed, it has," said Mr. Cadbury.

"I hate to leave you right now, Mr. Cadbury," said Richard. "But my Pa will be at the train station, and I want to say goodbye. Sally Jane, are you coming with me?"

"No," said Sally Jane. "I'll stay here with Mr. Cadbury until some of the actors show up."

Mr. Cadbury bowed his head to the young woman. "I appreciate your support."

•••

At the train station, Richard dashed to the platform to say goodbye to his father. "Pa, you'll never guess what happened to me at the theater!"

But Paul held his hand up. "As amusing as your stories are, my train is leaving any minute."

Marie tugged Paul's arm. "Something happened, Paul. What is it, Richard?"

Richard struggled to catch his breath while producing a letter, and then filled in his parents on what had happened at the Calumet Theatre.

Marie retrieved the letter from Richard's hands and read it. "This letter is addressed to me!"

"All aboard!" the conductor called out.

Marie grabbed her husbands' hands. "Miss Modjeska wrote this letter to me three decades ago, encouraging me to continue working for woman's suffrage." Marie shook the letter in Paul's face. "Paul, you must vote for the 19th amendment."

Paul nodded, quickly kissed Marie, then hugged his son. "I wish I could have spent more time with you," said Paul, lifting his suitcase. "But I'm headed to Lansing to do something very important."

Richard smiled. "Thanks, Pa. I'll tell Victoria the first chance I get."

"Set that wedding date, son."

"Yes, Pa. Victoria will be more eager than ever to become your daughter-in-law."

Paul tipped his hat to his wife and son while he boarded the train. He found a seat and lifted the window. "I'm going to vote in favor of the 19th amendment." His wife blew a kiss to him.

The conductor called out, "All aboard," and the wheels of the train chugged out of town. Richard turned to his mother and offered his arm. "Shall I walk you home?"

Marie gratefully accepted his arm and patted his hand. "I'd say a special dinner is on the menu tonight. Why don't you invite Sally Jane?"

"Ma, should I really be encouraging her? Sally Jane and I broke up years ago."

"You didn't let me finish. I want you to invite Mr. Cadbury as well."

Richard nodded. "Excellent idea. Let's stop by the theater first."

•••

Richard and his mother walked up the steps to the Calumet Theatre and promptly into the box office. Mr. Cadbury, as always, had his head buried in paperwork.

"Hello," Mr. Cadbury offered with an aloof frown. "What can I do for you?"

"It's what we can do for you," said Marie. But Richard interrupted. "Hey, what's this?" he asked, pointing at the wall. It was the same cracked photograph that had been in Richard's dressing room.

"I thought you were playing a prank," said Mr. Cadbury, his forehead furrowed with lines. "When I came back from a supper break this afternoon, I noticed it on the wall."

Richard exclaimed, "I didn't hang up that picture," the young man said, his eyes widening. "My Ma and I just saw my Pa off at the train station. In fact, that picture was hanging in my dressing room this morning when the lights were out, and I was trying to find my way out. I thought you put the picture here!"

Mr. Cadbury remained silent, shaking his head.

"Has anyone else been here this morning?" asked Marie.

"No, only Richard and Sally Jane," said Mr. Cadbury, shaking his head. "Sally Jane left the building only minutes after Richard. It couldn't have been her."

"How strange," said Marie. "Mr. Cadbury, would you like to join us for dinner tonight?"

Mr. Cadbury's aloof expression softened. "I, uh—"

Richard said, "Please, Mr. Cadbury. If it wasn't for you, I wouldn't have a career in theater. You gave me my first start."

"So, I did," said the former boss. "Very well, I accept the invitation."

Richard turned to his mother. "Ma, I'll be back in a minute. I need to pick up a script from my dressing room."

Marie nodded as Richard headed to the auditorium, and then backstage to his dressing room. He walked in, happy that his mother had the thoughtfulness to invite his former girlfriend and former boss to their dinner table. Perhaps the two would find things in common.

As Richard grabbed his script, he was about to walk out of the room when he gasped. On the wall was a different, perfect photograph of Helena Modjeska. Who or what had put up this photograph in his dressing room? Richard felt goosebumps on his arms, but he nodded at the picture. Helena seemed happy, at least for the moment. Perhaps because Richard's father was on his way to Lansing to help give women the right to vote.

Learn more about **Donna Searight Simons** in our Author Bios section at the back of this book

Vicarious Vacationer

by Leigh Mills

Mackinaw Bay Boathouse - near Hessel | Photo by Leigh Mills

'm a cleaning lady. I clean vacation and year-round homes in the Les Cheneaux Islands area of Cedarville and Hessel, on the north shores of Lake Huron in the Eastern Upper Peninsula, an area dedicated to seasonal, outdoor, recreational entertainment and relaxation. For over 100 years, generations of families have enjoyed the water, land, and summer community. All my clients have unique vacation homes and cottages situated along the shores of the mainland. Each place is very special and most have an extensive Les Cheneaux history. Family photos and other memorabilia cover the walls. Vintage birchbark knickknacks and handmade furniture accent every room. Old books and stacks of games fill the shelves, their edges worn from years of use. Echoes

of love, laughter, and sibling rivalry linger in the air. These homes have a different feel than 'regular' homes and are similar to mini resorts. There's less personal flotsam, giving them a more neutral vibration, and a special coating from the families sharing their summers together year after year in the same house, layering memories like decoupage. I experience a tangible "Ahhh, I'm on vacation" feeling when I walk in the door. A feeling enhanced by all the summer toys arranged along the beaches, dotting the lawns, and floating beside the docks: boats, bikes, beach chairs and patio furniture, fishing gear, volleyball nets and more, ready to use and enjoy. Each client has a regular vacation schedule every year. Over time, I build a connection to each place and start to think of them as my own, even for just a few hours each gig.

I experience the homes and cabins in a way most of my clients can't afford—when it's empty of people and pets; just crumbs on the floor, rings in the toilets and dust everywhere. I like having the house to myself. I don't play music, the TV, or distract myself any other way. I just listen to the wind, waves, birds, and boats as I move from room to room. My cleaning shifts average about four hours, sometimes longer. During short breaks, I find a comfortable location by a window or on a porch and hang out, enjoying the peace, quiet and wonderful views of the Les Cheneaux Islands. I refer to these breaks as "little vacations" and have a favorite spot in each house. In the summertime, the scene through a picture window captivates me as I picnic on the living room floor and gaze out past the end of Hill Island into the East Channel. A huge porch facing Mismer Bay has a chair I find most comfortable on warm, breezy days. Mesmerized by the water, I experience total peace. Two different clients on Snows Channel each have a kitchen table facing bay windows where I can look across their emerald lawns toward the array of tethered boats along the shoreline. A spacious sunroom on Hessel Point with nine floor-to-ceiling windows, a comfy couch, and convenient coffee table for my snacks provides a panorama of trees, sky, water, and boats. My favorite spot is a small, old boathouse made into a cabin near Beavertail Point. Its weathered porch is just out of the wind and has a private view of the nearby nature preserve. Worn wooden chairs and table make it the perfect place for those short vacation breaks and bird watching.

Most of my clients visit in the summer season, but I do have a few who keep their vacation homes open year-round in order to celebrate the holidays, ice fish in the bays, attend Snowsfest in February, and snowmobile through the woods. I love the off-season because it gives me the opportunity to "vacation" in my clients' houses during quiet times when the streets are almost empty and the lake is covered with ice. One of these is a big, old house in Cedarville drenched in history situated across from the harbor. Nestled on a couch next to the front windows, I look out onto Main Street and daydream about what it was like to live here sixty or seventy years ago when there was a different view. And a Mackinac Bay house near Hessel has walls of windows facing the water. As I clean throughout the year, I study the changing seasons and watch the ice as it forms in the winter and moves off in the spring. The light is amazing, and I love taking pictures of the view each season has to offer. In all my homes, I "microvacation" even while cleaning, pausing to look out the various windows, drink in the array of watery vistas and continually soak up the vacation-like atmosphere, savoring every minute as I work my craft.

I'm not the only vicarious vacationer. My husband caretakes a paradise island estate. He says of his experience, "By virtue of it being inhabited part time, I have a magic ticket where I can enjoy all the uplifting aspects of the property. It becomes a sanctuary of solitude; my ideal work environment." I occasionally clean there and can attest to the fairyland feel. It's an early Les Cheneaux estate with several buildings, two docks, and deep-water access for sailboats. Old pictures show a totally different landscape, but today it's covered with huge cedar trees and scant undergrowth, creating a park-like effect. An original building over 100 years old was used as a lodge for trappers, loggers, and other pioneers traveling in the Les Cheneaux area around the turn of the century. It has since been remodeled, still referred to as the Lodge, and houses the family when they come to visit throughout the year. Another old two-story building aptly named the Boathouse was also remodeled and is now the guest house/recreation room with a big deck on each floor. I clean the Boathouse and favor the second story balcony for my vacation breaks. It looks out over the secluded harbor, home to many forms of birds, fish, and wildlife throughout the year.

Living in a vacationland year-round can feel like being on vacation every day, especially when our long-time clients give us access to their docks, hot tubs, fishing gear, shorelines, homes, and hearts. "Feel free to use the canoes!" they exclaim. Our summer season is so busy we don't get much time to play, but we do take little trips around the Les Cheneaux in our motorboat, *Swan*, pausing to anchor every so often and pretend we just cruised in from another exotic location. We don't have to pretend too hard. During the off-season, we do security checks on several properties. These regular visits offer a continuously shifting landscape as the weather and light evolve. One place near the end of Saint Martin's Point gets blasted by an arctic Northwest wind during the winter, it's always much colder there than my front yard. That same place in the summer is caressed by a soothing lake breeze, removing any drippy sweat arriving with me when I visit the owners. It's great to experience the changes. Our neighbor and closest client's property is a seasonal playground. In the heart of winter, we hike in and access the frozen wonderland of their private bay. We stay out all day and enjoy the property in ways they can't—tromping through the snow, taking turns pulling and riding a sled loaded with goodies while looking for the best winter picnic spot.

Even our own domicile is a vacation home of sorts. It's a small cabin tucked away on twenty-two acres just east of Cedarville. The original structure is over fifty years old and was used as a fishing getaway through the summer, hunting headquarters during the fall. We purchased it the spring of 2020 when things were a bit crazy and couldn't get a realtor to show it. We decided to go and look by ourselves, adventuring on deserted highways. The property was easy to find so we walked in through the snow and took a brief look around. Since the shutters were off the windows, we peeked in and saw an adorable, fully furnished cabin. I had trepidations about buying it without feeling and smelling the inside, but when I opened the door for the first time and took a deep breath, my thought was, "Ahhh, I'm on vacation." There's no water view, but we can access the Lake Huron shore by walking just 15 minutes in either direction along the highway. Throughout the spring, summer, and fall, our footsteps take us past an ever-changing variety of wildflowers as birdsong fills the air. Winter months are our favorite because we love playing on the ice. Several nature preserves are within close driving range, and our very own property gives us hours of hiking pleasure since it's situated against state and forestry land.

Summer's End (Cedarville Harbor) | Photo by Leigh Mills

Sweet Lyman · Mismer Bay (Hessel) | Photo by Leigh Mills

Anyone can vicariously vacation anywhere. It's all a matter of attention and attitude. I'm someone who finds each moment worthy of attention and wonder, enjoying where I am and what I'm doing. When cleaning houses, even the funky jobs become less bothersome if I practice breathing in beauty and light, breathing out troubles and woe. I focus on experiencing life as a perpetual vacation, not just one day, week or month out of the year. When fully present, there is no other place to be and every moment is special, not fancy or filled with things, just the specialness of how we can be open and receive joy in the smallest ways. To be glad we're alive, attuned to the greatness of life and the glory of the Universe is the attitude I carry with me and share with the world. We can all use more vacations.

Learn more about **Leigh Mills** in our Author Bios section at the back of this book

Bricks across West Oak Street

by Raymond Luczak

Yellow chunks now made great sidewalk
   chalk,
we carried them from across the street,
through the trail of thistles and weed stalks.
The powder on our palms was sweet;

we'd carried them from across the street.
In the grass they lay perfectly paired,
   squared.
The powder on our palms was sweet.
Winter's threat had not yet chilled the air.

In the grass they lay perfectly paired,
   squared
for the stacks of split wood now askew.
Winter's threat had not yet chilled the air.
We put on gloves for the relay, new

for the stacks of split wood now askew.
Each piece of wood travelled from truck to
   arm;
we'd put on gloves for the relay. New
to us was the soreness building in our arms.

Each piece of wood travelled from truck to
   arm
as it leaned against the garage's back wall.
In us the soreness, building in our arms,
threatened to make our wobbly weight fall.

As it leaned against the garage's back wall,
the wood rose high, just above our heads,
threatening to make its wobbly weight fall.
Tin sheets on top held it in good stead.

The wood rose high, just above our heads,
while we raked away the loose bark and
   chips.
Tin sheets on top held it in good stead
as the night's cape made its daily trip.

While we raked away the loose bark and
   chips

out of the grass, we thought of winter
as the night's cape made its daily trip.
The bricks underneath would not falter.

Out of the grass we thought of winter.
The February snows towered quite high;
the bricks underneath would not falter.
We awaited that change in the gray skies.

The February snows towered quite high,
soon melting into slops of drippy snow.
We awaited that change in the gray skies
where in the basement the wood would go.

Soon melting into slops of drippy snow,
the wood turned a dark weathery gray
where, in the basement, the wood would go
unnoticed in the dark walkways.

The wood turned a dark weathery gray
that August as we relayed it to the window
unnoticed from the dark walkways.
The furnace was soon readied for its glow.

That August, as we relayed it to the window,
the dirty bricks were now exposed.
The furnace was soon readied for its glow
as grass blades bore sharp noses;

the dirty bricks were now exposed.
The weight of seasons had broken them in
   half
as grass blades bore sharp noses.
Those storm-beaten bodies spoke epitaphs.

The weight of seasons had broken them in
   half,
through the trail of thistles and weed
   stalks.
Those storm-beaten bodies spoke epitaphs,
yellow chunks now made great sidewalk
   chalk.

Colonial Skateland

by Raymond Luczak

The place was a beast,
shackled with walls
so thin that I could feel
gasps of ice-cold wind
cracking through
each puff of air I sputtered
when I tried to balance
myself in my second-hand
hockey ice skates.
I didn't understand then
the power of ankles
holding still, like the beams
of steel girding up
the roof high above us
while the dinky speakers
placed up high
in the corners played
whatever song popped up
on the jukebox inside
the front room where
we sat on battered benches,
pulled our thick-socked feet,
forced them into our skates,
and laced them up so tight
until there was little room
for blood to circulate.
I wobbled across the linoleum floor,

already slashed a thousand times
over and then some, before
I grabbed the edge of the fence,
plywooded and painted.
No matter how I tried,
I always fell. I didn't feel sturdy
enough like I had on my bike.
I wanted to glissando among
the skaters flowing together
to the latest disco song
trying to pulse some warmth
into the bone-chilled air,
somehow becoming a breath
of fire cutting through
from my mouth downward
into my feet. I would leap up,
my body no longer encumbered
with layers of knits, socks, mitts
but instead graced with scales,
razor-edged and fireproofed.
I would sprout wings and a tail,
swinging back and forth,
knocking down the walls
and the speakers, its music
still throbbing while I roared.
I would dragon my life anew.

Gogebic County Fairgrounds

by Raymond Luczak

The cowlicks of grass couldn't hide
the dry crumbs of brown and pale
underneath. It hadn't rained in a while.
The midway area, forlorn
of its rides and Ferris wheel,
spread around lonesomeness.
In between our brags about
the colleges we were gonna attend
now that we'd just graduated,
with our moment to flee Ironwood
like bats boomeranging out of hell
fast approaching while
Annie Lennox demanded out loud
on our transistor radio—
*but there's just one thing … who's that
    girl?—*
we dug deep around the stumps
on the fairground's peripheral edge
near the awkward slopes that doubled
as a parking lot in the back.
It was grueling work.

We took turns shoveling.
The soil wasn't easy to break.
Beads of sweat fell like tears
off the tips of our pimply noses.
We couldn't drink enough water.
When we were able to tilt the stump
from side to side, our job was done.
Someone would come around with a
    truck,
swinging a closed claw awaiting
to open and pull the jagged stump
out of the hole. We had to shovel
the piles of dirt right back into the hole.
We thought our job was to hide
the remains of our boring lives.
We never knew how the roots
of a tree, torn asunder,
could reconnect in the bliss
of soil, remembering
in the joy of rains to come.
They would absolve us.

Learn more about **Raymond Luczak** in our Author Bios section
at the back of this book

Two Bells

by J. L. Hagen

◆❖◆

The day I started on the *Ojibwe,* one of the Island passenger ferries out of Loyale, deck hands loading freight knocked what must have been a thirty-pound beef roast into the East Bay. It was shortly before eight, first run in the morning.

The freight was stacked high on the dock. The engineer, Jimmy Soderberg, and a deckhand, Derek St. Antoine, were rolling a hand cart stacked with boxes and tubs across the steel gangplank. At the last minute, Jimmy, the youngest crew member, topped the load with the roast, like a maraschino cherry on a chocolate sundae. They pulled it down the landing, building up speed to roll it over the transition lip onto the ramp. It struck off-center, and the roast bucked into the air, then dropped like a cannonball into Lake Huron. It floated there, wrapped in its white butcher paper, trapped between the dock and the eighty-foot ferry hull, bobbing below the surface like an old-time medicine ball.

"Holy shit!" Jimmy said. He giggled, hand over his mouth.

Derek snuck a peek across his shoulder, a grimace on his face. "We're gonna catch hell now."

"Goddamn it, what's going on here?" barked Hank Doherty, the dock manager. Doherty's job was to crack the whip and keep everything moving. His face, straight out of the cradle, disguised his true demeanor, but his nickname, "Doberman," alerted everyone. A deep scowl was etched across his face and lips, through which protruded a half-chewed cigar.

"Some freight fell off the cart," said Leonard Geroux, the older of the two deckhands.

Doherty peered over the dock edge. "What the—?"

"That last chop twisted the stern as the cart hit the ramp."

"Bullshit." Doherty turned to me. He jerked his head toward the line of tourists stretching down the sidewalk. "Makinen, get the passengers boarded. We'll deal with the fuckin' freight later." He stomped off to the next crisis.

Jimmy hitched up his pants and slunk by me toward the engine-room hatch.

"You're a lucky damn pup this morning," I muttered.

He pumped his fist and grinned. "Every morning."

We hustled everybody aboard, mostly commuters and tradesmen. A few looked over the edge when they passed by, but the tourists were mainly jockeying for the best seats to catch their first glimpse of the Island. They probably thought the package was ruined and would be pitched in the dumpster.

As the ferry pulled away from the dock, Doherty and a couple of his flunkies fished it out with a long dip-net. It would undoubtedly be the centerpiece of a large buffet tonight at one of the Island's luxury hotels. In a strange way, it portended what was to come that summer of 1975.

•••

I finished coiling the stern line and laid it on the cleat post, then slipped into the purser's cage to count tickets. Leonard and Derek slid a steel panel across the bow opening. The panel closed off the deck to any wave surge.

Leonard fished a pack of cigarettes from the pocket of his company shirt and offered him a smoke. Derek shook his head, then brought out his own. They slouched there against the hull panel and watched the waves roll by.

Once the ferry was underway, the crew had nothing to do for a half-hour. Some record-keeping might take me ten minutes, but even the engineer typically had no duties after the captain set course. With the Detroit Diesel screaming at full speed, the engine room was hellishly loud, so Jimmy generally came up to hang out with the rest of us. Occasionally, one or two crewmen might wander up to the pilot house to take the helm and relieve Tommy.

Derek was a few years out of high school, where he had been a decent shooting guard for the Warriors. Like most kids in Loyale with no college plans, he was following the typical path of a summer job that would ensure the minimum thirteen workweeks to draw unemployment all winter.

Small and trim, Leonard pulled his weight and didn't grouse or make excuses. His hair was peppered gray and brushed back from a lean, tanned face, made darker by his Native American ancestry. Derek was also part-Indian, as was the captain, Tommy Blanchard. But Tommy was in a whole other category.

Jimmy and I were both fair-haired Scandinavians. Everyone called him "Swede." He was still in high school, but his old man, Carl, was a long-time employee. He helped Jimmy pass the license exam and land the engineer's job after a year on the deck. Derek had three years under his belt. I was the newbie, looking for an easy summer gig before my college senior year.

Jimmy stood over six feet and carried about fifty extra pounds, the bulk of it in a "spare tire" held up by a cinched-tight leather belt. His liquid blue eyes, long smokey-blonde hair, and the beginnings of a double chin added ornamentation to his massive, round face. He was the one guy who everybody hoped would show up at their party. As Leonard confided a few days later, "That kid's going to get us all fired—or killed."

•••

Working on the ferries was a new world for me. It only took a few days to learn my job, but compared to the University, the work culture was like something from Mars.

I noticed right away that everyone wore sunglasses. All the time. Odd, because in the Straits, it's usually cloudy. Even on sunny days, it's not blindingly bright.

One morning, mid-passage, Jimmy and I were leaning over the stern deck panel between the purser's cage and the engine-room hatch. He was smoking a cigarette, while I watched a forty-foot sailboat laying on canvas for a run down Lake Michigan.

"Hey, what's with the sunglasses?" I asked.

"You mean—these?" He took them off and blinked a few times, then held them up for inspection.

"Yeah, you guys all wear these Air Force-style wire frames with mirrored lenses. It's like a cult thing. Is there a secret handshake—or what?"

He stared at me, and bellylaughed. "Oh, man, Maki, you college boys don't know squat."

I squinted, lips pursed.

"For girls, Dumbass! They can't tell if you're checking 'em out. Tommy learned me that the first day. Says he wouldn't have lasted two minutes, let alone twenty years without them shades. The dude's legendary."

"Really ...?" I tilted my head. "His face's pitted. He's paunchy. His front teeth gap...."

"Yeah, but where it counts, he's got a serious piece of equipment." Jimmy pointed across the deck at a coiled fire hose hanging from a wall bracket. "*Serious* equipment."

Derek sauntered over. "If you go up to the pilot house right now, odds are he'll have a girl there, maybe a couple, taking the helm, snapping pictures. Next thing you know, he'll be asking her, 'Would she like a personal tour?'"

Jimmy nodded.

I rolled my eyes. "Riiight...you guys are just shitting me."

"No, for real. Have you heard about that girl he met one summer who came back a few years later?" Derek asked.

"She's up in the pilot house," Jimmy added, "and he unzips his pants and whips it out right in front of her."

Derek checked to see if I was buying it.

"There's like a hundred people on the top deck," Jimmy continued. "He's standing two feet above them in the pilot house, smiling, waving, staring through the windows. The whole time, it's dangling out of his pants like a two-pound ring bologna."

Derek laughed. "He's a crazy bastard."

Jimmy peeled off his glasses, stared directly at me. "He says she glanced down and seen it. Her jaw dropped. 'Gosh, Tommy,' she says. 'You always were a bit too forward.'"

After the last trip, I walked across to Dabney's Rexall and bought a pair of sunglasses, ones with silver-mirrored lenses.

•••

The Straits tourist season typically lasted about ninety days. It ramped up after Memorial Day and tapered off by Labor Day. Everybody had to make their money in the summer—or wait until next year.

The *Ojibwe* had the shortest schedule, four trips over and four trips back, but like the other ferries, ran seven days a week. While it was uplifting to be on the water all day, for most of the passage, there was nothing to do—except stare at girls through my new sunglasses.

I should have realized Tommy had long ago solved the problem. As soon as we docked in Loyale, completing our first roundtrip, Derek hopped off the boat and double-timed toward Main Street.

Jimmy killed the engine and popped through the hatch. I pointed up the sidewalk. "Where's Derek going?"

"He'll be back. Don't worry about it." He smirked like a chicken thief with a craw full of feathers.

We loaded a few carts stacked with freight, including some fifty-pound bags of sugar for the fudge shops and suitcases for passengers staying overnight. Fifteen minutes later, Derek strolled toward us with a brown grocery sack under his arm. He stashed it in a bin full of life preservers.

It was time to take tickets. I hustled across the gangplank and gave the passengers instructions to keep the line moving. As usual, the tourists all made their way to the upper deck, and we had the lower deck to ourselves.

Derek hauled out the bag, opened it, and handed a PBR tall boy to Jimmy and me.

"Bring one up to the captain," Jimmy said. "We don't want him getting ornery."

"Headed there now," Derek said. A few minutes later, he hustled back down the stairs and popped the top on a beer for himself.

"Man, what a life," I said. "All day long, hitting on girls, drinking beer, and getting paid for it."

"Yeah, College Boy, see what you're missing?" Jimmy said.

"Captain says this one's on him," Derek added. "But the rest are on you, Maki."

"What?" I twisted around, thinking they were throwing me another knuckleball.

"He told me, 'Soderberg will show you.'"

My face tightened. I turned to Jimmy and shot him a look.

"Don't sweat it," he said, waving me off the ledge. "It's all worked out."

"Yeah, but I want to know who gets the two extras," I said, pretending to play along. I motioned in Leonard's direction. He was having a smoke near the breast line.

Jimmy rolled his eyes. "What extras, College Boy? Leonard ain't had a drink since his last DUI. That leaves three each."

I stuck out my tongue. "You guys drink warm beer?"

"Didn't notice the cooler in the purser's cage?"

"For the crew's lunches," I said.

They both cracked up. Jimmy gave me a shove. "That's right, College Boy." He held up a tall boy, ready to toast.

•••

Later, Jimmy pulled me aside to explain the system. "Tommy nailed it a long time ago."

Besides taking tickets and manning the stern line, the purser collected cash from late-arriving passengers. On almost every trip, stragglers who failed to purchase a ticket panicked and jostled desperately to board when they heard the departure horn.

Local tradesmen didn't bother trekking to the ticket office. No way would they be caught standing in line with the tourists, known locally as "Fudgies" for their seventy-five-year-old addiction to the Island confection.

On my first day, they gave me an antique, bar-shaped, metal ticket punch gripping a stack of paper receipts. When a passenger arrived breathless without a ticket at the gangplank, I was supposed to collect the money and slide two triangular punches on the tool to mark the correct fare, then tear off a receipt. The cumbersome device weighed about two pounds and had no doubt been used by Noah during the Great Flood.

"So, here's the deal," Jimmy said. "When a tourist whines, 'I ain't got a ticket,' you collect the funds, stash the cash in your pocket, and waive them aboard. If they want a receipt, hand them one, but then you mark it on your trip report—don't try it on the workers. Trust me, we'll have enough every day to buy two sixes at the Main Street Party Store. Fred Fairman will have them bagged before 9:45. You give Derek the money, and he'll make the delivery run. One last thing. Tommy says *always* keep an eye popped for 'Thimble.' Don't try it if that bastard's anywhere on the dock."

Francis Trimble, the general manager, was cursed with a lisp, hence the nickname. He had married the eldest daughter of the Marchant family patriarch (Senator Marchant). The story around town was that the owners had to give him *something* to do besides play golf and believed the ferry service was the least vulnerable of their holdings to a fatal screw-up. For the most part, it was a monopoly, so there wasn't actually much for him to do. Over the past twenty years, he had done it well.

So, this was the official off-the-books responsibility of the purser. Was it worth the risk for a few free beers every day? Apparently so, and Derek started making his daily morning run.

Even though the crew, except for Leonard, was well toasted by the end of each shift, the work was simple and there were few, if any, mishaps.

That is, until the day we made the fuel run.

•••

One morning in mid-August, Tommy and the crew huddled up for an announcement.

"Plan on some overtime tomorrow night, boys," he said. "After the last trip, we have to load fuel tanks and take 'em to the Island."

Easy duty. No passengers, just ten or twelve tanks full of gasoline for emergency vehicles, the airport, etc. Everything else on the Island ran on horse or bike power.

As Tommy briefed the crew, I caught a gleam in Jimmy's eye. The smirk on his face as he muttered an aside to Derek clued me something was definitely up. But the first passengers were waiting to board, so I wandered off to take tickets.

The next morning, Jimmy and Derek appeared unusually buoyant. They continued yukking it up with the tourists all day, and Derek shot off the boat ahead of the passengers on our first return trip. Fifteen minutes later, he trotted up the sidewalk with a bag under each arm. One of them disappeared with Jimmy into the engine room.

"What's up, Swede?" I asked.

He beamed. "For later, you'll see."

The advantage of the purser's station is that he can observe almost everything that happens on the boat. The purser, unless he is blind, doesn't miss much.

As we docked on our last run to the mainland, the passengers, eager to disembark, were jammed together by the exit. Everyone's attention was focused on Leonard and Derek hauling the ramp across the gap between deck and dock.

Jimmy popped out of the engine room. I was standing by the stern line cleat, gazing out the port-side opening.

"Makinen, help slide this panel back."

"What for?" I asked.

"You'll see."

We unfastened the panel and started to shift it forward. A three-foot gap opened next to the purser's cage.

"Far enough." He beckoned toward shore. Twenty feet away, from behind some overgrown juniper bushes next to a storage shed, two girls crouched over and slipped across the dock. They looked to be around sixteen.

"What the—?"

Jimmy raised a finger to his lips. One at a time, he handed them aboard.

The taller one sported a Jimi Hendrix T-shirt and long brown hair parted in the middle. She tucked it behind her right ear as she scuttled by me. "Hi, I'm Shelly."

"Darlene," said the shorter one, blonde, with thick bangs that reminded me of Joni Mitchell. She blushed. Everywhere that counted, she hung out of a pair of white jeans and a pink and orange tie-dye top.

Jimmy ushered them toward the engine room. The strong floral scent of *Ambush* trailed in their wake. "Be down in a minute," he said. "Have a PBR while you're waiting. Don't touch nothing."

He helped slide the panel back into place. We locked it.

"Who the hell is that?" I mumbled.

"Nobody. Ready for some fun?"

"If Tommy spots them, he'll go apeshit."

He let out a guffaw. "He don't care. Where do you think I learned it?"

I shook my head.

"Don't sweat it, Maki, it's all cool." He hitched up his pants, tucked in his T-shirt. "Gotta go, party time. Company waiting." His grin was wide as a November white cap.

•••

The last tourists disembarked shortly before six p. m. Leonard, Derek, and I wheeled a dozen hundred-gallon tanks onto the lower deck and wedged them with chocks to keep them from rolling.

"Hope you had a cig on the last run, boys," Tommy said. "I'm required to mention that official regulations prohibit smoking." He winked at Leonard and tossed Derek a bundle of red flags. "Run 'em up the poles."

Derek lowered the Stars and Stripes and company pennant. He raised the hazardous-cargo flags on the bow and stern. After we cast off, Leonard climbed up the stairs to the pilothouse.

A minute later, Jimmy popped out of the engine room, his two groupies in tow. They were already glassy-eyed. "Hey, Maki, ever been up top?"

I tipped my head his way, looking for a clue why he would ask the obvious. "What's the punchline?"

"No punchline." He leered at Derek. "Follow me."

The five of us scrambled up the back stairs to the upper deck. It was enclosed by a large cabin behind the pilothouse. Jimmy walked around to the stern and stood on the railing. He gripped the green steel flagpole, threw a leg up, and hoisted himself onto the roof. Derek lifted the two girls, then he and I followed suit. The top of the boat was sheathed with steel plate. You could roller-skate on it. From there you could see Lake Huron and the Island on one side and the Bridge and Lake Michigan on the other. Overhead, a cloud of soot-tinted diesel smoke spewed from the stack and dissipated behind us.

"Whoaa, awesome," Darlene said, taking a three-sixty at the shimmering lake.

The airflow blew Shelly's hair across her cheekbones. "Must be incredible at night."

"Yeah, pretty cool," I said, absorbing the evening light that coated the indigo water with liquid gold.

"It's going to get a lot cooler," Jimmy said. He flipped a side glance at Derek. On cue, Derek extended a cigarette lighter. Jimmy hauled a jumbo joint from his pocket and fired it up. He sucked in a fatal hit. As he passed it to Derek, the acrid odor of marijuana wafted toward me. Derek cupped his hands and pulled a man-sized drag off the doobie, then passed it to Shelly.

Shelly sucked in a mighty lungful and passed it to Darlene. Jimmy reached for the joint from Darlene and passed it to me.

"Aren't we not supposed to smoke?" I asked.

They all exploded into laughter. Clouds of pot smoke spewed over the stern, emulating the diesel exhaust that rolled toward the horizon.

"Just asking," I said. "We have a thousand gallons of gasoline on board."

"Right, College Boy. If you're going to play 'good citizen,' at least don't bogart the weed."

"Nah, it's cool," I said. I pulled a nice riff on the hand-rolled. It was decent, not as fine as the primo campus stuff. But it produced a clean, mellow buzz. "Good shit," I said between pinched lips and handed it back to Jimmy.

For ten–fifteen minutes, we sat cross-legged on the roof, passing the spliff around. Then another. I looked up ahead and saw a ferry barreling toward us. "Hey, everybody lie down. There's a boat coming our way."

We lay side-by-side and continued to share the ganja. Those in the middle—Jimmy, Darlene, and Shelly—scored a hit each way as the joint moved from Derek to me and back again. By the time we shinnied down to the upper deck, I was cranked as a new Porsche with Julie Christie in the passenger seat. The girls were giggling hysterically, like they had just seen Jimmy pull Leonard's pants down.

Jimmy wrangled them to the lower deck and into the engine room. Derek and I stepped up to man our lines for the dock landing. Leonard's face revealed his thoughts on seeing the two girls follow Jimmy. He turned and shouted something at Derek, shaking his extended arm toward the stern. Derek followed his index finger back to me, staring with a vacant grin like he had gut-slammed one too many Moon Pies.

I gazed out the port opening as we approached the breakwater. The *Potawatomi* was docked in the first berth and taking on passengers. It might be a squeeze.

The *Ojibwe* rounded the breakwater past the Channel Lighthouse. Tommy signaled *Half-Speed* with the Chadburn—then *Slow*. As the ferry decreased tempo, I rocked forward and stumbled to keep my balance. The stern line lay looped in my hand for the toss to a dockhand.

We came up on the other ferry's stern. Tommy signaled *Two Bells* to throw the engines into reverse. Instead, the boat lurched ahead, straight at the *Potawatomi*.

"What the—?" I grabbed the stern cleat. Tommy spun the wheel hard to starboard. Derek tumbled headlong and tripped over the gangplank. Leonard grabbed for the bow cleat.

Tommy signaled again. *Two Bells* rang out from the engine room. The boat lurched again. We plunged toward the beach. As we slipped past the bow of the *Potawatomi*, I could have high-fived the crew. Tommy swung the boat to port. Then back to starboard to try and straighten her out. Ahead lay the last slip. Then the shore. In between, lay Barry Marchant's Boston Whaler. Barry was the owners' grandson.

Beyond the Whaler's bow, five feet of water was all that remained before the *Ojibwe* rammed the beach and smashed through the bar windows of the Wonderland Hotel. In five seconds, Tommy would be joining the other barflies there. For the third time, he signaled *Two Bells*. The ferry drifted in neutral. In the glimmering surf bobbed Barry's boat, poised to become fiberglass toothpicks.

As we flew by the line of passengers waiting to board the *Potawatomi*, I threw my line at the dock hand. He dropped it on the bollard. Derek and Leonard did the same. The three lines stretched like taffy at the county fair. The engine finally caught and roared to life, churning out a tsunami of eddies and foam behind me. I collapsed forward onto the deck.

Leonard and Derek tumbled as well, grasping at something to break their fall. The first line of fuel tanks broke loose from their chocks. One rolled toward Leonard. The safety chain stretching from port to starboard caught the runaway tanker—then snapped. Steel links spun halfway across the deck and rang against the hull.

Derek scrambled up. He shoved the gangplank in the path of the oncoming tanker's wheels. It thumped against them. The tanker bounced onto the ramp, then rolled back and crashed into the other two loose transports.

The engine-room hatch opened. Up popped Jimmy, tucking his shirt into his pants. "What happened? What happened?" He twisted from side to side, fear chiseled on his moon-shaped face, eyes drilled as two piss holes in the snow.

"What the hell do you think happened, Jackass?" I shouted. "You didn't let the flywheel spin out before you hit reverse."

He glanced through the port opening. "Holy shit, did we hit Marchant's Whaler?"

"No, you're goddamn lucky," Leonard said, sticking a finger up in his face. "I almost got run over by one of them pigs. I'd like to kick your ass." He pointed at the tanker, now tangled with two others in the front row. "We got a thousand gallons of gas on deck and you're fucking in the engine room with double jailbait? Jesus H. Christ!"

"Get those tankers off the boat," I said, "before another shitstorm hits. And, for Chrissake, Swede, keep your stowaways down below."

We ran toward the gangplank. Tommy hustled down the stairs. He headed straight for the port opening and slid the panel backward. Hopping across the opening, he doubletimed it up the dock toward the Anchor Tavern. We pulled the ramp across and rushed to check Marchant's boat. The *Ojibwe*'s bow sat less than twelve inches from the stern of the Whaler—like nothing out of the ordinary had ever happened.

•••

The dock hands helped unload the fuel with a winch, then rolled empties on deck for the return trip. Twenty minutes later, Tommy strolled out of the bar and ambled over to the crew. I braced for a rain of hellfire.

He slipped off his sunglasses, unwrapped a stick of chewing gum, and glanced toward the horizon. "Nice evening," he said, shoving the gum in his mouth. "Let's head for home."

As we made our way back to the mainland, I joined Leonard in the pilothouse. Tommy was nursing his last beer.

"Getting any lately?" he asked.

"More than I can handle," I lied.

"Me too. Here, take the helm. I need a smoke." As he let go the wheel, his hand quivered with a slight tremor.

He and Leonard stepped out of the pilothouse and leaned along the port rail, each with a cigarette in hand. So much for marine safety regulations.

I stood behind the controls, holding the course to the mainland. After three pints of beer and half a joint, I felt ripping high. The engine throbbed and rumbled beneath my feet, and the helm kept me braced, solid as a century oak. But in my head, my brain was spinning like a merry-go-round in the Milky Way. When word got back to Thimble, someone was sure to be sacked. As we approached the East Bay, Tommy relieved me—not a moment too soon. A few minutes later, we tied up for the night.

As the crew unloaded the empties, Jimmy and I sneaked the girls out through the stern. As Darlene wobbled toward me, I caught her arm. She puked on my shoe.

She looked up. "Sorry, Maki," she said.

•••

Next morning, everyone seemed to have a case of amnesia. The eight o'clock run was smooth as vanilla pudding. When we rounded the breakwater, headed to the dock, a long line of passengers stretched from Marine Pier almost to Main Street. Some convention or other event had apparently ended last night, and attendees were headed back first thing to their respective cities.

We hustled everyone aboard. Several stragglers jumped into line, lugging suitcases and full shopping bags from the Island souvenir shops and fudge kitchens—but no tickets. I looked across the busy pier. Nary a sign of Francis Trimble.

"Not a problem, sir," I said to the first one. I motioned his party forward. "Hurry along. You can pay me cash." He peeled off a couple of twenties for himself, his wife, and kids. I handed back his change. "Step directly on board," I said, waving him across the ramp with one hand as I pocketed his bills with the other.

I pulled the same routine on two other groups, checking each time for Thimble lurking in a doorway or other hidden observation post near the company offices. As I hooked the chain across the gate, a small, slim figure with thinning hair and a permanent pout stitched on his face leapt from behind a dray loading beer kegs.

Thimble!

"What are you doing, Makinen? What are you doing?" he said, rushing toward me in his madras-plaid shirt, pressed tan slacks, and newly shined boat shoes. "You didn't give thoth pathengerth a ticket!" His piercing, pale-blue eyes glared at me through a hail of freckled skin acquired from too much time on the fairways.

"I know," I said. "The line was so long, I had to keep everything moving. The customers don't like to stand waiting for me to punch out a bunch of receipts. This clunky device really slows down the process." I held up the antiquated tool. "Frankly, it's poor customer service."

"Everyone *mutht* have a ticket," he said. "All pathengerth *mutht* be accounted for. You were told that."

"No worries," I said. "As soon as we cast off, I go back to the purser's office and punch out a ticket and a receipt for every single one. Of course, anyone who wants a physical ticket, I stop the line and give them one. But most people think it's just more clutter to haul around on vacation."

He hesitated, searching for an argument. "You might micth up the ticket money with your perthonal fundth."

"I lock my wallet in the purser's office in my lunch box."

His eyes narrowed. "Okay, but no more trickth like that." He wheeled about and paced back to his office. After we cast off, I hurried up to the pilothouse.

"What did Thimble want?" Tommy asked.

"Theemed to think I wath pocketing ticket money," I quipped.

"Shit, now he'll be watching us like a chicken hawk," he said. "He probably heard about our dance with catastrophe yesterday, too. Better lie low, especially Soderberg. That kid's out of control. Tell the crew."

I nodded, relieved. "Think Swede'll get fired?"

"Hell, no. His old man's our union steward." He scowled. "But the rest of us might."

Summer would wind down in a couple of weeks, and I would soon head back to the U. It was time to pull the lever on the Chadburn and ring *Two Bells*. I only hoped Jimmy had sobered up and was listening in the engine room.

Learn more about **J. L. Hagen** in our Author Bios section at the back of this book

Historical · Ishpeming at the ski jump

The Frost Line

by Nina Craig

Shirts hang on for dear life
    Over a clothesline

Snarls of hair frozen stiff
    with pine pitch wash out
    in gasoline

Reiterate why you married
    me in the first place
    If it was *only a lie,*
    a big lie – underlined

As sure as the sun rises
    grass grows, river flows
    You promised to love him as your own—your bloodline.

Rows of cabbage heads
    and potato eyes stare
    blankly from baskets
    along the tree line

Root cellar, dug deep
    into the earth, a constant
    forty degrees year round
    protects from the frost line.

Learn more about **Nina Craig** in our Author Bios section
at the back of this book

Letters to Harrison #11

by Art Curtis

4/25/21

Dear Jim,

Trout opener was yesterday, and I didn't go. I did not want to admit to myself, standing waist deep in a river, that I am not a very good fisherman, even though I can wade the walk and cast the talk. Do you practice catch and release, I'm asked; no, I practice no catch so no release. Jeez, Jim, one day on the South Branch some gussied up Orvis model lectured me on the fish I had in my net and when I went to put the fish back in the water to appease him, he said, you can't do that, that fish won't live because that braided net has scraped all the mucus off its side. It had been years since I'd taken a trout, and here I was feeling like I'd undone all my tree hugging, all my recycling, all my conservancy gifts, all my letters to the editors, my whole life dedicated to conservation thanks to *Boys' Life* where I first learned about it. So, I took the trout home and ate it. You had "truite au bleu" with wild leek and new potato and I had "trout with the blues," turned up Muddy Waters, who probably ate carp out of muddy waters, and gulped my whiskey in frustration.

The next day I went to The Northern Angler where I had to order special-sized Eco-clear net bags made from environmentally friendly non-PVC materials for my various sized nets. I kept thinking of the poor steelhead, the poor bass and the miserable perch and bluegill swimming around with no mucus on their scales. My guilt spent nearly $80 that day, and on the way home I had to admit, once again, that I don't catch enough fish to worry about releasing them. I'm no threat to the number of fish available. The moral dilemma, if there is one, belongs to those 10% of the fishermen who catch 90% of the fish and not to my brethren, the 90% of the fisherman who catch 10% of the fish.

I won't wear that guilt any more than I would wear the latest fishing apparel: the gear necklace, the fanny pack that turns into an in-the-stream fly tying table, the vest with three dozen pockets, the pack-in-its-pocket rain jacket, the Tilley hat, the finger free gloves that prevent sunburn on the back of your hands and, if it's winter, your palms stay warm while your fingers go numb. Nor do I need the several hundred dollar fly rods and their equally expensive cast aluminum reels specifically balanced to the flyweight rod for short casts on brushy streams, the mid-weight outfit for your everyday river and the heavyweight Spey rods and reels for waters so wide and turbulent that a misstep could drown you while your buddies laugh about how you just had to have that shot of whiskey in your morning coffee.

Did I mention the various lines — weight forward in sinking and floating, double taper in sinking and floating, level in sinking and floating, shooting heads, sinking heads, weights from two to fifteen? Christ, Jim, give me an angle worm, a hook, a sinker, a bobber, a tag alder switch, and some of that 4 Cord Braid that my grandmother made for American Thread and leave me be! How did fishing get so complicated or did the marketing people encourage the outdoor writers to try this and that and write about their experience? Since fishing is a lot more fun if the telling of it turns tall, all of a sudden, one needs this gear to have the same experience. But that doesn't explain the high fashion. I've never read a story about a guy-girl interaction in an outdoor magazine where the love scene has happened because of what either is wearing or were wearing. Come to think of it, I've never read a love scene in an outdoor magazine; however, I have had a few night crawler exciting fantasies about women wearing nothing but hip boots.

So, I didn't fish. I was going to fish today but snow, rain, never got above forty; so, wuss that I am, I didn't go. It's supposed to warm up by midweek. I'll go then and admit my life waist deep in cold water. You're missed, Jim; I need another slob to fish with.

Yrs.

Art

Letters to Harrison #32

by Art Curtis

11/10/21

Dear Jim,

It would have been a serious breach of patriotism for these pleasant peninsulas I see all about me to not have written you, a true Michigan boy, on the anniversary of the sinking of the Edmund Fitzgerald during a fierce November storm in 1975, seventeen miles NNW of Whitefish Point.

This letter is really a memorial for those twenty-nine able seamen who drowned, apparently all very suddenly, in the cold waters of Lake Superior who never gives up her dead. You even milked that idea in the first Brown Dog (BD) adventure when BD hauls the well-preserved corpse of an Indian out of Superior's waters, loads it into a stolen ice truck and convinces himself that the stiff is his father. Fortunately for all of us, they left the Fitz exactly as she and her crew were, only hauling up her bell as a commemorative gesture.

You were born and raised in this state and I'm a late comer, not having arrived until I was thirty, but I know at least half a dozen mariners who shipped on the big lakers through spring ice and those late season storms. I also knew a tugboat captain well enough to wear his big thick green chamois shirt after he died; a husband and wife who captained the Neebish Island ferry and several Coast Guardsmen, officers and crew, so I suspect you knew some mariners as well. The state is full of them. One time many years ago, I wandered into an old bar in a dilapidated wooden building in Bay City and by the time I left, I'd been promised a job next season on a half dozen freighters by some well lubricated crewmen laid off for the winter, all of whom promised me a good word with the master of their vessel. I think of all these people on November 10th and wonder if they felt fear when the waves "turned the minutes to hours" and crashed high up on the wheelhouse windows.

Early on in my efforts at writing poetry, at a time when I was so depressed, I wrote a romantic poem in which I envisioned suicide by drowning—swimming as far out from the church and graveyard in Middle Village as I could go until, exhausted, I slip under the waves where:

"A trout will rise from the deep,
carry me to where blue turns black,
where pressure will compact
and what's left will sink to the bottom."

Just so you know I got over that fantasy when I read the vivid description of what happens when one drowns in Sebastian Junger's book, *The Perfect Storm.*

I'm noticing that my draft is dated 3/16/94, so that was six years before you published *The Beast God Forgot to Invent*, the first of three novellas in a book by the same name. There's no way you could have known of my poem, so I'll take the story of Joe LaCort's apparent suicide by drowning, his body found near Caribou Shoals some thirty miles out from the harbor mouth, as further proof that we are brothers from different mothers. We both loved to swim and swimming figures deeply in our imaginations. You turned yours into *The River Swimmer,* and swimming and floating, or swimming a horse way out into deep water figure over and over again in your oeuvre.

I think my love for swimming was genetically instilled in me by how my parents carried out their courtship, one summer, on Lake Wangumbaug in Coventry, CT. My mom's folks had a cottage in the little development on the east side of the lake and my dad, who was working in the test houses at Pratt & Whitney Aircraft, was rooming with a group of guys in a cottage on the other side of the lake. My dad's rifle was mounted with a high-powered scope, so he would raise the rifle and aim it on the barrel float that was anchored some distance off from the communal club house that sat on development property. If my mom was on the float, he'd swim across the lake to spend time with her. Imagine doing that today — not the swimming part, using the rifle as a spotting scope! I tried swimming across a lake in NW Pennsylvania but three

quarters of the way across I panicked when a speed boat failed to see my frantically waving arm until the last minute. Scared, I turned around and swam back. I barely made it; I could never get my rhythm back after my panic. That was my longest swim. My shortest occurred after slipping off a rock into the waters of the Cape Cod Canal while fishing. To be clear, I didn't swim at all quite then; I simply climbed back up on the rock and waved to my horrified mother and sister that I was okay. The short swim came immediately after I turned back around to fish and saw my wallet headed in a tidal hurry towards Scusset Beach some seventeen miles further on. Imagine the shock on their faces when I dove back in. Fortunately, I could swim faster than the current was moving and was strong enough to return against it.

It's been pretty much established that the Fitz's crew and captain weren't given the chance to swim; she broke in half and plunged to the bottom taking all with her. Each was memorialized when a bell chimed twenty-nine times in Gordon Lightfoot's "The Wreck of the Edmund Fitzgerald." His ballad did much to make these five lakes known to the world at large. The first time I ever heard anything about these lakes was in a primary grade grammar book where, for whatever reason, I read the following:

"I thought I saw a Democrat
a voting in a booth.
I looked again and saw it was
a steamboat from Duluth."

Can you imagine the fun Republicans would have if they ever caught wind of that ditty? Of course, being an overly curious kid, whose parents had recently bought enough groceries at the A&P in East Hartford, CT, to qualify for Volume D of the "free" Funk & Wagnall's encyclopedia, I looked up Duluth and learned some about Lake Superior. And then, to prove the cosmos cooperates on a high level, I found a baseball card sized picture of a whaleback freighter on the ground outside of Ski's Restaurant where the penny and nickel candy and gum machines were located. Some poor kid must have pulled the wrong lever and gotten a pack of gum featuring ships instead of ball players. I wasn't surprised that the whaleback didn't look at all like any Democrat or Republican I'd ever seen.

I'm grateful for Lightfoot's commemoration of the men lost and for his awakening the rest of the country to the fact that we've got some mighty big and beautiful lakes in these parts, but I also hope that by the time Arizona and Montana and the rest of the west runs out of water, they've forgotten just how much fresh water is in these lakes. I'll tell you something, Jim, if they ever decide they want to be siphoning off some of Superior's waters, I'll buy a full-page ad in the New York Times warning them that that water is full of dead bodies. I know you'll back me up, Jim. Thanks! You're missed.

Yrs.

Art

Letters to Harrison #37

by Art Curtis

12/11/21

Dear Jim,

HAPPY BIRTHDAY, my dear friend! You'd be eighty-four if you'd stuck around and I'm but one person in a very large group of admirers who wish you had. You once said that "sipping seemed quite unnatural to a mouth disposed to gulping," so to honor you I will subdue my angst and refrain from the gulping that I usually do, to more quickly arrive at some level of flatlining my flailing emotions, and instead sip the age symbolic, eighty-four sips, of Russell's Reserve.

Since I cannot hope to do you any more honor than Amy Hundley, John Freeman, Peter Lewis, and Joseph Bednarik did last Wednesday in a launch of the Copper Canyon Press release of *JIM HARRISON: Complete Poems*, I will tell you something that honors you, in a very different and private way, that happened on my fiftieth birthday in the Dunes Saloon.

I'd been to Marquette where earlier in 1994, I'd juried an art exhibition at what was then the Lee Hall Gallery on the campus at NMU. I'd been offered a juror's show as part of my honoraria, and I'd gone back to pick up ALL my artwork because none of it had sold. How appropriate, now, to remind you of something you said in an essay entitled "Here I Stand for a Few Minutes."

"Everyone involved knows that the arts
        are a cruel mistress
and few of us indeed earn room and board
        from our strophes
and etchings, and if you make a buck or
        two there is the
additional worry that your work is pri-
        marily soiled toy for the
elitist children who can afford twenty-five
        dollars for a novel
or a book of poems."

My "etchings," as such, were some very sophisticated nudes of beautiful women photographed with Polaroid SX-70 film, the surface of which had been heavily manipulated in the academic manner in vogue at the time. But I digress. They are, however, still available for sale and I'd love for you to own one.

Several years earlier I had driven in to Twelve Mile Beach and at the top of the ridge before the final descent, a stand of mature birches was catching the color of the setting sun, the bark all bathed in a rosy pink. How I wanted to photograph them, but I was with my wife and my aging parents, and it had been a long day, so I didn't stop. Now I was alone, it was the same time of year, and it was the same beautiful weather we'd experienced years earlier, so I detoured off of 28 onto H-58 (Jim, do you know that now it's paved the whole way? Jeez ... "pave paradise and put up a parking lot" just so all those damn trolls with their enormous campers with AC and satellite TV can drive through the wilderness. Shit on all of them!). I turned north on the road to the beach and got to the ridge at the perfect time, but the birches were all gone and in their place were young hemlocks and firs. Lord was I disappointed; but I photographed the lake, the sand, the stones, the woods and the curve of the road until the end of twilight and then drove into Grand Marais to look for a place to stay. Someone pointed me to Hilltop Cabins just out of town on the east side. I rented a cabin and then asked the proprietor if there might be a place to eat at this late hour and he pointed me back downtown to the only place that would be lit up and said, "I'm sure they'll find you some food."

So it was that I entered the Dunes Saloon, a name I knew but did not recognize as such, given that at a little past midnight, I was very tired and very hungry. I stopped just inside the door because I thought I recognized the chunky guy in the loose-fitting shirt and camper pants sitting just before the bar curved and talking animatedly with two younger fellows sitting around the curve. The gentleman I thought I knew I could only see in profile, but he sure looked familiar. I have an-ingrained habit of preferring to sit where I can watch the door. I want to see first and have time to search my data banks before I'm noticed. Now, I was at the door but not yet noticed, and the data banks were working overtime—former client, former student, former adversary (the guy looked like he could handle himself)—who? I'd stared long enough that he turned. My God, Jim, it was you! The man most prominent on my list of people I would like to know. You knew you'd been recognized; I nodded and took a table on the wall opposite the bar. I was full of emotion, but I ordered a double Jim Beam up and thought through my options. Almost as quickly as my drink arrived, I'd resolved not to interrupt. It was your conversation and though the two younger men struck me as hangers-on what did I know, and more importantly how would I have felt if some stranger to both of us had interrupted our conversation? I had just placed my order with the waitress when the man who'd rented me the cabin walked out of the kitchen door just behind the two acolytes and said to you, in particular, "They've got a lead on who stole the money." I'd walked into a novel.

Back then my hearing was acute, so even though I was seated some distance away, I could hear every word. The money stolen had come from the Dune's cash register. The owner and chief cook and bottle washer said he'd figured the robbery had taken place about 5:30 that morning, just before he'd come in to put on the coffee and turn on the grille for breakfast, that he'd been running a little late and had he not been, he might have foiled the heist. He said the dick the State Police sent didn't find any evidence of jimmying either, so they were suspecting an inside job or perhaps a former employee. Whoever the culprit was hadn't gotten much—maybe $50 and some change, "'cause there wasn't much; I'd taken the weekend's proceeds home and left just enough to start the day. Thank God your bar bill payment wasn't in there, Jim! If it was someone local, they'd be hoping for such a treasure trove."

The discussion went on through my burger and fries and a second double Beam. I could tell everyone was hoping for an out-of-towner by the way various theories were advanced as to how someone could manage to carry the deed off and not leave any good evidence. I found the theorizing comforting—protect one's own, what's near and dear. The locals struggle as it is, and it wasn't much money.

That was before the internet and being able to pull up the appropriate police report in a Google search. I could have called the owner and asked; but that might have fed into the hopes of an out-of-towner and visions of me as ballsy enough to be so dissatisfied with my haul as to spend the day fishing the Sucker or the Hurricane and coming back to observe, spend the night, or part of it, and repeat the deed hoping for greater rewards. Now, thanks to your demise and my failure to introduce myself when I had the best chance, I'll never know. You're missed, Jim! Happy Birthday!

Yrs,

Art

Learn more about **Art Curtis** in our Author Bios section at the back of this book

Historical · Rockland Unknown family

Way Leads on to Way

A choose your own adventure story

by Brandy Thomas

*(When it's time to make a choice, follow the choice number
to the corresponding numbered paragraph.)*

Susan was a happy child with a childhood remarkable only for being the epitome of normal. Loving parents, a sibling she mostly got along with, stability, no major traumas, and she wasn't spoiled by her parents. There had been the normal difficulties of growing up, character building, but not character warping or destroying.

In the summer shortly after her sixteenth birthday, Susan found an old map at the local library book sale. It looked weathered and old but seemed to be artificially aged. It had some modern geography that she recognized and several parts that seemed to be places from fantasy books she had read or places that just seemed made up to fit the map. It was unique and beautifully made. Whoever made the map had drawn it by hand. The more she looked, the more details and fun illustrations she found. There was a tiny dragon circling a lonely mountain, sea monsters in the oceans, and sirens lounging on rocks along the shoreline. A detailed view of the city sharing her town's name showed the library where she was currently standing, carefully labeled.

She bought the map, took it home, found an empty picture frame, and hung it on her bedroom wall. There it hung for the next two years. Susan's eyes would drift to it when she was working on homework, or just daydreaming. It was always there and still a subject of fascination. When she turned eighteen, she graduated high school and there were choices to be made. Susan knew she should go to college (1), but she also wanted to take a year before college to explore some of the real places on her map (2).

(1) Susan visited college campuses and finally decided to attend the local state university to study geography. All those years of studying the map hanging on her bedroom wall made her realize that making something that incorporated both science and the arts could be a career for her.

Although she loved the art of mapmaking, geography as a major focused more on the sciences. There was a push to use modern technology to make ever more accurate maps of the world and mapmaking was used in more things than she ever imagined. She found there were subspecialties of geography where maps were used for everything from mine plans, to tracking climate change, to city planning, and traditional cartography. Once again, she found herself with a choice; stay in geography (3) or change her major to pursue an art degree (4).

(2) So, she made a plan, mollified her parents with promises, and started to explore. She started locally with the places she knew and started to compare the map with reality. Walking through familiar neighborhoods and finding new places in a town she thought she knew well. There were some differences between the map and reality which were interesting and seemed to capture more the feeling of a place than what was physically there. The old, abandoned mansion at the edge of town was marked on the map as the ruins of a castle and the library as a cathedral but other things were just as they were in real life.

A year passed and Susan once again had a choice to make. She wanted to continue exploring but knew this was not a stable easy life (7), and she knew college was probably the better choice (1).

(3) Staying in geography was the more practical choice. So, she continued in her degree, graduated, and got a job as a cartographer. Most of her time was spent in an office looking at satellite data and updating modern maps. She also got to go out in the world occasionally, working on projects mapping new areas or places that had some sort of anomaly that the computers couldn't figure out.

Susan soon realized that these anomalies were spots where reality seemed to get a bit thin, and some people could see and go places that were not there in the world she knew. She thought back to the map she had hanging in her childhood bedroom and all the fantastic places on it. She wanted to go explore these thin places and made an argument to her company that she was doing valuable research on anomalous mapping spaces. She wasn't about to try to explain she thought she could get to other worlds. They would think she was crazy, and if she was honest with herself, she wasn't too sure about her own sanity. At the same time if she didn't look, she would never know for sure.

They agreed and for a while funded exploration of these anomalies, but they eventually wanted to move on to more profitable plans. Susan was torn on continuing to explore (7) or continue at her job (10).

(4) After thinking and debating long and hard about it, Susan moved over to the art department. She graduated with a degree in art and art education. Her final project being a large fantastical map of her childhood neighborhood. She then went on to teach art at a high school in the next town over, as well as working on her own creative projects. Susan loved teaching (5) but also really wanted to focus on her own art (6).

(5) The years rolled by, and Susan had a family of her own. She continued to teach and was beloved by her students and was often the teacher mentioned when adults talked about when looking back to the person who had the most impact on them as a child.

More years passed and she welcomed grandchildren and retirement, and … (11).

(6) Susan continued to teach while she slowly started producing and selling more of her own artwork, to the point where she could quit teaching and work on art full time. Although she loved interacting with the kids, it drained too much from her. She just wanted to be able to focus on her own art.

Maps, with ever fantastical variations, were her overarching themes. Making something that was often so utilitarian into pieces of art brought her joy, and fame.

She moved near a large city and found herself occasionally wandering the city streets and noting how the liminal spaces could be shown on a map. How that little line of a street didn't really convey the space. Her maps tried to capture those spaces where she felt like she was drifting between worlds. The street that always seemed to have a low mist lurking at its edges became a narrow path along the edge of a swamp in her maps. The sterile block around the most expensive high rises in the city became a castle surrounded by a high wall and road surrounding it cobblestones that hurt the feet to walk on too long.

Critics raved about the social commentary present in her maps and the way she seemed to capture the soul of a place.

The years ticked by, and Susan found herself in the enviable position of being able to work only when she wanted to. Her life was filled with the love of friends and family. Although she had never married or had children, she took pride in her nieces and nephews (11).

(7) Everyone in her life was shocked that she continued exploring with no clear plan for her future. She tried to explain the pull she felt to explore but most just shook their heads and mumbled something about "wasting potential" or "crazy." She ignored them and continued slowly expanding out of her town, being gone for longer and longer times with no word to those at home.

She worked odd jobs here and there to keep herself fed and for the essentials. Eventually she bought a van and made it into her home, so she could travel without having to come back to her parents' house. She promised to check in with them and her sister regularly, so they knew she was safe.

The years rolled on and Susan found some places that weren't on the map or not the same. A drive down a dirt road, instead of leading to a small average town on the great lakes, led to large port city with tall sailing ships and residents who weren't all human. Without her noticing, her van had turned into an enclosed wagon.

She found in her travels that you could sometimes predict when you were going to travel somewhere else but often not. The same with coming back to what she thought of as her home world. No matter where she was, she found people the same; some good, some bad, most somewhere between.

After a several years Susan realized that if she wanted to stay in one place and do something other than explore the worlds, she needed to make a choice between continuing to travel (8), going back to her home world (10), or finding the world she loved most and staying there (12).

(8) Susan decided nothing was better than exploring and continued on the road. Although it was hard in many ways, it was also a wonderful life. Her nieces and nephews randomly received packages in the mail with toys and books and trinkets that were always interesting, always seemed to be the perfect thing, and something that none of their friends had or had even heard of.

She journeyed through the years finding new friends and finding family along the road. She slept where the stars were strange, and in campgrounds run by the U.S. Forest Service. Till one day she found herself camped for the evening on the edge of a towering forest with leaves of gold and crimson, looking out over a great inland sea. She was more tired than usual, but as she thought to herself, she wasn't young anymore and leaned back against her home and... (13)

(9) Sometimes Susan found things that were hidden in plain sight, a path, a town, or even a paragraph that wasn't where it was expected to be. Finding those places wasn't always easy, not because they were difficult to see but because they blended in with the expected. No path led directly to these places. Why would anyone take a second glance at that alley they walked past every day on their way to work, or the average-looking house at the end of the street. But she found those secret places could lead her anywhere she wanted to go. To restart her story from the beginning, or to skip to different choices along the way. But the one thing she found with all her choices is that they led to the same thing in the end and, at least for Susan, that was a beautiful thing.

(10) She decided that stability was more important to her and stayed. The places were not going anywhere, and she could always come back and visit them later (11).

(11) She was happy with her life and continued to wander streets in the city, as well as park trails, lonely country roads, and even the occasional deer path. Susan was always looking for a way into that other world she could catch a glimpse of out of the corner of her eye, the place that showed up in her maps.

Finally, one day, she was walking along the bike path next to the lake in her hometown, a place she had walked hundreds, if not thousands, of times before, when she came around a curve in the path and looked up to see a majestic castle and city before her. Normally the only thing around the curve was the new traffic circle the town had recently built.

She walked through the city gates and wandered the streets in awe. Although she didn't really fit in with the local people, they answered her questions and thought her a little odd, perhaps, they would get people like that in town occasionally.

After a day spent exploring the town and castle Susan had walked out of the gate and realized she could stay in this strange new place (12) or could continue around the curve into her own world again. She still got the occasional glimpse of that other place but that was the only time she ever managed to walk there (13).

(12) Susan traveled on looking for the place she wanted to call home, eventually finding a small cottage by the sea, just a half-day's journey from a small city. The world was similar to where she grew up, just a bit more magical. A land of small magics where fairies lurked around the garden flowers, a good word made your bread rise faster, or your clothes mended themselves. But there were no epic battles or sorcerers raising mysterious towers, at least not anywhere near her part of the world. It wasn't always an easy life, but she was content and many years later … (13)

(13) As Susan lay dying, she looked skyward and thought how lucky she was to have the life she lived.

Learn more about **Brandy Thomas** in our Author Bios section at the back of this book

Historical · Escanaba dog sled race to the finish

Art Fair Summer

by Kathleen Carlton Johnson

The public enters
moving with dollars,
to separated tents.

Collecting pottery with green intent,
artificial landscapes with realistic views,
books repeat stories of the human,
Crafts done in ribbons, glass,
copper rotating chimes,
diverse chatter spread on tables.

What is bought are intentions,
What is sold, creative.

Items deposited on shelves painted yellow,
On walls, in tiled kitchens, blue comforter bedrooms,
Reaching into the private.
All items exchanged,
capable of being bargains.

April in the U.P.

by Kathleen Carlton Johnson

Slate Blue
sky ground
trimmed in white
more snow coming
comedy of April.

Learn more about **Kathleen Carlton Johnson** in our Author Bios section
at the back of this book

Keepsakes

by Chris Kent

A routine drive, two-lane black top leading through the Upper Peninsula of Michigan. Heading home. Lake Michigan, its vast expanse rolled gently to her left, waves lapping against ivory colored sand. Smoke-like clouds heaped on the horizon. Balsams on the right, lining the ribbon of pavement, broken by an occasional settlement.

Lauren grew up in a small town. In the sixties she taught art in a rural high school. Many of her students graduated, then headed to a far-off place to fight a war they did not understand, the war in Vietnam. Driving alone, she thought back on those days. Violent demonstrations. Unpopular war. Those boys.

She almost missed a hand-painted sandwich board on the shoulder of the road, red letters, AUCTION. She made a U-turn following the sign down a two-track road. Bumping along the dusty trail she thought about auctions. Some treasures? A line of vehicles parked ahead. She pulled in behind the last truck.

A fall breeze chilled the air, she reached over the seat for a sweatshirt. Walking up the overgrown driveway she heard the measured cadence of an auctioneer.

"25-25-25 dolla', who 'll gimme 25? I have 10, now give me 15-15, gimme 15."

She stopped in front of the old farmhouse. Weathered siding had lost the last remnants of paint. A wooden shutter clattered in the breeze. Fragments of flower-patterned curtains hung in the window. Behind the homestead, rows of household items and farm tools lined the yard. She wandered through furniture and boxes, once cherished keepsakes. A family's life spread around the yard, open to the inspection of prying eyes.

A gilded frame leaned against a farm wagon. Behind the fractured glass, a portrait; a father, a mother, and a boy. Father in a sweater, cardigan, buttons fastened. Mother's dress, a flower print, tied at her waist. Her hair rolled under. The dress and hair styles dated the picture to the late 1950s. "Did they live here? Are these the artifacts of their lives?" she mused aloud. Looking toward a crowd around another farm wagon, she stumbled. Regaining her balance, she heard a voice from behind, "All right Miss?" A hand gripped her arm.

"No problem, I'm OK, thank you." she turned to see a man, work shirt tucked in uniform pants, "Gary" stitched above his shirt pocket.

He bent to retrieve her sunglasses, "Here you go, watch your step, eh." he turned, rejoining the crowd.

She smiled, nodded, mumbled a second thank you.

The auctioneer, forty something man, pencil thin mustache, wearing a pink western shirt, brass buckle on a belt that puckered his pants above his scrawny hips. A black string tie and on his head an oversized cowboy hat. Standing on the farm wagon, surrounded by boxes, buckets, and tubs, he held a small box above his head and called for a bid.

"Gimme 5-5-5, gimme 5 dollars. Gimme 2. Pay attention folks. Look at this."

Reaching down to the wagon bed he picked up an aqua green canning jar. He added it to the box, nesting the glass among the contents. "Can't you see this beauty on your window ledge? Now give me 2 dollars, 2-2, give me 2."

Drawn to the box; was it the color of that jar? Whatever it was had her attention. Why not, she thought as she raised her hand, index finger extended.

The auctioneer pointed, "I have a dollar, give me 2."

Why did I do that? she thought. I don't need that box; I don't need any stuff.

A voice from somewhere in the crowd called out "two."

"I have 2; give me 3–3 dollars."

Her hand shot up above her head, fingers raised. She shouted, "Three."

The auctioneer continued pleading for a four-dollar bid, then without warning, shouted "sold" pointing in her direction. Tucking the box between her feet she continued to watch the sale. As the voice of the auctioneer shouted sold over and over, she pondered the precious keepsakes being distributed. Keepsakes—those cherished things carefully preserved for the memories they hold or the price that was paid. Their value is only to those who know, understand, or own their history. The things that meant so much, were so important, now just another carton of stuff going for a buck or two.

"Did you know the folks that lived here?" She asked the man standing next to her, a slender fellow about her age, gray ponytail spilling from beneath his cap.

"No, the house been empty since I moved here. Fella told me it was an old couple. Sale bill said the name was Johnston, must be no kids—at least nobody cares about all this stuff. Too bad, don'cha think. Eh?"

"They moved here in the 70's", interjected a man standing to their left, his stout frame filled a pair of denim overalls "Didn't have any kids, well maybe a boy but never saw him. The old man died a few years back. He ran a business outta' that shed, sharpened saw chains and knives. She had chickens, sold eggs. They kept to themselves, never went to church, hardly came into town. She'd been in a nursing home since the old man died. She died a year or so back. House been vacant ever since she went to the home. I heard they found family, a niece, in Seattle, said she never been here. Sell the place."

"Wonder what brought'm here?" Lauren asked.

"I don't know, somethin' musta' happened, I'll tell ya. Da wife, she tried to get'm to church. Wouldn't do it. Said they didn't believe no more. Sad folks. Bought eggs. Brought my saws to him. But never made friends." He dropped his head, chin on his chest. "We tried."

"That picture over there the folks?" She nodded at the man telling the story, pointing toward the framed photo.

His thumbs hooked behind the buckles on his overalls, he leaned back, "Could be, like I said, never saw the kid. They were older when they came here."

"You were saying," she turned toward the tall man. "Too bad to see these possessions that must have meant something, spread around the yard."

"Makes ya think about the stuff you collect. Eh?" The man removed his cap, brushed back the hair loose from his ponytail and pulled the cap back on. "Wonder what my kids'll do with my junk?"

"Look at me, buying this box. No idea what's in it." The box under her arm, she nodded at the two men, "Better be on my way. Gotta' distance to drive. You fellas enjoy the rest of your day. Who knows, your kids might want the stuff," she smiled.

He sighed. "You be safe now, Miss." Touched the brim of his hat.

"Thanks. Enjoyed talking."

She walked away. "He's right," she said to herself. "Kinda' sad."

Back on the highway, the auction sign fading in her rearview mirror, two hours of driving ahead.

Her thoughts were mired in the tall grass surrounding the ramshackle farmhouse. Couldn't escape the photo in the gilded frame. Had they lived in the house? That young boy? Where was he? Wasn't there anyone who cared? She mulled thoughts as miles passed under the tires. Then thoughts about keepsakes of her own crept into her mind, all the things she and her husband had collected. She recalled the conversation at the auction, "makes you give thought to all your stuff" the fella had said. Would the kids care? Would it be spread out on the grass someday? She turned into their driveway, her mind still focused on keepsakes, what do they mean?

From the county road, it was a mile to their house. In the garage, she removed the jar and set the box on a shelf. She walked toward the house. Her attention diverted as their German Shorthair vaulted across the driveway, his welcome always brought joy.

Her husband Krug, a big man, tall, his imposing frame intimidating. The grip of his massive hand demanded attention. Intense blue eyes peered from under his always present Vietnam Vet cap. A man who spent forty years of his career in a suit was now comfortable in a buffalo plaid shirt and hunting pants. He stood leaning against the door frame. "Getting worried; thought you'd be home earlier."

"Stopped at an auction." She stooped to stroke the dog.

"You what?" Krug questioned.

"Stopped at an auction," she repeated.

"What kind of an auction? You didn't buy another horse?"

"Household auction."

"And?" Krug quizzed.

"A box of junk with this old Ball jar," she held up the jar. "Made me sad, a family's life auctioned off. Their keepsakes."

"So, what else is in the box?"

"I'll look through it tomorrow. Don't know why I bought it. The jar caught my eye. I talked to a couple guys at the auction about all the things being sold. Made me think about our stuff we've collected over the years. Things that are precious to us but mean nothing to anyone else. What will the kids care? What is a keepsake? Maybe it's about memories we try to hold on to. Think about Charlie, your brass statue of a Vietnamese warrior. You carried him all those months. He's a piece of art but he's more to

you. His value is memories, the price you paid."

"You're right. Memories. Good luck. Guys had things they carried—things they hoped would bring'em luck – keep'em safe. Sometimes they worked, sometimes they didn't."

"I smell chili. Perfect for tonight." She stepped toward Krug, put her arm around his neck.

"Glad you're home. Quiet without you."

Morning broke cool and still. Coffee on to brew, she slipped on her shoes, walked through the dew-covered grass toward the garage, each footstep leaving an imprint. Retrieving her auction purchase she turned toward the house, footprints already fading. The impact of her steps lasting but a moment.

She poured coffee, turned on the television, reviewed her purchase—a few buttons, pocketknife, belt buckle, a medal—a striped ribbon with an image of George Washington on a purple heart, a brown envelope with a rusty metal clasp, and a small box. She opened the box; a folded piece of fabric fell to the counter. She unfolded the cloth to find a dog tag, like the one in her husband's dresser drawer, from Vietnam. Jerry Johnston – US65748621 – Protestant – AB. All anyone in the military needed to know. Name, service number, religious preference, and blood type. Everything reduced to four lines on a piece of metal. She glanced at the TV, coverage of the current war in Afghanistan. Seven American soldiers killed. *War*, she thought, *never changes*. Her mind drifted back almost fifty years to grainy images on a television screen. Pictures from the other side of the world. A nameless village of bamboo huts. A talking head reporting a clinical impression of the conflict. The reality of war in tiny print at the bottom of the screen. Lower left the number 864, enemy killed. Lower right a second number ... 57 U.S. soldiers. The score, day's body count. True cost of war.

Fifty-seven American soldiers lost, boys. Surely one from some small Midwest farm town not far from where she had lived. By no fault of his own, thrust into a place he never knew existed, Vietnam. Soldiers lost, added to the thousands lost before, a sum, the result of decisions made by Washington politicians. The list of lost did not include the names of their sons or brothers. It did include those without a student deferment, wife, or children or without an ivy league education, a wealthy or politician father.

As quickly as each of those lives was lost, the numbers disappeared. Without emotion, a disconnected reporter moved to the day's next story—protesters in the streets. It was the same today. The newsperson shifted to a story on the current housing market. Seven lost soldiers left behind.

The Vietnam War caused bitter fury, dividing a nation. She and her husband recently started talking about it, the Vietnam War, their war. Perspectives far apart forty years ago. She was not a protester, never a critic of soldiers, but of a war she could not understand. As a high school teacher, she watched innocent boys leave for a far-off world they had never heard of, to fight a war few understood. During her tenure, seeing the impact of war. Young boys returning maimed, psychologically damaged. Or not returning, leaving a mourning family bearing the burden of ultimate loss. Krug's perspective, a soldier, an officer, a job to do. Driven to do the best against nearly impossible circumstances. Feeling, as a country, a responsibility to the people of South Vietnam. An obligation to wear the uniform of his country as generations before had done. To a young man, a personal challenge, which soon became an ordeal to survive. A man who came home wounded, to a country in turmoil, a country that mistreated terribly the veterans of a war they did not choose. Over the years, Krug and Lauren had reconciled their positions, although the demons of war, for her, impossible to understand.

She looked at the piece of stamped metal. Who was this soldier? Why was his dog tag preserved? Are keepsakes items you want to hold close or are they sometimes things you would rather not possess?

Light bathed the kitchen as the sun eased over the ridge. The jar sparkled jewel-like on the windowsill. Mist unraveled like a skein of yarn over the river. The dog rose from his resting spot, stretched, his muscles flexing.

"How would I find out what happened to a soldier?" Lauren spoke as her husband walked into the room.

"What did you say? A soldier? What are you talking about?" Krug sat, elbows resting on the countertop, his hands wrapped around his coffee mug.

"This dog tag was in the box I bought." The metal dangled from the ball chain around her fingers. "How can I find out something about Jerry Johnston? If he lived in that house, where the auction was? There was a picture, a couple with a young boy."

"Let me see the tag," setting his mug down. He rubbed his fingers across the metal, thinking about his dog tag in the bottom of his dresser drawer. Been there for years, always made the move, every time he relocated, it ended up back in the bottom of a bureau drawer. A touchstone, a connection to another time. Over the last forty plus years that experience had never left him. The ghosts ever present. Demons easily jarred from their resting place by the most unlikely episode. Today the simple touch of cold metal.

A blur of mental images ... a letter from the President. You are hereby ordered for induction into the Armed Forces; a change from civilian to military life; the mass of young men, shaved heads, feeling of your first set of dog tags, cold metal touching your bare chest; then the naked feeling if you did not have them. How they became a keepsake for those returning to be placed in a drawer and for those that did not, an inventory—one for a record and one for a body returning home.

Back to the moment as his wife repeated her question, "Can I find information?"

"We have his name and service number; that's a beginning." He raised his coffee to his lips and gazed at the river, thoughts of another river he waded into as a young lieutenant.

"Krug, is there any way to tell from the dog tag when a person was in the military?" She pulled a stool close to Krug, her shoulder touching his.

"No, dog tags look similar. What else is in the box? Maybe clues."

"These things: buttons, pocketknife, belt buckle, and a purple heart medal," she pushed the objects toward Krug. "Oh, this envelope, probably nothing," opening the flap on the envelope, removing two papers. The first, a school report card for Jerry Johnston.

"That's the name on the dog tag," pointing at the paper.

Taking the document from Lauren, Krug said, "Looks like a good student, all A's and B's. Can you read the name of the school on the report card?"

"I think it says Southridge Elementary."

"What's the other paper?"

Unfolding the second paper, "His birth certificate."

"Where was he born?"

"Charlotte, Michigan."

"When?"

"1950"

"My age. Vietnam. We can check the Wall website for his name," as he powered up the laptop. "We'll start with Michigan, assuming he lived here when he was drafted."

His fingers drumming the counter as he waited for the computer. A Google search generated the address, www.thewall-usa.com. The search easy, enter the name and state. They watched the screen. Within seconds the database of 58,195 names was analyzed and Jerry Johnston appeared - Army Sgt. E5, age 20, Caucasian male from Charlotte, Michigan, Panel 02W Line 86.

"The date matches that birth certificate. Let's see what else is on the page," he clicked the bar at the bottom of the screen. He read aloud, "Tour began on February 28, 1970, and he was a casualty on December 12, 1971, in Binh Dinh, South Vietnam, Hostile Ground Casualty, Misadventure, Body recovered."

"What does that mean 'misadventure'?"

"He may have been killed by friendly fire."

"That seems like such a waste. It's hard for me to understand. How could that happen?"

"You can't understand, you weren't there." Krug's response abrupt. "Things happen, it's dark, noise deafening. You're not sure where anyone is," his eyes fixed on a distant point, his finger rubbed the rim of his cup, circling.

"Krug, what does it say in that Personal Comment section?" she asked to redirect the conversation.

He blinked; his hand moved to the keyboard.

"It's comments people have posted. A couple posts from guys that were with him in Vietnam. Listen to this."

The only man killed, in Vietnam, that week. I remember it, like yesterday. Watching the hill get hit, being afraid. Finding out that Jerry was killed. I didn't know him well, but still, I'll never forget him. God bless you.

Friday, September 03, 1999

"This one is interesting. Talks about a *Life* magazine."

I have the Life magazine, titled, THE ONE BOY WHO DIED on my desk. I'm haunted by that smiling face on that issue, dated, January 21, 1972. I think each of us needs to look at it occasionally to remind us, the terrible price of war. There were many faces like Jerry's, the year I spent in Viet Nam. (Will Carmack)

Monday, January 16, 2006

Scrolling on, "Look, here's the cover of the magazine. It's his picture, Jerry's."

"That's him. He looks like the boy in the picture at the auction. I wonder if the parents moved to the U.P. after he was killed. I talked to this guy at the auction; he said they didn't have much to do with anyone. Wouldn't go to church. Something about not believing any more. Losing the boy would explain all that. Here's another post, it's from December 2012."

I think of you always, especially on this day. I'm sorry Jerry. (Bill Waldron, bwaldron@gmail.com) December 2012

"Krug, what do you think that means, 'I'm sorry Jerry'. It was just posted last December."

"It was the anniversary of his death. Remember, December of '71. Probably someone from his unit, who was there."

"This is crazy; I'm obsessed with this guy. I look at that picture from the magazine. He could have been one of the boys I had in class back in the late 60s. This explains why the dog tag was so cherished. It was all they had left, a keepsake of their only son. Just as we talked about earlier, keepsakes can be something you would rather not possess, a reminder of such terrible loss. Something you cling to in hopes of providing meaning to a meaningless event. I'm going to email the guy who put that last post on the page."

"Why? What would you say?"

"I'm going to tell him I have the dog tag. Maybe he wants it?"

"You are obsessed. Forget it. He might not want to hear from anyone."

"I have to," she whispered as she began composing an email to explain the auction purchase, the dog tag, her search. Should she send him the dog tag?

Closing the cover on the laptop, sliding it down the counter, "Okay, let's have breakfast and get the day started, I'll put this away."

Weeks passed. The dog tag remained on the desk. Now and then she would pick it up, turn it over and over in her hand, thinking about the lost son, the price of war, Bill Waldren. Krug would remind her; he probably doesn't want to communicate about this. Maybe he is trying to move on. We don't know the circumstances. Let's let Jerry Johnston rest.

Days later the heavy treads on the ATV gripped the gravel as she approached the mailbox. Usual mail and a small package addressed to her, no return address.

She cut the tape on the ends of the package and removed the box. Lifting the cover she found a folded piece of paper, a photograph, and a bracelet. The photo, Jerry Johnston and another soldier. Rifles across their chests, gaunt, dark eyes distant, military pants, dusty boots, dog tags hanging around their necks.

She touched the bracelet, course texture, dark, almost black, woven of hair-like material, four knots evenly spaced. Turning it over and over in her hands, feeling the rough surface, examining the strange material, finally placing it next to the photo. Studying the photo, she saw what she had not seen earlier. The bracelet, on Jerry Johnston's wrist.

Next the folded paper, a hand-written note. The greeting, 'Dear Lauren'. Quickly her eyes moved down the page to the scrawled signature, Bill Waldron.

I was surprised to get your message. I thought after all these years people would forget. You and I will never meet but now we have this connection. Hardly a month or even a week goes by without me thinking about Jerry. This is a picture of him and I. I look at it now and see two boys. That's what we were. They called us men, but we were just boys. Doing things that boys shouldn't have been asked to do.

I remember the night Jerry died. Our platoon had been out in the bush for three or four days. It was hot. We were tired. We set up for the night on a hill. Just after dark we got hit. Hard. You could never understand what that's like unless you were there. The confusion, the noise. Everyone tired. Afraid. In the dark, you don't know where anyone is.

She thought about what Krug had said. Just like he had described. The noise and confusion. Reading on,

After it was over, I found Jerry. He must have crawled forward from his fighting hole. I don't know why. He didn't have to die that night. It wasn't his fault. I've tried all these years to find a way to believe that it wasn't mine either.

I'm sending the bracelet he always wore. It was supposed to be his good luck charm. It's yours now. I'm in the VA hospital in Bangor. I'm going to die. I don't have much longer. The war seems to never really go away. I'm dying from cancer I got from Agent Orange. Maybe it's just making things even for me and Jerry.

Jerry's memory is now yours. Take good care of him.

Bill Waldron

She put Jerry's tag on the counter next to the bracelet and photograph. What now? She had been given the responsibility of these keepsakes. Her only connection, the dog tag from the auction.

A rush of air chilled the kitchen as the dog raced into the house disrupting her thoughts.

"Did you get the mail," Krug called from the doorway.

"I did."

"Anything of importance?"

"Well certainly interesting. Look at this. From the guy on the website, the Wall."

Hanging his coat on a hook by the door he walked toward the kitchen, "What guy?"

"The guy who wrote the post about Jerry Johnston," she handed Krug the bracelet.

He held the bracelet "I only saw a few of these, its woven from elephant hair, popular with the Vietnamese."

"He sent this too," holding up the photograph, "And a letter. Read it."

Krug settled on the bar stool, studying each word carefully. Finally, he leaned back, looked directly at his wife, "So what are you going to do?" His tone firm.

"These things, these keepsakes, don't belong to me. I shouldn't have them. I should have sent the dog tag to Waldron and been done with it. Why did he send me this stuff?"

"You said after you stopped at the auction, something about how sad it was there wasn't anyone to care about the keepsakes. That's what he's telling you. So, as I said before, what are you going to do?"

"There must be someone. I need to give them back. They aren't mine. We have a houseful of keepsakes that no one will want."

Winter dragged on. Temperatures slowly beginning to rise. Trees still bare, black skeletons dancing through the woods. Remaining snow, dull gray masses. Ribbons of obsidian water appearing in the river. The bracelet and her thoughts about Jerry had haunted her throughout winter.

She learned, according to legend, people who wear elephant hair bracelets are to be protected against illness, misfortune, and harm. The four knots represent elements of nature: fire, sun, water, wind. She learned too that Amelia Earhart wore an elephant hair bracelet; however, she mistakenly left it behind when she took off in 1937. Lauren couldn't help but wonder, was Jerry wearing his bracelet that day in Vietnam.

During the winter, the bracelet had prompted discussions between Krug and Lauren about war, and the aftermath. The country mired in another war, often linked in their conversations. During this time, she convinced her husband she had to rid herself of the responsibility; the keepsakes had to go to their rightful place.

Lauren stowed her carry-on and settled into her seat; seatbelt fastened. It was the right decision; she would return the keepsakes. She felt the vibrations as the plane taxied down the runway then lifted silently through the clouds. She reached across the seat touching Krug's hand.

A light rain fell as they descended the long granite walkway. Damp air laden with the pleasing aroma of cherry blossoms. His grip on her hand tightened, although not his first visit to this place, emotions were raw. She hesitated, the vastness of the black granite, the endless roster, the pall. Her lower lip rolled between her teeth; she chewed the tissue. Her eyes diverted, gazing at gray clouds rolling overhead. The sense of loss permeating the space was overwhelming.

Loosening his fingers, pulling his hand away from hers they parted, a preconceived plan. He to find a fallen comrade, she to search for Panel 02W Line 86. Touching the pocket of her rain jacket she felt the keepsakes.

Silently she walked, the endless polished ebony panels unfolding before her. She felt smothered, as if every lost soul were crowding closer. The ghosts of thousands asking *why*? She had no answer. Raindrops glistened against the blackness of the stone rolling gently to the ground—landing on cherished keepsakes, gifts to the lost.

There it was. Panel 02W. Her bent knee rested on the wet concrete. A chill spread through her body. She shuddered, shoulders shook, her eyes overflowing. She brushed her fingertips along the letters on line 86, his name, Jerry Johnston. Wondering if there had been, in these last forty years, another finger tracing the letters? A woman standing a few panels from her stepped closer placing a small piece of paper and a black crayon in her hand. Holding the paper over the name she carefully rubbed, the letters slowly became visible. His name. She folded the paper slipping it into her pocket.

She felt guilt. *We all should,* she thought. A passive protester. That was her role. Boys left that classroom to travel to the other side of the world to be changed forever. She had done nothing. Now some of their names were chiseled here while others lived to be haunted by demons for a lifetime. That gentle face of the soldier on the cover of *Life* magazine, it would never leave her. Nor would thoughts of all the joys he never knew. But today she would return his keepsakes.

She spoke softly the words she had memorized, written by a Major Michael O'Donnell, a man who knew, for his name was among those here.

"If you are able, save for them a place inside you and save one backward glance when you are leaving for the places they can no longer go. And in that time when men decide and feel safe to call the war insane, take one moment to embrace those gentle heroes you left behind."

Her hand deep in the pocket of the slicker clutched the bracelet, the purple heart, and the dog tag. "I brought these for you Jerry. I'm sure your mother would have if she had been able."

She rested the bracelet and the purple heart in the space where the Wall and earth met, a space that must have been designed to accept such mementoes. She then draped the chain holding the dog tag carefully over the armlet and slid the wrinkled photograph under both. A gentle touch on her shoulder, her husband had returned. She stood facing Krug, their eyes met; her hand touched the folded paper in her pocket then reached for his hand, fingers intertwining. Without a word spoken they walked up the concrete walkway. Away from the keepsakes, though neither, from the memories nor the demons.

Learn more about **Chris Kent** in our Author Bios section at the back of this book

Historical stereoview · Jackson Mine

Massive

by Ben Bohnsack

Massive—Like a great white pine,
    straight and tall,
    branches reaching toward the sky,
    showing beeches and birches and maples all around
    how to be a tree.

Massive—
Like the sky itself,
    A void so vast
    you can travel light years
    and still not near its edge
    or exhaust its creative resources.

Massive—
Like your own imagination
    when you let it go
    to create new experience
    and give leadership to friends and family
    out of that inexhaustible resource in your soul.

Dead Tree Standing
by Ben Bohnsack

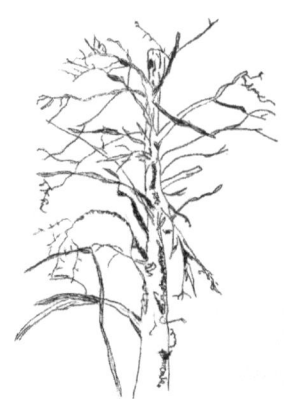

It's the skeleton of an old dead tree I see ...
    no leaves or needles, little bark remaining, out of sap.
Though it is dead and gone, still it stands,
    symbol to a long past, able and strong,
    but vulnerable, for after all, its life is gone
    and only its remains remain.
What if we were like that?
    If after we were dead, we still stood,
    flesh and sap rotted and dried
    yet standing as bones
    for those who came after to see and remember,
    stripped to the skeleton,
    a haunting reminder for those who come after
    until they wish we'd just be gone.
Better to be put into boxes in the ground
    and scattered as dust and ashes,
    out of sight until only spirit and memories remain.
So, live while you still have vegetation and bark and sap!
    Live worthy of standing tall and proud.
    Live in the shadow of those dear ones
        who once forested our land,
        and did well for you and for me.
Then be gone happily, knowing you leave no stump,
    no skeleton, no dead wood to fall and die again,
    only, and best of all, a spirit, a memory,
    to be lived out by seedlings on a quest of their own
in the places they are planted.

Learn more about **Ben Bohnsack** in our Author Bios section
at the back of this book

In Camp

by Edd Tury

Charles M. Rollen finished raking the tent floor and reached next to his sleeping bag, fumbling for what was left of the whiskey. It was ten o'clock in the morning. The sun shone through the spruce tops, barely illuminating the inside of the dirty canvas tent. C.M. got his glass and went out for some icicles. He snapped several off the tent fly and broke them into his glass. He poured two fingers of the whiskey over the ice, took a long sip, and looked back into the open tent flap. The tent always looked better after the floor was raked.

C.M. sipped more scotch and studied the bottle. It wouldn't last the day. A trip to town was in order; he hoped his brother Ned would be up for it after his day in the woods. The lack of camp whiskey was usually good motivation. He drained his glass and sloshed the remaining ice at the firepit. Chickadees flew into the small spruce tops, peeping their displeasure at being chased from the tent floor detritus C.M. had raked to the pit.

C.M. walked over to where his buck hung from the buck pole. For the hundredth time that week he pounded its frozen chest and admired the great antlers. It was a big deer; the largest buck any of them had killed. He shot it three mornings ago on the river ridge east of camp. He was lucky. There were few deer in these woods and the good bucks almost never made the mistake this one had made: it walked past C.M. in good shooting light. The camp celebration lasted long into the night. Most of the camp whiskey was

gone that evening. Luckily his brother didn't like scotch all that well. One bottle survived intact.

He admired the camp. It was an old-fashioned, rough tent camp. He liked that. He liked being part of an old-time deer camp. He, his dad, and his brother were quite comfortable. Not like the first couple of years when they didn't know what they were doing. They were warm at night, ate well, and hunted hard all day in the big woods. They saw few other hunters and liked it that way.

C.M. went into the tent. The trash box was full again. He inspected the trash carefully before he dumped it into the woodstove and cracked the front air hole. He took his time. Yesterday, after he emptied the trash into the stove, he was outside the tent straightening up the campsite when he heard a loud bang from inside the tent. Startled, he turned to see a large puff of smoke and ash burp out of the stovepipe. Three more explosions in quick succession, silence, then one more. He went back into the tent knowing that all five of his brother's lost cartridges had exploded in the stove. Ned had looked for his leather cartridge holder that morning. It was the type worn on a belt and it must have slipped off Ned's belt into the trash box when Ned took off his woolen hunting pants the night before.

He checked the stove for holes, but there were none. When the fire died down, he scraped the ashes out the front cleanout into the camp shovel. He carried the shovel of ash into the good light and sifted through and found the exploded cartridges. Instead of propelling the unconfined bullet, the burning gunpowder blew the bullet casings open at their necks, releasing the energy quite harmlessly. C.M. thought back to all the old cowboy movies and TV shows he saw as a kid where the hero threw pistol ammo into a campfire or fireplace. The exploding movie ammo usually sent a bullet through the bad guy's heart. What a bunch of crap, C.M. realized. At least it was some excitement the previous day.

C.M. turned on the portable radio and tuned it to the local station, a 5000-watter out of Iron River. The surrounding ridges made for poor reception. He caught snatches of the broadcast as he bumped around the camp. If the weather was right, he could pick up the Thanksgiving football game. He didn't care about the football game, but the radio was some company. But he soon tired of the noise and shut it off. He poured more scotch.

It was noon. The sun was just high enough to clear the treetops on the ridge overlooking the tent. The day was mild—mid-thirties—and C.M. was comfortable walking around camp in just his woolen shirt and long john bottoms. He scratched his two-week-old beard and ran his fingers through his matted hair. If they went to town, he planned on buying a shower at the Iron River Hotel.

In the swamp below the tent, snow was melting in the sunny patches. Warming air crept up the slope from the forest floor carrying odors as complex as the texture of the swamp. Decomposition, hard water, moss, and lichen combined with the smell of the muddy red earth. Trees, in every state of being, formed most of the confusion that was the river bottom. Home to a myriad of organisms, it all seemed quite benign today. But it was a different place when shadows lengthened and cooling air eased back to the low ground. In the evening deer would get up and begin their search for food. Coyotes, owls, and a few wolves would do the same. Poachers came

out at night, too. Headlights and spotlights freezing the deer for an easy kill. Illegal, because it was so effective.

The big tent was pitched in the middle of an old logging road. It was fifteen feet wide and covered the road from drainage ditch to drainage ditch. Forty yards behind the tent, the road disappeared into the vast Paint River swamp. County maps still showed this road hitting the river and crossing at a bridge. If that was the case, it must have been fifty years ago. There were no traces of the road going all the way to the river; no signs of a bridge survived.

C.M. walked up to the buck pole again, a beer in one hand, the scotch in the other. He wished he had another deer tag. He could still be hunting. He wondered if he could resist shooting a buck if it showed up near the campsite. His dad would tag it. He kept his rifle loaded, leaning on the woodpile under the tent fly. The downside of scoring early was not being able to hunt any more. While he considered his response to the unlikely occurrence of a buck walking into camp, he heard the low rumble of a truck, a sound quite distinct from the forest noise. He looked up the two-track to where it disappeared around the first bend into the pines. The black pick-up truck popped out like a ground spider from its funnel and rolled to a stop twenty yards from the tent. For a moment C.M. thought there was no one in it. The sun glare and dark side windows blocked any view into the cab. The rattle and clap of the idling diesel reinforced the feeling of being visited by an unmanned machine.

He hesitated, then approached the truck. A slight feeling of unease slowed his steps. Country music and cigarette smoke poured from the cab as the tinted glass window slid into the door.

"What the hell you doing camped in the middle of the road?" the driver asked. He wasn't smiling as he stuck his head out of the window to survey the camp. "We're trying to get across the river."

"Well, this is as far as you can get, with or without our tent here. The road ends right behind it." C.M. said. He watched the second man try to read a map. "You guys want a beer?"

"No thanks. Just opened one." The driver opened his door and got out. An empty Old Style rolled out onto the ground. "That your buck?" the driver asked, walking over to where the buck was hanging.

"Yes sir. Got it three days ago." C.M. followed the driver to the buck pole. The second man joined them. A cigarette dangled from his mouth, which he only removed when he took a drink of his beer.

"It's a good one," the driver said. "We used to get bucks like this up in Baraga. You should haul him into town. The paper's having a contest. You might win something."

C.M. didn't answer; the thought of these guys being interested in a local buck contest struck him as funny. He looked back to where the truck sat idling. The driver's door was open. A rifle leaned against the front bench seat. Loaded no doubt. Just some road hunters.

"Probably stop in town on the way out of camp," C.M. said finally. "My dad and brother won't mind."

The driver hit his partner on the shoulder and pointed down the road behind the tent. He could see the swamp from where they were standing. "Looks like he's right. Can't go no further from the looks of it." His partner grunted and took a long pull from his beer can, still staring at the buck.

The driver walked to the front of the tent and stuck his head through the tent flap. "You guys camp around here last year?"

"First time on this spot. We were on the Forest Service road last year." C.M. got two beers and offered them to the driver. "Have one on me."

"Thanks." The driver took them one at a time and put them in his side pockets. His other hand held a beer and cigarette. He moved toward the truck and his silent partner pulled himself away from the buck pole and joined him. They climbed into the pickup and proceeded to crab it back and forth

on the narrow road until it pointed back up the way it came.

"Nice buck. Thanks for the beers." The driver finally smiled and then they were gone. Diesel exhaust hung in the air. C.M. was relieved they were gone. He finished his beer in several large gulps.

Last year someone entered their tent when they were in the woods. The intruder took their meat and whiskey, ignoring an expensive rifle and other gear. C.M. and his partners felt violated. A code was broken. Whoever was responsible just wanted them to know they were not welcome in the area. Nothing else happened, but they moved the camp deeper into the woods this year. C.M. was glad he was in camp to greet the road hunters.

•••

C.M. hadn't heard a rifle shot all day. There were never many during the second week of the season. Yesterday he heard his brother's rifle at dark. He hoped for a buck, but his brother had shot the head off a partridge while walking in on the east-west road. It went for stew.

All that was left to do was get dinner started and drive the truck to the pickup point at dark. There he would wait for his brother and his dad to haul in out of the woods. The truck saved them a mile of walking. It meant a lot at the end of the day.

C.M. wished he were in the woods. He had filled his tag early. And with the buck of a lifetime. He didn't mind taking care of the camp and his hunting partners. He was happy in camp. But still he wished he were hunting. He would hunt again next season. C.M. pulled a chair out of the tent and made another drink with extra icicles and all the rest of the scotch. He sat in front of the tent facing the buck-pole. He sipped the scotch and waited for the evening.

Learn more about **Edd Tury** in our Author Bios section at the back of this book

The Gift

by Allan Koski

I am a gift from a power unseen,
endowed with a spirit restless and free,
spending a small part of eternity,
in a world of unending beauty.

I am led to drink from crystal streams,
bathed in warm summer rains,
caressed by the gentle breeze,
and sheltered by stately trees,

I know the breath of a deer on a cold winter's day,
the twinkling of a small star far away,
the song of the wind among towering pines,
and the green glow of a throbbing firefly at night.

I know the tranquility of the pathless woods,
the laughter of the cascading stream,
the deep silence of the vast prairie,
and the exhilaration of an eagle flying free.

I am awed by the polished silver moon,
warmed by the brilliant yellow sun,
suspended in its blanket of blue,
from which my life is continually renewed.

I am a gift from a power unseen,
possessed with a spirit restless and free,
alive in a world,
that many never see.

Learn more about **Allan Koski** in our Author Bios section
at the back of this book

U.P. Publishers & Authors Association Announces 4th Annual U.P. Notable Books List

MARQUETTE, MI (January 4th, 2023)— the **Upper Peninsula Publishers & Authors Association** (UPPAA) announces the 4th Annual U.P. Notable Books List this week. UPPAA board member **Mikel Classen** (Sault Ste. Marie) initiated the effort as a response to the lack of representation of U.P. writers in other Michigan state literary circles. Classen said, "Traditionally, recognition of Michigan books has been dominated by the university presses downstate and we would like to take this opportunity to highlight literature that focuses closer to home for us."

Evelyn Gathu, Director of the Crystal Falls District Community Library, will continue the library's alliance with UPPAA to co-sponsor the U.P. Notable Book Club (www.upnotable.com/book-club/). The club is available to any U.P. resident and features monthly Zoom meetups with national bestselling U.P. Notable authors such as **Karen Dionne** (*The Wicked Sister*). Members borrow the books from their local libraries or purchase at local stores prior to discussions. Presentations include author readings, a conversation on the making of the book, and a live Q&A with the audience.

To build this fourth annual list, UPPAA consulted with Upper Michigan booksellers, book reviewers, writers, and publishers to winnow down the notable books to a bare ten titles. You can find reviews of many of these books on the UP Book Review (www.upbookreview.com). It must be emphasized that the list is unranked, each title deserves equal merit as U.P. Notable Book. These ten books have been deemed essential reading for every U.P. lover and we highly recommend you ask your local librarian or booksellers for them today!

1. *The Big Island; a Story of Isle Royale* – Julian May and John Schoenherr (UMN Press reprints, 2022)
2. *North of Nelson: Stories of Michigan's Upper Peninsula* – Hilton Everett Moore (Silver Mountain Press, 2022)
3. *We Kept Our Towns Going: The Gossard Girls of Michigan's Upper Peninsula* – Phyllis Michael Wong (MSU Press, 2022)
4. *Dissecting Anatomy of a Murder* – Eugene Milhizer (Ave Maria School of Law Press, 2019)
5. *Shipwrecked and Rescued, Cars and Crew: The City of Bangor* – Larry Jorgensen (Fresh Ink Group, 2022)
6. *Dorothy is Moving Mountains, a True Story* – Dorothy Paad and Matthew Forgrave (DEP-Books 2022)
7. *The Biting Cold* – Matthew Hellman (Beacon Publishing Group, 2022)
8. *Superior Voyage* anthology – Marquette Poetr's Circle, Ed. by Rick Rastall (self-published, 2022)
9. *Empire Mine – Cascade Range: Michigan's Largest Iron Mine* – Allan Koski (self-published, 2022)
10. *Cady and the Birchbark Box: A Cady Whirlwind Thunder Mystery* – Ann Dallman (Modern History Press)

U.P. Notable Classics

The U.P. Notable Books Committee also includes an initiative called *U.P. Notable Classics* that highlights just two of the most significant U.P. themed works that have remained essential for at least 10 years. It is the committee's hope that these books can bring enjoyment to a new generation of readers.

- *Bloodstoppers and Bearwalkers: Folk Traditions of Michigan's Upper Peninsula* by Richard M, Dorson (University of Wisconsin Press, 2008)
- *Ice Hunter: a Woods Cop Mystery* by Joseph Heywood (2nd Ed; Lyons Press, 2008)

All books submitted to the *U.P. Book Review* are considered for nomination to the U.P. Notable Books list. You can find the latest reviews and subscribe to be notified of future reviews by visiting www.UPBookReview.com

U.P. Reader is Accepting Submissions for Volume 8

The *U.P. Reader* is an annual publication that represents a cross-section of writers that are the membership of the Upper Peninsula Publishers and Authors Association (UPPAA). This annual anthology showcases and promotes the writers of the Upper Peninsula. Each issue is released in paperback, hardcover, eBook, and audiobook editions in early Spring following the deadline. Copies of the *U.P. Reader* will be made available to booksellers, UPPAA members, libraries, and news services. The *U.P. Reader* has received more media coverage each year since the inclusion of the Dandelion Cottage Award. We hope the *U.P. Reader* will be a great place for you to showcase your original short works, too.

Submission Guidelines

- **Email submissions are no longer allowed.** Please submit your work through our submissions gateway which is www.uppaa.org/submit/ If you email your submission, you may be asked to re-send it through the gateway.

- Submissions will receive a receipt that the submission has been received. If a receipt is not received within three business days of submission either resubmit or contact editor@UPReader.org

- Must be a **current member of the UPPAA** to submit.

- Submissions **must be original** with no prior appearance in web or print. Submissions will be accepted for **up to 5,000 words**. Writers who submit work which has previously appeared in blog posts, web pages, eBooks, social media, or in print will be disqualified.

- Submissions **can be any genre**: fiction, nonfiction (memoirs, history, essays, feature articles, interviews, opinions) and poetry.

- All submissions will be **reviewed through a jury** and the submissions will be chosen through this process. Writers will be notified as to acceptance or rejection, but reasons for rejection will not be discussed.

- We prefer **Microsoft Word Document** (.DOC) files only or plain text files (.TXT). Do not submit PDF files. If you have some other type of text file, please inquire.

- **Please include a 50-75-word bio** at the end of the submission. Bios longer than 75 words will be trimmed by the editor. Any web addresses or email address in bios must be the most simplified form possible. (Do not include the http://)

- **Authors may only submit photos as part of a written submission** with the understanding that they will be converted to black-and-white. We reserve the right to limit the number of photos per story that will be used. Photos should be at least 300 DPI and no smaller than 2 inches on a sided (i.e. 600px minimum). If the Author is not the photographer, we may ask for a simple one-page "Photo Release" form to be sent in. Contact us in advance if you think you need more than 3 photos for your story. Author headshots are neither required nor used.

- **No more than 3 submissions will be accepted** from one person. If more than 3 are received, the jury may choose to disregard all of them. We are looking for quality, not quantity.

- **Poetry submissions count as one submission per poem. If a poem cycle is submitted it needs to be formatted either as one poem with multiple sections or as separate poems not numbering more than three.**

The U.P. Reader will require FIRST time rights in all formats, including but not limited to print, eBook, and audiobook for 12 months after publication. After 12 months, the author may use the work in any form they desire, including on the internet, print, and digital media. UPPAA retains the right to use it in perpetuity. For Example, we anticipate a "Best of U.P. Reader" to be issued for the 10th anniversary.

Publication Schedule for *U.P. Reader* Volume 8

- Submission deadline: Nov. 15th, 2023
- Dec 21, 2023   Jury / peer-review process begins
- Jan 15th, 2024 announcement of selected submissions
- April 1, 2024, official publication date

Young U.P. Author Section

Junior Division Winner
- **First Place: Halle Wakkuri**, Grade 8 (DCCHE—Delta County Christian Home Educators Homeschool Co-Op) for "The Karate Club." Sponsor: Lena Quinlan
- **Second Place: Serah Oommen**, Grade 8 (Houghton Middle School, Houghton) for "Overcoming Hardships in Life." Sponsor: Jessica Klein.
- **Third Place: Betty Harriman,** Grade 6 (Bothwell Middle School, Marquette) for "Mushroom." Sponsor: Adam Dompierre

Senior Division Winners
- **First Place: Jaclyn Jukkala**, Grade 9 (Houghton High School, Houghton) for "The Window." Sponsor: Jessica Klein.
- **Second Place: Lilli Gast**, Grade 9 (Houghton High School, Houghton) for "Azalea Tea and Other Poisons." Sponsor: Jessica Klein.
- **Third Place: Miah Billie**, Grade 10 (Homeschool, Ironwood) for "Shadows of the Mind." Sponsor: Elizabeth Billie.

Participating Schools – Senior Division
- Dollar Bay
- Gwinn High School
- Houghton High School
- Ironwood (Homeschool)
- L'Anse High School
- Marquette High School
- North Central Area Schools
- Northwoods Academy (Homeschool)
- Plummer Academy (Homeschool)

Participating Schools – Junior Division
- Bothwell Middle School, Marquette
- Delta County Christian Home Educators Homeschool Co-Op (DCCHE)
- Escanaba
- Houghton
- Keweenaw Learning Center
- Northwoods Academy (Homeschool)
- Republic-Michigamme

UPPAA is extremely pleased to announce the winners of the 6th Annual Dandelion Cottage Contest that celebrates the creative writing of the U.P.'s newest generation of writers! Each winner will take home a cash prize, a commemorative medallion, and a hardcover edition of the *U.P. Reader* in which their submission appears. Additionally, the winner of the Senior Division will have their name inscribed on the traveling trophy which will reside in their school in the coming year. Starting in 2019, we inaugurated two divisions for the contest: Senior (grades 9-12) and Junior (grades 5-8). New for 2022, we have added a full rank of winners for the Junior division which formerly had a single overall winner.

This year, we saw 26 high school submissions from nine different public and homeschools. Some schools submitted up to 4 entries from their students. The 11 Junior division entries came from seven different schools. We had six of our 37 total submissions from homeschooled students. The judges would like to thank each and every student who submitted their work. There were so many great entries in each division that the judges had a difficult time whittling down the list to just three winners.

The Window

by Jaclyn Jukkala

◆❖◆

Oliver Sutton felt his heart racing with each step he took, feet smacking the damp sidewalks of New York City. His breath was steadily getting rougher as he hit his ten-mile mark. His skin dripped with sweat, and his ears filled with the quiet jazz music and the loud, annoying city traffic, horns beeping and the slow trickle of too many people talking too loudly, too early in the morning.

"I am the best," he thought to himself, as he slowed to a stop. The air was cool as small raindrops hit his skin, mixing with his sweat, and causing him to shiver. He rounded the corner at a slow jog and felt his deep pockets for his gold key rings. He twirled them around his fingers before unlocking the door and stepping into his expensive apartment.

Pictures of himself lined the pale blue walls, and he smiled remembering each moment. He kicked off his shoes and continued down the hall. He stopped short at the most recent picture in the gold frame. He was standing on the podium at the 2021 Olympics for the long-distance runners. He was holding a silver medal, which was wrapped around his neck, smiling the fakest smile he had smiled in his entire twenty-five years.

He frowned. The picture was a reminder that he wasn't the best. "Not then." he reassured himself confidently, "but I am now."

He looked down at his watch and frowned again. It was only half-past seven; he still had another fifteen minutes until he had to leave for the gym. He backed down the hallway and re-laced his shoes.

"Oliver Sutton doesn't give up." he said aloud, firmly. He locked his apartment door and let his feet hit the pavement at a run. Rain was pouring down from the clouds like machine gun fire, cooling him off. He stopped at a stoplight and when it was clear to cross, he took it at a slow jog. He heard the screech of tires and saw the bright lights of a car.

That was the last thing he remembered.

•••

He felt himself open his eyes, but he couldn't see anything. His world was dark, and his body ached. Panicking, he tried to move, but his body wouldn't let him. He was trapped in his body, and he couldn't see where he was. He had no memories of what had happened; his mind was as dark as his eyesight. He shook inside, taking sharp breaths of fear. His heart was pounding faster than it did during the 2018 Finals. His mind was numb and blurry.

"Relax, Oliver, relax," a calm firm voice broke his panic. "You're safe here."

"Where's here?" he croaked painfully, trying to calm his breathing. He took deep, sharp breaths, causing his shaking to recede.

"You're here at New York Central Hospital," the woman's voice replied gently. "Can you see how many fingers I'm holding up?"

"I can't see anything," he snapped hoarsely, bitterly. The words hurt his throat to say, it felt like he was ripping open a wound and pouring gallons of salt inside.

The woman was quiet for a minute, but Oliver heard the scratching of a pen against paper.

The screech of tires against the wet city streets.

"Oliver," the woman said again, "My name is Nurse Sara. People with your condition sometimes run into a problem," she hesitated, trying to form the right words.

"My condition?" Oliver grumbled painfully. "I'm perfectly fine! I need my running shoes so I can train. The Olympics are seven months away!" he coughed roughly. He could feel his lie as it shattered his dreams. He could tell he was in no condition to even move.

"Oliver, I believe you may have temporary blindness, or permanent, but it's too soon to tell. As for running, you won't be doing that for a very long time," Nurse Sara relayed sympathetically.

Oliver's heart sank to his toes and started to race again. His skin felt cold and sweaty, and Nurse Sara's footsteps retreated to somewhere close in the room, quickly and nimbly. The footsteps returned and he felt a sharp poke in his left—or was it his right? —arm.

He fell into a deep sleep.

•••

He awoke, but his world was still dark. He lay still, taking in the truth of the moment. His eyes were open, he forced them open, but he still saw nothing. He knew he would never be the best again, never even close, not even second best. He sank deeper into his pillow and tried to fall asleep. It was a reassurance when he fell asleep. He could see his dreams in color, just not reality.

"Why?" he mumbled furiously. "Why did this happen to me?"

"Nobody knows why things happen the way they do," a soft, sweet voice broke the tense air of the stuffy hospital. The voice wasn't the voice of Nurse Sara, far from it.

"Who are you?" he turned his head to the sound of the voice.

"I'm Laurel," the voice replied. "You're Oliver Sutton, the Olympic runner."

"*The* Olympic runner," he thought, "not a former Olympic runner, but *the* Olympic runner." He finally responded to the voice of Laurel, "Okay."

He fell silent and moved himself back to his pillow.

"You were brought here last night." Laurel spoke again. "They say you're blind." Oliver didn't reply. He didn't have a reply.

"Here is the recovery room," she informed him cheerfully, "I just had a lung transplant."

"I need a new body transplant," he retorted stiffly. Laurel laughed lightly.

"That wasn't meant to be funny," he snapped, his throat straining. "I was serious."

"You got hit by a car."

"I know."

"You have three broken ribs."

"Okay."

"And both of your arms."

"Okay."

"And an ankle."

"Okay."

"And your left kneecap is shattered."

"Okay."

She fell silent.

"Is that all?" he asked, "or do you have more of my condition to share with me?"

"You're blind," she offered.

"Yep." He wanted to shout at her innocently sweet voice. How did she know this about him? "What do you see, Laurel?" he asked softly.

"People," she answered confidently, "lots of them."

"What are they doing?" he asked. He was desperate to see the world, even if it was through imagination.

"They're outside the window," came the dreamy voice, "There's an elderly couple walking a big, white poodle. There're two little kids, one boy and one girl, flying a brightly colored kite..."

The days were spent with her telling the things outside the marvelous window. He waited all night, or what he thought was night, for Laurel to wake up and begin talking. He craved her words that painted pictures in his mind with such clarity, it often surprised him when she stopped talking and the pictures faded from his imaginative reality. There were many times he thought he was seeing out the window himself.

Some days it was the elderly couple, who she named Ruth and Adam, and their poodle, Jack.

Some days it was the green summer trees turning into brilliant fall colors. One day it was an entire football team.

Others it was a trample of kids, running excitedly, or two teenagers holding hands.

The list went on, each day differing from the other.

Snow had begun to fall upon New York City, she said one day. It was a memorable day, that one. He had begun to see again. He could see the faint outline of his bed frame, and when he told her, she got really excited in that sweet voice of hers.

"That's great, Oliver, soon you'll be able to see the window too!"

The days went by as Oliver's vision improved, every few days he could make out a little more color.

One day Nurse Sara entered the room for the morning checkups, and she shouted out in panic.

The machine that was hooked up to Laurel, controlling her heartbeat, had gone blank, in a straight line. She had informed what seemed to be the whole world, shouting in panic in her loud voice.

The blank beeping had started earlier, but Oliver didn't know what it was, and it was driving him crazy. He could see the faint outline of Nurse Sara rushing to the bed beside him.

Oliver didn't know what was happening. People were rushing in and out of the room, and watching their shadows gave him a headache, not to mention the beeping machine. He was thankful when it shut off, and the people filtered out. Taking Laurel's bed with them—wait, where was she going?

"Nurse Sara!" he called out loudly, "where is Laurel going?"

"She's gone," came the choked reply of the strong nurse, "she left us."

Oliver felt the choking feeling in his throat. He blinked back the tears, but they came anyway. He heard Nurse Sara sniffling as she went out the door, and it quietly shut behind her. His heart was heavy, and his little vision blurred.

The days went by at a snail's pace. His vision became clearer by the day, but his mind was still fuzzy, until one day, he could see as clear as he could before the accident. He awoke that morning and opened his eyes. He was greeted with the white ceiling, as clear as day. He pulled himself up and looked for the window that Laurel had described so vividly.

There was no window.

The room was enclosed with white-washed white walls, surrounded by empty metal beds, with flimsy woolen blankets laid neatly over them. The lights were bright overhead, and the machines hooked up to him beeping.

He did a double take, searching the walls once again. And again. And again. There was no window. No matter how hard he searched or how frustrated he got, no window materialized.

Laurel had lied about the entire outdoors. She had entertained him hours on end with lies. He was furious, but only momentarily. After he was angry, he became thankful. Thankful to Laurel, for keeping his mind alive, and expanding his imagination. He was sure he would've sunk into a deep depression without her and her colorful imagination.

The weeks finally ended, and it turned into days before his release. Then the day was upon him, and he found himself being wheeled out of the hospital in a wheelchair. His sister, who he hadn't acknowledged in years, was waiting for him, waiting to take him home, with a smile on her face.

She pushed him through the bustling streets of New York City for the first time in almost a year. He looked at the city, with amazement. The change in the city was minuscule, but the change in his mind was massive. He saw the city, what he had thought was just home, nothing else, and looked at it with new eyes.

The traffic that he was once annoyed with was a wonderful noise that filled his ears. The ginormous skyscrapers that had shadowed his sun, towered over him, sparkling in the daylight. The people who had gotten in his way when he trained looked so familiar while yet so different. He didn't recognize many faces, but he recognized their way of movement, scrambling down the sidewalks, in and out of buildings, talking in an excited chatter.

Finally, he was home. At home with a new meaning.

JACLYN JUKKALA is a freshman at Houghton High School. Writing is one of her many hobbies; others include skiing, hunting, playing hockey, and reading.

Sault tow of lumber ships

Azalea Tea and Other Poisons

by Lilli Gast

◆❖◆

Millicent strolled through the gardens, outwardly seeming calm as could be, though she was anything but. Her status as advisor and informant to the crown was becoming bothersome.

The foreign delegation was due to arrive any moment, though she had just found that they had no good intentions about their visit. Now all she had to do was figure out what they were plotting to do against the royal family.

Easy, she thought sarcastically. She was as excited for their visit as she'd be to commit murder. Millicent now had to hurry to be on time to greet these people, and hopefully to decipher their intentions. She went to her rooms, changed, and very nearly ran to the reception hall.

Serena, a close friend of Millicent's and advisor to the queen, was already there, and waved her out onto the steps, whisper-shouting at her.

"Milly! You need to stop cutting it so close! They're nearly here!"

Milly calmly whispered back, "Oh, don't be such a mother hen! I'm here now, aren't I?"

"You and I both know you were supposed to be here twenty minutes ago! Now hurry up and get to your place, at least."

They got to their places in the row of people behind the queen just in time for her to greet the foreigners. The sun was beating down on the stone steps, and the atmosphere was as muggy as the kitchens after a feast had been made.

"Greetings! I hope your journey was pleasant." Queen Raleigh hailed the oncoming delegates. They were from a foreign kingdom that neighbored them on their west border.

She was standing on the palace steps, adorned in formal garb. The six delegates approached, coming up to the palace steps. None of them were armed, at least not that Milly could detect. Who knew what they were hiding in the trunks still in their carriages. Their leader appeared to be a graying man of average height who seemed to be in his fifties, who approached before the rest.

He bowed in acknowledgement. "Our greatest respects, your highness. I am Sir Emmett, advisor to the King and leader of this humble delegation. We come bearing gifts."

The Queen replied, "Pleased to make your acquaintance, Sir Emmett. Our greatest thanks and appreciation for the gifts, as well."

The man, Sir Emmett apparently, brandished a finely wrapped box, as big as a dinner plate. "In addition to our other offerings, we've brought you our most prized delicacy, our azalea honey. It adds the most wonderful flavor to tea."

Milly's immediate thought was *what in the world is azalea?* I've heard of no such thing.

More suspicious than ever after hearing of their apparent plotting, she wondered why in the world they would give something like food, especially azalea honey of all things. Food was just about the most uncommon gift there was, seeing as jewels and fancy things appealed to people's greed so much more. She'd have to make a mental note to ask what azalea was later.

Later, the delegation had been shown their rooms and was settling in before they'd have to congregate for teatime once again. Millicent had just briefed her queen on the situation with the suspect delegation. Milly was now preparing for afternoon tea, helping the maids set out the teacups next to the correct placement at the table, as the delegation's seats had been strategically placed. Once this was done, she went to the washroom to freshen up before going to await everyone at the base of the grand staircase.

They soon made their way down, and as Millicent directed them, went to the dining hall for tea. It was especially important that everyone sat down according to the planned seating arrangement as she and Serena had planned. They were served specialty tea and biscuits and made small talk. Now it was just a matter of time before Milly would find out whether this delegation really had nefarious intentions. She had put that strange

honey in half of the delegates' tea, just to make sure it wasn't poisoned. *Better safe than sorry*, she thought.

Sooner or later, she started to notice some of the delegates were moving slowly, and one of them was staring into the distance and drooling rather disgustingly. Apparently, that strange honey was poisonous. Millicent was both repulsed by their underhanded strategy and glad she'd discovered their plot so early on. She subtly signaled to the Queen, who'd earlier approved this plan, what was happening. Raleigh nodded, looking a little green, before asking the table, "How is the tea faring?" One of these poisoned delegates was sitting right across from Milly. He looked to the Queen, "I'm feeling just a bit queasy, I think I'll head to the washroom." He quickly scurried off, holding his mouth with his hand.

The Queen smiled demurely, "We did add in that lovely honey you brought to the tea. I do hope you don't mind."

The leader, Emmett, stood up, clearly panicked. "My lady, who exactly drank tea with the added honey?"

"I do believe a few men in your delegation did, it seems to be causing some adverse effects."

He spluttered, "Why…what…how dare you!"

Millicent smiled as she raised her teacup. This was positively a perfect calamity. Now all she had to do was wait for something a little stronger than azalea to come into effect. Suddenly, Queen Raleigh collapsed. At least five people rushed to her side. The situation with the foreigners had been enough to distract the Queen from testing her own tea and biscuits for poison stronger than azalea honey. It did inconvenience Milly that Raleigh had become an issue, but oh well. Out with the old, in with the new. This monarchy had been ridiculous anyway.

LILLI GAST is a freshman at Houghton High School. Reading is her favorite pastime, but she also likes to go skiing, snowshoeing, and hiking. She runs cross country in the fall. Science is currently her favorite subject.

Shadows of the Mind

by Miah Billie

◆❖◆

Chapter 1

Wind that sliced like steel on fresh flesh. Snow, though cold as ice, burned when it met skin. Wind that hissed like a thousand snakes past uncovered ears. Snow like a long white sheet stretched beyond the seen world. Snow and nothing else. The worst of it was that one could never escape it.

Her unbound silver hair was tugged in every direction. Her bare feet did not sink nor bleed onto the snow. The one sanctuary the girl had was a thick bear hide. But even that did not stop the wind from coiling around her and sinking its razor sharp teeth into her ripe flesh.

She had crawled through the frozen hell for a time that was lost to her. She could not remember the beginning and doubted she would see the end. The girl had no recollection of her life before the cold land. She did not even know her own name. The only thing that raced through her mind was the longing, but for what she could not say. And she needed it more than the wind tormented her.

Walking without any sense of direction, the girl caught the bitter scent of salt on her frozen nose. For a moment she waited, unmoving, with her breath locked in. Silver eyes tightly shut, and ears open. She for the first time in the cold land heard beyond the screeching wind. Large waves crashed upon the earth with a distant roar. Her eyes broke free of the iron clench she had laid upon them. The sun that was once enveloped in dark clouds blazed brightly in the sky above her. The wind was gone along with the scars it bore her.

Clutching the bear hide, the girl soared like an arrow to the salt filled waves. The seen world tore into a place beyond her imagination. She abruptly stopped. Towering cliff walls loomed high above the cold sea. Black sand pushed the raging sea away from the mountain cliffs. She inched towards the edge and looked upon the sand and sea. The girl knew that she had to be down there, but there was no path down that was clear to her. She leaned forwards.

A deafening crack ripped through the air, burning her ears. And suddenly she was falling. The girl twisted through the void she was prey to. Her screams filled the space around her. Her bear hide met the black sand before her. The girl plowed into the ground with a loud thump.

There was no pain, only the tickle of icy sand on her exposed flesh.

She shook off the black sand and crawled to her bear hide. Wrapped in the warm fur the girl spied a figure by the water. As she stood, the figure turned towards her. The girl slowly approached, as it approached her. She was filled with nothing short of uncertainty. In the middle of the beach, they stood. The figure was a tall man around her age. (She was not sure what her age was, but even so they seemed close.) The man was like a twin to her, silver eyes and hair, pale moon skin; it was haunting how similar they looked.

The man looked at her knowingly. "You do not seem to know me." He said in a soft and gentle tone.

The girl quietly asked, "No. Do you know me?"

The man smirked. "The damage that she inflicted upon you is beyond what I imagined."

"Who?" She demanded. "Who are you? What is this place? Who am I?" She quickly added.

"I am Roland, a friend to you. You are Linairu, the Dove. And this is the End."

"The Dove? What is the End, and who hurt me?" She repeated.

Roland sighed. "The End is the edge of the subconscious. A prison made by the Raven. It is constantly changing to keep you trapped within. It is full of tricks and illusions. Magic is stripped from the ones that are banished here, and in your case, memories."

"You keep referring to people as birds as if I know what you are talking about."

"There are three of us that go by the names of birds. You, Kyrith, and I make one soul. You are the Dove. Pure and kind. Kyrith is the Raven. Cunning and hateful. I am the Snowy Owl. Neither light nor dark. Together there is balance. You were banished to the End by Kyrith. She is corrupting the soul. Only with your help can I stop her." With more time Linairu was sure she would have

remembered being a part of a soul. Roland offered his hand to her. Linairu slowly extended her hand out, but then stepped back. Roland was clad in a black suit, while her hide was gray.

Roland stepped toward her. Suddenly he scared her in a way the cold land never did. "What are you doing?" he asked.

"You are a very good liar." She answered.

"Excuse me?"

"I respect that you know the limits to your talent and didn't wear the mask of the dove."

Roland played dumb. "Linairu, I have no idea what you mean."

She said as clearly as possible, "You are the Raven and I the Owl." Linairu ran past him towards the waves. He chased her, screaming curses and horrible things. Linairu dropped the gray hide and dived into the icy water.

Chapter 2

The sweet scent of honey and the songs of birds woke Linairu. She lay on the warm forest floor. When she entered the sea, hands of leaves grabbed her legs and forced her into crushing darkness. The next thing she knew she was falling through fluffy clouds to the floor of the forest. Landing had knocked her unconscious. When she woke her hair was braided down her back. Gray pants, boots, and shirt had been put on her.

The girl stood with her head raised to the stars. Gold, green, silver, and blue leaves reflected the light of the moon. Linairu crept through the dense woods. Night birds coed as she passed their high perches. She needed to find Kyrith and stop Roland from corrupting the soul. Linairu followed the smell of honey, for it woke her from the darkness. The stars burned brighter the farther she trailed into the forest.

The stinging sound of bees cut through the air. Trees parted in a perfect circle around an evergreen stump. Bees of pure gold swarmed low in the small opening. Linairu stepped into their sanctuary. Bees landed on her; she held one in the palm of her hand. Linairu dared to cross the parting. As she passed the stump, Linairu noticed a decaying raven sprawled out beside it. Black goo oozed from the carcass. It crawled up the bee's home in vain like streams. Bees that landed on the stump were devoured by the goo. The bees that were on her darted to their fallen friends, and in turn were consumed. Soon every bee was a part of the growing goo. Linairu could do nothing to stop it.

The dark substance had grown into a towering being when the goo melted away. Roland, wrapped in a darkness like none she had seen before, steeped off the fallen evergreen. Linairu turned to the trees. The sparkling trees laced themselves into a cage. The jeweled leaves withered away into black shrivels that cascaded to the ground. Linairu wanted to scream. Roland, it would seem, would stop at nothing to keep her on the side lines. Although she should have expected him to find her. Did he need or keep her from Kyrith?

With a cat-like stride and smirk painted on to his face, Roland inched toward her. With one hand he cupped her cheek. "Oh darling, did you seriously believe you could escape me?" Linairu pushed his hand from her face.

"Stop following me." She hissed.

With a soft laugh Roland calmly said, "And why would I do that?"

"What do you need me for?"

His cruel smirk remained on his cold face. "Let's play a little game, Linairu." She despised the sound of her name on his tongue. He leaned into her and whispered into her ear. "You run, and I chase." Roland shoved her into the cage of trees. The branches pulled her through their bars.

Linairu dropped to the forest floor. She lay with her back to the ground and face to the star filled sky, but that was for a mere moment. Linairu sprang to her feet and ran. She knew there was a trap of some sort, but she did not want to be alone with the Raven.

Trees moved to block her path. Their branches knitted a labyrinth before her. Linairu looked behind to find only darkness. The farther she ran away from the dark, the stars burned brighter above the maze. It was the warm stars that made her feel secure, but they betrayed her to Roland. If he thought that the dark scared her, he was mistaken.

Linairu knew nothing of herself, and yet she knew that she was never scared of the dark. Never scared of it swallowing her whole or losing her way. But rather what lurked there, of the things that would make her fear the cold and sunless world. If Roland thought she would stray into his reach, then, he was false. Linairu freely walked toward the void. To become unfindable, she must be unpredictable.

Chapter 3

The violent wind pushed and pulled her side to side. Linairu stumbled through the void erratically. The darkness consumed the very air she breathed, but not Linairu. She glowed like a torch that would light her path ahead. Every ounce of goodness oozed out of her pores to fight off the darkness. The distant crack of thunder tore through the howling wind, with a startling roar.

Cold rain buried her warmth down to her bones. She braced herself for every drop of water that pelted her. Even with the rain and wind she could not tell up from down, left from right. Linairu could not even feel the ground beneath her feet, assuming there was any at all. Through the pain and frustration, Linairu found inner strength to pull herself deeper within the darkness, for nothing else would.

The natural horrors that plagued the darkness did come from a source that was determined to push her back. It felt as if the storm came from one direction, but then another. Linairu stood as still as a wolf watching its prey. Beneath her unfeeling toes there was still nothing. The End was never what it seemed. Everything was in front of you, but if you were not looking, you would never see it. Changing her view, Linairu waited. Past the pool of darkness was Linairu wrapped in dim light. All around, she found herself looking right back at her. Mirrors on mirrors lined a dome like bug eyes.

Wind and rain propelled on and off the mirrors, moving faster with every lunge. The mirrors moved when Linairu did. She moved back and forth looking for a fault in the dome. She found none in the structure, but rather the material. Mirrors are made of glass, and glass can break. The moving of the dome with every step she took kept her at the center. Linairu went to her knees. Pushing her hand down as far as she could, she still felt nothing. Linairu raised her forearm above her head. Her fists went through the panel with one stroke. Now that, she felt. She stood, blood dripping into the mirror. The hole she made brought on a spiderweb of cracks that quietly grew. Linairu stomped on the nearest crack. The panel gave way for darkness to grab her. Shadows within shadows grew darker the farther she plunged.

Light broke through the shadows. Linairu landed face first into golden sand that burned with the heat of a thousand suns. She had made it out of the End. The only remains of the mirror world were the smashed panels that were buried in her flesh like thorns. Linairu rose, spitting sand out of her mouth. An overwhelming feeling raced through her. Energy bolted through her body stopping at the tips of her fingers. It was more familiar than anything she had witnessed thus far. Magic like what Roland had, but unlike his, hers was not dark. At least not entirely.

Linairu hovered her hand over her wounds. Agony rolled through her as rigid shards of glass were drawn from tissue. As the last glass thorn fell to the burning ground, Linairu's head grew light upon her shoulders. Her vision frayed, and her body ached. Beads of sweat rolled down her brow.

Out of nowhere, a new world engulfed her. It was not of her present time, but of her past. She, Roland, and Kyrith sat around a round table made of white crystal. Engraved on the back of all their chairs was a bird of their nature. Rainbow tinted stone wrapped around them in the form of a castle in the sky. Floor to ceiling windows lined the crystal wall. In front of each was a white clothed figure bearing the dove across their chest. Linairu was in the realm of good, for there was no safer ground.

Roland was draped in the same black suit as before. His cold face gave away not even an inch of emotion. Linairu donned smoke gray armor with the owl stamped on her breastplate. She lacked a sword and shield, but

that was to be expected. Kyrith was identical to Linairu, besides from the short cut hair. Even with the likeness to Roland nothing in her was cold. She glowed with kindness and joy, but Kyrith seemed drained. She was draped neck to toe in silver white dove wings that formed a gown.

It was Roland who spoke first. "Why my dears, have I been summoned to this quaint little meeting?"

"Roland, we both know there is no vail that befolds your eyes on what your shadow creatures have done and are still doing." Linairu barked back.

"Shadow Soldiers." Roland moaned.

"It does not matter what they are called. They are still killing the priest and priestess of the White Cloth." Kyrith's voice was laced with kindness and worry.

"My Shadow Soldiers have done none of what you say. Anyhow, if your Order of The White Cloth are dying, then why not consider all the options." Silence swept over the hall.

"Oh, my dear Kyrith, I take it that you have not. Is it truly impossible that this is not a battle between good and evil, but rather one conjured by morally gray?"

"What are you suggesting?" Asked Linairu.

"We both know what I mean. There is no vail stuffed in your ears, Linairu." A cocky smile plagued Roland's face. He continued with sinister joy sewn through every word. "I am no fool. Why would I openly attack you Kyrith? Who has the most to gain from our fighting?" Kyrith's gaze shifted to Linairu.

Roland had planted the seeds of deceit in her mind. Linairu began to dig them out. "No, you are not a fool. That is why you openly attack. So you can place the blame on me while your bigger plan escalates. Don't tell me you are planning to take control of the soul. And with only one of the three to fight, you could easily do it." Before he could water the soil with his silver tongue, Kyrith stood.

"Roland, you are no longer welcome here. Leave." With a flick of his hand, Roland transformed into a raven. Eyes ablaze he darted to the nearest window opening and threw the panel into the vibrant clouds.

Kyrith sat, giving Linairu her full attention. She asked with hope painted on her face.

"Lin, do you think he is going to take control? What will happen to us, to the soul?"

"If he does, then the soul is lost. He will consume our power, and in doing so kill us."

"How do you know such things?"

"Never you mind. Do not worry; he will not win; as long as I have breath in my lungs, I will fight."

Chapter 4

Like the cold land, the hot one was endless. Time was lost to Linairu. She knew it had been a good amount of time, since her wounds had healed. The sun would collapse, and the moon would rise, how many times, she could not say. Linairu inched further south with every passing day, but it was not enough. Roland could have reached Kyrith and become a step closer to control.

After she saw her past, it all came back to her. All of what had happened, and what would, if her schemes paid off. There was not one doubt in Linairu's mind of what she must do, and quickly. When she came back to the present, Linairu found her armor and weapons on the sand. She quickly pulled her armor on, attached sword and shield to her back, leaving room for a dagger on her hip.

The sun fell from the sky only to rise again. It did so hundreds of times leading up to the day Linairu looked upon crystal clear water, and above it a castle in the sky. The desert dissolved into a calm sea that reflected the purple-pink sunset before her. At the shoreline a rowboat sat waiting for her to board. As Linairu approached, she noticed there were no oars. In the land of light things worked themselves out. Without an ounce of surprise, the boat moved when she sat. Slower than Linairu liked, the rowboat sailed toward her long-desired destination. The closer she had gone the more tainted the water grew. Blood swept through the tide. Priest and priestess of the White Cloth lay in the shallow water.

Magic consumed her flesh. As an owl, she soared up through the sky to the crystal castle. The window panel, shattered from Roland, made an easy door for her. The once beautiful room was drenched in blood and gore. Fallen champions from the Order of The White Cloth to Shadow Soldiers carpeted the stone floor. If there were any survivors, none lay in the council chamber.

Linairu marched through the castle in search of wounded and Kyrith, only to find none. Linairu stood in front of the last hiding spot Kyrith could be. "Dove, I know you are in there." The portrait of Kyrith moved ever so slightly before Kyrith stepped out of herself.

She hugged Linairu, squealing. "Lin! Oh, I thought you were dead! A day after the meeting Roland attacked only to leave. What happened to you?"

"After I left the castle, I went to Roland."

Kyrith broke away.

"To talk sense into him, but clearly, I failed. He banished me to the End and stripped me of my memories to keep us apart. He must have called off the attack to meet me at the beach." Linairu made the End feel like an eternity of ever-changing obstacles that never stopped, but it was only an illusion of the mind. Moving past what you thought you saw, or thought was the only way through. She knew her idolized prison would be used against her one day.

Like the Order of The White Cloth and Shadow Soldiers, Linairu had an army of her own, the Ash Guard. If she was to save the soul, she would need them. "Kyrith, are all of the White Cloth gone? What happened to the Ash Guard?"

"Our armies are gone. I am sorry, Lin, there was nothing I could do." That was nothing short of a major setback.

Linairu groaned.

"Oh Lin, it will be okay. Good always defeats evil."

Suddenly, Linairu knew how to gain control. "Dove, you have to challenge Roland to single combat."

"What?"

"Good always wins."

"But what if it doesn't? Roland will win if I lose."

"I will be there the whole time."

Kyrith pondered the notion before replying. "You better not cheat. Promise me you will not cheat, Lin."

"I promise."

"Well then let's see what really conquers evil."

Chapter 5

Evil and good met at neutral ground, the Circle Square. Despite its name, the large top of the mountain was smoothed down to an oval. No walls ran along the perimeter, only open sky and death. At the center of the Circle Square, Roland and Kyrith stood ten feet away from each other. Linairu stood the same distance away from them both. Standing in the shape of a triangle showed the balance that flowed between them and their powers.

They skipped the formalities; they all knew the rules. Fight to the death. "Are we to duel in the open or not?" Roland asked prior to the start of the battle. Kyrith looked to Linairu.

"Since you tried to trap me in a labyrinth it is only right you should duel in one." Without an argument Roland nodded. With a sharp stroke of her wrist a labyrinth rose around the competitors.

At the top of the tall walls, Linairu crept after white and black lights. Roland and Kyrith's magic quickly flashed with loud pops. They raced through the labyrinth with the speed of light. Linairu rose to her full height with her arms raised to the cloudy sky. As the spell she cast left her, clouds were ripped from the sky and pulled towards the labyrinth.

The fog settled when the screams started. Linairu dropped to the floor and followed the cries to Roland. She found him alone (the fog did its job nicely) clutching his throat. In between screams, blood gurgled out of his mouth. "You!" He managed to say.

"Yes, it is me. Did you forget I was here?" she replied.

"You did this!"

Linairu put a hand to her chest as she sarcastically said, "What, who, me, the gray?" She closed the gap between them.

"Just because you are good, does not mean there is no darkness within you." He spat.

With a smile on her face, Linairu whispered to Roland, "Oh more than you can ever imagine my dear." She unsheathed her dagger from her hip and slid the blade across Roland's throat. She held him upright, waiting. Black smoke slid out of his gaping mouth like a snake breaking out of old skin. Black blood ran down his chin and throat, seeping through his fingers. With her free hand, Linairu scooped up his powers. Roland hit the ground with a loud thump. She leaned her head back, and with both hands forced the smoke into her mouth. Linairu felt pain, anger, vengeance, swarm in her chest. Power followed the darkness, and it felt good.

Linairu turned to find Kyrith wide eyed. Fear covered any kindness there was in her. Her hands shook, but despite it, Kyrith found the courage to ask her why.

"Dove, good and evil can only ever fight each other. You will always do the right thing, opposed to Roland. The two of you only have one choice. But I will always be torn. I will always have the option to be evil or good. Which may seem wrong, but it depends on the situation I am in."

"You started all of this."

"No. Roland was plotting against you. That's when I saw the opportunity to take control."

"We could have worked together. We could have brought him to the light."

"Roland would have made the soul dark. Destructive and hateful things could only follow. You would have made the soul bright, kind, but naive. Seeing the good in people, giving them a second chance to redeem themselves is not always the best thing to do. People take advantage of the kind. To be good is to be vulnerable."

"Not everyone is bad Lin."

"Maybe."

"When you went to Roland after the meeting, you knew he would banish you. Didn't you?"

Kyrith was buying her time.

"I did. People can be so predictable. I could not let you suspect me. I knew Roland would be happy at the chance to banish me and fight you alone. Don't worry I knew you would survive without me while I got my memories back."

"You're evil."

Linairu gave her a sad smile. "Maybe with your powers I will be evened out." Linairu threw the same dagger that killed Roland into Kyrith's throat.

The blade fell to the ground with a clank. Kyrith stood before her in dove wing armor. The blade never had a chance at piercing her collar. "Magic can be so convenient don't you think?" Kyrith conjured a transparent crystal sword and shield. And so, they dueled for the crown of their realm.

Kyrith was no match to Linairu in swordsmanship, but she fought like a born warrior. The sound of steel on steel was a song in their ears. The girls wore every scrap and bruise like medals. Exhaustion crept through their bodies. Soon the only sound that echoed through the labyrinth was the sound of their uneven breath. They stopped, separated, and walked on either end of a circle they made in their mind.

Circling each other, Linairu broke the silence, "Give up! You can never win."

Kyrith gave her a weak smile. "You don't seem to be getting anywhere either. Roland weighing you down?"

"When I am done with you, send him my regards."

"Bite your tongue!" Kyrith hissed, calm and cruel. "With any hope, the bitter tang will give you a taste of your words."

"How mean of you," she said with a laugh.

Kyrith rushed at her, only to leap out of her reach. She darted to other end of the circle they had drawn, ending in the middle. Kyrith spread her arms out, "Let us not dance around death any longer."

Linairu's anger built up in her. She didn't care what it cost her; dropping her shield she charged, lifting her sword high. As she approached Kyrith, she knew her mistake. Kyrith went low, tripping Linairu, stood and bolted out of the circle. Linairu lay at the center of a glowing symbol. Trapped, she screamed. At the edge of the circle Kyrith spoke, "Winter brings death. It is cruel, unforgiving, and fierce. Yet it is endurable."

"No," Linairu pleaded.

"I, Kyrith the Dove, banish you to walk the End for all eternity. You will be plagued with all of your memories. As you know, magic is prohibited there. If you try to escape, you will be put somewhere worse, like Roland's formidable prison. Funny, you built your own cage. You will be free to rule over the End in any way you see fit. I hope your crown was worth it." With one last kind smile, Kyrith cast the banishing spell. Linairu's deafening screams went through the End without so much as an echo.

MIAH BILLIE is a sophomore enrolled in an online home school. Her favorite classes are Art History, World History, and English. She has always loved stories, and after conquering dyslexia, Miah was able to express her love of writing and books. Her favorite genres are fantasy, history, and dystopian. When she is not enveloped in a good story, Miah enjoys watching movies, theater, hiking, photography, and antiquing.

Historical · ironwood unknown man with gun and pouch

The Karate Club

by Halle Wakkuri

◆❖◆

Once upon a time there was a fridge. There was nothing special about this fridge, it was a normal fridge, just like any other. The fridge belonged to a karate teacher named Frank Bacon. Mr. Bacon had a wife and two kids. This story is not about the Bacon family. It is about the fridge. Inside the fridge there was a karate club led by Sensei Pickle. He had seven students: Tomato, Cheese Stick, Carrot, Butter, Lettuce, Ranch, and his top student, Mushroom. You see this karate club had a special job: they protected the whole fridge from any rotten food that tried to make other foods join their side. Lately it had been hard to recruit new karate students because everyone in the fridge had heard about Eggs' accident.

To get you caught up, everyone was practicing their flying sidekicks and Egg flew a little too far and rolled off the top shelf. Dr Pepper tried to save him, but it was no use. Egg had a big crack. You see, it was every foods' dream to be eaten, so every food in the fridge dreaded two things: going bad and getting eaten by Mr. Bacon's dog, Joe. To everyone in the fridge, he was known as Sloppy Joe. Anyway, it was almost Mr. Bacon's birthday, so Mrs. Bacon bought him a cake and put it in the fridge. When Sensei Pickle heard about this, he immediately called an emergency meeting of the karate club.

"Alright everyone," yelled Sensei Pickle, "you may have noticed it is almost Mr. Bacon's birthday and they have bought the cake earlier than usual, so that means the Rottens have more time to convince Ms. Cake that she doesn't want to be eaten."

Cheese Stick interrupted, "But who wouldn't want to be eaten!"

Ranch added, "Yeah, I mean, especially with the honor of being a cake."

Carrot agreed and said, "Yeah, it's easy being cake. Everyone wants to eat cake. It's not like people stick candles in carrots for birthdays."

Tomato said, "When Mr. Meat was thawing, I overheard him telling someone that a rotten found his way into the freezer and convinced Ice Cream to go bad."

Butter shuddered, "That's horrible! Ice cream is way better than cake. It's nice and refreshing."

Lettuce said, "Well, cake doesn't make your head freeze like ice cream does. My doctor said I have to stop eating ice cream because it makes my whole head freeze."

Irritated, Sensei Pickle said, "Anyway, we must protect Ms. Cake so the Rottens don't do any harm. Mushroom, I'm leaving you in charge of tonight's guarding."

Mushroom replied, "Thank you Sensei. You know, I think I have a plan on how to stop the Rottens first we have to…"

Then suddenly the light in the fridge got brighter and everyone ran into their spots. Sensei Pickle dived into his jar, Cheese Stick ran into place, Carrot cartwheeled into her bag, Tomato lunged into his drawer, Butter slid on the shelf, Lettuce leaped into place, and Ranch tried to hop into the door shelf, but the door was yanked open so fast that he missed and landed on the floor. His cap flew off and his insides oozed out. All the foods watched quietly, like statues not making one sound. Mr. Bacon's little girl put the cap back on Ranch and set him next to Sensei Pickle's jar. Spoiled Milk was right behind the jar, so he decided to push Sensei Pickle right off the top shelf. The jar flew out right onto the floor and smashed into a million different pieces. Sensei Pickle was now laying on the floor. Mrs. Bacon ran in and when she saw the mess, she sternly told the little girl to pick it up. Mushroom sat in place sadly, looking down at his sensei. Mrs. Bacon walked away, and the little girl was about to pick up Sensei Pickle with the intent to eat him, but right before her little fingers could grab him, the dog ran by and gulped him whole. The little girl shut the fridge doors and all the food quickly got away from Spoiled Milk.

Mushroom looked over at him and said to the karate club, "Come on let's go."

Lettuce, Tomato, Ranch, Cheese Stick, Carrot, and Butter all looked at him thinking of what to say.

Tomato said, "I have homework to do."

Ranch said timidly, "I don't feel great. It feels like my insides are outside of me."

Carrot quickly said, "I'm coming, Mom."

Butter explained, "You don't want me, I have butter fingers."

Lettuce said, "I have an awful headache."

Cheese Stick replied with enthusiasm, "You can count on me Sensei Mushroom."

Mushroom sadly replied, "Just Mushroom is fine."

So off went Lettuce, Tomato, Ranch, Carrot, and Butter. All that was left was Mushroom and Cheese Stick

Mushroom said, "We need to plan how to stop the Rottens from getting to Ms. Cake and I have the perfect plan."

Later that night, Cheese Stick and Mushroom stood, hidden in plain sight within two inches of Ms. Cake. They were waiting for any Rottens to arrive. Just then Spoiled Milk and someone else walked onto the shelf, but it was too dark to tell who the other food was. They walked up to who they thought was Ms. Cake when all of a sudden Cheese Stick came zip lining in on a noodle and kicked Spoiled Milk down to the ground. Then Mushroom came spiraling in!

In a tone of surprise Mushroom said, "Egg what are you doing here?" For the first time they could see Egg. He was a pale color with multiple fruit stickers on his head to keep his crack from getting any bigger.

"It's Evil Egg to you Mushroom!" replied Evil Egg. Just then Evil Egg did a perfect flying side kick hitting Mushroom and Cheese Stick. They fell down. By this time, Spoiled Milk had finally gotten up. They grabbed what they thought was Ms. Cake and drove away in their to-go car. Cheese Stick and Mushroom got up rubbing their heads in pain.

Cheese Stick was worried, "What will we do now? They took Ms. Cake."

Mushroom proudly replied, "That's what we wanted them to think."

He stepped out of the way so Cheese Stick could see Ms. Cake still sleeping in the corner of the fridge.

"It's not going to take long before they notice though; we need a new plan." Mushroom said, leader-like.

Cheese Stick asked, "Isn't there a bowl of soup from yesterday on the second shelf?"

Mushroom hesitantly said, "Yeah, what were you thinking?"

Cheese Stick quickly explained, "Well, if we take some of the noodles, we can make a tripwire to make them fall into the soup."

Mushroom said, "Hot Sauce can distract them."

Cheese Stick said approvingly, "Exactly. Tomorrow is cleaning day so when Mrs. Bacon sees the soup..."

Mushroom finished, "She will throw them both away. But how will we do it all by ourselves?" Just then Tomato, Butter, Ranch, Lettuce, and Carrot all showed up.

Ranch said, "We're here to help!"

Cheese Stick replied, "We'll tell you the plan on the way to the second shelf!"

On their way, Cheese Stick and Mushroom told them what to do.

It was all set up when Spoiled Milk and Evil Egg came running full force toward them. Hot Sauce sprayed them in the face, they tripped over the noodles tumbled into the soup, and sank deep down. The Karate Club had gotten rid of the Rottens. For now.

The next day they were all practicing their karate moves when five more foods decided to join. Sensei Mushroom was happy they were safe at last. Or so they thought. You see, today was Mr. Bacon's birthday, so Mrs. Bacon would not be cleaning out the fridge, and that meant they had an unknown enemy, Hot Head Soup.

The End... For Now

HALLE WAKKURI is fourteen years old and is homeschooled in Delta County. Some of her favorite things to do are basketball, karate, listening to music, playing with her puppy, and, of course, creative writing. In her free time, she is often outdoors, hanging out with friends, and in the summer, you can usually find her at her family cabin on Lake Michigan.

Homestead near Marquette (1860)

Overcoming Hardships in Life

by Serah Oommen

◆❖◆

Sometimes it is hard to remember that everyone experiences difficulties. When I was thirteen years old, my parents divorced. It impacted my emotional, social, and even academic life. I withdrew from my friends and family. I felt lost and forgotten. When my friends tried to step in, I would shut them out, and I felt that they could never understand my emotions. My guitar teacher finally talked to my parents about my loss of interest. My mom reached out to a child therapist, and that's where Cindy Lou came in.

Cindy Lou who? Cindy Lou Green became my support. She discussed managing my anxiety and stress with extracurricular activities, particularly exercise. My friends all played basketball, so I decided to give it a try. As practice began to start, I learned to manage my stress while on the court. A year later, it was time to try out for high school basketball.

"Girl are you ready for basketball?" asked Olivia Smith.

"Yes, I'm excited," I replied.

We hustled down the hallway to get a good spot at lunch. By the time we sat down at our spot, Maria and Eleanor were already there. As I scrolled through my notifications, I saw my daily quote: Ali Ibn Abi Talib AS — "Do not let your difficulties fill you with anxiety, after all it is only in the darkest nights that stars shine more brightly." I smiled.

"Why are you smiling?" Eleanor asked.

"Nothing," I said, still smiling.

Then I looked at my grades as Maria looked over my shoulder.

"D+ in English! How are you supposed to play at the big game this Saturday," she asked.

"Oh, ha-ha, I just saw that," I responded.

Truthfully, I had seen it way before. I had been struggling to get that grade up; my mom was over-worked, and my dad was not involved. I didn't know how to bring it up with Cindy Lou, so it had been stressing me for a while. This big game would be a huge opportunity, and if I had to sit on the bench, it would not be good. I didn't really know what to do about it anymore. At practice, Coach Collins called me over. The last thing I needed was this dreaded talk.

"Hey Laney, how are you doing?" she asked sympathetically.

"I'm good." What else was I supposed to say?

"Are you aware you're failing English?"

"Yes." My voice quivered.

"I don't want to have to say this, but if you can't get it up by Friday, you can't play on Saturday."

"I'm aware; may I get back to practice please?" The coach nodded.

I tried to be respectful, but my emotions were all over the place. I started shooting and swishing some threes to try to help me feel better. I asked Coach if I could leave practice so I could catch Mrs. Schmidt to talk to her about my grade. She agreed, so I left. I caught Mrs. Schmidt right before she was about to leave.

"Mrs. Schmidt, can I talk to you?" I asked desperately.

"Hey Laney, what's going on?" she asked.

"You probably know my grade is low; is there any way I could get it back to a C by Friday, our big game is Saturday, and I can't play with a D+."

"Yes, I see what you are saying. I know that you have been working hard, so how about you present your book report to the class for extra credit? I can't promise an A, but you might at least be able to get a passing grade," she suggested.

I mentally tensed at the word present. "Thanks Mrs. Schmidt," I took a deep breath. "I-I'll do that."

"Ok, you got this Laney."

As I walked home, I thought about the presentation. I had to finish some work for the presentation. It made me nervous though. I always tried to avoid presentations, but now I was forced to choose between my fears and basketball. When I opened the door to my house, my dad was sitting on the couch asleep with a beer in his hand. James, my brother, was playing on the ground with Hot Wheels. I changed and showered and checked the fridge for food. I made some mac and cheese for James and me. After cleaning the kitchen and folding some laundry, I sat at my desk to finish the presentation. It was already Wednesday. I would have to present tomorrow, and I was not ready. I sent Cindy Lou a message about what I should do. She walked me through a breathing exercise by breathing through my nose and out through my mouth. I practiced while finishing up the presentation. It was late, so I put James to bed and finalized my presentation. I was exhausted so I went to bed.

The next day I didn't feel like getting up, but I helped James get ready. My dad was already gone who knows where. We headed to school as I dropped James off at the elementary school. I practiced breathing again as I tried to forget about the presentation. During lunch, I kept quiet. I had already told my friends what was going on, so I ate my chips and left to contemplate in the bathroom. Olivia met me in there and comforted me.

Olivia and I left the bathroom and headed to English while I tried to not think about my presentation. Mrs. Schmidt called on me twenty minutes to the bell. I sunk in my seat, the chewing of gum and tapping of feet grew immensely louder. I walked up to the front of the room, my legs turning to Jell-O as I struggled to mutter the words, "My name is Laney..." I looked over at Olivia giving me a huge smile and thumbs up. I rushed through the presentation, trying to do it to the best of my ability. After school, I barely could practice. It was all I could think about. I was constantly checking PowerSchool to see if there were any updates. At the end of practice, I finally got the update. I got an A on the presentation! My grade was a C+. I could play in the game!

After seeing the grade, I told my friends and coach and they both congratulated me. I was proud to have worked for something I love. We played the game and won by a few points. I learned that I can do anything if I put my mind to it. Also, I couldn't have managed my anxiety without Cindy Lou. My experiences help shape who I am, and they have helped shape me into a better person altogether.

SERAH OOMMEN is an eighth-grade student at Houghton Middle School. She enjoys various activities such as basketball, snowboarding, singing, playing guitar, and writing. She currently serves as the president of the middle school student council and is also a member of the Houghton Band. Through her fictional short story titled, "Overcoming Hardships in Life," Serah weaves a tale of of strength and hope that resonates with anyone who has faced their own hardships in life.

Mushroom

by Betty Harriman

Dark gray clouds huddled close together in the sky. A gust of wind blew, making the blades of grass dance. Usually, Eck and their mother would stay at home below the most perfect mushroom, but today happened to be Eck's birthday.

"With all of these clouds a storm might be coming soon," Bue exclaimed pointing with her webbed finger at the sky. "Well, I'll be heading to bed now," Bue said while yawning.

"Well mother, as you might know since I've grown up now, I have no place to stay," Eck said, looking proudly at Bue.

"Well, you can't stay here, it's tradition for a toad to leave on their second birthday," Bue said solemnly. Even though Eck was scared of being alone, they understood and so they began to leap away.

"Okay, well, be safe out there!" Bue called just as Eck's body disappeared over the horizon.

"I'll find myself my own nice mushroom to stay under!" Eck declared. As Eck began to hop around the marsh, they spotted a turtle distracted by some sort of food.

"Hey!" Eck called to the turtle. The turtle looked up from his meal and immediately jumped into the water. Eck carefully stepped on tufts of grass to get to the place where the turtle was.

"Hey! I need to ask you a question!" Then a sudden movement in the murky water caught Eck's eyes.

Eck stared intently at the spot, "Hello, turtle?" Then it started to move, Eck leaped along the edge of the water, following the movement as fast as they could.

Eck had spotted land ahead and leaped onto it, the turtle surfaced, exhausted, "What do you want from me?" he asked.

"I wanted to ask you if there were any mushrooms nearby," Eck said, while tapping their foot impatiently.

"Umm, there are some over on that tree." The turtle frantically pointed with one of his small green feet at a nearby tree. Eck turned their head swiftly to see what seemed to be a mushroomless tree.

"Where are the mushrooms?" Eck asked, turning back around but the turtle had vanished. There was only a small ripple in the water. Eck sighed and waddled over to the tree to investigate, they looked all around and saw nothing but bark and lichen.

"Oh, lichen! I forgot it is a fungus." Eck remembered, "Well, that doesn't help me." They shook their head in disappointment and began searching again. Eck went further into the dense cedar forest. Soon Eck felt their stomach rumble, so they went to search for food; the best place to look was under logs. Their favorite food was worms so this was perfect for them. The leaf litter crunched under Eck's feet. After wandering around for a little they found a large log. Eck excitedly hopped over and began to push the log with all their might. They tried and tried but it wouldn't budge.

"Do you need help there, bud?" An unfamiliar voice sounded from behind. Eck was startled and jumped into the air. When they landed, they looked up to see a bird standing there, Eck recognized the feather pattern and assumed she was a robin.

"I do need help," Eck shivered with terror as they stared at the tall bird that towered over them, "But aren't you a robin? Robins can and will eat toads!"

"Ha! I'm a robin but I won't eat you. Even if I tried I couldn't!" The bird turned to her side so that Eck could see her beak, it was unusually short. Too short for her to even attempt to eat Eck. They sighed with relief and stood up straight.

"Phew! I totally thought you were going to eat me!" they sighed. "My name's Eck, what's yours?"

"My name's Ree!" The robin said as she blinked enthusiastically.

"Well, if you're hungry you can help me turn this log over." Eck turned around and looked at the huge log.

"Of course! I sure am starving," The robin exclaimed. Ree walked over to the log and pushed her head against it, right next to her Eck was pushing against the log. Still with both of their efforts, it wouldn't budge. Eck looked over at Ree, her originally orange chest feathers looked dull and gray in the shade of clouds.

"Since both of us can't do this together, you could go get someone. Preferably from the bog, someone who likes worms and bugs," Eck said, annoyed that they couldn't turn the log over.

"Sure!" Ree flew up blowing leaves everywhere.

Eck looked up at the falling leaves and sighed, "This is going to take forever!" As the leaves slowly fell, the sky cleared up to show clouds heavy with rain that hovered above. They waited, and waited while staring at the sky trying to determine when the rain would fall.

•••

"Hello?" Eck turned around to see Ree and a frog staring at them.

Eck stared at the frog and said, "Hello, my name's Eck, and as you may know we're trying to turn this log over for food, thanks for coming to help." Eck paused, "And thanks, Ree, for getting them."

"I'm Ima! And I'm starving!" Ima licked her lips and looked at the log, "Are you ready?" Eck, Ree, and Ima then walked over to the log and began to push it; with all their effort and energy, it shuffled over revealing a large sum of worms, beetles, and grubs. They all leaped into the crater the log left behind and they began to feast on the bountiful array of food. After they had stuffed themselves full, Eck started to chat about how they were trying to find a nice mushroom to call home.

"Hey, down by the river that leads to the bog there are plenty of mushrooms, there's probably going to be one that you can live under," Ima pointed out.

"Oh my, thank you! I better get going before this storm starts!" Eck said, grinning.

"So should I," Ree put in sadly.

Eck wondered why Ree was sad but brushed it off. "Well then, thank you all!" Eck then joyfully leaped away from them, making large, long strides to the bog. Then they reached the river that led into the bog. Eck bounded up the last stretch to the river and saw the most beautiful, perfect mushroom. It would fit them nicely. Eck looked at the surroundings, then froze as they recognized that this was the part of the stream where Ms. Marsh lived.

Ms. Marsh was a huge and mean muskrat that ate amphibians like frogs and toads. She was feared by almost all. She was so bad that children got told stories of her and her strong appetite for anything. Eck was raised to stay far, far away from there.

"Excuse me?" A voice sounded. Eck spun around to see none other than Ms. Marsh. They began to leap away as fast as possible. Eck looked over their shoulder and saw Ms. Marsh chasing after them, determination in her eyes as she sprinted towards Eck. Eck turned back around and put in their last burst of energy, but it was not enough, the noise of Ms. Marsh's run was right behind Eck. They closed their eyes in fear and felt sharp teeth graze their foot. Eck opened their eyes and screeched. The muskrat skirted to a stop and jerked Eck's leg over which spun around Eck and wrenched their leg. They trembled in pain then kicked hard, hitting Ms. Marsh in the face, knocking her unconscious. Eck limped away in fear and pain past the bog and back into the cedar forest for safety.

There, among the tall trees lay the body of Ree, fallen on the ground. "Ree!" Eck yelled in distress as they leaped over, forgetting the pain in their leg. "Ree! Oh, Ree are you okay?" Rees' dull eyes gave no expression but pain. Eck frantically searched Rees body, they saw a bent wing. The twisted limb looked so unnatural. "Ree! Your wing, it's broken!" Eck said solemnly. "My mom will help you." Eck quickly put the large bird on their back, but they collapsed under her weight. Eck knew what they had to do; Eck left Ree and strode over to the bog, "Ima!" They called.

"Yes?" Ima answered from within the tall grass. "Oh, Eck I thought you were—" Ima started to say, relieved, but Eck cut her off.

"No time to wait; Ree has a broken wing, we must take her to my mother. She can heal well!" Eck and Ima rushed to the forest without saying another word.

"Ree!" Ima said as they pulled up to Ree.

"I can't lift her alone; I'll lead you to my mom's house!" Eck and Ima worked to pull Ree over to the marsh as fast as they could. They were careful not to pass Ms. Marsh's territory as they walked by the river that led to the bog.

"I know this is probably not the right time, but I just wanted to apologize for telling you to come by here. I heard Ms. Marsh yelling in anger about a toad who had narrowly escaped her. I was worried for you, I'm sorry. I didn't mean to get you hurt, I really didn't," Ima confessed.

"Oh, it's fine; it was partly my fault, I didn't recognize Ms. Marsh's land. I forgive you." Ima sighed with relief, but then looked at Ree and frowned, their friend was greatly injured and needed care. "Right up here!" Eck led Ima up to the mushroom; they had recognized their old home.

"Bue!" Eck called, "Where are you? We need your help Bue!"

Bue appeared from her moss bed, "Oh my, Eck who is this? What has happened?"

"No time to explain, Mom. She needs healing!" Bue obeyed and began to heal Ree as Eck and Ima explained their whole story. Bue had also healed Eck's injured leg with a maple and pine salve she created.

"Hello?" Ree mumbled getting up from the makeshift bed Bue had created.

"Ree! Oh, you're okay! What happened?" Eck asked.

"Oh, I slipped and fell out of a tree. I-I last remember seeing the clouds. Has it rained?" Ree said with a hint of pain in her voice. All of the animals quickly looked at the sky and saw the clouds now probably so full with water they would spill out their rain any time now.

"No, it hasn't. What were you doing up in a tree?" Ima asked. Ima stared at Rees limb, it was put in place with a stick wrapped around cobwebs, and then leaves to act as a sling.

"Well, I'm embarrassed to admit but, I'm looking for a home, too." Ree shuffled her legs and looked at the ground.

"Well, I'm also looking for a home!" Ima laughed out.

"Coincidence?" Eck giggled, "We all are!" The group laughed and laughed. "We could all look for each other's houses together!" Eck suggested.

Then the group agreed and Bue took an approving glance and said, "Then go ahead, before this storm starts!"

•••

Ree, Eck, and Ima thanked Bue, then took off and arrived at the bog to find Ima a new home. "You should get a home near the cedar forest so we can all live close together," Ree suggested. So, they went to the very edge of the bog, and they all began to search between tufts of grass for a nice home.

"Is this good?" Ree asked, showing Ima a small mud indent between two grass tufts.

"Eh, I'm not sure that it has enough privacy,"

"Oh," Ree said disappointed.

•••

"What do you all think of this?" Ima pointed at a hole in the mud that seemed to go deep.

"Try it out!" Ree laughed.

Ima shoved her head deep into the hole, "Wow!" Ima said in awe. "It's huge!" Ima began to tug and tug her head out. But her head was stuck. "Help, my head; It's stuck!" Ima yelled. Simultaneously Eck and Ree tugged Ima out. "Thanks!" Ima said with gratitude. "Well, I guess this one won't work." Ima chuckled while shaking the mud off of herself.

As they all started to search again, but they had to no longer because Eck found the perfect home! "Ima, come check this out!" Eck encouraged. Ima and Ree hopped over, and Eck presented a grass tuff on top of clay-like mud, the grass curled over which made a private place for Ima to stay.

"It's perfect!" Ima's voice was filled with warmth as she hopped over and went in, "I'm going to love it here; thanks Eck and Ree!"

As Ree, Eck, and Ima exchanged goodbyes Eck couldn't help but feel sorrow and worry, "What if Ms. Marsh comes?" Eck asked Ree as they walked to the forest. Ree remembered Ms. Marsh from the old children's tales,

"Don't worry, Ms. Marsh doesn't even know Ima and Ima is about as far away as possible from her." Eck looked on with worry clouded in their eyes, "Seriously, Eck she's going to be fine!" Ree stopped and rested her uninjured wing on Eck's shoulder, "She'll be okay!" Ree encouraged.

"Okay!" Eck smiled as the worry faded away.

•••

Eck and Ree searched among the trees by looking into the sky that was cluttered with branches full of leaves. "Since I can't fly yet, I need a tree with step like branches," Ree explained.

"Okay," Eck continued to search, "That one!" Eck pointed at a large tree with many branches that led up to a very bushy branch.

"I'm going to check it out!" Ree hopped up each individual branch to the branch that looked like it had a great potential for a nest. "Hello?" Ree asked. Eck looked up confused, but Ree wasn't talking to them.

"Peep!" Something sounded, "Peep!" "Peep!" "Peep!"

A large black bird with sleek, smooth black feathers crashed onto the branch with a fury of feathers, "What are you doing with my babies?" The bird screeched.

"Oh! I-I'm sorry I didn't realize someone lived here!" Ree replied with fear.

"Well, you better get going now! And don't come back here!" The huge bird shooed Ree away from the nest with her four chicks with poofy black feathers. Eck assumed that the bird was a raven or a crow who had already made that tree branch her home.

Ree and Eck walked away and started to search again. "What do you think about this one?" Ree then showed Eck a nice branch that had leaves in a circular position which would be awesome for a nest.

"But there are no stairs!" Eck pointed out.

Ree sighed, "Oh, I didn't realize that."

•••

Eck became weary of the clouds above. They had been anticipating rain all day, but it had not come; now it was getting dark, and they had still not found a home. Eck was thinking about what they wanted in a house when they spotted a large tree, with beautiful steps and a branch with leaves that made a circle shape that was big enough to fit Ree perfectly if she made a nest on it. "Ree! Ree!"

Eck showed Ree the huge tree. "This will be wonderful! Thank you, Eck! I hope you find a home that's close!" Ree smiled hopped up the branches of the tree and began building her nest out of the leaves.

Eck was filled with joy for their friends but was also worried about having to find themselves a home. Eck came around a corner to find a mushroom at last. The mushroom was a large coral mushroom; they leaped under it, but its thick network of stems was too cluttered and it had so many holes that it wouldn't work to protect Eck from anything. Eck continued to search and search; they came up to a log with a shelf mushroom. Eck waddled up and stood under it, then they looked up to see that it was way too tiny to protect Eck from the elements. They waddled on to see a nice mushroom about the size of Eck's body, "Finally!" Eck sighed, relieved.

"Excuse me?" A rabbit came from under it, "This is going to be my home!" The rabbit boasted. Eck angrily hopped away.

•••

"Wow!" Eck exclaimed, striding over to an amazing mushroom. They settled under the rusty orange mushroom and sat. Suddenly, the mushroom began to float up. Eck looked up to see a human! "Eek!" Eck started to leap away; they looked back to see the human placing the mushroom into a basket while smiling with glee. Eck blinked in disgust, "Humans!" They rolled their eyes and carried on.

Eck then came up to a morel mushroom, "I'll try it out!" Eck said, trying to cling on to any hope. But Eck was too tall and wide to fit under the moral. Eck wasn't even phased anymore; they just kept on walking. All hope had left Eck's body when they heard a "drip drop" sound they looked up at the sky as the clouds started to rain. Eck caught a glimmer of red and looked over to their left at the most beautiful, large, red, shiny, and perfect mushroom they had ever seen. Eck opened their mouth in awe. They were stunned by the beauty of it. A raindrop landed on Eck's head snapping them out of it, reminding them to head under. The pitter patter of rain soothed them as they settled down under the mushroom for a rest.

Eck thought about their day; it had been extended and hard but fortunately they had made two new life-long friends. Eck had concluded that the day had been very successful and that many days from now would also be as successful. They also hoped that in the future Ima would have a nice home, decorated with all her findings. And that Ree would make a beautiful nest that was comfortable. The noise of the rain consumed Eck as they drifted off into the darkness of sleep, peaceful and fulfilled at last.

BETTY HARRIMAN is an eleven-year-old sixth grader at Bothwell Middle School in Marquette. Her hobbies include skiing, hiking, and biking with her family. She also enjoys spending time with her three cats, Bean, Boots, and Kirby. Betty loves to read, write, and make art.

Historical - Hancock - Unknown Man with Dogs

Author Bios

JOHN ADAMCIK learned to love Michigan's Upper Peninsula through Jeanneen, his wife of thirty years, and also through her U.P.-native family. Originally from Midland, the Adamciks live in North Carolina and have two adult children. They visit family in the U.P. as often as possible. John earned his BA in English at SVSU, where he wrote for and edited the *Valley Vanguard*. He has recently been published in *O.Henry* magazine.

BEN BOHNSACK is a retiree in Marquette for whom ideas, words, art, and life all flow together, waiting to be expressed and lived out. Once a pastor, now mostly a grandfather, woodcut artist, and community volunteer, his creative impulses come and go but are always at heart of who he is. ben@sandriverfriends.com, sandriverart.com

TRICIA CARR is a long-time Gwinn area resident who grew up reading Agatha Christie and her natural bent in writing is traditional and cozy mysteries, and short stories of many types. Her husband and daughters, her three cats, and her Pomeranian, Sir TripsALot, (called so because he does) cheer her on.

MIKEL B. CLASSEN has been writing and photographing northern Michigan in newspapers and magazines for over thirty-five years, creating feature articles about the life and culture of Michigan's north country. A journalist, historian, photographer and author with a fascination for the world around him, he enjoys researching and writing about lost stories from the past. He is the creator of the *U.P. Reader* and is a member of the Board of Directors for the Upper Peninsula Publishers and Authors Association.

In 2020, Mikel won the Historical Society of Michigan's George Follo Award for Upper Peninsula History. He has just released a new book, *True Tales: The Forgotten History of Michigan's Upper Peninsula* in 2022.

NINA CRAIG is Ojibwe/Odawa, enrolled in the Sault Ste. Marie Tribe of Chippewa Indians and of Swedish/Scottish descent. Her family has deep roots in the Upper Peninsula and northwestern lower Michigan. Since 2016, Nina has been taking writing from The Writers Center in Bethesda, MD and at the Kalamazoo Institute of Arts. She resides in Kalamazoo to be near her children and grandchildren and writes poetry, short stories and is working on her memoir.

ART CURTIS was writing ad copy when he turned to poetry in 1991 after reading Jim Harrison's *"Letters to Yesenin,"* during a major personal crisis. His work has appeared in *Peninsula Poets, Walloon Writers Review, Dunes Review* and *TADL: Poets' Night Out*. He lives near Bellaire with his cat, Mr. Strider, and finds Petoskey stones in his sandy garden nearly 400' above Lake Michigan.

JULIE DICKERSON grew up in Flushing, Michigan. She has four children and currently lives on an eighteen-acre hobby farm in Jackson with her husband, where they enjoy gardening, reading, and hiking. Their home in the Upper Peninsula of Michigan provides time for canoeing, biking, fishing, and spending time with family and friends in the splendor of the Great Lakes Region.

DEBORAH K. FRONTIERA was terribly afraid of bees as a child, but often offered cracker crumbs to ant hills. She has used insects as characters before (but in a future world post-people) rather than in the "real" world of today. This story was inspired the day she saw a slew of bees slurping up nectar from the hummingbird feeder outside her kitchen window. Check out her other insect characters on her website: www.authorsden.com/deborahkfrontiera

ELIZABETH FUST has a bachelors in writing from NMU. Though not a native Yooper, she refuses to leave the place. She is a self-published children's book author, frequent short story contributor to UPPAA's *U.P. Reader*, and a feature contributor to the *Marquette Monthly*. Elizabeth is Communications Coordinator for Kall Morris Inc, an orbital debris research and solution development company in Marquette, Michigan. Follow Elizabeth's writing on Facebook and Instagram at Elizabeth Fust Books.

J. L. HAGEN is the author of *Sea Stacks*, stories referencing the fictional community of Loyale, Michigan. His novella, *Runtley Goes Rogue*, received a 2022 gold medal from the Florida Writers Association. "Chelsea's Rescue" was named one of 2020's best sci-fi short stories. A graduate of University of Michigan and University of Chicago, he grew up in St. Ignace. He and his wife Joy commute between Lake Michigan and Tampa Bay. His email is j.l.hagen@outlook.com.

MACK HASSLER and his wife began spending summers in the U.P. in 1989, but Mack only discovered his footing with creative writing in the region gradually. With critical essays on Schoolcraft and Curwood, he now has seen some of his poems take off. Sadly, his wife died in the fall of 2022, but he continues to write hoping she senses his work still in the big woods.

RICH HILL lives along the shore of Lake Superior in Michigan's Eastern Upper Peninsula with his wife Judy. He graduated from Northern Michigan University with a BFA in Art and Design. In his free time, he jams with fellow musicians (drums), reads, and plays pickup tennis. Thus far, he has published four books, which are available on Amazon and RichardHillBooks.com

KATHLEEN CARLTON JOHNSON is both a visual artist and poet. She has been published in the Origami Poems Project, has twelve chapbooks published, and has published work in *MacGuffin, Rattle,* and the *William and Mary Review*, to mention a few venues. Her poems have been heard on Public Radio 90: Voices from the Past. She was a presenter at the UPPAA Conference in 2022.

SHARON KENNEDY has written a newspaper column for Gannett Media and is working on a sequel to her book, *The SideRoad Kids: Tales from Chippewa County*. Her latest book, *View from the SideRoad: A Collection of Upper Peninsula Stories* was published last year. In keeping with the "sideroad" theme, the working title of her next book is *Memories and Observations of a Side Road Newspaper Columnist*.

CHRIS KENT lives with her husband on the Brule River near Iron River. She retired to the U.P. from a career in marketing and public relations in downstate Michigan. Chris is active in her community, feeling a deep responsibility to give back. Inspiration to write came from a local writing group and a home where woods, water, and sky come together to provide opportunity and motivation to create. She has been published in several anthologies and magazines.

ALLAN KOSKI (1951 – 2023) graduated from Michigan Technological University. He has authored two books and has numerous published historical and professional papers. Most recently served as the President of the Advisory Board at the Michigan Iron Industry Museum appointed by Governor Gretchen Whitmer.

EMILIE LANCOUR is an author, photographer, educator, and mom from the Copper Country in the U.P. of Michigan. She has published two books so far; a memoir after the loss of her husband titled, *It's Okay to be Okay, Finding Joy through Grief* and a collection called, "A Cup of Miracles". She can often be found on the shores of Lake Superior collecting rocks and enjoying the sunset.

TAMARA LAUDER is a professional artist in the Northwoods of Wisconsin who enjoys combining her passion for writing with her artwork. She is published in a variety of genres and is the author and illustrator of an inspirational pictorial book. Inspired by the beauty of the Keweenaw Peninsula, her writing was selected for the *Houghton Selected Shorts Story Contest* performed at the Rozsa Center at Michigan Tech University.

ELLEN LORD is a Michigan native. She grew up in the Upper Peninsula. Her writing has appeared in *Dunes Review, Walloon Writers Review, R.K.V.R.Y Quarterly Literary Journal, PSM Peninsula Poets* and *TDAL Poets Night Out* chapbooks. She won the Landmark Books Haiku Contest in 2017 & 2019. She is a member of The Poets Society of Michigan, Freshwater Poets in Traverse City, and Charlevoices Writers' Group in Charlevoix. She likes to spend time exploring the wilderness near her ancestral home in Trout Creek, Michigan.

RAYMOND LUCZAK grew up in Ironwood and Houghton, Michigan. He is the author and editor of many books, including *Chlorophyll: Poems about Michigan's Upper Peninsula* and *Compassion, Michigan: The Ironwood Stories* (both titles available from Modern History Press). His book *Once Upon a Twin: Poems* (Gallaudet University Press) is a U.P. Notable Book. An inaugural Zoeglossia Fellow, he lives in Minneapolis, Minnesota.

MARIA VEZZETTI MATSON writes about her family in Michigan. However, she is not in any way related to the Dogman. Matson's published books about her Italian immigrant history include *Gelsomina's Story of Caesar Lucchesi* and *Alone to America.* She's a proud Italian Yooper. Her website is MariaVezzettiMatsonAuthor.com

ROSLYN ELENA MCGRATH lives in Marquette, Michigan and delights in the rhythm, rhyme, and magic in life and its interplay with her written, visual, and healing work. She's the author/illustrator of three card decks and six books, the most recent being her first book of poetry, *Sizzle, Soar, Glow, Roar: Earth Pulse Arias.* Roslyn also publishes *Health & Happiness U.P. Magazine,* and supports self-actualization at Empowering Lightworks, LLC. You can learn more at EmpoweringLightworks.com.

BECKY ROSS MICHAEL grew up in Michigan, where she raised a family and taught in U.P. public schools. She now gardens and works on her sunny balcony in North Texas. Writing for adults and children, Becky's pieces appear in print and online. In addition, she enjoys the challenge of working as a freelance editor. Visit Becky at platformnumber4.com

LEIGH MILLS lives, cleans, and vacations in the Eastern U.P. with her husband, Eric. They moved from Colorado in 2020 where Leigh was a columnist for the *Crestone Eagle* newspaper and a contributor to the *Colorado Gardener Magazine.* She loves writing about her cleaning adventures and taking pictures of the Les Cheneaux landscape.

M. KELLY PEACH is one of the lucky ones who is able to live his retirement in the U.P. He enjoys his children and grandchildren, hiking, reading, collecting books and baking. Visit his website: mkellypeach.com; Twitter @MichaelPeach He has work published or forthcoming *Suicid(al)iens, Resist with Every Inch and Every Breath, Moss Puppy Magazine, Riddled with Arrows 5.3, The Lovers Literary Journal,* and *Once Upon a Crocodile.*

DONNA SEARIGHT SIMONS is the author of *Copper Empire* and has given historical Copper Country presentations at libraries throughout Michigan. She works at Oakland University (Rochester, MI) and looks forward to vacationing in the Copper Country every chance she can get.

T. KILGORE SPLAKE ("the cliffs dancer") lives in an old mining row house in the copper mining village of Calumet in Michigan's upper peninsula. Splake has become a legend in small press literary circles. Street Corner Press in Sister Bay, Wisconsin recently published two books about Splake written by Robert Zoschke. *The Road to Splake* and *Splake Eyes* contain a collection of poems and photographs that trace Splake's path from a backwoods poet to international literary acclaim. Splake's most recent book, *A Poet of the Wild,* was edited by Walt McLaughlin.

MICHAL SPLHO is an analyst in the creative industry, who has gained professional experience in publishing and graphic design area. He is an expert in project management in publishing, creative and design solutions. Splho has typeset all the interior layouts of *U.P. Reader* volumes 1 through 8. He is based in Bratislava.

BILL SPROULE is a Professor Emeritus, Department of Civil and Environmental Engineering, Michigan Technological University, Houghton, Michigan. He is a member of the Society for International Hockey Research and the Houghton County Historical Society, and author of *Copper Country Streetcars, Houghton – The Birthplace of Professional Hockey, Michigan Tech Hockey: 100 Years of Memories, and Michigan Tech Football: The First 100 Years.*

NINIE GASPARIANI SYARIKIN works as a writer, translator, and researcher. Prior to living in Michigan's Upper Peninsula, she lived in Washington, DC for 25 years. Texas was the first American soil that she stepped on in the summer of 1987 when she attended a six-week English language immersion program at The University of Texas at Austin. Ninie is a mother of three sons, one of whom was a Peace Corps Volunteer in Uganda, East Africa.

BRANDY THOMAS is a professional editor who lives and works in Marquette, Michigan. In addition to editing the written word, she is also an audiobook narrator and editor. She is the voice of the *U.P. Reader* (*Hello everyone!*) as well as a writer of poetry and short fiction. For more information about Brandy, visit www.ThomasEditing.com.

TYLER R. TICHELAAR is a seventh-generation Marquette resident and award-winning author. He has spent his life capturing the people and history of Marquette in both fiction and nonfiction works, including *The Marquette Trilogy, The Best Place, Haunted Marquette, When Teddy Came to Town*, and *Kawbawgam: The Chief, The Legend, The Man*. Tyler is also a professional editor and the owner of Superior Book Productions. Visit him at www.MarquetteFiction.com.

EDD TURY descended from Hungarian Gypsies. He is a Michigan native and avid Transcendentalist who often finds himself exploring the wilderness on foot, bike, or kayak. He graduated from the University of Michigan during the turbulent sixties and continues to work as an electronics guru whose goal is to dance in the moonlight. Edd's writing has appeared in *Dunes Review, Open Palm Print, Poet's Night Out* chapbook, *Detroit Metro Times, Michigan Out of Doors* magazine, *Michigan Woods n Waters*, and the *Ann Arbor news*. Edd lives at the end of the road in Charlevoix County.

VICTOR R. VOLKMAN is the president of the Upper Peninsula Publishers & Authors Association (UPPAA) since 2019 and has been on the Board since 2009. He is the Senior Editor at Modern History Press (Ann Arbor, MI) which is the publisher-of-record and indexer for the entire *U.P. Reader* series. He is a graduate of Michigan Technological University (class of '86). He can be reached by email to victor@LHPress.com.

AUGUST WHITNEY splits his time between Houghton, Michigan and Milwaukee, Wisconsin, where he works as a lift operator and a kayak guide respectively. His writing has appeared in the *Incandescent Review* and the *UWM Honors Newsletter*. Direct any inquiries to augwhitney@gmail.com

Help Sell
The U.P. Reader!

❖❖❖

The popularity of the *U.P. Reader* is growing, but we need it to grow more.

Help us sell the *U.P. Reader* by selling the *Reader* alongside your other books. The *U.P. Reader* at its wholesale price allows those who wish to carry it to make a nice profit on the sales. Bookstores and individuals can all benefit from helping the U.P. Reader grow.

If you have writing that has been published in the *U.P. Reader*, you should be selling copies of the Reader alongside your other work. This not only helps get exposure for your writing but for all the others that were accepted alongside yours. Part of the mission of the *U.P. Reader* is to get the many voices of the writers of the UPPAA in a single publication so that readers would have a place to find and sample the incredible talent that makes up the authors and poets of the Upper Peninsula.

Taking a few *Readers* to an event can make the difference in selling. Those who have been selling the *U.P. Reader* have seen good sales and considerable interest in the publication from readers and customers. Many customers ask the seller if they have a piece in the book to sign it. As the U.P. Reader is helping you as a writer, you can be helping the *U.P. Reader*.

Do you have local booksellers in your area? Encourage them to stock the *U.P. Reader*. Bookstores that are selling the Reader are seeing brisk sales. Many of the bookstores have restocked their issues several times and are saying how much they enjoy them. They are profitable and returnable. The *U.P. Reader* is a win-win situation for bookstores.

Take a copy of the *U.P. Reader* to your child's English or Language Arts teacher. The Dandelion Cottage Award is open to all children in U.P. schools and homeschool. There is never a fee to participate!

Back issues of the *U.P. Reader* are also still available. They can still be ordered right alongside the new issue and can be combined to sell as a set. There are many who still haven't discovered the *U.P. Reader* yet, and a package set is a nice way to introduce them to the joys of reading a *Reader*. These can still be purchased wholesale just like the current issue.

There are hardcover versions of the *U.P. Reader* as well. These are beautiful bound versions of the *U.P. Reader* that are a wonderful keepsake for the real *U.P. Reader* fan. Again, these can be ordered wholesale and sold right alongside the paperback versions.

To order, go to UPReader.org/publications on the web and put in your order. Contributing authors will be emailed a discount code and their orders will be discounted to the wholesale price (50% Off!).

Please help us, help you make the *U.P. Reader* a success!

Come join
UPPAA Online!

UPPAA

The UPPAA maintains an online presence on several websites and social media areas. To get the most out of your UPPAA membership, be sure to visit, "like," and share these destinations and posts whenever possible!

Web Sites

- **www.UPPAA.org**: learn about meetings, publicity opportunities, publicize your own author events, add your book to the catalog page, read newsletter archive.
- **www.UPReader.org**: complete details about deadlines, submission guidelines, how to place a print advertisement, where to buy U.P. Reader locally, and more.
- **www.UPNotable.com**: all the information about the U.P. Notable Book Club meetings
- **www.UPBookReview.com**: publishing 36 reviews of books by U.P. writers or about the U.P. every year!

Facebook Pages

- **UPPAA**: www.facebook.com/UPSISU/ —OR—type in **@UPSISU** into the Facebook "search" bar
- **UP Reader**: www.facebook.com/upreaders/ —OR— type in **@UPreader** into the Facebook "search" bar

Twitter

Twitter

- Message to **@UP_Authors** or visit https://twitter.com/UP_Authors

Comprehensive Index of U.P. Reader Volumes 1 through 7

Listen to *U.P. Reader* audiobooks

...while you drive the Seney Stretch, walk the treadmill,
or just work around the house!

**Each unabridged edition is professionally narrated and edited
by U.P. resident Brandy Thomas**

Available from Audible.com and iTunes
No subscription required!

www.ingramcontent.com/pod-product-compliance
Lightning Source LLC
Chambersburg PA
CBHW080916020726
47502CB00008B/2465